The World Beyond The End

Todd Thorne

Ada Forge Books

First edition 2026

Foreword

2013 — 2026

This story began in 2013, long before the world had any real understanding of what a global pandemic could look like or how deeply it could change everyday life.

At the time, the idea felt distant. Something that could happen in theory, something you might read about in a novel or hear discussed in passing, but not something that would ever truly reach into every corner of the world. The concept behind this book came from that place, imagining what would happen if a virus started in a remote part of the world and spread quickly across continents, carried by the simple fact that people can move from one country to another in a matter of hours.

In this story, the virus is far more devastating than anything we have experienced, yet. It leaves more than ninety-nine point nine percent of the population gone, and what remains is not just an empty world, but a changed one. The structures that once held society together disappear almost overnight. What follows is not just survival, but transformation. Some people rise to become better than they were before, while others reveal the worst parts of themselves when there are no rules left to hold them in place.

The early pieces of this novel were written during long nights working third shift. There were hours that needed to be filled, and I needed something to keep my mind active and focused. This story became that outlet. It started as a way to stay awake, to pass time, and to explore an idea that stayed with me longer than I expected.

After those early drafts, the manuscript sat for years. It was placed on a shelf and, for a long time, forgotten. Life moved on, as it does, and the story remained unfinished.

About a year ago, I came back to it.

What started as a rough draft became something worth finishing. I spent time refining it, shaping it, and bringing it to a place where it could finally be shared.

What you are about to read is the result of that process.

A story that began in quiet hours, set aside for years, and then brought back to life.

Todd Thorne 04/2026

Contents

Prologue

Foya, Liberia

Foya, Liberia

The morning was already hot when Kallon sat down on his stool.

He had been sitting there every morning for eleven years, in the same place, facing the same stretch of trees at the edge of the village. The routine had never failed him. But this morning, something felt wrong.

His legs didn't feel like his own.

There was a distance to them, as if they belonged to someone else and had simply been placed beneath him. He shifted his weight, waiting for the feeling to pass, the way small things usually did.

It didn't.

In the doorway behind him, his wife stood watching. She had been watching since he woke. He had noticed that too.

"Stay home today," she said.

Her voice was steady, but there was something underneath it.

Kallon shook his head.

His father had gone out on mornings like this. Sick. Tired. It hadn't mattered. The forest didn't care how a man felt. The children needed to eat. That was the rule.

"It's nothing," he said. "I'll be fine by evening."

She didn't argue.

Eleven years of mornings like this had taught her when words wouldn't change anything.

Kallon stood slowly, reached for his rifle, and moved to the door. As he stepped out, he touched the frame with his hand, the way he always did. A small habit, repeated so many times it no longer required thought.

Then he walked toward the trees.

The path felt longer than it should have.

Kallon stopped twice before he reached the edge of the forest, bending slightly just to catch his breath. The rifle felt heavier in his hands, as if it carried more than its weight. Even the light filtering through the branches seemed wrong. Too yellow. Too thick. As though the air itself had changed.

He told himself it was the heat.

He stepped into the shade.

The first bird lay beneath a fig tree.

Kallon slowed, then stopped.

It was on its side, wings folded close to its body, as if it had simply settled there to rest. There were no marks on it. No blood. No sign of a struggle.

It had just come down.

And stayed down.

He stood over it for a moment, then moved on.

There was another bird a little farther down the path. Then another.

By the time he counted six, something had tightened in his chest. Not from sickness. From recognition.

He had seen animals die before. He knew what it looked like when something passed through a place and left silence behind it.

He didn't say it out loud.

He kept walking.

The stream was still running when he reached it.

That, at least, hadn't changed.

But the hog at the bank had.

It was a large animal, heavy and well-fed, lying on its side in the mud. The heat had already begun to swell it. Its eyes were clouded, its skin stretched tight. Flies rose and settled over it in slow, restless waves.

Kallon stood there for a long time.

He understood what it meant when animals died like this. Not one. Not scattered. Together.

His grandfather had told him stories, once. About places where the birds stopped singing before anything else happened. Places where the forest itself seemed to hold its breath.

Kallon had never believed those stories fully.

Now he did.

But belief didn't change what waited at home.

His children had not eaten properly in three days.

The hog was there.

Close. Real.

Enough to feed them.

He told himself it was the heat. Animals died from heat. It happened every season. He repeated that until it almost felt true.

Then he dragged it home.

His wife didn't ask where it came from.

She saw the way he moved. Heard the cough when it came up from deep in his chest. For a moment, she raised her hand to her mouth, as if to hold something back.

Then she turned and began preparing the fire.

The meat went into the pot and cooked slowly. The smell carried over the fence and into the neighboring yards, drawing people the way it always did.

They came with bowls. With quiet questions. With hunger.

That night, they all ate together.

It was a good meal.

The kind where people laughed a little too loudly and filled their bowls again before they were empty. The kind where no one asked questions they didn't want answered.

For a few hours, everything felt almost normal.

By morning, Kallon could not stand.

He wasn't surprised.

Some part of him had known at the stream. Maybe even before that. Maybe the moment his legs first felt wrong beneath him.

It didn't matter now.

His wife sent for the doctor.

The man arrived late in the day, already sweating, carrying a bag that looked too small for what was coming. He listened to Kallon's chest, his expression tightening as he worked.

"It's a fever," he said at last. "Keep him cool."

He hesitated, then added, "Pray."

That was the moment Kallon understood.

People came to sit with the family.

They brought water. Touched his arm. Said his name as if it might anchor him in place.

Then they went home.

Within days, the coughing followed them there.

The doctor did not return.

One by one, the houses began to darken.

Not all at once. Not suddenly.

Slowly.

Like a fire burning down after the wood is gone.

Smoke stopped rising in the mornings. Doors stayed closed. Dogs moved through the village without being called, without being told where to go.

The birds did not return.

By the end of the week, there was no one left to die.

One

Gillette, Wyoming

Wyoming 1987

The bus moved through the night slowly.

Its headlights carved a narrow path through the darkness, just enough to keep them moving forward. Hudson Hollins sat near the middle, his bag at his feet, his hands resting loosely in his lap. The seat beside him was empty. It had been empty long enough that he had stopped noticing it.

Time had slipped away somewhere behind them.

Cities had come and gone without leaving much of an impression. Lights would bloom beyond the glass, stretch into patterns that almost felt alive, and then collapse back into nothing as the bus pushed forward. People climbed on, rode for a while, then disappeared again, each carrying a story Hudson would never hear.

He turned a quiet question over in his mind.

Was he unhappy?

No. Not exactly.

It was something else. Something harder to name. A space more than a feeling. The place between something ending and something else beginning, where nothing had settled yet.

He had been in that space longer than he wanted to admit.

Across the aisle, a man leaned forward slightly.

"You headed somewhere far."

It wasn't quite a question.

Hudson looked at him more closely this time. Younger than he first appeared. Straight posture, the kind that didn't come naturally. Clothes clean, worn with intention. A patch on his sleeve.

"Gillette, Wyoming," Hudson said.

The man nodded, slow and understanding. "That's a ways."

He smiled then, easy and unforced, like something in his life had recently shifted back into place.

"I'm headed home. Omaha."

"Military?" Hudson asked.

"Yeah." The man touched the patch lightly. "Finally."

They let the conversation settle for a moment as the bus continued forward.

"What takes you to Gillette?" the man asked.

"A job," Hudson said. He heard how flat it sounded, even to himself. "A chance to start somewhere new."

"Wyoming's mostly wind and bison," the man said, still smiling. "But there are worse places to start over."

Hudson noticed the difference but didn't correct it.

Start somewhere new.

Not start over.

He let it pass.

The man leaned back and closed his eyes not long after. Hudson turned back to the window.

His reflection hovered faintly in the glass, drifting in and out as light shifted outside. There and not there at the same time.

He thought about the apartment waiting for him. The job he had accepted over the phone in a voice that sounded more certain than he felt. The people who didn't know him yet.

He would have the chance to be someone new.

Or he would learn that whatever he carried with him wasn't the kind of thing distance could leave behind.

He wasn't sure which one unsettled him more.

By the time the bus rolled into Gillette, dawn was beginning to gather itself along the horizon in thin gray layers.

The town didn't announce itself.

Low buildings. Wide streets. A water tower catching the first light. Nothing that insisted on attention.

Hudson found that, unexpectedly, a relief.

He stepped down onto the pavement and paused.

The air felt different. Colder than he expected, but cleaner too. Not just in temperature, but in something harder to describe. A kind of emptiness that came from distance, from the absence of everything he had grown used to tuning out.

He stood there for a moment and breathed it in.

A voice called from the curb.

"You Hudson?"

He turned.

A young man stood beside a car, already smiling, already in motion.

"Yeah."

"Dean." He crossed the distance and took Hudson's bag without asking. "Welcome to Gillette."

He slowed a step and gave Hudson a quick look, like he was checking something off in his head.

"Human Resources said I'd know you when I saw you," he said, a small grin forming. "Around six foot, black wavy hair, medium beard, blue eyes. Built like you've actually worked for a living."

He nodded once, satisfied.

"They didn't mention Tennessee, but I can see it. You look like you belong out here anyway. Like you could step onto any Wyoming ranch and no one would think twice."

He shifted the bag on his shoulder.

"Sorry about the bus. I think they design those seats specifically to break a man."

Hudson almost smiled. "Sixty hours."

Dean winced. "Then you've earned breakfast."

He said it like it wasn't a suggestion.

They drove through town in a company car, Dean talking easily as they went. He pointed things out as they passed, not like a tour, more like someone filling space because silence didn't quite fit him.

"That diner over there," he said, nodding toward a low building on the corner, "coffee's terrible, but the eggs are honest. That's about as good as it gets around here."

He pointed again as they turned.

"That bar everyone goes to. And that one, "a quick gesture across the street," the bar everyone says they don't."

Hudson looked out the window as they moved.

The streets were wide. The sky felt bigger than it should. The light had a different quality to it, shaped by open space instead of buildings.

"Not much here," Dean said, "but it has a way of getting into you."

Hudson nodded slightly, still watching.

I could be someone different here, he thought.

He wasn't sure if that was hope or just something he needed to believe.

Maybe both.

They stopped at a small diner near the edge of town.

Inside, the air was warm and carried the steady rhythm of a place that didn't change much from day to day. Dean talked while they ate, filling the space without expecting much in return. Hudson found that he didn't mind listening.

"You got family coming out later?" Dean asked.

Hudson shook his head. "Not anymore."

Dean nodded once and left it there.

No follow-up.

No attempt to pull at something Hudson hadn't offered.

Hudson felt a quiet appreciation for that.

After breakfast, they pulled up in front of the apartment.

Dean left the car running as Hudson stepped out and looked at the building. It was ordinary in every way that mattered.

That felt right.

"Walking distance to work," Dean said from the window. "Around here, that's a selling point."

Hudson glanced up at the sky. It stretched wide above the building, already shifting toward pink along the edges.

"Tomorrow's your first day," Dean added. "You'll be fine. People here are good."

He said it simply, like it wasn't something he needed to prove.

Hudson nodded.

Dean pulled away, leaving him alone on the quiet street.

Hudson stood there for a moment, bag in hand, the cold air moving lightly across his face.

This is where it starts, he thought.

Whatever it is.

He picked up his bag and went inside.

Liberia

Far from Wyoming, a truck rolled to a stop at the edge of a town.

The engine went quiet.

The men stepped down one at a time, their movements controlled, deliberate. Protective suits sealed at every joint. Their faces hidden behind visors already clouded with dust.

The air was still.

No voices.

No movement.

No children.

That was always the first sign.

Children should have been everywhere. Running. Calling out. Getting in the way. Their absence came before anything else.

Before the doors hanging open.

Before the cold cooking pots.

Before the truth settled in.

The men walked slowly through the first row of structures.

They did not speak.

Inside the first shack, the smell reached them before the details did. Not blood. Something else. Something the body becomes when it has nothing left to give but still tries.

Three bodies lay on the floor.

A man near the door, one arm stretched toward it. A woman against the wall, folded into herself. A child at the back.

Too small.

That was the part that landed hardest.

There were no wounds.

No signs of struggle.

Just stillness.

Around them, dried in uneven shapes across the dirt, a pale residue had settled and cracked.

One of the men crouched.

"Respiratory," he said.

Flat. Professional.

The lungs had filled. The body had tried to force it out. That effort had been the end.

They moved on.

Each building told the same story in a different arrangement.

Two here. Four there. An old man alone. A young woman at a table, a cup still upright in front of her.

Small details remained.

Shoes placed neatly by a door.

Fabric half-folded.

Objects that insisted people had lived here.

Outside, dogs watched from a distance.

Birds lifted briefly, then settled again.

The men returned to the truck.

One of them picked up the radio.

"Field Team Four. We've confirmed. Same as the others."

Static answered.

Then a voice.

"No survivors?"

"None. One hundred percent."

A pause.

"Cause?"

"Severe respiratory failure. Massive fluid expulsion. Same pattern."

The pause stretched.

"This stays contained," the voice said. "We downplay findings. If this spreads without control, we lose the response."

The man looked out at the empty town.

"There's no way to make this smaller."

"Understood. Move to the next site."

The line went dead.

The engine started.

They drove on.

Behind them, the town settled into silence again.

The birds.

The dogs.

The heat.

The slow reclaiming of everything that had been left behind.

Far away, Hudson stepped off a bus in Wyoming.

He stood in the cold air.

Breathed in once.

Then again.

Breathing was safe.

For now.

Two

Life Wreckage

Gillette, Wyoming. 1987

The alarm went off at six.

Hudson shut it off before the second ring and lay there for a moment, eyes open, staring at a ceiling that didn't belong to him yet. It was his second morning in Gillette, and the first one that actually asked something of him.

He sat up slowly and swung his feet to the floor. The room was small and spare, still carrying the smell of fresh paint mixed with something older, something that belonged to whoever had lived there before him. That didn't bother him. He hadn't come here for comfort. He had come because it was far enough away that no one knew his name.

He moved through the routine without thinking. Shower, shave, dress. That was the goal most mornings. Don't think, just move. Let the steps carry you forward until the day takes over and the rest of it quiets down.

He stopped at the window before leaving. Across the street, a light flicked on in a small house, and a truck backed slowly out of a driveway, tires crunching against gravel. Somewhere nearby, a radio played low enough that he couldn't make out the words. The world was waking up, doing what it always did, not caring who was watching.

Hudson pulled on his jacket and grabbed his keys, then stood at the door for a moment with his hand resting against the frame. He had done this before, different door, different life.

The air was cold and clean as he walked to work through streets he was still learning, past buildings that didn't mean anything to him yet. That was one of the few clean things about starting somewhere new. For a little while, nothing carried weight. No memories attached. No history pressing in from the edges. Just streets, buildings, and a town that hadn't had time to become complicated.

He knew it wouldn't last. It never did.

Somewhere back in Tennessee, there was still a house, a divorce, and a son he wasn't allowed to see. He kept it in check. Not gone, just kept quiet so it didn't take over everything else.

He kept walking and didn't look back.

Greeneville, Tennessee. 1982

The day everything went wrong had started like any other Saturday, and that was still the part that stayed with him. There had been no warning, no sense that anything was off. Just a normal day unfolding the way normal days always did.

Football on the television. Friends gathered around. Plates of wings, empty bottles, someone's jacket thrown over the back of a chair.

Hudson sat slightly apart from the center of it, the way he usually did. He had always been more comfortable watching than talking. His wife used to call it his watching face, the look he got when he was taking something in without needing to be part of it.

He had been drinking since early afternoon. Not enough to draw attention, just steady, the kind of drinking that fills the space between now and whatever comes next. She had asked him to be home by six, and he had said he would.

"Another one?" someone asked, already reaching into the cooler.

Hudson knew he'd had enough. Some part of him knew that clearly. But the game had gone into overtime, the room was warm, and the moment felt easy in a way that made the next decision feel smaller than it really was.

"Sure," he said. "One more."

He thought about his wife and his son, but the thoughts came and went quickly. There was time. There was always time. That was the lie the afternoon told him, and he let himself believe it.

When the game ended, everything broke apart the way it always did; handshakes, see you next week, someone clapping him on the shoulder on the way out.

"Drive safe," someone said.

"Always do," Hudson answered.

He stood beside his truck for a moment in the cooling air, the sky turning orange along the edges. He knew he'd had too much. He could feel it, not in a dramatic way, but in something quieter. The kind of awareness that comes when a man tries to be honest with himself and doesn't quite follow through.

The right choice was obvious. He had a quarter in his pocket, and there was a payphone not far away. One call and someone would come get him. Simple.

He got in the truck anyway.

He told himself he was fine and started the engine.

The highway stretched out ahead of him, empty. He set the cruise control and rested his hands lightly on the wheel. He felt steady, and that was the problem. He felt just in control enough to believe he was.

Up ahead, a side street met the highway, and a compact car sat at the stop sign. He noticed it, registered it, saw the sign clearly, red, solid.

You've got a stop sign, he thought.

The car pulled out.

No hesitation. No warning. It just moved.

Hudson hit the brakes. The wheels locked, and then there was no space left between him and the moment. The impact came all at once; metal folding, glass flashing white, the airbag slamming into him hard enough to take his breath and his hearing at the same time.

Pain followed immediately, both legs at once, sharp and wrong. He tried to move but couldn't. The truck had collapsed around him, trapping him in place.

He smelled burned rubber and coolant, something else beneath it that didn't belong. Blood ran into his left eye, and he couldn't lift his arm to wipe it away.

Voices came next, distant at first, then closer. Someone shouting. Someone calling. He tried to answer, but nothing came.

Red lights pulsed through what was left of the windshield. Hands reached in, careful, controlled. Someone told him not to move while another voice barked orders.

They cut the roof away. He heard it more than he saw it, metal tearing as it gave.

Then the sky opened above him. Wide, pale, faces leaning in.

As they lifted him out, a single thought surfaced, clear and uncomplicated.

You had a stop sign.

He held onto it. The only clean thing in the moment. The part that wasn't his.

The ambulance doors closed.

He didn't understand yet how long he would carry that thought.

Three

Life Changes

Gillette, Wyoming. 1987

Hudson sat in the apartment with a work folder open in his lap and the lamp on.

He wasn't reading anymore. He'd stopped a while ago. But he kept the folder open because closing it meant the workday was officially over, and once that was over there was nothing between him and the quiet.

The quiet was the hard part.

He'd learned to measure days differently since getting out. Not by what he accomplished. Not by who he talked to. Just by whether anything went wrong. A day where nothing went wrong was a win. Didn't matter if that sounded like a low bar. He'd lived long enough to know it wasn't.

The job had gone fine. Better than fine. The work made sense to him, electrical systems and load calculations and the kind of problem that had a right answer if you were patient enough to find it. He liked that. He'd spent enough years in places where the rules shifted depending on who was watching. It was good to work with something that didn't care about any of that.

The company ran federal prisons. He'd known that when he took the job.

He'd taken it anyway. Make of that what you want.

He closed the folder. Set it on the table. Looked around the apartment.

Nothing on the walls. No photos. No objects from anywhere else. Everything had gone somewhere over the years, one piece at a time, until there was nothing left to take. He didn't miss the stuff itself. He missed what having stuff meant. That your life was stable enough to accumulate things. That you had somewhere to put them.

Harry would be twelve now.

Hudson didn't have to calculate it anymore. He just knew. Seven years old when they took Hudson out the front door in handcuffs. Twelve now. Five years of growing up without his dad around, and not in the good way, not in the divorced-parents-two-houses way. In the my-father-went-to-prison way.

That thought didn't ration the way other thoughts did. It showed up whenever it wanted.

He got up and went to the window. Stood there looking at the street until Gillette went dark and quiet and the only sounds were the occasional car and the wind off the open land beyond the edge of town.

It wasn't a bad life.

He told himself that straight. No sarcasm in it. He was out. He had a job. He had a roof and food and no one telling him when to sleep. After four and a half years, those things weren't nothing.

He just wished they felt like more.

He turned off the lamp and went to bed.

Greeneville, Tennessee. 1982

The morning they came for him had started like every other morning.

That was the part he kept coming back to. No warning. No bad feeling when he woke up. Just sunlight through the windows and the smell of coffee and his wife moving around the kitchen and his son getting ready for school.

He was at the table eating breakfast with both legs in casts, propped up on a kitchen chair he'd dragged over. A few days home from the hospital. Each of those days had felt like evidence that the worst was behind them. The accident had been bad. The recovery was hard. But they were getting through it.

He believed that. He needed to believe it. At that point the two things were the same.

His wife poured his coffee without being asked and sat down across from him. She had a look on her face that she was working to keep neutral.

"Heard from the detective lately?" she asked.

"Not since the hospital."

"Just wondered if they needed anything to close it out."

"It was an accident," Hudson said. "They ran the stop sign. If there was a problem, somebody would've said something by now."

She nodded. Looked at her coffee.

Something was moving behind her eyes that she wasn't sharing. He saw it and didn't ask. They were both doing that, holding things back to protect the other one, or maybe to protect themselves. Hard to tell the difference after a while.

The blood draw. He knew about it. The nurse had told him at the hospital, flat and professional, just delivering information. Hudson had put that number in a box in the back of his head and left it there. He'd told himself he hadn't been impaired. That the crash would've happened to anyone. That point zero eight was technically the limit, and technically wasn't the same as guilty.

Eleven days of telling himself that story.

He was close to believing it.

His son came through the kitchen with his backpack on, kissed his mom, said goodbye to Hudson with the careful cheerfulness of a seven-year-old who'd figured out that the adults in his house were fragile right now and it was his job not to make it worse.

Hudson watched him go.

His wife left a few minutes later. Hudson rolled the wheelchair to the living room window and watched her back out of the driveway. The street was quiet. Sprinkler going in a neighbor's yard. Birds somewhere.

We're going to be okay, he thought.

He meant it.

The knock came forty minutes later.

Three hard hits. Not a neighbor knock. Not a delivery knock. The kind that isn't asking.

Hudson was halfway to the door in the wheelchair when it came in.

Not opened. In. The frame split at the latch and the door swung hard and fast and men in body armor poured through, moving like they'd done it a hundred times, because they probably had.

"Police! Get on the floor! Floor, now!"

Hudson's hands went up before he'd made a decision to raise them. Body just did it.

"I can't," he said. "My legs. I can't get down."

Nobody listened. A hand grabbed the wheelchair and the world tilted and he went forward, palms hitting the hardwood, both casts slamming into the floor. The pain was total. He stopped being able to think for a second. Just breathed. Focused on the grain of the wood six inches from his face.

He'd refinished that floor. Three summers ago. His son kept running in to ask how much longer it would take.

Handcuffs went on.

He didn't fight it. There was nothing to fight with.

He lay there and listened to his house being searched. Drawers opening. Boots crossing rooms. All the private stuff of a life being opened and looked at by strangers.

They carried him out. Not helped. Carried, like furniture.

His neighbors were outside. He didn't look at them.

The car door closed. Through the window he watched his house get smaller. The front door was still hanging open, broken, interior dark.

That's when it finally landed.

Not the accident. Not the moment he got in the truck. This moment, right here, watching his house disappear through the back window of a police car while his son was at school not knowing yet.

He should have called someone for a ride.

That was it. Plain. No excuses around it. Two people were dead and he was in handcuffs and his son was going to come home today to something he'd never be able to unlearn.

He should have called someone.

He sat with that the whole way to the station.

The interrogation room was cold on purpose.

They put him at the table still in the wheelchair, casts resting at a bad angle, wrists cuffed to the table. Nobody asked if he was comfortable. He was a case number now. Case numbers didn't get asked that.

The detective came in, sat down, opened a folder. Didn't introduce himself.

"Blood alcohol. Point zero eight."

"That's the limit," Hudson said. "Right at the limit."

"Over the limit. Legal maximum is point zero seven nine."

Hudson heard himself say it: "If I'd taken one less sip it would've been legal."

The detective just looked at him.

"A woman and her daughter are dead," he said. "The car that pulled out. She ran the stop sign. That's documented. But your reaction time was impaired."

"I was paying attention," Hudson said. "I saw the sign. I had the right of way."

"You did," the detective said. Not agreeing. Just placing it next to the other fact. "And you were over the legal limit. Both things are true at the same time."

That was the sentence. Both things are true at the same time.

Hudson had spent eleven days building an argument where the first fact cancelled out the second one. The detective just set them side by side and the whole structure fell apart.

Hudson asked for a lawyer. The conversation ended.

The jury took less than a day.

His lawyer had told him straight: the facts weren't good, sympathy wouldn't be enough, the best he could do was be honest about that day and hope it counted for something. Hudson had tried. He'd sat in that witness box and told it plain, no justifications, no architecture.

Hadn't mattered.

Twelve years, if he caused no problems, worked a job, he could parole out in four.

The judge read it like he was reading a grocery list. Just doing the job. Hudson took it the same way.

Prison had its own rhythm. Head down. Clean record. Do the time. His legs healed up enough to walk, though the limp never fully went away. The headaches came and went.

His wife filed eighteen months in. Papers came in the mail. He signed them and sent them back and sat for a long time after.

He'd known it was coming. Didn't make it smaller.

His son stopped writing in the second year. Hudson didn't blame him. Nine years old, father in prison, mother rebuilding. There's only so much a kid can carry across that kind of distance. Hudson kept writing for a while anyway. Stopped when it started feeling like he was writing for himself.

When he got out he had some cash, a list of conditions, and a suspended license that would follow him for years. The restraining order took care of the rest. He couldn't go back.

So he went west.

Gillette, Wyoming. 1987

He lay in the dark in the Gillette apartment and ran through it.

The woman. Her daughter. Harry, his son, in a house Hudson wasn't allowed near. The driveway. That was the one he always came back to. Standing there in the cooling air, full knowledge, the right choice obvious, a payphone fifty yards away.

He'd gotten in the truck anyway.

She had pulled out in front of him. That was real. That was true. But he'd been drinking since early afternoon and he'd known it when he turned the key and he'd gone anyway, because he was the kind of man who told himself he was fine when the evidence said otherwise. That quality had been there long before the accident. Prison hadn't fixed it. He was still working on it.

Slowly. One day at a time.

He used to hate that phrase. Too simple. Too much like a bumper sticker. Then he spent enough time in a place where one day at a time was literally the only option, and he came out the other side understanding it differently.

You can't fix the past. You can't reach it. All you've got is today.

So you make today count. Then you do it again tomorrow.

Sleep came eventually. It always did, once he stopped fighting the accounting and just let it finish.

Outside, Gillette was quiet.

Inside, Hudson breathed and waited for morning.

FOUR

Flu Expansion

GILLETTE, WYOMING. 1987

Sixty dollars. That's what it cost.

Hudson bought the bike on his third day in Gillette from a guy selling it out of his garage on the west side of town. The man called it a mountain bike. There wasn't a mountain anywhere in sight. Hudson didn't bring that up. The tires were good. The frame was solid. It moved when you asked it to.

That was all he needed.

What he'd missed, more than he'd realized, was the ability to just go somewhere. No license. No asking for rides. No owing anyone anything. Four and a half years inside had taken that away so completely he'd stopped noticing the hole it left.

The bike didn't fix everything. It wasn't the same as having a truck and a license and nothing stopping him. But it was his, and it moved under his own power, and when he rode it nobody needed to know where he'd been.

That counted for something.

The ride home from the garage was rough at first. The scar tissue in his legs had its own opinion about pedaling, stiff and angry at the start, better once things warmed up. He pushed through it. Pain like that wasn't a stop sign. It was a negotiation. Keep moving and eventually it backs off.

By the time he got back to the apartment his palms were red from the grip and he was breathing hard and he felt something he hadn't felt in a long time.

Not happy. Something more specific than that. The feeling of having handled a problem himself, start to finish, without asking anyone for help.

He leaned the bike against the wall and stood there looking at it.

Good enough.

He rode to work the next morning.

The air had that early Wyoming cold to it, the kind that makes everything sharp and clear. His breath came out in little clouds. His legs found the rhythm faster than the day before.

Gillette looked different from a bike. Slower. More detailed. From a car, the town was just buildings and roads you passed through. On a bike you caught the stuff in between. A hand-painted sign in a diner window. A dog sitting in a front yard like he owned the whole block. Two guys outside a hardware store having the kind of conversation that looked like it happened every morning.

People noticed him. A few nodded. A couple waved, the easy wave of a small town that hasn't had a reason to be suspicious yet. Hudson nodded back and kept pedaling.

At work, a guy looked out the window at the bike locked to the rack.

"You rode that here?"

"Seems easier," Hudson said.

The man laughed and said something about Hudson being the healthiest guy in the office by Summer. Hudson accepted it and went to his desk. That was the kind of moment he wanted right now. Light. No weight to it. Just a thing that happened and moved on.

In the evenings he rode without any particular destination. Past churches with potluck signs. Past a grocery store. Past a bar where somebody had apparently decided it was going to be that kind of night because the music was coming through the walls. He rode until the light died and the town settled into its evening version, then rode back.

Not happy. He wasn't going to pretend that. But he was moving. Under his own power. Learning the streets, which ones connected and which ones dead-ended and which ones surprised you if you followed them far enough.

After years of being told exactly where he could and couldn't go, that was more than nothing.

He'd stopped expecting big things. Turns out small things hit harder than he remembered.

The bike leaned against the wall each night, dusty from the roads. Hudson went upstairs, sat in the quiet, let the day finish.

Tomorrow he'd ride to work again.

Monrovia, Liberia.

The room was already too warm when they sat down.

Ceiling fans going, moving the heat around without doing anything useful about it. Dr. Rourke stood at the front, jacket still on. People who knew him knew what that meant. He thought this was serious enough to dress the part.

"Field reports only," he said. "No speculation."

Dr. Porter from the CDC had a red-taped folder open in front of her. Ambassador Hale from the UN sat across from her. At the far end of the table, Minister Kaba sat with his hands folded, not saying anything. He had the look of a man who already knew what was coming and was waiting for everyone else to catch up.

The TV on the wall was muted. The headline scrolled at the bottom of the screen.

MYSTERIOUS ILLNESS REPORTED IN WEST AFRICA.

Rourke pointed to the map behind him. Liberia in the center. Everything around it still clean, still unmarked.

"We are classifying this as a regional outbreak," he said. "Severe. Highly lethal. Contained."

Porter looked up. "That assumes symptoms show up fast."

"Which is why we're here," Rourke said.

Fresh printouts went around the table, still warm from the machine. Hale looked at the numbers and asked about mortality rates in the voice of a man who already doesn't want the answer.

Rourke read the page before answering.

"Fatality rate," he said. "Over ninety-nine percent."

The room went quiet.

Kaba unfolded his hands and folded them again. "Entire towns have gone silent," he said. "No radio contact. No messengers. Nothing."

"We have teams headed there now," Rourke said.

Porter shook her head. "They're not headed there. They're arriving. And they're finding the same thing everywhere they go."

Hale leaned forward. "Can we keep this inside Liberia?"

Nobody answered right away. The fan clicked overhead. Outside, a helicopter lifted off, loud for a second, then gone.

"That is still our working assumption," Rourke said.

Porter looked at him. Didn't push it. Not yet.

The door opened and an aide came in fast, dropped a telex on the table in front of Porter, and left.

She read it once. Read it again.

"Confirmed cases outside Liberia," she said.

"Confirmed how?" Hale asked.

"Same presentation. Same respiratory failure. Same progression. Guinea, two locations. Sierra Leone six hours ago."

Kaba spoke without looking up. "People move between those towns every day. Markets. Family. It's just how it works."

"Expected movement," Rourke said.

"There's also an unconfirmed report from Lisbon," Porter said. "Man collapsed after getting off a plane. Dead before quarantine could happen."

"Unconfirmed," Hale said.

"Yes. But the timing fits."

Rourke looked at Porter. "What are we seeing on incubation?"

"Longer than we thought," she said. "Days. Maybe more. Long enough for someone to board a plane, fly across the world, clear customs, get a hotel, eat dinner, sleep, wake up the next morning feeling completely fine."

She let that land.

Kaba said what everyone was thinking. "Then border screening is already too late."

Nobody argued.

An aide put a portable radio on the table. Static, then a voice.

"Field Team Seven. We're in Nzérékoré. Same findings. Entire district. No survivors."

Rourke closed his eyes for a second. "Any mutation?"

"Negative. If anything, it's spreading faster than earlier reports."

The radio cut out.

On the TV behind them, the muted anchor was standing in front of a map that now stretched beyond Liberia's borders. Red markers appearing as she talked.

"NNN has affiliates in thirty countries," Hale said. "Once this hits the international feeds..."

"It already has," Porter said. "Lisbon isn't speculation anymore."

Rourke walked to the map. He paused. Then he erased the containment line he'd drawn at the start of the meeting and moved it outward. Nobody said anything about the erasure.

"We're not tracking containment anymore," Porter said. "We're tracking spread."

"We need to be careful with our language," Hale said.

Rourke looked at him. "Language won't slow this down."

Someone turned up the TV volume without asking.

The anchor's voice filled the room.

"This is National News Network. We are receiving reports of a rapidly spreading respiratory illness now confirmed in multiple West African nations. Officials stress there is no cause for panic."

Footage rolled behind her. A clinic packed with patients. Stretchers in the hallway. Doctors moving fast, faces tight. The footage lasted maybe four seconds before cutting back to the anchor's steady expression.

Hale was already on his feet. "They weren't cleared to show that."

"They have satellite feeds," Rourke said. "They don't need our clearance."

Kaba turned away from the screen. "My people aren't panicking because of rumors. They're panicking because they're watching their neighbors die and nobody is telling them what it is."

Phones started ringing around the room. An aide picked one up and held it slightly away from his ear.

"Rome wants clarification," he said. "London's on the other line."

The radio cut in before anyone could respond.

"Field Team Eleven. Dakar. First confirmed cases in the city. Local hospitals can't handle the volume."

Porter looked at the map without speaking. Dakar. Port city. Air hub. One of the most connected points on the continent.

She didn't say it. She didn't have to.

"Here's the mechanism," she said instead. "People feel fine. They move. They get on planes and buses and trains. They arrive somewhere new and feel fine for another day or two. By the time they get sick, they've already passed it to ten other people who are now on their own planes and buses." She looked around the table. "Every traveler is a delivery system. None of them know it."

Another telex. Porter read it and placed it face-down.

"Northern Spain," she said. "Multiple deaths. Hospitals overwhelmed."

"We can't release that," Hale said.

"NNN has someone in Barcelona," Porter said. "It's already out."

On the screen the anchor's map kept expanding. Red markers popping up one by one while the room argued about managing information that had already stopped being manageable.

Hale killed the sound again.

"We've lost the narrative," he said.

Rourke looked at him. "The narrative was never ours. We just thought it was."

Nobody argued.

The meeting went on for hours and ended without a conclusion because there wasn't one available.

Telex pages kept coming. The radio kept bringing in new locations. Rourke stood at the map with a legal pad, writing numbers he didn't show anyone. The people close enough to see them looked away.

"Every major travel corridor," he said. "Weeks. Not months."

"Does cold weather slow it?" Hale asked.

"No data supporting that," Porter said. "We've been hoping. It's not there."

Kaba looked up. "What do I tell my people?"

The room had no answer. Not because nobody cared. Because there was no answer that was honest and also useful, and everyone in that room knew it.

"This is not an outbreak," Rourke said. He set the pencil down. "An outbreak has edges. You work from the perimeter in. This has no perimeter. This is an event."

The radio went again.

"Field Team Nineteen. Northern Spain, spread confirmed beyond Barcelona. Secondary cities reporting. Two hospitals closed."

Hale stared at the TV. The map on screen was almost solid red now.

The meeting broke up without anyone officially ending it. People gathered their papers and headed for the door, moving toward work that wouldn't be enough, and knowing it, and doing it anyway.

Five

Doris

Gillette, Wyoming. 1987

Hudson was deep in a load calculation when he noticed someone standing next to his desk.

He looked up.

Doris.

A folder rested under one arm. She watched him with the patience of someone who had been there a while and didn't mind waiting.

He'd been aware of her since his first day. The way you notice someone who makes a complicated place run like it isn't complicated at all. She handled the administrative side of the office with a kind of quiet efficiency, always where something needed attention, gone as soon as it didn't.

He respected that.

"Settling in okay?" she asked.

"So far," he said. "Nothing's blown up yet."

She smiled. "Around here that's a good sign."

She shifted the folder slightly. There was a pause, but not an uncertain one. More like she had already decided what she was about to say.

"Few of us grab dinner on Thursdays," she said. "Diner on Main. Coffee's decent. You're welcome to come."

Hudson hesitated.

Not because he didn't want to. He'd had enough evenings alone in that apartment to know that sitting across from someone sounded better than it should.

He hesitated because saying yes had gotten unfamiliar.

"Sure," he said. "I'd like that."

"I'll pick you up at six," she said. "Easier than navigating."

She turned, then glanced back once.

"Wear whatever you've got on."

He watched her head back to her desk, blonde hair catching the overhead light for a second before she disappeared into the rhythm of the office again.

When he looked back at his diagrams, the lines didn't hold his attention the way they had before.

She pulled up right at six.

The car was older, paint faded from years in the sun, the door closing with a solid, reassuring weight. Inside, it smelled faintly of her perfume, mixed with paper and the warmth of a car that had been sitting out all day.

A country station played low on the radio.

Hudson had been hearing it through his apartment walls all week and still hadn't decided how he felt about it.

"Gillette treating you okay?" Doris asked as she pulled onto the road.

"Quieter than I expected."

She laughed. "Everybody says that. Then they either leave in a month or they're still here twenty years later saying the same thing to the next new person."

"Which are you?"

"Twenty years," she said. "Give or take."

The town moved past them slowly.

"I'm basically the unofficial tour guide," Doris said. "Which mostly means knowing what used to be here."

"Lot to guide?"

"Not really," she said. "That's kind of the point."

There was no apology in it.

Just acceptance.

The diner sat at the edge of Main Street, glowing warm against the evening.

A bell rang as they stepped inside. The air carried coffee, grease, and something steady that didn't exist anywhere else.

Doris was greeted by name before they reached the booth.

They slid in across from each other. The menus were worn at the corners. The waitress poured coffee without asking.

Hudson took that as a good sign.

A television hung in the corner, tuned to NNN. The volume was low. The anchor's mouth moved, but the words didn't reach the tables.

Hudson noticed it, then let it go.

They ordered. Doris didn't look at the menu.

They talked about work first.

The limits of the system. What the company actually needed. What had been left out of the job description. Doris filled in the gaps without overexplaining, the way someone does when they know exactly what matters and what doesn't.

Eventually, the conversation shifted.

"Grew up close to here," Doris said, her hands wrapped around the mug. "Left for college. Spent a few years in Denver thinking I'd made it. Then came back."

"What brought you back?" Hudson asked.

"Mom got sick. I came for that." She paused. "She got better. But by then I wasn't in a hurry to leave."

"That surprised you?"

"More than it should have." A small smile. "I used to think bigger automatically meant better. Denver taught me that wasn't true."

Hudson nodded. "I've lived in places like that."

She studied him briefly.

"You seem like someone who knows that already."

"Most things I've learned came the hard way," he said.

She didn't argue.

Instead, she turned her mug slowly in her hands.

"My parents named me after my great-grandmother," she said. "Doris. Never thought much about it growing up. Just one of those names you inherit."

Hudson looked up slightly.

"But now," she continued, "people tell me I remind them of Doris Day."

A quiet breath, almost amused.

"I didn't see it at first. Still don't, most days. But I hear it enough that I've stopped arguing."

Hudson leaned back slightly.

"Life's funny like that," he said. "Names stick around long enough to become something else."

She looked at him, waiting.

"I always thought Doris Day was one of the cutest actresses in those old movies."

It wasn't said like a line.

Just simple.

She held his gaze for a moment, then smiled.

"I'll take that," she said.

Something settled between them after that.

The conversation moved easier.

Hudson looked down at his plate.

"I was married," he said. "Have a son. Things ended badly. I moved out here because staying back there felt like staying in a room that kept reminding me of everything I got wrong."

He hadn't meant to say that much.

Doris didn't interrupt.

"Don't see my son anymore," he added. "That part doesn't get easier."

"I'd guess not," she said.

No sympathy layered on top.

Just truth.

"I'm not running anymore," Hudson said. "At least that's what I tell myself."

She gave a slight smile.

"The fact that you can say that probably means something."

He looked at her.

She wasn't easy to read.

Present, but not exposed.

"What about you?" he asked.

She let out a small laugh.

"That's more complicated than it sounds."

"You don't have to answer."

"No, I know." She turned the mug again. "I was with someone for a long time. Ended about three years ago. Not a fight. Just... slow. Then done."

She paused.

"I figured out I'm better at being alone than I thought. Whether that's healthy or just something I got used to... I don't know yet."

"Probably both," Hudson said.

She nodded.

"Probably both."

The TV volume jumped.

Not gradually. Someone cranked it, the way you crank something when what's on it has suddenly changed into something very important.

Every head in the diner turned.

Red banner across the bottom of the screen. BREAKING NEWS. The anchor looked the same as always, controlled, professional. But the set of her jaw was different.

"We are receiving new and troubling information regarding the outbreak now being referred to as the Liberian Influenza," she said. "Officials now confirm the illness is far more severe than previously reported. Health agencies are acknowledging for the first time that the virus is spreading rapidly across multiple continents."

The diner went quiet. Not loud-panic quiet. Still quiet. The kind of still that happens when something distant suddenly isn't.

A fork stayed frozen halfway to someone's mouth. The waitress stopped mid-step, coffee pot in hand, and stood at the counter staring at the screen. The guy in the booth by the door said something to the woman across from him, low, and she didn't answer.

"Sources indicate an extremely high mortality rate," the anchor said. "International travel restrictions are under review as cases continue to rise in Europe, Asia, and parts of South America."

Behind her, a map. Red markers everywhere. Not scattered. Everywhere.

Hudson had been tracking this the way you track a storm that keeps getting adjusted on the forecast. You watch it, you note it, you tell yourself it's probably going to turn. The map on that screen wasn't turning.

"This is no longer considered a localized outbreak," she said.

Nobody in the diner spoke.

Hudson looked at Doris. She had both hands flat on the table, coffee forgotten, eyes on the screen. Not scared exactly. The look of someone running a calculation.

Then she looked at him.

Something passed between them that had nothing to do with the broadcast. The two of them had been sitting here, in this warm diner on an ordinary Thursday, talking about their lives, and the world had shifted while they weren't watching. The distance they both counted on, each in their own way, had gotten smaller.

"Don't know what to make of that," Doris said.

"Neither do I," Hudson said.

The waitress came by, asked if they needed anything. Neither of them answered for a second. Doris shook her head and the woman moved on.

They paid and went outside.

The street looked the same. Same cars parked at the curb. Same lights in the same windows. Nothing visibly different. Hudson had felt this before, in a different context. The moment where before and after split apart with no visible seam between them.

Doris drove Hudson home with the radio off. Just road noise. Neither of them tried to fill it.

She pulled up outside his building and left the engine running.

Then she turned it off.

Hudson looked at her.

"You want to come up?" he asked.

She took a moment. Looked at the building. Looked back at him.

"Yes," she said.

They went upstairs without talking. The building was quiet. Hudson unlocked the door and held it. She stepped in. Door closed behind them.

The apartment was dark and still. She set her purse on the table and looked around at the room. The spare furniture. The nothing on the walls. No photos. No clutter. He watched her take it in.

No judgment in her face. Just recognition. Like she understood what a room like this said about a person without needing it explained.

Hudson turned on the lamp. Low light. Softer.

Outside, the news was still running. Maps still spreading. Whatever was happening out there was still happening and would keep happening until morning.

In here, it was quiet.

Two people who had both been careful for a long time, standing in a small apartment in Wyoming, and the careful distance between them feeling like something that didn't need to stay.

They didn't talk about the broadcast.

There were better things to do with the evening.

Six

Hudson Calls Home

Gillette, Wyoming. 1987

The television no longer returned to regular programming.

Hudson noticed it when he woke, the screen already lit from when he had fallen asleep watching it the night before. The anchor's voice was steady and unbroken, no commercials, no weather, no familiar transitions back to ordinary life. National News Network had abandoned its usual rhythm sometime in the night and had not returned to it.

He sat on the edge of the bed in yesterday's clothes and watched.

The banner at the bottom of the screen had changed.

GLOBAL HEALTH EMERGENCY.

Officials appeared one after another behind podiums and microphones, each speaking in the measured cadence of people trying to project calm while describing something that did not accommodate calm. Words like vigilance and preparedness repeated with the hollow regularity of phrases chosen for their weight rather than their meaning. No one said panic. No one said the thing that the maps behind them were already saying.

The maps were worse each time they appeared. Not slightly worse. Significantly worse. The red had spread in the night the way weather spreads, indifferent to borders, filling in around the places that had tried to hold it back.

Hudson made coffee and stood in the kitchen doorway watching a panel of experts speak carefully over each other. He recognized the specific quality of the disagreement: not a disagreement about facts but about how quickly to say them. They all knew. The question was the pace of the telling.

Then the screen cut to the seal behind the podium, and the panel dissolved, and the room the anchor sat in went quiet for a moment before she said: "We go now to the White House."

Gillette, Wyoming.

President Reagan stood before the cameras with the controlled gravity of a man who has rehearsed the weight of what he is about to say and has decided to carry it visibly rather than conceal it. He did not smile. He did not use the cadence he used for reassurance. This was a different register, slower, each word set down deliberately.

"My fellow Americans," he began.

Hudson sat at the kitchen table. He had seen this setting before, the podium, the seal, the careful arrangement of the room to signal that what was happening was serious but managed. He had seen it during other moments that turned out to be less serious than they looked, and moments that turned out to be more. He had learned to listen for what was not said rather than what was.

"We are facing a serious global health threat," the president said. "One that demands decisive and immediate action."

He spoke of coordination. Of allies and partners and the full resources of the federal government. The language was firm in the way that language is firm when firmness is the only thing left to offer.

Then: "Effective immediately, all nonessential international travel into the United States will be suspended."

Hudson set his coffee down.

"All incoming flights from affected regions will be halted. Additional restrictions will be implemented as conditions require. Essential services will continue to operate, and I want to assure the American people that we are taking every step available to us."

He went on. Borders. Screening protocols. The importance of unity. The promise of regular updates. What he did not say pressed against every sentence he did say: no timeline, no threshold for reversal, no sense that this was temporary in any way that could be measured.

When the address ended and the anchor returned, her tone was unchanged but her eyes had sharpened.

"This marks the first suspension of international travel in the modern history of the United States," she said. "Enacted for public health reasons, effective as of midnight tonight."

Hudson turned off the television and sat in the quiet. Outside, a car moved along the street. Somewhere down the block, someone's morning was proceeding without apparent interruption.

He thought about Harry.

He thought about where Harry was, and how far that was, and whether far was still a meaningful category.

He got up and got ready for work.

The news did not slow while he was away from it.

It accumulated, each development arriving before the previous one had been absorbed, each new footage package carrying the same essential information in a different location. India. Brazil. The long lines of ships idling at the entrance to the Panama Canal, waiting at a gate that had been closed with the sudden finality of something that had been pretending to be optional.

China had moved first, and moved completely. Satellite images on the evening broadcast showed highways emptied, airports sealed, cities that had never been quiet now producing no visible evidence of the millions living inside them. An analyst said they were buying time. Another said they were past the point where time could be bought.

The canal footage returned throughout the day, the camera finding the same guards standing at the same barriers from slightly different angles, as if a new perspective might change what the images meant. It did not. The canal had always been spoken of as a passage, the place where the world's movement narrowed and continued. Now it was a wall, assembled after the thing it was meant to stop had already moved through.

"Despite these measures," the anchor said, in the version Hudson caught on the small television in the break room at lunch, "health experts confirm the virus is already present north of the barrier."

Someone behind him said, "Jesus."

He did not turn to see who.

Doris appeared in his office doorway in the early afternoon, leaning against the frame with her arms folded loosely. She looked at him for a moment before speaking, the way she had looked at him across the diner table the previous night, with the specific attention of someone who has recently decided to pay closer attention.

"You look like you've been somewhere else all day," she said.

"I've been here," Hudson said.

"Physically," she said.

He smiled despite himself. "The news this morning."

She nodded and stepped inside, lowering her voice out of habit rather than necessity. The office around them was occupied with its own business. "Did you hear the Secretary of Health?"

"I missed that."

"Pandemic," she said. "Official declaration. They're calling it the Liberty Flu." She paused. "I think they're hoping the name makes it feel more manageable."

"Does it?"

"No," she said.

“Did they explain the name change?”

“I think people were worried the name Liberian Flu would cause issues for Liberia,” she said.

He exhaled slowly and set down his pencil. "What I saw this morning already looked worldwide. The declaration just makes it official."

"Wyoming's still quiet," Doris said. She said it the way you say something you're not entirely sure you believe but want to test out loud.

"For now," Hudson said.

She looked at him. The two words sat between them with the same weight they had carried at the diner.

There was a brief pause, comfortable in a way that would not have been possible two days earlier.

"I was thinking," Doris said, "that maybe tonight we don't both need to go home to our own separate televisions and watch the world fall apart alone."

Hudson looked at her. He was aware of what the previous night had changed and what it hadn't, and of the specific quality of what she was offering, which was not urgency but company. Two people who had both spent too long being alone and had recently discovered they didn't have to be.

"I'm going to do some work at home," he said. "There's a project I want to stay ahead of."

She raised an eyebrow slightly.

"You're welcome to come," he said. "The work will keep."

The corner of her mouth moved. "I'll bring food," she said. "Something that isn't diner coffee."

"That would be better," he said.

She pushed off the doorframe and turned to go. Then she paused without looking back. "For what it's worth," she said, "last night helped. The fun part, I mean."

Hudson understood what she meant. "Yeah," he said. "It did."

He watched her walk away and sat for a moment before returning to his work, which took longer than it should have because the numbers on the page kept losing their place in his attention.

Gillette, Wyoming.

He was home by six and sat at the table with his notebook open and a pen in his hand that he had not yet used. The apartment felt the way it always felt when he returned to it: functional, quiet, arranged around the absence of anyone else. He had stopped noticing that quality most evenings. Tonight it was present again, the way it had been in the early weeks before Doris.

He thought about Harry.

He had been thinking about Harry since the president's address that morning. Not continuously, but in the way a bruise makes itself known: the thought would recede and then something would press against it and it would be there again, sharp and specific. Harry was twelve years old and living in eastern Tennessee with Carla and the man she had married, and the distance between there and here had always been the kind Hudson understood as legal and emotional and geographic and largely unsolvable.

Tonight it felt like a different kind of distance.

The maps from the morning were still in his head. The red filling in. The anchors choosing their words carefully. The President's voice saying, effective immediately, in the way of someone who had run out of alternatives.

He picked up the phone.

He had Carla's number memorized despite himself, the digits arranged in his mind with the particular persistence of things you have tried to let go of and haven't managed. He dialed and listened to it ring and told himself he was prepared for however it went.

He was not.

She answered on the third ring.

"What do you want, Hudson." Not a question. A declaration of inconvenience.

"I just got off work," he said. "I was hoping I could talk to Harry for a minute."

The pause was brief and sharp, the pause of someone deciding which form of no to use. "You can't just call here whenever you feel like it."

"I know," he said. "I'm not trying to cause trouble. I just want to hear his voice. One minute."

"You know this isn't appropriate. You know how my husband feels about this."

Hudson kept his voice level. "I'm not calling about you or your husband. I'm calling about our son."

"It upsets him," she said. "When you call, it upsets him, and then the whole evening is ruined. Do you understand that? Do you care about that at all?"

He took a breath. "Carla, there's a sickness spreading across the world. I've been watching it all day. I'm worried. I just want to know he's okay."

She laughed, and the laugh was the kind that had no humor in it, the sound of someone dismissing something without examining it. "There is no sickness."

"That's not what's being reported on every channel."

"Oh, please," she said, her voice rising into the tone he remembered, the tone that meant she had already decided and was now explaining her decision to someone too limited to have arrived at it themselves. "My husband has been following this very closely. This is United Nations propaganda. This is about control. About getting people scared so they hand over their freedoms without asking questions. Do you understand what I'm saying to you? This is manufactured."

Hudson was quiet for a moment. He looked at the wall. Outside, a car went past on the street, unhurried.

"I'm not asking you to agree with me," he said. "I'm asking to speak to my son."

"You watch too much NNN," Carla said. "That's always been your problem. You believe whatever they tell you. You don't think for yourself. My husband says--"

"Please," Hudson said. The word came out smaller than he intended. "One minute. Please."

There was a silence, and Hudson thought for a moment that something in it might shift. That some remaining part of whatever they had once been to each other might still be accessible. That the word please might land somewhere.

It didn't.

A new voice came on the line. Lower. Unhurried in the way of a man who has nothing to prove because the outcome is already settled.

"You listening to me?" the man said.

Hudson straightened without meaning to, some old instinct. "I'm listening."

"Good. You do not call this house. Not for any reason. Not ever. You are not part of this family. You are not part of my wife's life. And you are not part of that boy's life. You had your chance and you threw it away and that is done. If you call here again I will make sure there are consequences you are not prepared for. Am I being clear enough?"

He said it without heat, without the raised volume of anger. That was the thing that settled cold in Hudson's chest. Not the words but the delivery: flat, methodical, the voice of someone who had said things like this before and had found that calm was more effective than fury.

"I want to speak to my son," Hudson said.

"Your son," the man said, with a pause between the two words that made them sound like a category being contested. "Your son is fine. He doesn't need you calling here and upsetting the household. He doesn't need you at all."

The line went dead.

Hudson held the phone to his ear for a moment, listening to nothing. Then he set it down on the table, his hand resting beside it.

He sat without moving.

Harry was twelve years old. He was in a house with that voice. He was being raised by a man who spoke like that in the privacy of a phone call to someone he had already won against, which meant the version available to people he had not yet won against would be worse.

Hudson knew, in the way that a person knows something that cannot be acted on, that the restraining order and the miles and the legal language that had settled the custody arrangement were all working together to keep him away from his son. He also knew that calling again would accomplish nothing and might make things worse for Harry.

The knowledge of both things at once was a particular kind of helplessness. He had felt it before. It had not become easier to hold.

He looked at the window. The town was quiet outside, the street unchanged, the ordinary evening proceeding without him. Somewhere out there, Doris was getting into her car with food she had said she would bring, planning to sit with him through a night that had already gotten heavier than she knew.

He was glad she was coming.

Seven

No More Work

Gillette, Wyoming. 1987

NNN was running a debate.

Two guys at a desk. A moderator. Chyron at the bottom: LIBERTY FLU: HOW FAR SHOULD GOVERNMENT GO?

Hudson watched from the couch and tried not to throw something at the television.

Blue Tie was the one who'd been right. Mandatory quarantine. No delays. No exceptions. He'd seen the same hospital footage Hudson had seen and he couldn't understand why that footage wasn't enough. His voice had that tight, controlled quality of a man trying not to shout.

Red Tie never raised his voice once. He talked about freedom. Government overreach. Slippery slopes. He wasn't entirely wrong about any of it. Governments do keep emergency powers. That happens. But the virus outside wasn't waiting for that argument to resolve itself, and Red Tie was applying the right principle to the wrong moment.

Neither of them was going to convince the other. That wasn't the point of the segment.

"Quarantine remains voluntary at this time," the anchor said when it was over. "The administration has emphasized personal responsibility."

Reagan came on in replay footage, steady behind the podium.

"America is a nation built on freedom," he said. "We will not be quick to abandon the very principles that define us. People must be able to attend church, send their children to school, and gather with their families. Once freedoms are taken, they are not easily returned. That is a slippery slope we will not go down."

He paused.

"Yet."

Hudson stared at the screen.

Yet. One word. What it meant was: we know the slope is real. We know we're standing at the top of it. Everything else I just said is provisional.

An honest word. The most frightening word in the whole address.

Then Byrd came on. Senate Majority Leader. No composure on his face at all.

"This country needs to be locked down tighter than bark on a pine tree," Byrd said. "Nobody out of their house. Not for work. Not for church. Not for a Sunday drive. This is not a debate about freedom. This is a debate about whether there will be people left to be free."

The anchor moved on to the next segment.

Outside, a church bell rang on schedule.

Hudson turned the volume down. Sat in the quiet. Listened to a country that hadn't decided yet what it was willing to give up.

He went to the grocery store Tuesday morning. Early. Before the crowds.

The lot was already half full.

He stood at the entrance and looked at the cars and understood that everyone had had the same idea about going early. He went in anyway.

The sound was wrong the moment the doors opened. Too many people, too fast, in a space built for a slower pace. Carts banging into each other, nobody apologizing. A kid crying in the cereal aisle while her mom loaded boxes without looking down at her. Two guys at the end of the pasta section, talking low and tight about whether there was more in the back, neither of them making eye contact.

Hudson worked the edges. Rice. Canned goods. Coffee. He stayed out of the main aisles where people had stopped moving, frozen in front of shelves like the choice between soup brands was suddenly the most important decision they'd ever made.

The shelves were already half empty.

Not from normal shopping. From fear shopping. The paper aisle had been cleaned out. The medicine section was stripped bare of anything that touched fever, cough, or anything respiratory. People's fear was running about three days ahead of the official messaging. Hudson noted that and kept moving.

He didn't take more than he needed. That made him stand out among the people with overloaded carts, but he didn't care.

At the register the cashier was maybe nineteen. Gloved hands that shook slightly, just enough to notice. She had the look of someone who came in because calling out felt like losing, and was now reconsidering that math.

"Busy morning," Hudson said.

She nodded, eyes on the scanner. Then, quietly, talking more to the belt than to him: "They say it's not here yet."

"People just want to feel ready," he said.

She handed over his change and held it for a second, not quite passing it across. "Do you think it's as bad as they're saying?"

He thought about what to tell her. She'd be back here tomorrow, scanning groceries for whoever came through. Nothing he said would change that.

"Being careful doesn't cost anything," he said. "Not being careful does."

She looked at him then. Really looked. Something in her face settled a little. Not relieved. Just like someone had finally said the actual thing instead of talking around it.

"My mom keeps telling me to come home," she said.

"Listen to her," Hudson said.

He loaded up his backpack outside and rode home fast. The streets weren't empty but the people on them had a different quality now, heads up, aware. Like everyone had started calculating something they hadn't been calculating before.

He washed his hands before he even took his jacket off.

Gillette, Wyoming.

The San Juan, Puerto Rico footage hit that evening.

NNN had a camera inside an emergency room or somewhere close enough that the images were clear. Hudson had been preparing himself for something like this, he was wrong. He wasn't prepared..

Stretchers in both directions down the hallway. Not temporary. Permanent. Patients on them with IVs hanging from whatever was available. Doctors squeezing through the gaps moving with the efficiency of people doing a job they trained for but never actually expected to do. A nurse crouched on the floor next to a patient because that's where the patient was.

Hudson leaned forward.

A hospital administrator came on outside the building. She looked like she hadn't slept in two days and had stopped tracking it.

"Do not come unless it is an absolute emergency," she said. "We cannot handle the volume. If you come here tonight for anything less than an absolute emergency, you are taking a space from someone who is dying."

Flat. Direct. No softening. She'd stopped thinking softening helped.

The anchor repeated the message: stay away from hospitals unless you're dying. Behind her, more footage. Ambulances parked outside closed entrance doors. A tent going up in a parking lot in the rain at eleven at night, people hammering stakes into wet pavement under portable lights.

Then the phrase that made Hudson sit very still.

Doctors choosing who to treat.

Not a triage. Choosing.

He turned the volume down but didn't kill it. He needed it in the room. He got up and started putting groceries away, placing each item deliberately. Rice. Canned tomatoes. Coffee. The dried beans he'd grabbed from an aisle nobody else had touched.

If the hospital wasn't an option, staying out of the hospital was the only move.

He washed his hands when he finished. Hot water, longer than needed.

On the screen behind him, another city. Another hospital. Another warning from someone who'd run out of softer ways to say it.

By midweek the office was a ghost town.

Thursday morning: lights on, systems running, five people in a building that had held twenty-three on Monday. The silence wasn't complete but what sounds remained were wrong. Phones ringing twice and stopping. Hallway echo that had never been there before.

Doris was there. That was the first thing Hudson checked when he walked in. He noticed that he checked it.

She was at the coffee machine with her coat still on, holding an empty mug. When she saw him come through the door something in her face changed. Like he was the first recognizable thing she'd seen all morning.

"Just us," she said.

"And some ghosts," Hudson said, looking down the empty hall.

She almost smiled. Poured coffee for both of them.

They worked through the morning. Maintaining routine because routine was the last thing holding the shape of a normal day. By ten the phones stopped ringing. One guy left around eleven without saying anything. The man whose wife was sick came back from a phone call, grabbed his stuff, and walked out. Nobody asked.

Three left by lunch. They sat at the conference table with food they weren't really eating.

"People are scared," Doris said.

"Can't blame them."

"The ones who left today," she said, "they're not cowards. They've got someone at home they're more scared for than themselves."

"That's generous."

"It's accurate." She folded her sandwich wrapper without eating the rest of it. "I keep asking myself whether any of this matters. Whether the infrastructure we're maintaining actually does anything useful anymore."

"Power matters," Hudson said. "Hospitals need it. Whatever hospitals are still running."

She looked at him. "You actually believe that."

"I need something useful to believe," he said.

She was quiet. Then: "I've been thinking about who I'd call if it got worse. The list is shorter than I expected."

Hudson knew what she meant. He felt the same thing. The circle pulling in tight, and near the center of it, someone he'd known less than a month.

"You're on my list," he said.

She met his eyes. "Good. You're on mine."

Not a big moment. Not a speech. Just two people acknowledging what was already true.

The workday ended without anyone officially calling it. They just reached the point where staying felt dishonest. The three of them left together. Hudson and Doris locked up. The click of the door echoed down the empty hall.

Outside, the parking lot was wide and quiet under the gray sky.

"Call me when you're home," Doris said.

"Yeah," Hudson said.

He rode home in the cold. Aware of his breathing. Aware of the empty roads. Pretty sure the office wasn't going to reopen.

The shelves were worse two days later.

Not slowly worse. Structurally worse. Hudson stood in the store and looked at sections that had been restocked and were already going bare again, the turnaround between full and empty measured in hours now.

NNN explained it that night. Truck drivers not showing up. Distribution systems running on fewer people than they needed. A warehouse manager on camera, not hiding his frustration: we can't stock what we can't move, and we can't move it if people won't come to work.

Same story with fuel. Manufacturing. Each piece of the chain that failed put pressure on the next one.

Hudson thought about the cashier with the shaking hands. Hoped she'd gone home.

He opened his cupboards and took stock. He had enough. He'd been building it up quietly, trip by trip, not from panic but from the same thinking he applied to everything: figure out what you actually need, get that, stop.

Not comfortable. Prepared.

The difference was everything.

The phone rang two nights later.

He picked up before the second ring.

"Hey." Doris. Her voice had that stretched quality it got when she'd been alone with her thoughts too long.

"Was about to call you," Hudson said.

"They shut us down," she said. "Official message tonight. Management said there's no point maintaining the pretense." A pause. "Their word. Pretense."

"I figured it was coming."

"I kept thinking it would hold a little longer," she said. "Stupid."

"Wanting things to hold isn't stupid."

He heard her TV in the background. Same anchor. Same tone.

"Mexico," she said. "Did you see?"

"Some of it."

"Whole regions just going dark. No signal. No reporters. Like watching the lights go out room by room from outside the house."

"The border," Hudson said.

"Military's too spread out. Too many gaps. Wyoming's still quiet." She exhaled. "I keep saying that to myself like it means something."

"Means something today," Hudson said. "And will mean something tomorrow."

She laughed. Short. Real.

"You always do that," she said.

"Do what?"

"Find the part that's still positive." A pause. "I needed that tonight. I didn't know how much until I heard your voice."

He sat with that.

"I need it too," he said. "In case that wasn't obvious."

"Getting more obvious," she said.

They talked for another hour. Not about any of it. About dinner. Hudson's tales from college. A summer she remembered from Colorado for no particular reason. Just two people keeping the world outside the window where it belonged for a little while.

After they hung up, Hudson sat in the quiet with the phone in his hand.

He'd spent years getting good at needing less. It had been useful. Got him through things that required running lean.

He was starting to think he'd gotten too good at it.

By Friday he'd made up his mind.

Supplies lined up along the wall. Organized by what he'd need first, what would last longest, what he couldn't replace. Water in every container he owned. Batteries next to the radio. Candles in the kitchen drawer. Door locked. Windows checked.

He stood at the window watching the street. A car went by. A man walked a dog, unhurried, like this was still a regular day. Maybe he didn't know yet. Maybe he knew and was walking the dog anyway.

Hudson didn't judge either way.

He ran through what he knew. Hospitals over capacity in most countries. Supply chains failing. The virus moving through people who felt fine, who had no idea they were carrying it. Every contact was a risk now. Every trip outside was a roll of the dice.

The smart move was to stop rolling.

He wasn't scared. He checked for that and it wasn't there. What was there instead was clarity. He'd been in situations before that required him to get honest about what was actually happening and stop telling himself the comfortable version. This was one of those situations.

Eight

The Border

USA, Mexico Border 1987

NNN couldn't keep up with Mexico City.

The footage came in pieces. Aerial shots of a city that had stopped working. Traffic lights still running their cycles over empty streets. Buses sitting with doors open where they'd stopped, drivers gone. Smoke from fires nobody was left to explain.

"Hospitals were overwhelmed within hours," the anchor said.

The footage behind her was worse than overwhelmed.

Patients on floors. On sidewalks. Doctors on camera for a few seconds: no space, no staff. Then the doctors stopped appearing.

After that, no official word. Because there was nobody left to make it official. Power failures. Water going out. Police dispatch silent. Neighborhoods going quiet in hours, not days.

"The Mexican government has not issued a statement in forty-eight hours."

She wasn't reading from notes anymore. It sounded like she was just saying what she knew.

Streets full of stopped cars. Open stores with no one inside. Bodies in some shots. In others, just the spaces where bodies had been.

Mexico City was gone.

NNN never said that word.

They didn't have to.

The border was next.

Military vehicles at the crossings. Long lines of soldiers in the heat, rifles low. The anchor said the border was secure.

A correspondent standing in the wind and dust said secure was a relative word for a line that ran two thousand miles through open desert.

The camera kept finding the gaps. Fence ending at rocky ground. Starting again a quarter mile later. Nothing in between but open land and hope.

"The border measures are part of a layered response," the anchor said.

Layered wasn't sealed. Everyone knew it. Nobody said it.

The sun went down. The desert didn't care.

They crossed at night.

Two of them. Moving slow. Stopping when something shifted in the dark, going again when it turned out to be nothing. They'd watched the patrols earlier, found the gap where the fence stopped for nearly a mile.

"This is it," the taller one said.

The other nodded. He was thinner than he'd been a month ago. "USA still has power," he said. Saying it out loud. "Still has food."

"Still has people," the taller one said.

They went low and fast. Boots on rocks. No sound. When they made it across, neither of them spoke. The stars were the same on both sides. That was the kind of thing you noticed.

"My mother would have come if she could," the thinner one said.

"Mine wouldn't have made it," said the other. "She was already sick when it started."

A country that didn't know they were in it yet.

"Nothing left back there," the thinner one said. Not sad. Just true.

"Then we keep going."

They walked north toward the lights.

The thinner one coughed.

"Cold air," he said. "Just that."

"Everyone back home started that way."

"That was different." Another cough, short, controlled. "This is exhaustion. We haven't slept right in a week."

The taller one watched him and didn't say what he was thinking. Might be wrong. Nothing useful to do with it if he wasn't.

"Get to the city. Then we rest."

The cough came back twice before they hit pavement. Each time a little worse.

El Paso, Texas.

El Paso at dawn. Ordinary. Stores opening. A few cars. A city that hadn't been asked yet to be anything other than normal.

The Kmart lot was already half full. People inside moving fast, carts overloaded, faces tight. Doors sliding open and closed without stopping.

Disinfectant smell that wasn't keeping up with how fast people were touching things.

The thinner man coughed as they passed a woman reaching for rice. Turned his head away. She glanced at him. He was already looking somewhere else.

She put the rice in her cart and kept moving.

Checkout line packed in close. The thinner man wiped his nose on his sleeve. The woman behind him shifted. The man in front didn't turn around.

They paid cash. Walked out into the sun.

The doors opened for the next person.

And the next.

The bus station was standing room only.

People moving toward family. People moving away from wherever they'd been. People just moving because standing still felt worse. All of them in the same building, same air, same rows of seats pressed close together.

TV in the corner. NNN. Volume low, captions running a few seconds behind. Everything the anchor said arriving with the feeling of something already past.

The thinner man coughed when he bought his ticket. Quick, controlled, wave of the hand, nothing to see. The clerk tore the stubs without looking up.

She'd been there since six. Hours left on her shift. She'd touched hundreds of people's cash already. Wouldn't occur to her to think about that until it was too late to matter.

On the bus, every seat filled. Shoulders touching. Shared air in a sealed space going nowhere fast.

The coughs came back. Deeper each time. The woman across the aisle moved toward the window without quite meaning to. Nobody said anything. Saying it out loud would have made it real.

Rest stop. A man forgot his wallet. The thinner one bought his coffee without being asked. They laughed. The man touched his arm in thanks. They went back to their seats.

Houston at evening. City lights wide and bright. Still here. Still lit. Still looking like somewhere worth arriving.

Friends waiting. Hugs. Food. Music. Everyone talking at once, telling stories, naming who hadn't made it, who still might. The thinner man smiled and ate and coughed once into his fist and turned away. Nobody noticed. Why would they? Everything was fine now.

The virus didn't need anyone to notice.

Breath. Touch. Laughter. Shared air. The most human things in the world.

The bus brought it there.

Love finished the job.

The first El Paso reports were easy to dismiss.

Uptick in respiratory cases. Seasonal. Nothing unusual. Officials said it. People believed it because they wanted to. That wanting was the most expensive thing in the whole disaster.

Within hours: clinics short-staffed. ERs closing to non-critical cases. The same message on repeat, worn smooth from overuse: stay home unless you're dying.

Then Houston showed up in the same reports.

They called it a cluster. The cluster doubled. Then they ran out of words for it.

The maps on screen filled in fast. Not like a wave. Like a web. Jumping along travel routes, appearing wherever people had gone, and wherever the people they'd met had gone after that.

"Contagious before symptoms," an expert said. He'd been saying it for weeks. "By the time someone feels sick, they've already passed it to a dozen others."

That night the anchors stopped saying if.

The Liberty Flu was already inside the country. It had been for days.

Washington, D.C.

NNN stayed on longer than it should have.

No schedule. No segments. Anchors came and went. The studio lights were on backup power and everyone knew it.

The anchor who stayed had been doing this twenty-two years. He read now like a man going through the motions because stopping felt worse than continuing.

"Unprecedented loss of life across the United States," he said. "And the world. No framework exists for what this is."

The graphics died behind him. Off camera, someone started coughing and didn't stop. Then movement. Then silence from that direction.

The anchor looked at his paper. Set it down.

"President Ronald Reagan and First Lady Nancy Reagan have died."

He stopped.

Five seconds. Maybe more. Then he picked it back up, because someone had to keep going until they couldn't.

"Details are limited."

The feed cut.

Different room. Different everything.

Bunker under Colorado Mountain.

Concrete walls. Bare lights overhead. The echo of a sealed space built deep in a mountain, carved out specifically so that certain people could survive things that would kill everyone else.

President George Herbert Walker Bush at a plain metal desk. No seal. No flags. Dark suit, no tie. The look of a man who hadn't slept in days and had stopped trying to hide it.

Behind him: people. Aides, officials, their families. All of them there in the mountain, sealed away and safe while the country above them burned.

He looked straight into the camera.

"My fellow Americans. I'm speaking from a secure location. I want to be clear about what that means."

He paused.

Not for effect.

It felt like he was deciding, in that moment, how much truth he was willing to put into the world before it went quiet.

"It means a selected group of government officials, essential personnel, and their families have been brought to a protected facility," he said. "We are safe. We are underground. We are monitoring conditions from a location that is not accessible to the general public."

He let that sit.

No softening.

No attempt to make it easier to hear.

"I'm not going to pretend that's fair," he continued. "It isn't. The people in this room did not earn their place here. And the people who didn't make it did not deserve what happened to them. I won't stand in a bunker and tell you different."

His hands rested flat on the desk in front of him.

They didn't move.

"This was not contained. It was not slowed in time. We prepared for outbreaks, for war, for disasters we could see coming. This was something else. By the time we understood what we were facing, the systems that hold everything together were already failing."

Behind him, barely noticeable unless you were looking for it, a heavy door opened and closed. Someone moved through the background. Quiet. Controlled. The sense of a place still operating, even as everything above it had stopped.

"What I can tell you is this," he said. "We are not abandoning the country. We are tracking conditions on the surface as long as we have the ability to do so. When it becomes survivable again, we will come back up. We will work to restore power, water, communications, and some form of government."

He paused again, but this time it wasn't hesitation.

It was weight.

"That work will take years," he said. "Possibly longer than any of us expect. We understand that. And we are committed to it regardless of how long it takes."

The room behind the camera stayed silent.

"Medical data collected before communications failed suggests that a small percentage of the population, roughly one in ten thousand, may carry a natural resistance to this strain. We don't know why. We don't know how to identify it ahead of time."

He leaned forward slightly.

"If you're hearing this, there is a real chance you are one of them."

He let that land.

"Hold onto that."

His eyes stayed fixed on the camera now.

Not scanning.

Not reading.

Focused.

"To whoever is listening," he said. "Now. Later. Wherever you are when this reaches you."

A breath.

The kind a man takes when he knows there won't be many more chances to speak.

"What was built can be built again."

He didn't rush it.

"Not the same. Not soon. But it can be done."

He glanced down briefly, then back up.

"Be decent to each other. Share what you have. Help the people close to you. The person next to you is not your competition."

A slight pause.

"They're all you've got."

The signal flickered once, barely noticeable.

"We will continue broadcasting as long as we are able," he said. "After that... you will be on your own for a while."

Another breath.

Quieter now.

"We haven't given up."

A final look into the camera.

Steady.

Resolved.

"God have mercy on us all."

The image held for a moment longer than it should have.

Then it cut.

The feed held on him. The bunker behind him. The sealed door. The people who got to live underground while everyone else took their chances.

Then it cut.

The anchor was back. He straightened his papers out of habit. Opened his mouth.

The lights went out.

All of them. Instantly. No warning.

Screen black. No goodbye. No final word. Mid-sentence, mid-thought, just gone.

Dark.

Silence.

A blank screen in an empty studio with nobody left to watch it.

Gillette, Wyoming.

Hudson was on the floor when it happened.

He'd moved off the couch at some point without deciding to. Back against it, knees up, radio on the table. Some part of him had already understood the TV wasn't making it through the night. Radio needed less to stay alive.

When the screen went dark he stared at it.

The radio kept going. Some voice relayed through whatever towers were still standing. He left it on. A voice was something.

He picked up the phone and dialed Harry's number.

It rang.

Kept ringing.

Nobody answered.

He sat there with the phone in his hand afterward. Didn't put it down right away.

He didn't know if the house in Tennessee had power. Didn't know if Carla and her husband had done what needed doing. Didn't know if Harry was okay or scared or sick or what anyone had told him about any of it. Didn't know if Harry knew his father was alive in Wyoming right now, sitting on the floor, trying to reach him.

No way to know.

Then he dialed Doris.

She answered on the first ring.

"Still here," she said. Before he spoke.

He closed his eyes. "Still here."

He heard her exhale. The sound of someone who'd been holding something and finally didn't have to.

"I watched it go dark," she said.

"Me too."

"Did you hear what he said? About the bunker?"

"Yeah."

"They're all down there," she said. Not angry. Stating it. "Safe in a mountain. Monitoring conditions."

"While the conditions kill everyone up here."

"Yeah."

A long quiet. Radio in the background. Nothing moving outside.

"He said they'll come back," Doris said. "When it's safe. Rebuild everything."

"I think he meant it."

"Doesn't change what it is."

"No," Hudson said. "It doesn't."

They stayed on the line. Didn't talk about the bunker anymore. Just stayed connected, two people in the dark in separate homes in a town that had gone mostly quiet.

"I tried calling my sister," Doris said after a while.

"Answer?"

"No."

He didn't say anything about Harry. She knew.

Nine

Phone Call

Gillette, Wyoming. 1987

One ring. Hudson picked up.

"Hudson."

Her voice was wrong. He knew it before he could name what was wrong about it. Stretched thin. Held together by effort.

"I'm here," he said.

He heard her take a breath. It caught. Wet and shallow, like air moving through something it shouldn't have to move through. She'd been sick three days. Each call worse than the last. He'd known. He hadn't said it out loud until now.

"I think I'm going to die," she said.

Flat. No drama. Just Doris telling him the truth the way she always told him things.

He closed his eyes. Slid off the couch to the floor, back against the wall, without deciding to.

"Talk to me," he said.

"There's nowhere to go," she said. "No doctors. I tried calling. Nothing." A pause. The effort in that pause. "Nobody's coming anymore."

He didn't tell her she was wrong.

"I didn't want to be alone," she said. "That's why I called."

"You're not alone. I'm right here."

She exhaled. Something she'd been holding went with it.

"That helps," she said. "More than you know."

He listened to her breathe. Trying to memorize it.

"I'm scared," Doris said. "Not of dying. Just of how it goes at the end. Whether it hurts."

"I'll stay with you the whole time," he said. "I'm not going anywhere."

"Okay," she said.

The cough came a few minutes later.

He'd heard it every day for three days. Each time worse. This was worse than all of them. It started deep and wouldn't stop, and when it finally did she made a sound that wasn't a word. Just a person gathering what was left after something had taken a lot.

"Sorry," she said. "That probably sounded bad."

"Don't apologize to me."

"Old habit." Something almost like a smile in her voice. "Can't help it."

"Keep it," he said. "I like your habits."

She started to laugh. The cough took it. When she came back she was quieter. The voice a little smaller. Something used up and not coming back.

"Talk to me," she said. "About something normal."

So he did.

He talked about the diner. The booth by the window. The cuddles on her couch. The afternoon they had fed ducks at the park and how one had chased Doris. He talked about the moment Doris laughed at something he said, sudden and real, and how he knew he was going to like knowing her. The drives around the county. Eating fried chicken at Cluck Palace and making fun of the strange uniforms. The nights spooning in bed.

Her breathing steadied a little as he talked. Not better. Just less alone.

"I liked the nights," she said.

"Me too."

He talked about the morning she'd shown up in his office doorway and said he looked like he'd been somewhere else all day. How she'd been right. How he hadn't expected to be seen that clearly by someone he'd known less than a week. How she always said the actual thing instead of something easier.

"You showed up," Doris said quietly. "That's what I'll remember. The world was falling apart and you just kept showing up."

He couldn't answer for a second.

"I'm glad I did," he said.

"Don't waste it," she said. Her voice smaller now. Pulling inward. "Being alive when so many aren't. Don't waste it. Promise me."

"I promise."

"I don't know what comes next," she said. "I don't know if I believe in anything specific. But I hope it's quiet. And warm. And nobody's afraid."

He didn't say anything. There was nothing to add to that.

"I want to close my eyes," she said. "But don't stop talking."

"I won't," he said.

"Okay," she said. "Okay."

She went quiet.

He kept talking. Wyoming mornings. The sky out here before the sun clears the horizon. The bike. The day he bought it. Small things. The things that made up the weeks they'd had.

Her breathing came through the phone.

Then it was harder to hear.

Then he was listening to a connection still open in a room that had gone still.

He stayed on the line. He'd promised. He kept talking softly until stopping felt like it was okay. Like she'd gotten far enough.

When he lowered the phone the apartment was the same as it had always been. Supplies along the wall. Lamp on. Blank TV. Everything exactly where it was.

He sat on the floor.

The grief was there. It didn't have a shape yet. Just pressure, everywhere at once.

Gillette, Wyoming.

First time outside since the flu hit the country.

The door opened like it always had. Air came in cool and clean, carrying pine from somewhere distant. He stood on the threshold and looked at the street.

The day was beautiful.

That was the part that got him. Clear sky. Wide and blue. Sun on everything, warm and even, not caring what had happened. Birds in the trees doing what birds do.

They didn't know. The birds just kept going.

He stood there until the strangeness of it settled. Then he got on the bike.

The streets were empty the same way they'd been empty for days. But it felt different today. Before, the emptiness was something he'd watched from a window. Today he was inside it.

He rode slow toward her street.

Her house was the same. Small. Kept up. Flower beds along the front walk, yellow and purple, still leaning toward the sun. Her car in the driveway at the angle it always sat.

He leaned the bike against the fence.

Front door was unlocked. She'd known he'd come.

The house had a different quiet to it.

Not empty. Full. Full of someone who wasn't there anymore. A glass of water on the counter. A cardigan over the back of a chair. A crossword half-finished on the table, pen resting on it at the angle of someone who meant to come back.

He stood in the kitchen and looked at it all.

Then he walked down the hall, one hand trailing the wall. Not for balance. Just to touch something.

At the bedroom door he stopped. Hand on the frame.

He'd been on the phone with her when it happened. He'd been moving toward this moment since she called. He'd thought maybe that would make it easier.

He pushed the door open.

She was in the bed, covers to her chin, and the first thing he thought was that she looked like herself. Her hair on the pillow. Her hands. He could have told himself she was sleeping.

She wasn't sleeping.

Eyes open. Fixed on the ceiling. The marks of what the last hours had cost her were on the pillow, on the sheets. Tissues piled on the nightstand. Towel near her shoulder, dark and wrung. Medicine bottles lined up, caps off, every dose taken, none of it enough.

The phone receiver was on the floor beside the bed. Long pink cord next to it. The same phone.

Hudson stood at the foot of the bed and looked at her.

He looked at her the way you look at someone you need to keep. The angle of her face. Her hands. The things no photo ever gets right. He let himself understand fully what he'd lost. No protection. Just the whole of it.

She'd seen him clearly from the start and stayed anyway.

He chose the spot beside the flowers.

They were still standing. Still turning toward the sun. She'd planted them and tended them and they were still here.

The shovel went in slow. He worked without hurrying. Nobody to hurry for.

When the grave was right, he went inside and wrapped her in the sheets. Careful. Both hands. She was lighter than he expected. That hit him in a way he hadn't prepared for.

He carried her out and lowered her down slowly.

Then he stood at the edge and looked up at the sky. Same blue as all morning. Beautiful without asking permission.

"You were honest with me," he said. "From day one. You saw what I was carrying and you didn't ask me to pretend it wasn't there. You just sat across the table and talked to me like I was worth it."

He stopped. Started again.

"I needed that more than I knew."

Wind blew through the flowers.

"I don't know what I believe about what comes after," he said. "But you said you hoped it was quiet and warm and nobody afraid. I hope that too. And if anyone gets what they hoped for, it should be you."

He picked a few blossoms and laid them on the sheet.

"Thank you for showing up. For staying. For calling me when you were scared."

He picked up the shovel.

"I'll try not to waste it. I promised. I mean to keep it."

He filled the grave. Placed stones. Pressed each one down with both hands.

Stood there until it felt right to leave.

Then he got the bike.

He rode through town because he needed to see it. Not through a window. Not on a screen. Actually see it.

He passed the hardware store. The young guy who'd walked him down an aisle once, patient, pointing out the difference between two similar parts like it genuinely mattered. Store dark. Door locked. The young guy most likely dead.

Near the hospital it got worse.

Cars at wrong angles. Doors left open. People on the sidewalk and near the entrance, where they'd stopped. A stretcher outside with the wheels locked. Police cruisers with the lights dead. Cones set up in a pattern that had made sense to someone once.

Somebody had tried. You could see it. Came here with training and equipment and intention, and kept going as long as they could.

Hudson stopped his bike and looked at it.

Turned around and rode back. Slow. Through streets that had been his for a few weeks and were now something else. A town that had been alive. Was now the record of it. Houses still full of every ordinary thing people owned, waiting for someone who wasn't coming back to use them.

At his building he leaned the bike against the railing and stood in the stairwell.

Doris was in the ground by her flowers.

The cashier with the shaking hands. He didn't know. He hoped she'd gone home to her mother like he'd told her to. He hoped her mother had been somewhere worth going.

He climbed the stairs. Went inside. Sat down in the same chair he'd been in when she called. The one he'd slid off onto the floor.

Hudson didn't move till morning.

TEN

Reality of Being Alone

GILLETTE, WYOMING. 1987

He stayed inside for weeks.

Not because he was afraid. Fear would have required energy, and he didn't feel like he had any left to spend. What held him there was something quieter, something heavier. A kind of exhaustion that settled deep in his bones and made even the simplest choices feel unnecessary. The world had ended, and nothing inside the apartment demanded that he acknowledge it.

Days lost their edges. He slept when sleep came, sometimes for hours, sometimes not at all. He woke in the dark and in the middle of the afternoon with the same dull acceptance. Meals happened when he remembered to eat. Canned food. Snack food. Anything that didn't require effort or thought.

He read, though even that came in pieces. One book kept finding its way back into his hands, *Earth Abides*. He had read it before, years earlier, when the idea of collapse had still felt distant, almost theoretical. Now it felt different. Closer.

He recognized the kind of quiet the book described. A world not destroyed by violence, but emptied. No single moment where everything ended, just people disappearing one by one until what remained felt unreal. Gillette felt like that now. The buildings were still there. The streets still stretched where they always had, but the life that gave them meaning was gone.

He would set the book down and stare at the wall, as if something might move there if he waited long enough. Nothing ever did. Outside, there were no cars, no voices, no distant hum of power from other apartments. He watched old VHS movies he had seen too many times to count. Sometimes he paid attention. Most of the time he did not. The sound was enough. It filled the space just enough to keep it from closing in completely.

Time stopped behaving the way it used to. Without work, without schedules, without anyone expecting anything from him, the hours folded together. The grief stayed, but it changed. It was no longer sharp or coming in waves. It spread out instead, settling into everything he did. A constant pressure rather than a wound.

Hudson did not try to push it away.

He let it stay.

The power went out without warning.

The refrigerator stopped humming, and the digital clock on the microwave disappeared. It was not dramatic. The apartment did not change all at once. It simply lost its background noise, and in that loss, everything else became sharper.

Hudson waited.

Nothing returned.

As the light outside began to fade, he stood and moved through the apartment, flipping switches out of habit. Each one answered him the same way. Nothing.

He stood at the window and looked out over the street. There were no streetlights, no glow from neighboring buildings, no sign of electricity anywhere. The town was dark in a way he had never seen before. Not storm-dark. Not temporary.

Complete.

Hudson understood what that meant.

He did not panic. He did not swear or throw anything. He simply accepted it. The grid was gone. He knew what it took to keep power running. People. Coordination. Fuel. Maintenance. Every part of that system depended on the same thing the rest of the world had depended on.

People.

And they were gone.

The apartment had been a kind of shelter, an illusion that something of the old world still remained. Now that illusion was gone too.

He sat in the dark and considered what came next. He could try to find a generator and make the place livable again, if fuel was still available. Or he could find somewhere already prepared, someone who had expected this and built for it. Either way, staying here no longer made sense.

The loss of power did what grief had not.

It forced him to move.

He lit a candle and watched it burn, the flame steady and small against the walls. By the time it went out, the decision had already been made. He would leave the apartment. Not the town. Not yet. But he would not stay still any longer.

He found the car at the far end of the apartment lot.

It was an older sedan, clean, parked straight between the lines. Nothing about it suggested urgency. It looked like it had been left with intention. He tried the door. It opened.

Inside, the air still held the faint smell of the last person who had driven it. He checked the glove box, then the console, not expecting much. Then he opened the gas cap.

The keys were tucked neatly inside.

He drove slowly through town.

Every street told the same story. Cars parked where they belonged. Houses intact. Lawns maintained. No signs of struggle.

Just absence.

Gillette had not been destroyed. It had been left behind.

He passed neighborhoods he recognized, places that had once felt ordinary. Now they looked preserved, untouched but empty.

He saw the generator before he saw the house.

It sat beside the garage, protected by a weathered enclosure. The kind of system installed by someone who planned ahead. Inside, the house was still.

In the bedroom, an elderly couple lay side by side. There was no sign of panic. No sign they had tried to escape. They had gone where they were most comfortable and stayed there.

Hudson stood in the doorway for a long moment, then nodded once.

He moved them carefully, speaking quietly out of habit more than necessity. He buried them together beneath a tree in the yard, choosing a place that felt right. When he finished, he stood there for a while before returning to the house. He closed the bedroom door and left it closed.

Cleaning took the rest of the day.

He worked steadily, not rushing and not avoiding anything either. He wiped surfaces, washed dishes, and opened windows to let fresh air move through the house. By the time he was done, it no longer felt untouched.

Outside, he checked the generator. The natural gas line still held pressure. He tested it, then started the system. The sound came low and steady.

Inside, the lights flickered on. The refrigerator started again. The house came back to life, not as it had been, but enough.

Hudson stood in the living room and let that settle.

Survival did not require force.

It required knowing what to do.

He did not rush the scavenging.

There was no reason to. He moved through the town carefully, taking what he needed and leaving the rest. Kmart stood open, its automatic doors frozen where the power had failed. Inside, everything was still. Carts sat abandoned, some half-filled, some empty.

He took canned food, dry goods, and water. Nothing extra.

The water system had already failed. Faucets now gave nothing but air.

Other houses told the same story. He knocked before entering, even though he knew no one would answer. Inside, he found the same endings again and again. Beds. Floors. Stillness.

He took tools and supplies.

Nothing personal.

He left the rest where it belonged.

Gillette, Wyoming.

That afternoon, he sat on the porch. The generator hummed softly behind the house, the sound fading into the background until it barely registered. He had a book open in his hands, but he was not reading.

Hudson noticed the movement before he saw what caused it. Something shifted at the edge of the yard, just beyond the line where the grass gave way to dirt. It was not fast or sudden. It was careful. He lifted his head slightly, his hand still resting on the open book in his lap.

A black shape stood there, half in shadow.

A dog.

It did not move closer right away. It simply stood and watched him. Hudson stayed where he was. The world had been empty long enough that any movement felt like it needed to be respected.

The dog stepped forward slowly.

A German Shepherd. Large and well-built, but leaner than it should have been. Its coat was still clean, which told Hudson it had not been on its own long. A collar rested around its neck, worn but intact. No tag.

Its ears stayed up. Alert. Not aggressive. Just aware.

Hudson lowered the book to his lap and let his hands rest where the dog could see them.

"Hey," he said quietly.

The word did not carry far. It did not need to.

The dog stopped a few feet away, close enough now that Hudson could see its eyes. Clear. Intelligent. Tired. The kind of tired that came from waiting for something that never showed up.

Hudson did not move. He did not reach. He knew better than that.

The dog took another step, then another, circling slightly, not in fear but in habit. It checked angles, checked him, made sure what it saw from one side still held true from another.

Hudson let it.

After a moment, the dog stepped in close enough that its shoulder brushed against his knee. Then it stopped. Its head lowered slightly, and it pressed its muzzle gently against his leg.

Not asking. Not begging. Just there.

Hudson let out a breath he had not realized he was holding. He rested his hand slowly on the dog's head. The fur was warm. Real.

The dog did not flinch. It did not pull away.

It stayed.

"Sit," Hudson said.

The dog sat without hesitation.

That told him everything he needed to know.

This dog had belonged to someone. It had been trained, cared for, talked to. It had waited at doors, listened for footsteps, expected someone to come back.

Hudson's hand stayed where it was, moving slightly now, his fingers pressing gently through the fur behind the ears. The dog's eyes closed halfway for a second, then opened again, still watching, still present.

"You've been on your own for a bit," Hudson said quietly.

The dog didn't answer. It didn't need to.

They stayed like that for a while, without any sense of urgency. There was no reason to break the moment. A light breeze moved across the yard, and somewhere in the distance something metal shifted and settled. The world continued in small ways, even now.

Hudson reached down and scratched lightly along the dog's neck. The tail moved once, then again, not wild or excited, but measured, like the dog wasn't sure yet how much it was allowed to feel.

Hudson understood that.

He leaned back slightly in the chair and looked out across the empty street, then down at the dog again.

"You've had a name," he said. "Probably heard it every day. Someone called you, and you came."

The dog's ears twitched slightly at the sound of his voice.

Hudson nodded once, more to himself than anything else. "I don't know what it was," he said. "Doesn't seem right to pretend I do."

The dog stayed close, steady against his leg.

Hudson was quiet for a moment. He didn't feel the need to rush it. Then, without really deciding to, he said, "Shadoe."

The dog's head lifted.

Ears forward. Eyes on him.

Hudson noticed that. Not excitement. Not recognition of the word itself, but of the tone behind it.

He gave a small nod.

"Shadoe," he said again.

The dog held his gaze. Its tail moved once against the porch, a single solid thump.

That was enough.

Hudson rested his hand on the dog's head again, a little firmer this time.

"Yeah," he said quietly. "That works."

The dog leaned into him without hesitation.

The name settled into place as if it had been there all along.

Hudson leaned back slightly in the chair. "You can stay," he said. It wasn't a command, and it wasn't really an invitation, just something spoken out loud.

Eleven

Survival Shopping

Gillette, Wyoming. 1987

Hudson drove through Gillette with Shadoe riding quietly beside him, one ear twitching at the steady hum of the engine. The town passed by in pieces he recognized but no longer felt connected to, the grocery store, the diner, the intersection where traffic lights no longer cycled through red and green. Nothing was broken, nothing was burning, and that was what made it harder to understand.

The Ford dealership stood just off the main road, its glass intact, flags hanging still, and banners advertising deals that would never be honored. Hudson parked, and the sound of the door closing echoed louder than it should have. Shadoe stepped out with him, staying close as they moved between the rows of trucks.

Hudson ran his hand along the vehicles as he passed, reading the stickers out of habit, engine specs, pricing, financing terms, all of it belonging to a system that assumed tomorrow would come. He stopped when he saw it.

An '88 Ford F-250.

Extended cab, four-wheel drive, white paint untouched.

Brand new.

He opened the door, and the smell hit him first, that distinct scent that only came with something unused. Shadoe jumped in, turned once, and settled. Hudson gave a small nod. "Yeah," he said quietly. "That'll do."

He checked it anyway, under the hood, fluids, belts, everything. Perfect. When he turned the key, the engine came alive smooth and steady.

Reliable.

That mattered.

Behind the service bays, he found a generator still strapped to a pallet. He set it up beside the fuel pump, and within minutes the system came alive. He filled both tanks, then filled gas cans one after another until he had twenty gallons extra.

The sporting goods store came next.

The door opened without resistance, and inside smelled like rubber, canvas, and oiled metal. Hudson moved with purpose, not rushed, not careless, but deliberate.

He started with firearms, not because he wanted them, but because he understood the world had changed. People could be dangerous. Animals could be worse. Being unprepared was the quickest way to lose everything.

From behind the counter, he took a 9mm handgun, simple and reliable. He checked the action, the weight, the balance, then set it aside. Next came a .357 revolver, solid and mechanical, the kind of weapon that didn't leave room for doubt. He added it to the pile.

From the rack, he selected a 12-gauge pump shotgun, practical for close range, then a .30-30 rifle with a wood stock and lever action, proven and dependable for distance and larger threats. He paused before taking the last one.

A .22 rifle.

Lighter. Quieter. Meant for small game.

That one mattered more than the others.

Ammo came next. Boxes of 9mm, .357 rounds, 12-gauge shells in both buckshot and birdshot, .30-30 cartridges, and .22 rounds in bulk. He didn't take more than he could carry, only what he could justify.

Knives followed, a folding pocket knife and then a bowie knife, larger and heavier, meant for work that required more than precision. He tested the grip and kept it.

Then the rest.

A backpack with reinforced straps, built slowly and deliberately. A cold-rated sleeping bag, a compact tent, water purification tablets, flashlights with extra batteries, a first aid kit, rope, fire starters, tools that didn't depend on anything else working.

He moved to the pet section last.

Shadoe stood near the door, watching.

Hudson nodded slightly. "You're coming," he said.

He picked up a heavy-duty collar, stronger than the one the dog wore, and a working vest with usable pockets. Food and a collapsible bowl followed. Shadoe didn't move as Hudson approached. He knelt and replaced the collar carefully. The dog stayed still and accepted it. The vest took a moment to adjust, but once it was set, Shadoe shifted once and settled.

Ready.

Hudson loaded everything into the truck.

That night, he studied the map. "Daylight driving," he said quietly. "No risks we don't have to take."

Shadoe stayed close, which felt like agreement.

Morning came cold and clear. Hudson loaded the final items, weapons stored out of sight but within reach, fuel secured, pack accessible. He looked at the house one last time.

It would have been enough.

For a while.

But not for what he needed to do.

He got in. Shadoe was already waiting. The engine turned over, and Hudson pulled onto the road, heading east.

The highway stretched out ahead, empty and too clean. No traffic. No movement. The world hadn't tried to run. It had just stopped.

Hours passed through open land, fences, and sky that felt too large. Hudson didn't rush or push speed. Distance mattered more than time.

Then he saw it.

Wreckage ahead.

A line of vehicles tangled across the road. He slowed and worked the truck through carefully. Most of the damage was old, drivers who hadn't made it, a chain reaction that spread outward from one mistake.

He stepped out.

The air didn't move.

Shadoe followed, slower this time, nose low. "Bathroom break," Hudson said quietly. "Stay close."

The dog circled, stayed within range, and came back on his own.

Good.

They got back in, and Hudson eased the truck around the last of it, returning to open road.

By the time the sun began to drop, the land had changed. More hills. A different feel to the air. Hudson saw the sign before the town.

Sturgis, South Dakota.

Hudson drove slowly through the streets of Sturgis, letting the truck idle forward while he looked. The town felt like the others, still, intact, left behind. He passed smaller homes first, then larger ones set back from the road with longer driveways and yards just beginning to lose their order.

He chose one without overthinking it.

A large home near the edge of town. Two stories. Wide porch. Windows unbroken. No vehicles in the driveway.

Nothing disturbed.

He parked and shut off the engine. The silence returned immediately. Shadoe stepped down beside him, staying close, alert without being tense.

Hudson walked to the front door, knocked once, and waited. Not because he expected an answer, but because it felt necessary.

Nothing came.

He turned the handle.

The door opened.

The air inside was still, not stale, just quiet.

Hudson stepped in slowly, letting his eyes adjust. Shadoe moved ahead, pausing at the threshold before continuing, reading the space in a way Hudson couldn't. Hudson pulled a lantern from his pack and clicked it on. Soft light filled the entryway.

Warm. Contained. Enough.

The house was clean. No signs of struggle. No broken glass. Everything sat where it had been left, as if the people who lived there had stepped out expecting to return.

Hudson moved through the rooms, steady and deliberate. The living room held family photos, a couple, two children, smiles from another version of the world.

He didn't linger.

The kitchen was clean, counters wiped, dishes in the rack, a coffee mug near the sink. The pantry was full, canned goods, dry food, enough to last a long time if used carefully.

He looked down at Shadoe. "We have a family-sized box of fruit loops, Shadoe. We can't complain about that."

Shadoe did not seem impressed.

Near the back, Hudson found what he needed most, two sealed five-gallon water jugs.

Good.

Upstairs, the hallway stretched quiet. Shadoe moved ahead, checking each room. A child's bedroom. Toys left where they had been dropped. Another room, the same unfinished feeling.

Hudson paused, then moved on.

The master bedroom was clean, bed made, untouched.

He stepped inside, set the lantern down, and let the light fill the room.

"This will work," he said.

Shadoe circled once and settled near the foot of the bed.

Hudson went back downstairs, gathered food and water, fed the dog, then ate quietly at the table. When he finished, he rinsed the bowl out of habit.

Back upstairs, he set the lantern low.

Shadoe was already settled.

Hudson sat on the edge of the bed, taking in the room one last time.

A house full of life.

Now holding only quiet.

He didn't try to make meaning out of it.

He just accepted it.

He lay down.

The mattress felt strange at first, too clean, too untouched. Shadoe shifted closer.

That helped.

Hudson fell fast asleep.

Twelve
Nebraska

Midwest, USA. 1987

Hudson traveled across South Dakota, turned south, and crossed into Nebraska under a sky that felt too wide for the road beneath it. The land rolled gently, open and patient. Shadoe lay quiet in the passenger seat, head lifted, watching the horizon.

The first roadblock appeared at an on-ramp outside a small town. Concrete barriers stacked deliberately. Razor wire sagging where it had once been stretched tight. A jeep sat beside it, tires half sunk into the shoulder.

No bodies. No signs of panic. Just abandonment.

Hudson slowed but did not stop. He could imagine the moment they left. Orders given. Fuel running low. No relief coming.

At the Nebraska-Iowa state line the story changed.

Barriers reinforced with vehicles. A pickup nose-first into concrete, hood crumpled inward. Bodies near the road. One slumped against a van doorframe as if the person had tried to get out and simply could not go any farther.

Hudson stopped the truck and sat with his hands on the wheel.

This had not been chaos. This had been pressure. People pushing forward because staying behind meant death.

He eased down to the center median, shifted into four-wheel drive, pushed through the mud without trouble, and drove on.

The signs accumulated as Iowa opened up around him. A tractor sideways across a two-lane road. Hay bales stacked into crude barriers, some rolled aside where vehicles had forced through. On a barn wall, spray-painted in uneven red letters:

STAY BACK.

A mile later, another message contradicted it.

NO ONE LEFT.

At an intersection, pressed hard into plywood with a thick marker:

WE TRIED EVERYTHING.

He did not stop. He read as he passed and let the words settle without argument. These were not lies. They were records.

"People did what they knew how to do," he said. "They just didn't know enough."

Shadoe shifted in his seat, nose lifting as if testing the air.

The road ahead darkened gradually, then the smell reached him. Burned fuel. Char. The kind that lingered long after the fire was gone.

He eased off the gas.

The tanker came into view slowly. It lay across the highway on its side, split open along its length, metal peeled back and blackened. The road around it was scorched and cracked. The explosion had reached the bridge.

Hudson stopped well back and shut off the engine.

He and Shadoe stepped out together. Hudson walked forward carefully, studying the damage. The guardrails sagged. Steel supports beneath the roadway had warped from the heat. Sections of concrete had fallen away entirely, leaving a jagged edge where the highway simply ended.

He stood at the edge and looked down.

Below, a county road ran beneath the bridge, narrow, partially hidden by weeds. Beyond it, the land opened up again, flat and accessible. If he could get down the embankment he could pick up that road and go around the city entirely.

The embankment was steep. Loose dirt and rock, a serious angle, not meant for vehicles.

Hudson walked it on foot first, testing the ground, pressing his boot into the surface to judge how it gave. The upper section was the worst of it, dry and crumbling at the edge. Lower down the soil compacted and held better.

Passable. Barely.

He pulled the truck forward until the nose hung over the drop, then stopped. From inside the cab the angle looked worse than it had from the ground. The hood tipped down and the truck's full weight shifted forward against the brakes.

"Stay with me," he said.

He released the brake slowly and let gravity begin the work, steering rather than driving, keeping the front tires tracking straight. The nose dipped hard. Dirt gave way beneath the rear tires and the back end slid left before catching again. Hudson corrected without overcorrecting, hands steady, breathing through it.

Shadoe pressed himself flat against the seat without making a sound.

Halfway down, the right front tire found a soft pocket and dropped suddenly, lurching the truck sideways. Hudson's stomach went with it. He turned into it and pressed the accelerator just enough to push through rather than dig in. The tire caught. The truck straightened.

He held the line the rest of the way down.

When the ground finally leveled out beneath them Hudson sat still for a moment, both hands on the wheel, saying nothing.

Then he exhaled.

He guided the truck onto the county road and drove beneath the ruined bridge without looking up. On the other side, farmland opened ahead, quiet and usable.

"No more highways," he said.

Shadoe shifted beside him.

Hudson faced forward and drove on.

He made camp just before dusk, far enough from the road that headlights would not have found him even if there had been anyone left to drive them. He built a small fire and sat with his back against the truck tire, watching the flames settle.

Shadoe lay close to the warmth.

Hudson reached into his pack and found the marshmallows. A box of graham crackers. The kind of thing meant for evenings with other people.

He held a piece out. Shadoe sniffed it suspiciously, took it gently, chewed with visible confusion as it stuck to his muzzle.

Hudson laughed quietly before he could stop himself.

The stars emerged one by one, sharp and unfiltered, the sky wider than he remembered it ever being. The fire warmed his hands. The dog breathed steadily beside him.

For a few minutes the world felt almost normal.

When the fire burned to embers Hudson stayed where he was.

"I keep thinking I'll hear someone," he said, more to the dark than to Shadoe. "Just a voice. Anybody."

Shadoe rested his head against Hudson's knee. The contact was solid and real.

"You're good company," Hudson said, rubbing behind the dog's ear. "But I'd like someone who talks back."

Thirteen

Jerry

Nichols, Iowa. 1987

The two-lane road narrowed as Hudson drove east, the land drawing in around him. Fields pressed closer to the pavement now, fences running tight and straight, their posts weathered but upright. The towns came smaller out here, fewer buildings, fewer reasons to slow down unless you meant to stop.

A sign rose ahead on the right, its paint faded but readable.

WELCOME TO NICHOLS
POPULATION 375

Hudson eased off the accelerator.

Nichols looked untouched. Houses stood in place, paint intact, yards trimmed just enough to suggest someone had cared recently. No vehicles moved along the streets. No doors stood open. There was no smoke rising from chimneys or grills. No sound carried on the air. Not even birds.

Hudson rolled through town at a crawl, eyes scanning instinctively. This was the kind of place people disappeared into without being noticed. Too small to matter. Too quiet to draw attention. A place where someone could survive simply by staying put.

Shadoe lifted his head, alert, sensing the change.

Hudson slowed even more, the truck nearly idling now. For the first time in days, the absence felt different. Not empty exactly. Just waiting.

Nichols did not feel abandoned.

It felt occupied by something unseen.

Hudson passed the old Nichols School without meaning to stop.

The building sat back from the road, red brick rising three stories high, its windows tall and evenly spaced. An old rural school, built to last longer than the town around it. He registered it the way he had registered a hundred other empty structures along the way.

Then something moved.

Just a flash at the edge of his vision. Bright. Colorful. Gone before he could name it.

Instinct took over.

Hudson slammed on the brakes.

The truck lurched to a stop, tires chirping against the pavement. Shadoe pitched forward and caught himself. Hudson's hand was already on the dog's shoulder.

"Sorry, buddy," he said quickly, steadying him.

The engine idled, loud in the sudden stillness. Hudson stared through the windshield, heart pounding harder than the moment required. He replayed the image in his mind. Color. Motion. Not fabric caught in wind. Not light shifting.

A person.

The words came out before he could stop them.

"I think I just saw a person."

He shut off the engine.

The silence returned instantly, thick and complete, as if the world had been holding its breath. Shadoe perked up, ears forward, tongue out, watching Hudson instead of the building.

Hudson sat there for a moment, hands resting on the wheel, afraid to move and afraid not to. He had gone too long without seeing anyone to trust his eyes easily.

But the feeling would not leave.

Whatever had moved near that school had not been wind or shadow.

It had been alive.

Hudson opened the door and stepped out slowly, careful not to let it swing shut too loudly. Shadoe jumped down beside him and stood still, tongue tucked just past his teeth, watching Hudson for cues rather than the building itself.

The school dominated the block.

It was larger than Hudson had expected up close. A solid red-brick structure rising three stories high, its shape squared and deliberate, built in an era when communities invested in things meant to endure. Tall windows lined each floor, their glass unbroken, blinds pulled all the way open as if to welcome the light inside. The architecture was practical and proud, the kind of rural school meant to serve generations.

Hudson studied it from the curb.

"This isn't nothing," he said quietly.

He lifted a hand and pointed, barely moving his arm. "I think they went in there."

Shadoe followed the motion with his eyes but did not bark or growl. He simply stood, steady and alert, waiting.

Hudson felt the familiar calculation settle in. Distance. Cover. Entrances. Exits. The weight of the shotgun in his hands. The quiet truth that if someone was inside, they might be scared. Or dangerous. Or both.

He could leave.

He could tell himself it was better not to know.

But the need was stronger than the risk. He had gone too long without hearing another human voice. Too long without proof that survival had not been limited to himself and a dog.

Hudson took a breath and started toward the school.

Whatever waited inside, Hudson had to see it for himself.

Hudson reached the door and rested his hand on the handle for a moment before turning it. The metal was cool beneath his palm. He pulled it open slowly, letting it swing inward with a soft, hollow sound.

The smell hit him at once.

Old books. Waxed floors. Dust that had settled evenly instead of piling up. It was the same scent every school had carried when he was a kid, a mix of order and time, familiar and strangely comforting.

What was missing stood out just as clearly.

There was no cafeteria smell. No lingering grease or cooked food clinging to the air. Just clean stillness.

Blinds along the hallway windows were pulled all the way up, letting sunlight pour in. It filled the space without effort, warming the tile floors and softening the edges of the long corridor. The temperature was comfortable, neither cold nor stale, the building holding the day the way it was meant to.

Hudson understood immediately why someone might choose this place.

It was dry. Solid. Predictable. A place built for people to gather and stay.

He stepped inside and closed the door partway behind him, not wanting it to echo. Shadoe moved just off his left leg, close enough that Hudson could feel the brush of fur against his jeans. The dog's presence was steady, reassuring.

They moved slowly down the hallway, footsteps soft against the floor, sunlight stretching ahead of them.

Somewhere inside the building, something alive was waiting.

Nichols, Iowa.

The sound hit them halfway down the hall.

A laugh. Loud and sudden, echoing off the walls.

Not startled. Not nervous. Not afraid.

Joyful.

Hudson stopped so fast his breath caught. Shadoe halted with him, muscles tightening, ears forward. The laugh came again, followed immediately by a voice, warm and animated.

"That is soooo funny. I love that so much."

Hudson felt the tension shift inside him, not easing exactly, but rearranging itself into something unfamiliar. Confusion. Curiosity. This was not the sound of someone hiding or bracing for danger. It was the sound of someone enjoying themselves.

He leaned down slightly, keeping his voice low.

"We have a live one," he whispered.

Shadoe's tongue hung out, his tail still, eyes bright.

"Easy now," Hudson murmured.

Ahead, an open doorway broke the line of the hallway. Light spilled out from it, brighter than the rest of the corridor. Beside the door, a sign was mounted neatly on the wall.

LIBRARY

The laugh came again, softer this time, followed by the rustle of pages.

Hudson stayed where he was for a long moment, listening. Whatever waited in that room did not sound like a threat. It did not sound like fear at all.

It sounded like life continuing without realizing it was supposed to stop.

Hudson took a slow breath and started toward the doorway.

He edged closer to the door and stopped just short of the frame. He leaned slightly and looked inside.

A man sat at one of the long library tables, shoulders relaxed, posture easy. Sunlight spilled across the surface in front of him, illuminating an open book. Hudson took another step and saw the pages clearly.

A comic book.

Bright colors. Bold lines. The kind meant to be read slowly and enjoyed more than once.

Hudson moved fully into the doorway and rested his knuckles against the frame. He knocked softly, more a courtesy than a warning, and kept his voice low and even.

"Hello."

The man turned quickly, chair legs scraping lightly against the floor.

For a split second Hudson braced himself, expecting fear or suspicion.

Instead, the man's face lit up.

A wide, open smile spread across it, unguarded and genuine, as if Hudson's presence was the best surprise imaginable.

"Hi!" the man said brightly.

The word echoed softly in the room.

Hudson stood there, momentarily caught off guard. There was no calculation in the man's expression. No assessment. No fear. Just pleasure at seeing another person standing in front of him.

Hudson felt something loosen in his chest that he had not realized was still tight.

This was not what danger looked like.

This was innocence, untouched by the shape the world had taken outside the school walls.

The man stood up so quickly his chair tipped back, then caught itself against the table. He took a step toward Hudson, eyes bright, attention already shifting past him.

"Puppy dog," he said, pointing, voice filled with wonder. "A real live puppy dog. I love them."

Shadoe wagged his tail once and stepped forward, accepting the attention without hesitation. Jerry laughed, delighted, and knelt down to scratch behind the dog's ears, talking to him as if they had known each other for years.

"I'm Jerry," he said, looking up at Hudson with the same wide smile. "I'm twenty-three."

Hudson nodded. "Hudson."

Jerry nodded back, satisfied, then returned his attention to Shadoe. "He's a good boy. I can tell."

As they talked, Jerry explained his days in simple, matter-of-fact terms. He worked at the school before everything stopped. Did odd jobs. Cleaned classrooms. Helped the teachers when they asked. He liked keeping things in order.

"I live across the street," he said. "But I come here every day."

Hudson glanced around the library. The tables were clean. Books neatly shelved. Floors swept.

Jerry followed his gaze. "I keep it ready," he said proudly. "For when the kids come back."

There was no question in his voice. No doubt. Just purpose.

Hudson felt the weight of the words settle in. Jerry had not survived by misunderstanding the world. He had survived by holding onto routine, by believing in return, by choosing care over fear.

In a world that had come undone, Jerry had stayed exactly where he was meant to be.

Hudson listens without interrupting.

Jerry talks easily, comfortably, the way people do when they are not afraid of silence. He explains his days. Cleaning. Organizing. Making sure everything is ready. The words circle back again and again to the same idea.

When the kids come back.

Hudson begins to understand that Jerry does not see the world the same way he does. Or maybe he does, just through a different lens. Jerry does not speak of governments or sickness or borders closing. He does not talk about death in numbers. He talks about sleeping. About waiting. About keeping things nice.

The school is clean.

The halls are orderly.

Purpose still exists here.

Jerry has not survived by fleeing or stockpiling or preparing for violence. He survived by staying. By repeating what he knew. By letting routine anchor him when everything else disappeared.

Shadoe settles at Jerry's feet as if the decision has already been made. Jerry absently scratches behind the dog's ears, laughing again at something Hudson does not quite catch.

The sound fills the room.

Hudson realizes it is the first real laughter he has heard since before Doris died.

He smiles before he can stop himself.

Fourteen

Jerry's Adventure

Nichols, Iowa. 1987

Jerry rocks slightly on his heels, then points across the street.

"You wanna see my house?" he asks, like the idea has just occurred to him and might be forgotten if not spoken aloud. "It's right there."

Hudson follows the direction of his finger.

Across the narrow road sits a white farmhouse, L-shaped, its paint weathered but intact. It looks older than the town around it, the kind of house that once stood alone when fields pressed in from every side. Nichols must have grown up around it slowly, as if the house had been there first and allowed the town to stay.

Hudson nods. "Sure. I'd like that."

Jerry beams and starts walking immediately, already talking as if the invitation were settled business. He points out cracks in the sidewalk, a mailbox that leans too far to the left, a tree that loses its leaves early every fall. None of it feels important, and all of it does.

Shadoe moves easily between them, unhurried, tail low and relaxed. Hudson notices how natural the arrangement feels, like something practiced rather than new.

The yard is tidy. Grass cut short. No debris. No sense of panic or neglect. The porch is swept clean. A chair sits near the door, angled toward the street, as if someone once liked to watch the world go by.

Jerry opens the door without hesitation.

Inside, the house smells faintly of old wood. Sunlight spills through uncovered windows, warming the floors.

Jerry steps inside first and holds the door open with his shoulder, pride written plainly across his face.

"Momma liked it clean," he says. "So I keep it clean."

The house feels lived in. Not frozen in time, but cared for. Floors swept. Counters wiped down. Shoes lined neatly by the door. There is no sense of panic here, no piles of scavenged goods or frantic preparation. Everything has a place, and everything appears to be in it.

Hudson takes it in slowly.

Sunlight pours through open curtains, filling the rooms with warmth. The furniture is worn but sturdy. Family photographs sit where they were meant to sit. A calendar still hangs on the wall, dates crossed off neatly until the markings simply stop.

Hudson looks at Jerry, who is already kneeling to greet Shadoe again, rubbing the dog's chest with both hands.

"You've been doing a good job," Hudson says.

Jerry nods, as if this has always been understood. "Isn't hard. You just do it every day."

Hudson waits a moment, then asks gently, "Jerry, what do you think happened to everyone?"

Jerry looks up without confusion or fear. He answers as if the question is practical, not frightening.

"They got sick," he says. "Momma told me that could happen. Sometimes people go to sleep for a long time."

Hudson notices what Jerry does not say. He does not say disappeared. He does not say ended. There is no anger in his voice. No denial.

Only acceptance, shaped in words he can live with.

Jerry stands and walks toward the kitchen. "You hungry? I got crackers. And peanut butter. Momma liked peanut butter."

Hudson follows him, understanding something clearly for the first time.

Jerry is not helpless.

He has simply survived in a different language.

Jerry sits at the kitchen table while Hudson leans against the counter. Shadoe lies at Jerry's feet, tail thumping softly each time Jerry's hand drops down to scratch behind his ears.

"I never watched the news," Jerry says suddenly, as if continuing a thought already in motion. "It was always bad stuff. Loud people. Momma didn't like it either."

Hudson does not interrupt.

Jerry looks down at the table, tracing a small circle with his finger. "Momma told me sickness happens. Sometimes people get better. Sometimes they go to sleep for a long time."

He nods once, certain of it.

"Like Topper," he says. "He was my dog. He got old and went to sleep. We dug a hole for him. Momma said nice things." Jerry pauses, then adds, "Frisky too. And Thumper. He was my rabbit. He was soft."

Hudson feels something tighten in his chest but keeps his voice steady. "Your mom explained it that way?"

Jerry nods. "She said it makes it easier to understand. And it did."

He looks up then, meeting Hudson's eyes without hesitation. "After the school closed, Momma started coughing. She told me she might go to sleep like my pets did."

Jerry says this plainly. There is no drama in it. No tremor.

"She told me if I didn't get sick, I should dig a hole for her. And say good things. Just like we always did."

Hudson does not speak. He is afraid that if he does, his voice will fail him.

"One night she went to sleep," Jerry continues. "I checked on her in the morning. She didn't wake up."

Jerry shrugs slightly, as if acknowledging a hard fact of weather. "So I did what she told me. I dug the hole. I said nice things. I told her thank you for taking care of me."

His hand drops again to Shadoe's head. The dog presses closer.

"I didn't get sick," Jerry says quietly. "Not even a stuffy nose."

Jerry stands and walks to the sink, rinsing his glass before setting it upside down on a towel. The movement is habitual, practiced. Nothing about it feels improvised.

"The kids never came back," he says, as if mentioning the weather. "I waited a long time."

Hudson watches him. "You kept going to the school?"

Jerry nods. "Every day. It's my job."

"But there were no classes."

Jerry looks at him, puzzled by the question. "Yeah. But they'll come back."

He says it with the same certainty he used when he talked about his mother. Not denial. Just structure.

"So I cleaned," Jerry continues. "Swept the halls. Wiped desks. Took out trash. If the kids come back and it's messy, that wouldn't be right."

Hudson imagines the empty school, the sunlight on the floors, the order preserved in a world that had dissolved everywhere else.

"What about food?" Hudson asks gently.

Jerry shrugs. "I walked to the stores. I don't like stealing."

"No?"

"No," Jerry says firmly. "That's wrong."

He moves to a drawer and pulls out a folded stack of paper, bound loosely with a rubber band. He hands it to Hudson.

"I left notes," Jerry explains. "What I took. How much. I wrote that I would pay when the store people came back."

Hudson unfolds one of the papers. The handwriting is careful, deliberate.

Milk. Bread. Peanut butter. I will pay you later. Thank you.

He hands the papers back without comment.

Jerry smiles, satisfied. "That way it's fair."

Hudson feels something shift inside him. A realization settles quietly, heavier than any fear he has carried since Wyoming.

Jerry did not survive because he was stronger.

Or smarter.

Or more prepared.

He survived because he stayed.

Because he did not run.

Because he held to routine, to rules, to decency, even when no one was watching.

The world had collapsed, and Jerry had refused to collapse with it.

Hudson looks around the kitchen again. The clean counters. The open curtains. The calm.

In a country emptied by panic and movement, Jerry had remained rooted.

And that, Hudson realizes, is what kept him alive.

Hudson notices the light changing before Jerry does.

The sun slips lower, the edges of the rooms softening as shadows stretch across the floor. The warmth of the afternoon fades into something cooler, quieter. Outside, the town remains still, unchanged by the passing of hours.

"What do you do when it gets dark?" Hudson asks.

Jerry brightens, as if pleased by the question. He walks to a cabinet and opens it, revealing two old metal lanterns, clean and ready.

"I light these," he says. "Then I read."

"Read what?"

Jerry grins. "Comic books."

That figures, Hudson thinks.

"And then I go to sleep," Jerry continues. "When I wake up, it's morning again."

Simple. Complete.

Hudson hesitates, then says, "I've got food in the truck. Nothing fancy. Would you like to have dinner together?"

Jerry's face lights up instantly. "Really?"

"Really."

They step out back, where a small grill sits beside the porch, weathered but intact. Hudson opens the lid and checks it over.

"I didn't know that worked," Jerry says, watching closely. "Momma never let me use it."

Hudson gets it going easily. Soon the smell of heating metal and canned stew drifts into the evening air. He pours the contents into a pot and sets it to warm.

Jerry eats, but only in between reaching down to pet Shadoe, who sits patiently at his feet, tail thumping whenever Jerry looks at him.

"He's such a good boy," Jerry says again, as if it bears repeating.

Shadoe leans into the attention, content.

They eat slowly, talking about nothing important. The weather. The school. Dogs. The light fades completely, replaced by the soft glow of lanterns Jerry brings outside and sets on the table.

For the first time in a long while, Hudson feels something unfamiliar settle in his chest.

Hudson sleeps in the spare bedroom, the kind meant for visiting relatives who rarely came anymore. The bed is neatly made, the room clean and quiet. For the first time in days, he sleeps straight through the night.

Morning comes gently.

Sunlight filters through the curtains, warm and steady. Outside, birds move through the trees as if the world has not ended. Hudson steps out back and lights the grill again. Eggs sizzle in a pan. Spam browns beside them. He opens cans of fruit and sets them on the table.

Jerry comes out smiling, already talking.

After breakfast, Jerry leads Hudson around the backyard. A small chicken coop sits near the fence.

"They give me eggs," Jerry explains proudly. "I feed them every day. They don't like it when I'm late."

Hudson nods. "They look healthy."

They do.

As they sit again, Hudson hesitates, then asks, "What about your dad?"

Jerry doesn't seem surprised by the question.

"When I was little," he says, "Momma told me Daddy worked with lions and tigers. At the circus. He had to leave before I was born because the animals needed him."

He pauses, then smiles faintly.

"I didn't like that. I didn't like that the lions and tigers needed him more than me."

Hudson listens, saying nothing.

"Later," Jerry continues, "my friend Johnny Bee told me the truth. He said my mom and dad were teenagers. Daddy got scared. Cold feet. So he moved away."

"Where to?" Hudson asks.

"Dallas," Jerry says confidently. "Everybody knows it's hot in Dallas, so he wouldn't have cold feet there. And he liked cowboys. Dallas has real cowboys."

Jerry shrugs, unbothered.

"I never told Momma I knew. That way she could still believe the circus story."

Hudson looks at him, struck by the quiet kindness in the choice.

Jerry smiles and reaches down to scratch Shadoe behind the ears.

The rest of the day unfolds without urgency.

Jerry walks Hudson through Nichols as if giving a guided tour. He points out houses. Tells stories about who lived where. Mentions which families had kids at the school and which ones didn't. He shows Hudson the playground, the ball field, the maintenance closet where he keeps extra mops and cleaning supplies. He talks the entire time, filling the empty streets with sound.

Hudson lets him.

It feels good to listen to a human voice again. Even when it loops. Even when it wanders. Jerry's words are not noise. They are proof of life.

The next morning, Hudson tells him.

"I have to leave," he says carefully. "I'm heading to Greeneville, Tennessee."

Jerry blinks. "That's far."

"It is."

Jerry nods, thinking. "You coming back?"

Hudson shakes his head. "No. I don't think so."

Jerry frowns. "But the school needs me."

Hudson follows his gaze to the brick building across the street. Sunlight catches the windows. Clean. Ready.

"The kids will come back," Jerry adds quickly. "They always do."

Hudson waits, then says, "I don't think they are."

Jerry's words tumble over each other after that.

He can't leave the school. Someone has to keep it ready. What if the teachers come back and it's dirty. What if the kids are scared and need their desks the same way they left them. What if.

Then he stops and looks at Shadoe.

"But he'd be sad," Jerry says suddenly. "If you left him here."

Shadoe thumps his tail once, as if on cue.

Jerry starts talking faster now.

He's never gone anywhere except Nichols. Except Des Moines when he needed the hospital. He doesn't know Tennessee. What if he gets lost. What if he forgets the way back. What if the kids come back and he's not there. What if they need help.

He stops again, breathing hard, confused by his own thoughts.

"I don't know," Jerry says finally, rubbing his hands together. "I don't know what's right."

Hudson does not argue. He does not push. He only listens.

For the first time since Hudson arrived, Jerry falls quiet.

The question hangs between them, unanswered, heavy not with fear, but with choice.

Hudson breaks the silence carefully.

"Jerry," he says, "you read a lot of comic books, right?"

Jerry's head snaps up. "Oh yeah. I love adventures."

"The good ones?" Hudson asks.

"All of them," Jerry says. "The ones with action. And surprises. And when things get really bad but then they don't."

Hudson nods. "Drama."

"Yep. Lots of drama," Jerry agrees.

Hudson leans back against the truck and looks down the road stretching east. "What if this is one of those stories?"

Jerry tilts his head.

"What if this is your adventure," Hudson says. "Not in a book. Real life. You don't know what's coming. There will be surprises. Probably some hard parts too. But there will be good ones. New places. New people."

Jerry listens, eyes wide now.

"All you have to do," Hudson continues, "is get in the truck."

He opens the passenger door.

Shadoe jumps in immediately, tail wagging, settling into the seat like he belongs there.

Jerry stares at the open door.

At the dog.

At Hudson.

His hands flutter as he talks through it again, faster this time. The school. Momma. The kids. The road. Tennessee. Adventure. What if. What if.

Then he stops.

Smiles.

"Well," he says, "adventures always start when you leave."

He steps forward and climbs into the truck.

Hudson closes the door.

The engine turns over.

The road waits, wide and empty, ready to take them wherever the story leads next

Fifteen

Muscatine Survivor

Muscatine, Iowa. 1987

Muscatine was ahead, a large town along the river. The road signs had been counting down since Hudson left Nichols, dropping from fifteen miles to ten, and now five.

A weathered welcome sign stood beside the road as the truck entered town. ***Welcome to Muscatine. The Pearl of the Mississippi.***

Hudson rolls into town expecting the same emptiness he has seen everywhere else. Quiet streets. Parked cars. No movement. But this time, something is different.

The road ahead is blocked.

Not debris. Not wreckage.

A barricade.

It is crude but intentional. Shopping carts turned sideways. A fallen street sign. Plywood nailed together and dragged across the asphalt. Someone built this. Someone planned it.

Hudson eases off the accelerator and brings the truck to a stop.

Jerry leans forward, peering through the windshield. "That's not supposed to be there."

Before Hudson can answer, a figure steps out from behind the barricade.

Hudson's foot moves instinctively. The truck slips into reverse.

Then he sees the rifle.

The girl looks young. Too young. No older than fifteen or sixteen. Her hair is wild, tangled, like she has stopped caring how it falls. She wears a mismatched collection of clothes layered without logic.

The rifle rests in her hands.

It is not aimed at them.

It points at the ground.

That detail stops Hudson from backing up further.

The message is still unmistakable.

Someone is here.

Someone is armed.

Someone is nervous.

The engine idles loudly in the sudden stillness.

Hudson's grip tightens on the steering wheel. Jerry sits frozen beside him, eyes wide, breath shallow. Shadoe lifts his head, ears forward, sensing the shift in the world outside the truck.

Hudson exhales slowly.

The world has changed again.

Not with sickness.

Not with silence.

But with people.

The girl does not shout.

She does not rush.

She stands where she is and watches them, measuring.

"My name's Genie," she says finally. "I'm sixteen."

Her voice is flat, practiced. Like she has said it before. Many times.

Up close, Hudson can see the details more clearly. Her hair hangs loose and uneven, as if she cut it herself and stopped halfway through. Her clothes are a jumble of layers that do not match in color or season, pulled together for usefulness rather than appearance. Mud cakes thc bottoms of her boots. They look like something meant for farms, not streets.

The rifle in her hands is an AR-15 SP1.

Clean. Maintained.

Not a toy.

"It's for protection," she says, as if that explains everything.

Hudson opens his door slowly and steps out, keeping it between himself and her. The metal feels thin now, insufficient, but it is something. He raises his hands just enough to show them empty.

"Jerry, stay inside," he says without looking back.

Jerry's voice comes small through the open window. "I don't like guns."

Hudson hears him swallow. "They're too loud."

Genie snorts. "That's kinda the point."

She studies Hudson again, then shifts her stance. The rifle lowers fully. She sets it carefully against the barricade, never taking her eyes off him. Her other hand rests on her hip, where a handgun sits in a worn holster.

"I won't aim at you," she says. "But I'm keepin' this."

Hudson nods. He understands that kind of compromise. It is the closest thing to trust the world has left.

The space between them remains charged. Not with violence. With uncertainty.

Nobody moves closer.

Nobody relaxes.

This is how people meet now.

Hudson takes a single step forward, then another.

Slow. Measured.

His hands stay open and visible at his sides. No sudden movements. No reaching. He gives the girl no reason to imagine threat where none is offered.

Genie does not move from behind the barricade. She watches him with open suspicion, chin lifted slightly, eyes sharp. This is her line. She is not stepping past it.

Jerry eases out of the truck on the far side, keeping close to the door. Shadoe follows him, staying low, reading the tension in the air. The dog's ears flick, but he does not growl.

Genie breaks the silence with a loud laugh.

"Well," she says, "you might as well come inside if we're gonna talk."

She jerks her head down the street. "I got a place set up."

Hudson hesitates, then nods.

The shelter turns out to be a convenience store a block away. Inside, the shelves have been cleared to make room. A sleeping area in the back. A small kitchen cobbled together near the counter. It smells faintly of fuel and old snacks.

Genie reaches into her pocket, packs tobacco into her cheek, and spits on the tile floor without thinking.

Jerry stops short.

"That's nasty," he says, his voice sharp with genuine offense.

Genie laughs again, louder this time. "You serious?"

She looks Jerry over, head to toe, then turns to Hudson with a crooked grin.

"What is he," she asks bluntly, "some kind of retard or something?"

The word hangs in the air.

Jerry's face tightens. He takes a step back toward Shadoe, upset and confused. Hudson feels the shift immediately, like a line has been crossed that cannot be stepped back over.

He does not raise his voice.

He does not smile.

"That's not acceptable," Hudson says evenly. "His name is Jerry. He has Down syndrome. He's smart. He's kind. And he's with me."

Genie rolls her eyes, unconcerned. "Whatever."

But the damage is done.

The cruelty is casual. Unexamined. Learned and carried forward like a tool.

Muscatine, Iowa.

Hudson does not soften his tone.

"Jerry has Down syndrome," he says. "An extra chromosome, simply put, Jerry unlike us, is able to see the good in everything."

Genie snorts and spits again, this time into an empty cup.

"My dad used to say people like him are dangerous," she replies. "Crazy strong. Don't know their own power. You gotta watch them."

Jerry stiffens.

His face goes red, his hands curling into fists at his sides. "That's not true," he says, louder now. "My momma told me to stay away from people like you. You're not nice."

The words land harder than shouting ever could.

Genie's expression sharpens. "Excuse me?"

Hudson steps in before it can go further.

"That's enough," he says, his voice calm but unmovable. "We're not here to argue. And we're not here to judge each other's worth."

He turns slightly toward Jerry. "You're fine," he says quietly. "You didn't do anything wrong."

Then Hudson looks back to Genie, deliberately changing course.

"We're just passing through," he says. "We're looking for information. About other people. Other places."

The redirection is intentional. A way out. A refusal to escalate.

Genie studies him for a long moment, jaw working the tobacco in her mouth. Whatever fight she was expecting does not arrive.

The lines are drawn now.

Not between survivor and threat.

But between decency and cruelty.

Hudson has chosen which side he stands on.

Genie leans back against the counter as if settling into her story rather than offering it.

"My dad raised me," she says. "Just him and me."

She shrugs. "We were poor. Always were."

She talks about school like it was a hostile environment she endured rather than attended. Kids laughing. Teachers looking past her. The words *white trash* spoken loudly enough that she was meant to hear them.

"I didn't have friends," she says, not bitter so much as factual. "Didn't need 'em."

Hudson listens without interrupting.

Genie explains that trusting people was a mistake she learned not to make early. Everyone wanted something. Everyone lied. So she stopped believing anyone.

"That's how I made it," she says. "By not trusting nobody."

She grins suddenly, sharp and unapologetic.

"I burned the high school down," she adds.

Jerry's eyes widen.

"Watched it burn for two days," Genie continues, clearly pleased. "Best thing I ever did. All that place did was make people think they were better than me."

There is no regret in her voice. No hesitation.

She tells them she likes being alone. Likes not answering to anyone. Likes knowing the rules are hers now.

"But I ain't stupid," she adds. "I know where people are."

Hudson asks where.

"Galesburg," she says. "There's folks there. Kmart parking lot. Old people mostly."

She wrinkles her nose. "They're better than most. Kinder. Not like the others."

She taps the side of the generator humming in the back room. Explains how she siphons fuel from cars. How she keeps the lights on. How she takes care of herself.

Pride radiates off her.

Genie has not softened in the absence of the world.

She has hardened.

And she wears that hardness like armor, convinced it is the only reason she is still alive.

Hudson does not ask Genie to come with them.

The thought never surfaces between them.

Genie does not offer.

There is a shared understanding that requires no explanation. They are moving in different directions, shaped by different choices, holding different versions of survival.

Hudson thanks her for the information about Galesburg.

She nods once, already losing interest.

Jerry stays close to Hudson as they walk back to the truck. Shadoe glances over his shoulder but does not slow.

Genie remains where she is, leaning against the counter, watching them through the open doorway. She does not wave. She does not call out. She does not warn them again.

She does not need to.

Hudson starts the engine.

The truck pulls away slowly, then gathers speed as they leave the barricade behind. In the mirror, the convenience store shrinks until it disappears entirely.

Genie does not follow.

She does not chase.

She returns to her world, alone by choice, armed by fear, convinced that isolation is strength.

Mississippi River Crossing

They stop on the bridge spanning the Mississippi River without speaking about it first. Hudson eases the truck onto the shoulder and cuts the engine. The river spreads out beneath them, wide and steady, moving with the patience of something that does not care who is still alive to witness it.

Jerry steps out and walks straight to the railing. He leans forward carefully, gripping the cold metal with both hands. Shadoe sits beside him, head tilted, watching the water flow past.

Then Jerry gasps.

An eagle drops from the sky with sudden precision, wings folding tight as it strikes the surface of the river. For a moment it disappears in a burst of spray, then rises again, powerful and certain, a fish clutched in its talons.

Jerry laughs, loud and unrestrained.

"Did you see that?" he shouts. "Did you see that?"

Hudson smiles and walks closer. He watches the bird climb back into the sky, its wings cutting clean lines through the air.

"I've only seen them in books," Jerry says, breathless. "Never like that. Never real."

He shakes his head in disbelief. "This is the best part of the adventure so far."

They stay there longer than necessary, letting the moment settle, letting the river and the sky wash away the sharp edges of the last encounter.

Later, back in the truck, Jerry grows quiet.

"I don't like people like her," he says finally. "She was mean."

Hudson nods. "Some people let bad things turn them hard."

Jerry looks down at Shadoe, who rests his head on Jerry's knee.

"Well," Jerry says, "I like you. And I like him."

Hudson reaches over and pats the dog's shoulder. "That's what matters," he says. "We stick with the ones who treat us right."

Jerry smiles at that.

The truck rolls forward again, carrying them east, leaving the river behind, taking with it a small piece of wonder to balance the weight of everything else.

They merge onto Interstate 74 heading south, the empty lanes stretching ahead like both an invitation and a warning. The truck hums steadily beneath them, the tires the only sound left of human movement.

A flash of color pulls Hudson's attention to the roadside.

He slows.

A billboard stands just off the shoulder, its original advertisement buried beneath thick strokes of red paint. The letters are uneven, hurried, written by someone who had not taken the time to make them clean.

Hudson brings the truck to a stop and reads it again.

COMMUNITY IN GALESBURG

STOP IN GALESBURG

He studies the words a moment longer than he needs to.

They weren't meant to last. They were meant to be seen.

Jerry leans forward, squinting. "Where's Galesburg?"

Hudson reaches for the atlas on the seat, flipping it open and tracing the route with his finger before glancing back up at the road. "Not far," he says. "About an hour if the roads stay clear."

Jerry nods, satisfied, and settles back.

Hudson doesn't move right away.

He looks at the sign one more time, taking in the way the paint dripped in places, the way the strokes overlapped. Whoever wrote it had believed someone would come. Had needed someone to come.

Hudson shifts the truck into gear and pulls back onto the interstate.

The sign disappears behind them, but the message stays.

It settles into the cab, quiet and heavy, changing the feel of the road ahead.

Up until now, the world had been empty. Predictable in its own way. You saw the danger before it reached you. You moved around it or through it.

This was different.

This meant people.

And people were harder to read than anything else he had faced so far.

The exit sign for Kmart comes into view ahead, just as Genie had told them. Hudson eases off the gas, guiding the truck into the lane without saying anything.

Shadoe shifts beside him, alert now.
Jerry watches the road, his expression open, expectant.
Hudson keeps his eyes forward.
He doesn't know what they're driving into.
Only that it won't be empty.
He takes the exit.

Sixteen

RV Club

Galesburg, Illinois. 1987

Hudson eases the truck into the Kmart parking lot and lets it idle.

He expects disorder. Abandoned vehicles. Scattered carts. The careless remains of people who passed through and never settled.

Instead he sees order.

Four RVs arranged in a precise square near the edge of the lot. Backs facing outward. Doors facing inward. Clean. Evenly spaced. Close enough to form a wall.

It reminds him of old photographs. Wagon trains pulled into circles at night. Not for comfort. For protection.

Something moves between two of the RVs. Just a glimpse. A face, watching.

Hudson cuts the engine and steps out, hands relaxed at his sides.

"Hello," he calls.

A brief pause. Then a voice, steady and alert. "Walk around till you see the opening."

Jerry and Shadoe climb out beside him. They circle the square slowly, boots on gravel, and Hudson feels eyes tracking them the whole way. Unseen but present. This place has rules, and he understands one of them clearly before he ever steps inside.

It is not hoping to be safe. It is expecting trouble.

The opening is narrow, just wide enough to pass through single file.

Hudson steps in first.

The space inside opens like a room behind a door. Four people. Close enough together to suggest they have been living in each other's pockets for weeks. One laughs at something. Another stretches in a folding chair, legs out, ankles crossed.

Jerry stops walking. Counts softly under his breath. "Four," he says, almost to himself.

Shadoe sits beside him, calm but watching.

A man with gray hair and a straight back steps forward. Marine posture. The kind that doesn't leave.

"Tony," he says.

The others follow. Moses, who nods once. Dwight, who raises a hand. Mae, seated, who offers a small smile that doesn't quite reach her eyes.

They came from different roads. Different places. Followed painted signs on overpasses and billboards, words pointing toward Galesburg. Found each other here and stayed.

Tony was a Marine, Vietnam, then construction. Moses sold cars after the Navy, retired at sixty-eight and thought he was finished working. Dwight spent his life as an ironworker, high above the ground, trusting steel and the men beside him. Mae was a registered nurse who left early to care for her husband when he got sick, and stayed with him until the end.

The men grow quiet when their wives come up. Each one lost to the flu. Different places, same ending.

Hudson keeps his own story brief. Wyoming. Traveling east. His son. Jerry adds his in simple terms. The school. The kids. His mamma.

Then Tony's voice drops, just slightly.

"There's another group," he says. "Half a mile from here."

Moses nods. "Old neighborhood. Big houses. Fenced in."

"Generators," Dwight adds. "Security."

Mae's expression tightens. "And a man who runs it."

Hudson waits.

"Bruce," Tony says. "He decided early on who was worth keeping around." He pauses. "We weren't."

Moses keeps his voice flat, like he has practiced the telling until the anger stopped showing. "Said we were useless. Too old. Burning through supplies."

"Told us to move on," Dwight says. "While the roads were still passable."

Hudson looks around the circle of them. "But you stayed."

"We should have left," Mae says. "Probably." She folds her hands in her lap. "But then we started hearing things."

Tony leans forward, elbows on his knees. "Bruce started collecting people. Mostly young ones."

"Collecting how," Hudson says.

"People passing through," Moses says. "Looking for safety. Something that felt like the world used to." He pauses. "Some make it back out. Most of those leave the area fast."

"Some," Tony says, "he keeps."

Jerry frowns. "Keeps?"

"They're not allowed to leave," Moses says. "That's what we believe."

The words settle slowly.

Mae speaks without looking up. "Bruce is evil. That's not a thing I say easily."

A group of young men support him. Agree with him. Benefit from the arrangement. They protect him because he rewards them.

"You're talking about a dictator," Hudson says.

Mae nods. "And his protectors."

Hudson feels something that is not quite anger and not quite fear, but sits in the same neighborhood as both. He has met men like Bruce before. The flu didn't make Bruce. It just gave him permission to be his true self.

The conversation settles for a moment, the fire the only sound between them.

Then a door opens on one of the RVs.

The woman who steps out doesn't hurry. She takes in Hudson, Jerry, and Shadoe in a single unhurried look, the way someone does when they've already decided what they think and are checking whether they're right.

Red hair pulled back, strands loose around her face. Late thirties. Strong shoulders. The kind of posture that comes from years of standing in front of rooms full of people who needed answers and weren't always going to like them.

She crosses the space and stops at a comfortable distance. Not cautious. Just measured.

"Stephanie," she says. Her eyes move to Jerry. "Hi."

Jerry smiles immediately. "Hi."

Mae speaks quietly. "Bruce wanted her to stay with them."

Stephanie doesn't react to that. She's heard it said before.

"I was there six weeks," she says. "Long enough to understand what it was." She pauses. "I made myself more trouble than I was worth. Loud. Uncooperative. Argued about everything. Eventually they decided it wasn't worth the effort."

No pride in it. No relief either. Just the clean delivery of someone who made a decision and executed it.

"I'm from Bloomington," she says. "I taught chemistry." She glances at Hudson. "Like everyone else, I lost everything."

She leaves it there. The rest of the story is hers to share when she chooses, not before.

As evening settles, Tony lights the fire. The flames catch quickly and the RVs hold the heat inside the square. They talk about the old world for a while, the small things that once felt important, the systems that vanished in weeks.

Eventually Bruce comes back into the conversation, as he always seems to.

Jerry watches the fire, knees pulled close. "I think most people are good," he says. "I think they want to do good things."

No one interrupts him.

Moses stares into the flames for a long moment. "I wish that were true," he says quietly. "I really do."

Then Dwight speaks without looking up from the fire.

"They send someone over. Couple times a day."

Hudson glances at him.

"From Bruce's group," Moses says. "They watch the Kmart. Always have."

Tony adds, "They know when someone new shows up. Every time."

Hudson looks back toward the opening in the RV wall, the narrow gap they walked through an hour ago. They were seen the moment the truck rolled into the lot. Watched as they parked, as they stepped out, as they circled the perimeter looking for the way in.

Nothing here is accidental.

The fire crackles softly. The sound suddenly too small against the open dark.

Then another sound cuts through it.

An engine. Deep. Unmistakable.

Heavy tires on gravel, slow and deliberate, the way something moves when it wants to be heard.

Heads turn as one.

Tony stands. His voice is calm in the way that comes from having been afraid enough times that it no longer shows.

"That'll be them."

SEVENTEEN

Your Invited

GALESBURG, ILLINOIS. 1987

They heard the truck before they saw it.

It was a Dodge Ram, lifted high on oversized mud tires, moving slow and deliberate. In the old world it would have looked like overcompensation. Now it looked like a statement.

Shadoe went rigid at Jerry's leg. Didn't bark. Just locked in.

Three men climbed out before the engine fully died.

Mitchell first. Tall, wide through the shoulders, ball cap low, a heavy belt carrying weight on one hip. He moved like a man who expected space to be made for him.

Jordy second. Younger, wiry, shoulders up around his ears. The kind of guy who had turned a nervous disposition into something meaner.

Sloan last. Thicker through the chest, slower out of the truck, taking his time. He scanned the group the way you scan a room before entering it.

All three wore their weapons holstered and visible. Not raised. Not pointed. Just there. The way a reminder is just there.

Hudson stood half in the firelight, half in the gray afternoon, and watched them come.

What bothered him most wasn't the weapons or the truck or the practiced way they moved together.

It was how ordinary they looked.

Six months ago he would have passed these men in a hardware store and forgotten their faces before he reached the parking lot. Now they walked across dead pavement like they owned every square foot of it.

Mitchell led them toward the gap between the RVs without slowing. No call out. No asking. Just walking in, the way you walk into a place you've already decided belongs to you.

Mae stepped into the gap before he got there.

She was a small woman. She stood like she was six feet tall.

"Well look here," she said, voice bright as a slap. "The three minions of Bruceville. Right on schedule."

Jordy's face snapped. "We're no minion to nobody. We're building a real community."

Dwight chuckled from the doorway. "Nobody who wanted to live under Dictator Bruce's rules has showed up yet," he said. "But you keep trying."

Sloan lifted his chin. "We don't have a dictatorship. We have true socialism."

He said it the way people say things they've rehearsed. Hudson watched his eyes. The words and the eyes weren't telling the same story.

Mitchell spread his hands, smooth and practiced. "Easy. We take good care of everybody at the commune. That's all we're saying."

Hudson spoke for the first time.

"Then I'd like to go up there and talk to them," he said. "See if any of them want to join us down here."

The smile on Sloan's face didn't break. His eyes did.

Jordy cut in fast. Too fast. "We don't do that. Not yet. People are safe where they are. Protected from outside problems."

Hudson let a beat of silence pass.

"Sounds like the only problem," he said, "is the one inside your socialist project."

Nobody spoke for a second.

Mitchell's jaw shifted. Sloan's smile went thin and billboard-flat. Jordy opened his mouth and closed it.

Then Mitchell changed course entirely. He turned away from Hudson and looked past him at the older group standing in the shade near the far RV.

His voice went hard.

"You people need to be gone from here," he said. "Everything in this town is ours. The Kmart. The supplies. All of it. Bruce is done warning you."

Moses stepped forward.

He was small. He moved slow, the shuffle of a man whose knees had opinions. He blinked up at Mitchell with the innocent expression of someone who had just heard a noise they couldn't quite place.

"I'm sorry," Moses said pleasantly, "what were you saying?"

Mitchell stared at him. "I said you need to leave."

Moses tilted his head. "Hmm?"

"Leave. Go. This town is ours."

Moses turned to Mae with a look of gentle confusion. "Is he talking to us?"

Mae pressed her lips together to keep from smiling.

"I believe so," she said.

Moses turned back to Mitchell with a sympathetic expression, like he was about to deliver bad news to someone he felt sorry for.

"You'll have to forgive us," Moses said. "We all have dementia. Can't remember a word anyone tells us five minutes later." He gestured at the group behind him. "It's a real problem."

Mae actually laughed. Couldn't stop it.

Dwight put his fist over his mouth.

Jerry beamed like he was watching his favorite comedian.

Mitchell did not laugh.

He took one step forward and grabbed Moses by the front of his shirt.

Not a shove. A grip. Deliberate. A hand full of fabric hauling a seventy-year-old man up onto his toes.

"Think that's funny?" Mitchell said. Low. Close. The kind of voice that doesn't need volume.

Moses looked up at him.

He did not look afraid.

He looked interested.

"Son," Moses said calmly, "I have outlived two wars, one tornado, three bad marriages, and a doctor who told me I had six months to live in 2003." He paused. "You are not the worst thing that's ever grabbed my shirt."

Hudson was already moving.

He crossed the space in four steps and stopped directly beside Mitchell. Not behind him. Beside him. Close enough that Mitchell had to turn his head to see him.

Hudson did not touch him.

He did not reach for anything on his belt.

He just stood there, calm as a fence post in a storm, and looked at Mitchell with the flat, patient eyes of a man who has already decided how this ends and is in no hurry.

"Put him down," Hudson said.

Two words. No rise in the voice. No performance.

Mitchell held for a second. His grip on Moses didn't release but his eyes went to Hudson and something in them shifted, the way a dog's eyes shift when it realizes it may have misread the situation.

Jordy's hand moved toward his hip.

Hudson's eyes didn't leave Mitchell. "Tell your friend," Hudson said quietly, "that if his hand goes any further, this gets a lot more complicated than a dinner invitation."

Silence.

Jordy's hand stopped.

Mitchell released Moses.

Moses straightened his shirt with the unhurried dignity of a man who has made his point and knows it.

Sloan stepped in, smooth as oil over water, rebuilding the professional smile like nothing had happened.

"Anyway," Sloan said. "Bruce is hosting dinner tonight. Hudson, you're invited."

Hudson looked at him.

"Just me," Hudson said.

"You and anyone you'd like to bring." Sloan's eyes moved to Stephanie. "Stephanie is welcome, of course. It would be good to see her again."

Something crossed Stephanie's face. Gone before anyone who didn't know what to look for could catch it.

Mitchell added, looking at Jerry: "Jerry stays here. With the group."

Jerry's face fell a little. "But I like dinner."

Nobody acknowledged that.

"Two hours," Jordy said. "Come hungry."

Hudson didn't nod. Didn't agree. Didn't refuse. He took the information the way you take a look at something you intend to deal with later.

The three men walked back to the truck. Mitchell didn't look back. Jordy did, once.

The Ram rolled out of the lot, engine fading.

Nobody spoke until the sound was completely gone.

Moses straightened his collar and looked at his shirt like he was checking for damage.

"Well," he said. "That was rude."

Mae put her hand on his arm. Her expression had gone from entertained to something harder.

"You okay?" she said.

"Fine," Moses said. "My pride has taken worse."

Jerry was looking at Hudson with a different expression than usual. Quieter. Less cheerful.

"Are they going to come back and do that again?" Jerry asked.

"Probably," Hudson said.

"To someone else?"

"If we let them."

Dwight spat on the pavement. "We going to let them?"

Hudson looked toward the road where the truck had gone. "No."

Mae raised her eyebrows. "But you're still going to their dinner."

"Because of that," Hudson said. "Not in spite of it."

He looked at Stephanie and tilted his head toward the side of the nearest RV. She followed without being asked.

They stood in the shade away from the group, the winter sun low enough that it didn't reach them there.

Stephanie spoke first.

"They know where we sleep," she said. "They've known for a while. That wasn't a visit to warn us. It was a visit to show us they can walk in any time they want."

Hudson nodded. He'd already gotten there.

"Tell me about Bruce," he said.

Stephanie looked at the ground for a second. Then back up.

"I was there for six weeks," she said. "I got out. Most people don't."

"Why not?"

"Because by the time you understand what it is, you've already given up too much to leave." She crossed her arms. "It doesn't look like a trap from the inside. It looks like the only safe place left."

"What did you give up?" Hudson asked.

She was quiet for a moment.

"My car. My fuel. The medicine I had. They take inventory when you arrive. Call it pooling resources. Call it community." She paused. "By week three you're dependent. By week six you've stopped thinking about leaving because leaving means starting from nothing."

Hudson watched her face.

"What made you go?"

Something moved behind her eyes. She let it settle before she answered.

"A woman named Cora," she said. "She asked Bruce a question at dinner one night. In front of everyone. Just a question about the food rationing. Whether it was distributed fairly."

"What happened to her?"

"She was gone the next morning," Stephanie said. "Bruce told everyone she'd decided to leave. Said she wasn't a good fit for the community."

Hudson said nothing.

"Nobody asked where she went," Stephanie said. "That was the thing that told me what I needed to know. Thirty people sitting at a table and nobody asked. Because they already understood that asking was the wrong answer."

She looked at Hudson directly.

"That's what tonight is," she said. "He's going to feed you and compliment you and tell you he needs men like you. He's going to make you feel like you have a seat at the table."

"And then?"

"And then he'll ask you for something small. So small you won't notice it. And then something else. And then the circle around you starts to close."

Hudson looked toward town.

"Why invite me at all," he said, "if that's the risk?"

"Because you're a bigger risk outside," Stephanie said. "You've got people. You've got skills. You've got Shadoe, and everyone in that commune knows what a dog like Shadoe can do." She paused. "Bruce doesn't want you as an enemy. He wants you folded in. Useful. His."

"And if I don't fold?"

Stephanie's eyes held his.

"Then what happened to Moses today," she said, "will look friendly by comparison."

The words landed clean.

Hudson was quiet for a moment.

"Are you going to come?" he asked.

"Yes," she said. No hesitation.

"Why? Knowing what you know about that commune."

She looked at him steadily. "Because I know that community and you don't. And you're walking into it either way." She paused. "I'd rather be there."

Hudson looked at her for a long moment. He'd met people in his life who were brave because they didn't understand the danger. Stephanie understood it completely. That was something different.

"Alright," he said. "You come."

She nodded.

"We stay together," he added. "We don't accept anything we can't walk away from. We eat, we listen, and we leave."

"And if he won't let us leave?"

Hudson's expression didn't change.

"Then we find out what kind of man he really is," he said. "Tonight instead of later."

Stephanie studied him.

"You're not scared," she said.

"I'm careful," he said. "That's better."

They walked back to the group.

Mae had Moses sitting in a folding chair now, pressing a cloth to the back of his neck even though he kept insisting he was fine. Jerry was on the ground next to Shadoe with his arm over the dog's back. Dwight was leaning on the RV, arms crossed, watching the road.

Hudson looked at all of them.

"Stephanie and I are going to dinner," he said. "Not because we trust it. Because we need to see it up close."

"And if it goes wrong?" Dwight asked.

"Then it goes wrong and you'll know because we don't come back by dawn." Hudson looked at him. "If that happens, you take the group and you move. Don't wait. Don't come looking for us. You move."

Dwight didn't argue. That was how Hudson knew he understood.

Jerry looked up from the ground. "What about Shadoe?"

"Shadoe stays with you," Hudson said.

He crouched down and put his hand on the dog's head. Shadoe pressed into it for a second, eyes up, calm and reading.

"Stay," Hudson said quietly.

Shadoe sat.

Jerry wrapped his arm a little tighter around the dog's back, reassured.

Mae walked up to Hudson before he and Stephanie started toward town. She stopped close and kept her voice low.

"You know what he is," she said. Not a question.

"Getting a clearer picture," Hudson said.

"You know what he wants you for."

"Yes."

She looked at him the way women look at men they've decided to trust against their better judgment.

"Don't let him have it," she said.

"No," Hudson said. "I won't."

He and Stephanie turned toward town.

The sun was already dropping. The buildings ahead were going dark at the edges, the way buildings do when the light starts failing and nobody is turning the lights on inside anymore.

Somewhere up in those buildings, Bruce was setting a table.

Making it look like hospitality.

Banking on the fact that people who are tired and hungry and scared will sit down at any table that's offered.

Hudson wasn't tired. He wasn't hungry. And he'd stopped being scared of the wrong things a long time ago.

He and Stephanie walked into the dark.

Eyes open.

EIGHTEEN

Dinner Show

BRUCEVILLE 1987

The farther they drove, the cleaner everything got.

Hudson noticed it first in the sidewalks. No debris. No broken glass. Then the houses, intact, shutters level, fences unbroken. Then the lawns, actually trimmed, the kind of trimmed that required someone spending time on it while the rest of the world fell apart.

Stephanie watched the windshield and said nothing.

Hudson slowed when the security booth came into view.

It wasn't improvised. Thick glass. A covered overhang. An arm barrier painted white and red. A man standing beside it with a rifle held at a downward angle that meant business without quite saying so.

Hudson stopped a few feet from the barrier.

The guard stepped forward. Sunburned face, greasy hair, sharp eyes.

"Turn it off," he said.

Hudson killed the engine.

"Out. Both of you."

They got out. The guard looked them over the way a customs agent looks at luggage, searching for something he expected to find.

"Vehicles don't go inside," he said. "I'm Pickle. I'll walk you up."

Stephanie leaned close to Hudson. "This is part of it," she said quietly. "They make you leave the truck at the gate. You walk in on foot. It's designed to make you feel like a visitor in someone else's place before you've even met anyone."

Pickle's eyes flicked toward her. He didn't respond. He'd heard it before, or he knew it was true and didn't care either way.

Hudson looked through the barrier.

The neighborhood beyond it was another world. Wide driveways curving into covered garages. Stonework standing clean and proud. And behind the houses, rolling out wide and green and impossible, a golf course. Fairways like velvet. A flag in the distance standing perfectly straight.

Everything maintained. Everything preserved.

Not for survival.

For someone.

Pickle lifted the barrier. "Let's go."

They walked. Hudson counted sightlines, angles, the position of the booth. He glanced back once. His truck sat outside the gate like something discarded.

He faced forward.

Pickle didn't take them straight to the house.

He guided them to a small outbuilding first, a converted garage set back from the street, its door propped open. A folding table inside. Two chairs. A clipboard.

A man sat behind the table.

Small frame. Narrow shoulders. Hair combed neatly, too neatly for the end of the world. He looked up when they entered and stood immediately, the quick rise of someone who had been told to be welcoming.

"Hi," he said. "I'm Topher. I just need a few minutes with each of you before dinner. Just a quick intake. Standard for everyone who visits."

He smiled the apologetic smile of a man who knew he was an inconvenience and wanted you to know he knew.

"It's nothing formal," Topher added. "Bruce just likes to know a little about the people he invites. Background. Skills. That kind of thing. It helps him figure out how he can be useful to you."

The last sentence was perfectly constructed. How he can be useful to you. Not how you can be useful to him.

Hudson didn't catch it. There was no reason to catch it.

"This is something new, Bruce is adding to his ridiculous rules," said Stephanie to Hudson.

"If something happens, yell out to me."

Stephanie walked in. Hudson waited outside with Pickle, who stood against the wall and stared at the middle distance and offered nothing.

When Stephanie came back out her face was neutral. She didn't say anything about what had been asked.

Hudson went in.

Topher gestured to the chair across the table. Hudson sat. Topher sat. The clipboard was face-down. Topher didn't pick it up.

"So," Topher said, easy and friendly, "where are you from originally?"

"Tennessee," Hudson said.

"Long way from home. What brought you out this way?"

"Work," Hudson said. "Before everything. Electrical engineering. Had a job in Wyoming."

Topher nodded like this was casual conversation, not information.

"Electrical engineering," he said. "That's interesting. What kind of work specifically?"

Hudson shrugged. "Power distribution. Grid systems. Generator installs. Industrial controls. I ran projects for a company that managed federal facilities."

"Federal facilities," Topher said. Still just nodding. "So you know how to keep large systems running. Power for buildings, that kind of thing."

"That's most of it, yeah."

"That's a real skill," Topher said, and he said it with what seemed like genuine respect. "Most people I talk to, you know, they were in sales or management or whatever. Nothing wrong with that. But practical skills, technical skills, those are different now."

He asked a few more questions. How long had Hudson been on the road. Whether he had any medical training. Whether he knew anything about agriculture or water systems.

Hudson answered all of it. There was no reason not to.

After about ten minutes Topher stood and extended his hand.

"That's all I need," he said. "Thank you. Pickle will take you around to the back."

He smiled again. The same apologetic, harmless smile.

"Enjoy dinner," he said. "Bruce is a great host."

Hudson shook his hand and walked back out into the evening.

He didn't think about the conversation again until he was sitting at Bruce's table.

Pickle took them around the side of the house, hedge-lined path, swept clean, the controlled route that delivered them exactly where they were meant to arrive.

The back of the house. The deck.

Wide boards. String lights waiting overhead. A long table covered in white cloth and heavy plates. The golf course rolling out behind it all, green and unreal.

Bruce was already standing at the far end of the table.

Hudson recognized the type before he registered the man. Clean shirt. Combed hair. Not a trace of doubt on him. The look of someone who had decided long ago that things would go his way, and had found no evidence since to suggest otherwise.

He came forward with open arms.

"Welcome," Bruce said. "Welcome to Galesburg."

Smooth. Practiced. The words of a man who had said them enough times that they'd lost weight and gained polish.

He extended his hand to Hudson.

Hudson shook it. Calibrated grip. Firm without aggression. A handshake that had been refined over years of wanting to win every room.

"Hudson," Bruce said, holding it a half-second longer than needed. "I'm glad you came."

"Appreciate the invitation," Hudson said.

Bruce turned to Stephanie.

"Stephanie." Same warm smile. "Welcome back."

Two words carrying everything. I know you left. You're here anyway.

Stephanie shook his hand without expression.

Mitchell, Jordy, and Sloan were already seated. A few others too. People who looked clean and well-fed and careful about how much they showed it.

"Please," Bruce said. "Sit."

They sat. Hudson across from Mitchell, Stephanie beside him. Bruce stood at the head a moment longer, letting the scene settle.

Then he sat and lifted his water glass.

"To rebuilding," he said. "To survival. To the future."

A few people echoed it. Hudson didn't.

Bruce noticed. His smile didn't move.

The food came out carried by four residents in dark slacks and crisp shirts. Moving in a line, plates level, eyes down. Staff. Not neighbors.

Thick steaks. Roasted potatoes. Bread. Butter in a dish.

Real butter.

Hudson watched the table. Every hand hovering just above the silverware, suspended. Nobody eating. Waiting.

Bruce picked up his fork.

The table started eating.

Hudson took his fork and looked at Bruce.

"Is everyone in the community eating like this tonight?" he asked.

Soft question. Hard edge inside it.

"Everybody eats in their homes," Bruce said pleasantly.

In their homes. Not here. Not together. Not equal.

Stephanie's eyes moved to her plate.

Bruce folded his hands like a man who had a point to make and was in no hurry to make it.

"I was raised Pentecostal," he said. Almost casual. "Old-school. Structure wasn't optional. Men do what men are built for. Women do what women are built for. Everybody knows their place. The whole thing works."

Trained nods around the table.

"It's not oppression," Bruce said. "It's tradition. Without structure, everything collapses."

Hudson took a bite. Said nothing.

Bruce watched him not respond and seemed to find it interesting.

A server stepped to Hudson's side. Young woman, early twenties, eyes down.

"Would you like me to cut your steak, sir?"

"No. Thank you."

She stepped away.

Stephanie raised her chin toward the same server. "Could you cut mine?"

Half-second pause.

"I think you can cut your own," the server said. Soft. Practiced.

Jordy smirked. Mitchell looked at his plate. Sloan kept smiling.

Bruce said nothing.

Stephanie leaned toward Hudson.

"Men get served," she said quietly. "Women don't."

"I noticed," Hudson said.

Bruce waited until the moment settled. Then he turned.

"Topher," he said. "Tell them how you got here."

Hudson looked down the table.

Topher. The man from the outbuilding. The clipboard. The apologetic smile.

Topher set his fork down carefully and told his story. Peoria. The actuarial job. His wife and kids. The flu. The dying. The roads. He told it the way people tell things they've been asked to perform enough times that the grief is real but the words have worn smooth.

"I was ready to be done," Topher said. "Literally ready."

He looked at Bruce with the eyes of a man who had decided that what he was looking at had saved his life.

"And then I found this," Topher said.

"That's enough, brother," Bruce said. Gently. Cutting it off at exactly the moment it had done its job.

Topher stopped immediately.

Bruce turned to the table.

"Every person who comes here goes through an intake," Bruce said. "You both met Topher this afternoon."

He said it casually. Like it was nothing.

Hudson went still.

"It's not invasive," Bruce continued, pleasantly. "Topher just has a conversation. Gets a sense of who someone is. What they know. What they've done. What they can do."

He lifted his water glass slightly.

"And then he gives me a number," Bruce said. "A score."

Hudson looked at Topher.

Topher looked at his plate.

The conversation in the outbuilding replayed itself in Hudson's head. The casual questions. The nodding. The friendly interest. How he'd answered everything openly because there was no reason not to. Tennessee. Electrical engineering. Power distribution. Grid systems. Federal facilities.

Not a conversation.

An interview.

And he'd sat there and handed over every answer without a second thought.

"Most survivors score low," Bruce said. "Nothing wrong with that. They contribute what they can. They're fed and housed. They're part of the community."

He looked at Hudson.

"But occasionally someone arrives with real value."

His eyes didn't leave Hudson's face.

"You scored the highest we've ever recorded," Bruce said.

Hudson held his gaze. Kept his voice even.

"Based on a ten-minute conversation," Hudson said.

"Topher is very good at what he does," Bruce said. Still smiling. "He doesn't need long."

Hudson glanced at Topher again.

Topher was still looking at his plate. The way a man looks at his plate when he knows what was done with what he collected and has made a certain kind of peace with it.

Hudson looked back at Bruce.

"Electrical engineering," Bruce said. "Grid systems. Power distribution. Generator installs for federal facilities."

He said it back, word for word. The way someone recites a list they've memorized.

Hudson's own answers. Handed over freely. Sitting on that clipboard.

"In this world," Bruce said, "that's not a resume. That's a superpower."

He spread his hands across the table as if presenting a gift.

"Here's my offer. Any house on this street. Your choice. Roof, heat, security, food. Tools and materials. Personnel to support your work."

"Personnel," Hudson said.

"People to help you."

"Loyal to you," Hudson said.

"Loyal to the community," Bruce said.

Same thing. Both of them knew it.

"And I answer only to you," Hudson said.

"You'd have full authority over your projects," Bruce said. "I set the priorities. You execute."

Hudson was quiet for a moment.

"What happens to people who score high and say no?" he asked.

The table shifted. Pressure, not sound.

Mitchell looked up. Jordy stopped chewing.

Bruce's smile stayed exactly where it was.

"That hasn't happened," Bruce said.

"Yet," Hudson said.

One word. He held Bruce's eyes and left it there.

For just a moment something behind Bruce's smile went flat and still. The way water goes still before it freezes. Then he laughed, short and easy, and dismissed it.

"I like you," Bruce said. "You think straight."

He clapped his hands once.

"Paula," he called. "Bring the dessert."

She came through the back door carrying a tray.

The heels first. Black, expensive, red soles clicking across the deck boards in a place where heels had no business being. The dress short and tight and dark, belonging to a world that no longer existed. Hair down. Everything arranged to be looked at.

She was maybe twenty-two.

She moved with the careful precision of someone who had learned that moving carefully was safer than moving naturally. Eyes down. Tray level. She worked from Bruce's end of the table toward Hudson's, placing cake without being thanked, without being looked at in the face.

Bruce watched Hudson watch her.

"Paula made that herself," Bruce said. "That's what we do here. We don't just survive."

He smiled.

"We live."

Paula reached Hudson last.

She leaned forward to place his plate and her fingers moved across the back of his hand. Light. Quick. Deliberate.

Hudson's eyes dropped to the plate.

A small piece of paper folded under the rim.

He shifted the plate as if settling it, and the paper came free into his palm. Two seconds. Into his sleeve. Nothing to see.

Stephanie had seen it. Her face didn't change.

Paula walked back to the house without looking at anyone.

Bruce kept talking. The community. The future. The vision. The warm and reasonable voice of a man who believed every word or had practiced believing it until the difference was gone.

Hudson listened, ate his cake, and watched the door Paula had disappeared through.

It didn't open again.

Hudson stood when the cake was finished.

"Thank you for dinner," he said. "Good food."

Bruce rose with him. The smile, still there.

"Think about the offer," Bruce said. "No pressure. Sleep on it."

"I'll do that," Hudson said.

They both knew he wouldn't.

Bruce extended his hand. Hudson shook it. Same calibrated grip. Half-second longer than needed.

"My door is always open," Bruce said.

"Good to know," Hudson said.

They walked off the deck. Pickle fell in behind them. The walk to the gate felt longer than the walk in. Hudson didn't look back.

Pickle lifted the barrier. Hudson got in the truck. Stephanie got in. He started the engine and the sound felt like something returned to him.

He drove.

In the mirror, Pickle was already back at the booth. Already watching the road.

Back at the mansion, before the sound of the truck faded, Bruce turned to Mitchell.

"He's not going to accept voluntarily," Bruce said.

Mitchell nodded.

"He cares about those people at the Kmart," Bruce said. "The old ones. The simple man. The dog." He looked at the golf course in the last of the light. "People make worse decisions when they have something to protect."

"What do you want to do?" Jordy asked.

"Watch them," Bruce said. "All of them. Every hour. Don't let them leave the area."

"And if he still won't cooperate?" Sloan asked.

Bruce looked at him.

"He will," Bruce said. "When the alternative involves the people he cares about."

He said it the way you state something that has already happened.

"Clean this up," he said to the servers. "Quickly."

They moved immediately.

"People eat after work is done," Bruce added. Casual. Absolute.

Nobody argued. Nobody looked surprised.

Kmart

"Hudson! We watched Ghostbusters!"

Mae came out behind Jerry, reading Hudson's face before he spoke. Shadoe pressed through and found his spot at Hudson's leg. Hudson put a hand on the dog's head for a second.

"How bad?" Dwight asked.

"Bad enough," Hudson said.

He pulled the paper from his sleeve and unfolded it. Held it so they could see.

HELP.

The circle went quiet.

Mae's face changed. "Paula," she said. Not a question.

"You know her?"

"She came through here weeks ago," Mae said. "Young. Beautiful. Excited to be around people. Said she'd been alone a long time. We tried to get her to stay."

She stopped.

"She didn't," Hudson said.

"No," Mae said. "She did not."

Moses sat down slowly on his folding chair.

"A man like that," Moses said, "doesn't take no from someone like her."

Jerry looked between them, smile gone. "Is she okay?"

"Not yet," Hudson said.

Dwight rubbed his jaw. "You told him you're an engineer."

"He already knew," Hudson said. "Before I sat down. They run an intake on everyone who comes through the gate. A man named Topher. Friendly. Clipboard. Felt like a conversation."

He paused.

"It wasn't a conversation. He scores everyone. Skills, knowledge, usefulness. Feeds the numbers to Bruce."

Dwight stared at him. "And you answered honestly."

"I had no reason not to," Hudson said. "At the time."

"We've got three problems," Hudson said. "Paula. Bruce knowing everything about us. And him making sure we can't leave before he gets what he wants."

"What does he want?" Jerry asked.

"He wants me to restore his power grid," Hudson said. "Lights, heat, security systems. Make the commune self-sufficient."

"And if you don't," Mae said.

"He'll find a way to change my answer," Hudson said.

The circle was quiet.

Jerry looked down at Shadoe. Shadoe looked back. Calm. Steady.

"What do we do?" Jerry asked.

Hudson looked at all of them.

"Tonight we sleep and we watch," Hudson said. "Two-hour rotations. Nobody goes anywhere alone."

"And tomorrow?" Mae asked.

"Tomorrow, we act normal."

Nineteen

Toys and Dogs

Kmart 1987

Morning came in gray and cold, the kind of cold that sat down on the pavement and stayed there.

The RV clan woke up slow. People stepped outside wrapped in coats and blankets, breath coming in white clouds, faces carrying the usual mix of stiff joints and leftover worry from the night before.

Mae already had a pot going on the small burner. Dwight was lined up beside her opening cans, both of them working without needing to discuss it. Breakfast was whatever they had. Canned fruit. Sausage from a skillet. Powdered milk stirred into water until it turned the color of fog.

Mae handed out cups.

"Don't think about it," she said. "Just drink."

"Close your eyes and it almost tastes like real milk," Dwight said.

Mae shot him a look. "Don't ruin my morning with your honesty."

Jerry came out wrapped in his blanket like a cape, hair sideways, eyes still finding themselves. He walked straight to Hudson the way he always did when something was on his mind.

"Hudson," he said quietly, "I keep thinking about my chickens."

Hudson looked at him.

"I left them," Jerry said. "I didn't even say goodbye. They don't know where I went."

Mae paused what she was doing. Shadoe walked up beside Jerry and leaned his shoulder against the man's leg without being asked. Jerry's hand found the top of the dog's head and rested there.

"You had to go," Hudson said.

"I know," Jerry said. "I still feel bad."

Nobody tried to fix that. Some things just needed to be said.

After breakfast Mae clapped her hands once.

"Camper World," she said. "We get Hudson his RV today."

Jerry perked up instantly. "Like a house on wheels."

"Something with more space and more safety," Dwight said. "Hudson needs his own setup."

Moses raised his hand slightly from the folding chair where he'd settled. "I'll stay. Put beans on early. Let them cook all day."

Mae smiled at him. "Nobody's too good for beans."

The group sorted itself out fast. Hudson, Mae, Stephanie, and Jerry would make the run. Dwight and Moses held the camp.

Jerry climbed into the back of Hudson's truck with Shadoe at his feet and his blanket still around his shoulders. Mae took the passenger seat. Stephanie was behind them.

As the Kmart faded in the mirror, Mae stared at the passing town.

"People came back down here sometimes," she said. "Ones Bruce sent away. Or ones who left on their own."

"They talk?" Hudson asked.

"Not much. Scared. Like they couldn't get away fast enough."

Stephanie leaned forward from the back seat. "They wouldn't say what they saw. Just that they didn't want to go back."

"That's all you need to know," Hudson said.

Jerry spoke up from the back. "Bruce is like the villain in every comic I ever read."

Mae looked at him.

Jerry nodded seriously. "That's a bad thing."

"Yeah," Mae said. "It is."

Woodhull, Illinois.

Camper World sat in the northern part of the county where the roads were cleaner and the buildings still stood straight. The lot was wide, the signs still readable, the lamp posts standing like they expected traffic to return any day.

Hudson rolled in slow, eyes working the lot before the truck fully stopped.

Then he checked the mirror.

A Honda Civic turned in behind them. Tinted windows. Parked crooked between two empty spaces.

"We've got a tail," Hudson said.

Mae didn't look surprised. "Bruce."

"Making sure I don't leave the area," Hudson said.

Jerry looked out the back window. "Who's in it?"

"Doesn't matter," Hudson said. "We act like we don't see them. They don't exist."

Stephanie nodded. "If they know you've spotted them they change the game."

Hudson opened his door. "We're just shopping, they don't exist."

They walked into the RV rows and let Jerry lead the way, which was the right move. Nobody could look like they were just shopping better than Jerry.

He moved from one unit to the next with wide eyes and running commentary. This one had stairs. That one had a couch. One had a bathroom Mae described as smaller than her patience. Jerry found a model with recliners and declared it a movie theater.

Hudson let them have their moment. He walked behind, quieter, checking seals and frames and tires and power panels. Not admiring. Measuring.

Six units in, near the back row, he stopped.

Bluebird Wonder Lodge. Big enough to live in. Solid enough to move. He stepped inside, walked the length of it, opened panels, checked under the sink, read the generator access.

"This one," he said.

Jerry looked around at the space and nodded with full authority. "This is the one."

"He elected it," Mae said. "It's settled."

Hudson looked at Mae. "I want you driving it back."

Mae straightened. "Me."

"You can handle it. Park it at Kmart the right way. Complete the enclosure."

She tried to hide her pride. It didn't work.

"I'm not gonna disappoint you," she said.

Jerry bounced on his heels. "I'm riding with Mae. I'm co-pilot."

Mae pointed at him. "Co-pilot listens."

"Yes ma'am," Jerry said immediately.

They got it ready. Mae climbed into the driver's seat of the Bluebird Wonder Lodge and settled in like she'd been driving it for years. Jerry rode up front beside her, already waving out the window before they'd moved a foot.

Hudson and Stephanie took the truck.

The convoy rolled out of Camper World onto the open road. Mae had the RV, Hudson behind her, the world gray and quiet around them.

He checked the mirror.

The Civic was there. Same distance. Same patience.

"Still with us," Stephanie said.

"They want to make sure I come back," Hudson said.

After a mile Stephanie turned her head slightly.

"I'm trying to get to East Tennessee," Hudson said, before she asked. "My son was there when everything happened. I was in Wyoming. I don't know if he made it."

Stephanie was quiet.

"I'll help with Bruce," Hudson said. "I'm not walking away from this with Jerry and the older folks caught in it. But I have to get to Tennessee. I need to know."

"I'd do the same," Stephanie said. "I'd burn the whole road down to find someone."

"You know what the problem is with Bruce," Stephanie said.

"Tell me."

"He's the glue. If he disappears the commune collapses or worse, Mitchell and Jordy and Sloan start fighting over the pieces."

"Power vacuum," Hudson said.

"Exactly. Either way the commune is over. But the fallout lands on everyone living inside it."

Hudson nodded. He'd already been running that math.

"The community, if it is to continue, will need good people. Ones that will make decisions that benefit everyone," Hudson replied.

Henderson, Illinois.

They came out of the tree line on the right side of the road.

Not one or two.

A pack.

Fifteen, maybe twenty dogs pouring out of the brush at a dead run, cutting across the road in a ragged wave. Big ones, small ones, all of them thin and matted and moving with the frantic energy of animals that had been hungry a long time and had stopped caring about much else.

Mae had no warning.

The RV hit the edge of the pack going forty miles an hour.

The impact wasn't a crash so much as a series of thuds, heavy and wrong, the RV lurching right as Mae instinctively yanked the wheel. Forty-four feet of vehicle swung wide, the rear end fishtailing across both lanes, tires screaming on the pavement.

Hudson stood on his brakes.

"Mae!" Stephanie grabbed the dash.

The RV rocked hard onto the shoulder, chewed up gravel, and came to a stop at an angle half off the road with the nose pointed into the ditch. Not rolled. Not wrecked.

Hudson was already out of the truck.

He ran to the RV door as the pack split and regrouped. Most of them scattered when the vehicle hit but a dozen had stopped, circling back. Growling, heads low, teeth out. The kind of growl that meant they weren't afraid and hadn't been afraid of anything in a long time.

The door of the RV swung open. Mae came down the steps with a tire iron in her hand and fire in her eyes.

"I'm fine," she said before Hudson could ask. "Jerry."

Jerry appeared in the doorway behind her, wide-eyed, still holding the armrest from the co-pilot seat.

"That was bad," Jerry said.

"Stay inside," Hudson said.

The pack tightened. Eight dogs now, arranged in a loose half circle around the front of the RV, cutting Hudson and Mae off from the truck. The biggest one, a gray shepherd mix the size of a small wolf, stood at the center of the line. It wasn't barking. It was watching.

That was worse than barking.

Hudson had his hand on his sidearm. Mae raised the tire iron. Stephanie had come up on the flank, putting space between herself and Hudson so they weren't clustered together.

The gray dog stepped forward.

Then, from behind Hudson, came the sound of a door opening.

Not his truck.

From down the road, where the Honda Civic had come to a hard stop when the pack hit the convoy, both doors opened and Jordy and Sloan climbed out fast. Jordy had his rifle up. Sloan had drawn his sidearm.

The pack turned.

New targets. More of them.

Three dogs broke from the main group and sprinted toward Jordy and Sloan at full speed.

Jordy fired once and missed.

Sloan backed up hard and tripped over his own feet and went down on the pavement, his gun skidding away from him.

"Get it off me!" Sloan screamed.

One of the dogs had him by the sleeve. Not his skin, not yet, just the jacket, but it was pulling and shaking its head and Sloan was on his back on the asphalt screaming like it had already gotten through.

Jordy fired again. Missed again. His third shot hit close enough to scatter two dogs but the one on Sloan held.

The gray shepherd turned back toward the RV.

Hudson drew.

The rear window of Hudson's truck had been opened for ventilation earlier..

Shadoe came through it like he'd been waiting his whole life for exactly this.

He hit the ground running, a black streak moving low and fast, no sound at all until he was three feet from the gray dog and then the sound was everything, a bark so deep and hard it hit the chest like a physical force.

The gray dog froze.

Every dog in the pack froze.

Shadoe planted himself between the pack and the RV, every muscle locked, head low, showing everything he had. He didn't lunge. He didn't chase. He held the line and made it very clear that crossing it was going to cost more than any of them wanted to pay.

The gray dog held for three full seconds.

Then it turned and ran.

The rest of the pack followed in a wave, disappearing back into the brush the same way they'd come, and then the road was quiet except for the sound of Sloan still yelling on the pavement.

Hudson looked over at Jordy and Sloan.

Sloan had gotten himself up. His jacket was torn at the sleeve. His face was white. He was patting himself down like he couldn't quite believe he still had all his parts.

Jordy lowered his rifle.

He looked at Hudson.

Hudson looked back.

Neither of them said anything for a moment.

Shadoe stood his ground between the road and the tree line, still watching the brush, ears forward, making absolutely sure.

Jerry appeared in the RV doorway.

"Shadoe!" he called.

Shadoe turned his head once, checked Jerry, then looked back at the brush. Not done yet.

Mae was already walking toward the front of the RV, assessing the damage. She crouched down, looked under the front end, stood back up.

"It'll drive," she said. "Grille's bent just a touch. Nothing but some cosmetic stuff."

She looked at Jordy.

"You can thank us later," she said.

Jordy's jaw worked.

"We didn't need your help," Jordy said.

Mae looked at Sloan, who was still breathing hard and had a two-inch tear in his sleeve where the dog had been.

She said nothing. She didn't need to.

Stephanie walked up beside Hudson, quiet.

"Tell Bruce," Hudson said to Jordy, "that we drove to Camper World, we got an RV, and we came home." He paused. "That's all there is to tell."

Jordy stared at him.

"We're not going anywhere," Hudson said. "Yet."

He let that word sit.

Then he turned and went back to his truck.

Shadoc camc to him immediately, pressed against his leg, and Hudson put a hand on the dog's back.

"Good boy," Hudson said.

Shadoe's tail moved once.

Jerry was halfway down the RV steps.

"Shadoe saved us," Jerry said, with the complete certainty of someone stating a fact.

"Yeah," Hudson said. "He did."

"He's the best dog," Jerry said.

"Don't tell him that," Mae said, climbing back up to the driver's seat. "He already knows."

Hudson looked back at the Civic one more time.

Jordy was helping Sloan into the passenger seat. Sloan was still checking his arm. The rifle was back in the car. The aggressive energy they'd carried out of Bruceville had gone somewhere quiet and wasn't coming back anytime soon.

They'd followed Hudson out here to intimidate.

They were going back having been saved by the people they were surveilling.

That was going to be a difficult conversation with Bruce.

Hudson got in the truck.

"Ready?" Stephanie asked.

"Yeah," Hudson said.

He started the engine. Up ahead, the Bluebird Wonder Lodge rumbled back onto the road, Mae easing it off the shoulder with the care of someone who knew exactly what she was doing.

Jerry waved from the passenger window.

Hudson pulled out behind her.

In the mirror, the Civic fell in behind them. Same distance as before. But something had changed in the way it moved. Less deliberate. Less certain.

Like two men trying to look like they hadn't just been on the ground.

Hudson let himself feel something close to satisfaction and then let it go.

There was still Bruce. Still Paula. Still everything waiting back at the Kmart lot.

But right now Mae was driving a forty-four-foot RV home through a gray winter afternoon, Jerry was waving at nothing in particular out the window, and Shadoe was sitting in the back seat looking out the windshield like a dog who had done his job and knew it.

The convoy rolled on.

Twenty

Ester

Kmart 1987

Moses had the beans going by eight.

Big pot, low heat, the kind of cooking that needed time and didn't apologize for it. The smell spread across the Kmart lot slowly, warm and simple, the kind of smell that belonged in a kitchen rather than a parking lot but made do with what it had.

The camp felt thin without Hudson's group. Dwight walked the perimeter the way he always did, reading the edges of things. Tony leaned against the nearest RV with his arms folded, a man whose version of relaxed still looked like readiness. Moses stirred the pot and hummed something that might have been a hymn if it had more words to it.

The car rolled in just after ten.

Not fast. Not aggressive. Slow and uncertain, the way a person drives when they're not sure if they're welcome anywhere.

It stopped near the edge of the lot and a woman climbed out.

Dwight had her measured before she fully stood. Thirties, maybe forty. Large frame. Tired eyes. Moving with the careful deliberateness of someone whose body had become a project she was managing rather than a thing she inhabited naturally.

Six months pregnant. Maybe more.

Dwight stood very still for a second, which was unusual for him.

Moses looked up from the beans.

Tony pushed off the RV.

The woman kept one hand resting on her stomach, not for comfort but for confirmation. Like she needed to remind herself the weight was real.

"Is this the Galesburg community?" she asked.

"Yeah," Dwight said. "Come warm up."

She walked toward the firepit carefully, watching the ground, watching them. She'd learned to read people fast. That was clear from how her eyes moved. Not scared exactly. Calculating.

The smell of beans reached her.

Something in her shoulders released.

"That smells real," she said.

Moses smiled. "It'll be ready tonight. Beans need time."

"So do I," she said. Then she seemed to realize how that sounded and gave a short, tired laugh. "Sorry. I've been alone a long time."

Dwight pulled a folding chair out and she sat carefully, easing herself down like every movement was a negotiation.

"My name's Ester," she said. "I'm from east of Indianapolis."

She looked at the beans, then at them.

"I drove until the gas got low. Then I found more gas and drove again. Did that for a while."

Moses sat down across from her. "What made you stop here?"

Ester reached into her coat pocket and pulled out a folded piece of paper. She opened it and held it up. A hand-drawn copy of a sign she'd seen on the road. SURVIVORS. GALESBURG COMMUNITY. REBUILDING TOGETHER.

"I've been following these since Champaign," she said. "They're all over the highways going south."

Dwight's face didn't change.

"I know what you're going to say," Ester said, before anyone spoke. She folded the paper back up. "I've been doing this long enough to know when people are about to warn me about something."

She looked between them.

"So go ahead," she said. "Tell me."

Dwight told her. He didn't dress it up.

The signs were real. The community was real. Bruce was real. And people who went up there and said they'd stay didn't come out again.

Ester listened with the focused attention of someone taking notes in her head.

"You're sure," she said when he finished. "Not just rumors."

Dwight shook his head. "Not rumors. One of us lived there six weeks. Got out. Most don't."

She studied him, not doubting him, just making sure she understood what he meant.

"You've seen it yourself," she asked, "or you're going off what people told you."

Dwight glanced at Moses before answering. "We've been up there. Not inside for long, but enough to know it's real. We've talked to people who came back down."

Moses shifted forward slightly. "And that's the part you need to hear right. We haven't seen anyone being hurt. Not directly. Nobody screaming. Nobody being dragged around. It's not like that."

Ester watched him closely.

"But," Moses continued, "Bruce decides who has value. That's what matters up there."

Dwight nodded once. "If he thinks you've got something to offer, skills, strength, something useful, he'll ask you to stay. Real polite about it too. Makes it sound like a good thing."

"And if you don't?" Ester asked.

"They send you away," Dwight said. "No argument. No second look. You're just not part of it."

Ester absorbed that, her expression steady.

"So people choose to stay," she said.

"Yeah," Dwight answered. "That's the part that gets you. Nobody's forced at the start. At least not that we've seen. They go up there, they see the walls, the structure, the food, and they decide."

Moses added quietly, "But once they decide, it changes."

Ester's eyes shifted to him.

"They don't leave," Moses said. "Not like they came in."

Dwight leaned back slightly, choosing his words. "We've seen a few come out. Not many. And the ones who did didn't hang around."

"In what way?" Ester asked.

"They were in a hurry," Dwight said. "Didn't want to talk. Didn't want to explain anything. Just got what they needed and kept moving."

Moses nodded. "And that tells you something. People who are safe don't leave like that."

Ester looked down, her fingers moving slowly across her belly as she processed it.

“So you’re saying it’s not a prison,” she said, “but it’s not free either.”

“That’s about right,” Dwight said.

“It’s controlled,” Moses added. “And Bruce is the one doing the controlling.”

Ester was quiet for a moment.

Then she looked up again.

“Here’s my problem,” she said. “And I’m being straight with you because I’m too tired for anything else.”

She met Dwight’s eyes.

“I’ve lost two pregnancies,” she said. “Early. Both times. This one made it to six months, which is the furthest I’ve ever gotten.” She paused. “I don’t have a doctor. I don’t have supplies. I don’t have anyone who knows what they’re doing.”

Moses leaned forward. “We’ve got a nurse coming back this afternoon.”

Ester went still. “A nurse.”

“Retired,” Moses said. “But she’s delivered babies. She knows what she’s doing.”

Ester’s eyes shimmered. She blinked it back quickly, the way people do when they’ve learned that showing too much hope can cost them.

“Okay,” she said carefully. “That’s something.”

“We can get you what you need from the Kmart,” Dwight said. “Diapers. Formula. Blankets. Nobody’s touched the infant section.”

Ester nodded slowly. The calculation was visible now, clear and deliberate. She wasn’t reacting. She was weighing.

“If I stay here,” she said, “I have a nurse and supplies. But I don’t know if this camp is safe. I don’t know who else might come through.”

“Not yet,” Ester said.

Tony accepted that with a nod.

Ester looked toward the distant neighborhood. "If I go up there, I have walls and guards. But I lose my freedom."

"You lose more than that," Dwight said.

Ester met his eyes.

"I know," she said. "I heard you. But a nursing home has walls and rules too, and people still choose them." She looked back toward the horizon. "Sometimes you trade freedom for safety, and it's the right call."

Moses spoke softly. "Not when the walls belong to Bruce."

Ester didn't answer right away.

Then the Dodge Ram rolled in.

Mitchell climbed out first.

His eyes found Ester before they found anyone else. They dropped to her stomach and stayed there just long enough.

Then he smiled.

It was the smile of a man delivering good news to someone else.

"Well," he said. "Bruce is going to want to meet you."

Hudson's truck pulled in at the same moment, the Bluebird Wonder Lodge behind it. Hudson was already stepping out before the truck fully stopped. Stephanie beside him. Jerry jumping down with Shadoe at his heels.

Jerry saw Ester and his face lit up.

"Oh wow," he said. "A baby!"

Hudson looked at the Ram, Mitchell, Ester's belly, and he understood all of it in about three seconds.

Mae came around the front of the RV and saw Ester and her whole posture changed. Nurse instinct, immediate and total. She walked straight toward her.

Mitchell moved to intercept.

Mae didn't slow down.

She walked around Mitchell like he was a piece of furniture and crouched in front of Ester's chair.

"How far along?" Mae asked.

"Twenty-six weeks," Ester said. "Maybe a few days past."

"Any complications you know of?"

"Two previous losses. Early both times. This one's held."

Mae's face stayed professional but her eyes went careful. "You seeing any swelling in your feet? Headaches?"

"Some swelling," Ester said. "Not bad."

"We need to watch that," Mae said.

Mitchell cleared his throat.

Mae ignored him.

"She stays here," Mae said, to no one in particular, in a tone that meant everyone in particular.

Mitchell's voice came out smooth. "Bruce would like to meet her. She's free to make her own choice."

He looked at Ester.

"You heard what they said about us," Mitchell said. "I understand why you'd be nervous. But Hudson came to dinner last night." He gestured toward Hudson. "He walked out when he wanted to. Nobody stopped him."

Ester looked at Hudson.

Hudson said, "That's true for me, doesn't mean it will be true for you."

Stephanie stepped forward. "He also turned down a house on the nicest street in Galesburg and said no to Bruce's face. Most people don't get to do that."

Mitchell shrugged. "Bruce respects a man who knows his own mind."

Ester turned her head back toward the distant neighborhood. Hudson could see the math happening behind her eyes.

"I want to hear him out," Ester said. "Then I'll decide."

"Ester," Mae said, voice dropping.

"I know the risk," Ester said. "I've been calculating risk for months by myself." She looked at Mae. "I just want to see it. One conversation. Then I come back."

Mae stood up. Her jaw was tight.

"You won't come back," Dwight said.

Ester heard him. She didn't argue.

She stood slowly and looked at Moses.

Moses looked back at her with the helpless sadness of a man who has watched people walk toward things he can't stop.

"We warned you," he said quietly.

"I know," she said. "Thank you."

She walked to her car.

Mitchell was already at the Ram.

Ester followed him out of the lot.

Mae stood watching until both vehicles were gone. Her hands were at her sides, very still, the way hands are still when they want to do something and can't.

Hudson stepped up beside her.

"We'll get her back," he said.

Mae looked at him. Something in her face was already grieving.

"You don't know Bruce," she said.

Bruceville

Ester's car felt smaller the closer she got to the gate.

The neighborhood looked exactly like the signs had promised. Clean streets. Intact houses. No debris, no broken windows, no cars abandoned in the middle of lanes. It looked like a place that had been protected rather than survived.

Pickle was at the booth.

He didn't greet her. He pointed at the curb and said "Park." She parked. He said "Out." She got out. He said "Walk." She walked.

No welcome. No warmth. Just compliance expected and assumed.

The path around the side of the big house. The deck. The golf course. The whole careful presentation of stability and abundance.

Then the back door opened and Paula stepped out.

Ester had been braced for another man. Another guard. Another Mitchell.

She hadn't been braced for a young woman.

Paula was maybe twenty-two. Dressed too carefully for the end of the world, too polished, too arranged. But her eyes were different from everything else about her. They were tired in a specific way. Not the exhaustion of someone who worked hard. The exhaustion of someone who had stopped expecting anything to be different.

"Hi," Paula said. Her voice was gentle. Practiced.

"Hi," Ester said.

Paula's eyes moved to Ester's belly and something crossed her face that she didn't manage to hide. Not happiness. Not the usual reaction people had to a pregnancy.

Something closer to worry.

But it was gone in a second and she stepped aside.

"Bruce is in his office," she said. "I'll take you."

The inside of the mansion smelled like wood polish and cigar smoke and the particular staleness of rooms that were clean but not lived in. Warm, but the warmth of a thermostat, not a home.

Paula walked her down the hall and knocked once on a heavy door, then opened it without waiting for an answer.

The office was large. A real desk, solid and dark, covered with a spread-out jigsaw puzzle. Hundreds of pieces arranged in careful sections, the corners built, the edges filled, the center waiting. A crystal ashtray at one end held a burning cigar.

Bruce sat back in his chair and looked at Ester the way a person looks at something they have been hoping would show up.

Not at her face.

At her stomach.

"Sit down," he said.

Ester sat.

Bruce stood and came around the desk, not quickly, not aggressively, just moving to get a better look. He circled slightly to one side, eyes on her belly, the way a man circles a vehicle he's thinking about buying.

Ester's skin prickled.

"How far along?" Bruce asked.

"Twenty-six weeks," she said.

He nodded slowly. Satisfied.

"Healthy pregnancy?" he asked.

"So far."

"Previous children?"

"Two losses," Ester said. "Early."

Bruce waved that away. "But this one is doing good."

"Yes."

He went back to his chair and sat down. He picked up a puzzle piece and turned it between his fingers without looking at it.

"Do you understand," Bruce said, "what you are?"

Ester said nothing.

"You are the most important person in this county," Bruce said. "Possibly in this part of the country."

He set the puzzle piece down.

"Population collapse is the real threat," he said. "Virus kills over ninety-nine percent. But the survivors who don't reproduce, they finish the job the virus started. Twenty years from now there are no children, no workers, no future. Just old people dying out."

He looked at her belly.

"You change that," he said. "Every successful birth changes that."

Ester kept her voice steady. "I'd like someone who knows what they're doing at the birth."

"Of course," Bruce said. "We'll research it. Women did this for thousands of years without hospitals."

"Some of them died," Ester said.

Bruce smiled. "Some of them did. But you're strong. You've already held longer than expected."

Behind Ester, near the door, Paula shifted her weight.

Ester half-turned toward her.

Paula's face was carefully neutral. But her eyes weren't. They were doing something Ester recognized because she'd been doing it herself for months: calculating. Measuring the distance between where she was and where the door was.

"The camp down at Kmart," Ester said, turning back to Bruce. "The woman there is a retired nurse. She's delivered babies. I was thinking I could stay with them until the birth, then—"

"No," Bruce said.

The word was quiet. No anger in it. No hesitation either.

"The birth happens here," Bruce said. "Where I can ensure the conditions."

Ester's stomach dropped.

"I'm not saying I'll stay permanently," she said carefully. "Just until I know what I want."

"The birth happens here," Bruce said again. Same tone. Same certainty. "After that, your options are your own."

He picked up the puzzle piece again and turned it. Turned it. Found where it went and pressed it into place.

"Paula," he said, without looking up. "Check on Pickle, he's getting the south bedroom ready."

Paula said, "Yes sir," in a voice so flat it didn't sound like a voice.

Ester looked at her.

Their eyes met for just a moment.

Paula looked away first. Not out of indifference. Out of the particular practiced discipline of someone who had learned that eye contact with another woman in this house was something that had to be managed carefully.

Ester understood it instantly.

Everything the Kmart group had said hit her at once, not as a warning she'd heard before, but as a thing she was living.

Paula wasn't staff.

Paula wasn't a guest.

Paula was a demonstration.

Of what happened to women who came here and had no one to come for them.

Ester's voice came out quieter than she intended. "I'd like to go back to the Kmart camp."

Bruce looked up from the puzzle.

"I understand the nerves," he said. "New place, new people, new situation. That's a lot."

He spread his hands.

"But you're about seven months pregnant. You need stability. You need medical support. You need a safe place to deliver."

"They have a nurse," Ester said.

"They have a parking lot," Bruce said. "I have a house."

He smiled the smile that had no warmth underneath it.

"The baby comes first," Bruce said. "You understand that. I can tell you're a practical woman."

Ester stared at him.

He was using her own intelligence against her. Framing the trap as a reasonable decision. Making the bars look like walls she'd chosen.

She looked at Paula one more time.

Paula was already turned away, hands clasped, waiting to be useful.

Ester thought: that is what I will look like in six months.

Then Pickle appeared in the doorway.

"South bedroom's ready," Pickle said.

Bruce looked at Ester with the patient expression of a man who had already decided.

"Wonderful," Bruce said.

He stood, extended his hand.

Ester shook it because refusing felt like the thing that would make it worse.

Bruce's grip was warm and firm and lasted exactly one second too long.

"Welcome," he said. "We're glad you're here."

Pickle stepped back from the doorway and waited.

Ester walked toward it.

She passed Paula on the way.

For half a second she slowed, and Paula slowed too, and they were close enough that Ester could have spoken. Could have said something.

Paula kept her eyes forward.

Ester kept walking.

The hallway was long and the stairs were carpeted and the south bedroom was clean and warm with a window that looked out over the golf course. There was a bed. There was a lamp. There was a door with no lock on the inside.

Pickle closed it behind her.

Ester sat on the edge of the bed.

She put both hands on her belly.

She had been smart about this. She had calculated. She had weighed the options and made a decision based on logic, not fear, not hope, not desperation.

She had still walked right into it.

Because Bruce was smarter about this than she was.

He'd been doing it longer.

Twenty-One

An Offer Put Forth

Kmart 1987

The fire was small but it held the group together the way fires do, pulling chairs in close and making the cold feel optional.

Hudson stood at the edge of the light and waited until the last side conversations died. When he had everyone's attention he began.

"I'm going to offer Bruce my services," he said.

Dwight looked up from the fire like Hudson had said something obscene.

"No," Dwight said.

"Let me finish," Hudson said.

Dwight's jaw worked but he stayed quiet.

Hudson looked at Mae first, because what he was about to say was really for her.

"He wants electricity more than he's willing to say out loud," Hudson said. "Not generator power. A real system. Something permanent. And I'm the only person within a hundred miles who knows how to build it."

Mae's face had gone very still.

"That's leverage," Hudson said. "And we're going to use it."

Dwight shook his head slowly. "This is how people get pulled in. They think they're playing the game and then one day they look up and they're part of it."

"I know," Hudson said. "Which is why the conditions aren't optional."

He turned to Mae.

"You get access to Ester," he said. "Regular visits. Monitoring. Everything you need to keep her and the baby stable."

Mae's breath caught slightly.

"And when it gets close," Hudson said, "you stay. Not visit. Stay. You set up the delivery. You run it."

"Bruce won't like that," Mae said.

"Then Bruce doesn't get his power grid," Hudson said.

Moses leaned forward. "And us? What happens to the camp?"

"Nobody touches Kmart," Hudson said. "No visits. No threats. No Mitchell rolling up to make a point. As long as I'm working, this camp is left alone."

"And you live here," Stephanie said. Not a question.

"I work over there. I sleep here." He looked at the group. "No house. No moving in. I'm not becoming part of what he's built."

Tony spoke from the back, arms folded. "What does he get out of it?"

"Trained workers," Hudson said. "I'll need people to do the physical labor. He'll provide them and I'll train them."

Dwight's face tightened. "So he gets a trained crew."

"He thinks he does," Hudson said.

Dwight stared at him.

"People learn skills," Hudson said quietly. "They become less dependent on Bruce."

Jerry raised his hand halfway. "Can I help?"

"Someone has to hold this camp together," Hudson said. "That's you and Shadoe."

Jerry looked at Shadoe. Shadoe's tail moved once.

Jerry didn't look entirely satisfied but he nodded.

Mae's voice came out low and fierce. "When do I see her?"

"Tomorrow," Hudson said. "If Bruce agrees today."

"And if he doesn't agree?" Dwight asked.

Hudson looked at him.

"Then I walk away and he goes back to running his generators until the fuel runs out," Hudson said. "And I find another way to get Ester out."

Mae closed her eye's for a second

When she opened them her face was set.

"Do it," she said. "Get me to her."

Bruceville

He walked in alone, the same way visitors were made to walk. On foot, past the gate, past Pickle who looked at him like a stain on the carpet, through the neighborhood that smelled too clean and too quiet for a world that had collapsed.

Bruce was on the golf course.

Of course he was.

Green knicker pants, yellow shirt, spotless shoes, putter in hand. He could have been at a country club. The apocalypse had rearranged itself around him without leaving a mark.

Sloan stood off to the side, arms folded, face doing the thing it did when he was being paid to look like he wasn't bothered.

Bruce looked up when Hudson stepped onto the green and smiled wide.

"Well now," he said. "I knew you couldn't stay away."

"I'm not here for a house," Hudson said.

Bruce chuckled and took a putt. The ball rolled short of the hole. He made a small disappointed noise.

"Try?" He offered the putter.

"Never played," Hudson said.

Bruce grinned. "Neither had I. Amazing what you pick up when the whole world is yours."

He said it lightly but it wasn't a joke.

Hudson let it sit there. Then he started.

"You're tired of the generators," Hudson said.

Bruce's chin lifted slightly.

"They're a crutch," Hudson continued. "Fuel runs out. Parts fail. Noise draws attention. One bad week and you're sitting in the dark telling everyone it's temporary."

Bruce walked slowly along the edge of the green, rolling the ball with his toe.

"Go on," he said.

“I can build you a microgrid,” Hudson said. “Not the old system, and not right away. But something solid. Power you control across the whole neighborhood. Heat, lights, everything, without depending on fuel.”

Bruce stopped walking.

"And you want workers," Bruce said.

"I'll need people for the labor," Hudson said. "I train them, they do the physical work, I direct the technical side."

Bruce turned toward him fully now, the golf game forgotten.

"What do you want in return," Bruce said.

Hudson told him. Mae and Ester. Regular access. The delivery. The camp left alone.

He said it plainly, one condition at a time, watching Bruce's face as each one landed.

Bruce listened without interrupting. That was the thing that felt wrong. He usually talked over people, redirected, found ways to reframe. He was listening in the specific focused way of a man who had already decided and was waiting for the other person to finish.

When Hudson stopped, Bruce was quiet for a moment.

Then he smiled.

"Alright," Bruce said.

Hudson waited for the but.

It didn't come.

"Mae gets access to Ester," Bruce said. "She stays for the delivery. Your camp is left alone. You work during the day and go back to Kmart at night."

He spread his hands.

"Deal," Bruce said.

Too fast. Too easy.

Hudson stood on the perfect grass under the gray sky and felt the specific unease of a man who has just gotten everything he asked for and knows he should not have.

When you negotiate with someone like Bruce and they fold this quickly, one of two things had happened. Either you had more leverage than you thought.

Or they already had something you didn't know about.

Hudson kept his face neutral.

"Workers," Hudson said. "I'll need four people who can learn."

"Done," Bruce said. He turned his head. "Sloan. Bring them."

Sloan walked off without a word, the stiff stride of a man swallowing something he didn't like.

Bruce looked back at Hudson with the satisfied expression of a man crossing something off a list.

"This is going to be good for everyone," Bruce said.

Hudson nodded.

He didn't believe it.

But he filed it away. Whatever Bruce was holding, he'd find it eventually.

Sloan came back with four people walking behind him.

They moved in a loose line, not quite together, the way people move when they've been assembled rather than gathered. Three of them looked nervous. One didn't look nervous at all.

Bruce said their names like he was reading a property list.

"Theo. Thirty. Missouri." A lean man with rough hands, dirt worked permanently into his knuckles. He nodded at Hudson with the quick deference of someone who had spent years being told what to do by people with authority.

"Gideon. Thirty-six. Wisconsin." A bigger man, broad through the shoulders, face carrying the kind of tired that had nothing to do with sleep. He looked at Hudson without nodding, without smiling. Just looked. His eyes had the quality of someone who had stopped expecting things to be okay and was getting by on something else.

"Misty. Twenty-four. Geneseo, Illinois." A young woman with her hair pulled back and her chin up. She looked like she was trying to project confidence and was mostly succeeding. Her hands were folded in front of her, still.

"Shaz. Twenty-eight. Joliet." The fourth one. She stepped forward when her name was called without hesitation, which was already different from the others. Her posture was straight but not rigid. She looked at Hudson, then at Bruce, then back at Hudson, and the look she gave Hudson was clearly different from the one she'd given Bruce.

Bruce gestured toward Hudson like he was presenting a reward.

"These will assist you," Bruce said. "Train them. Use them."

Hudson stepped forward.

"I'm Hudson," he said. "I live at the Kmart camp, not here. I work here during the day and go home at night."

Misty blinked. "You don't live in the community?"

"No."

She glanced at Bruce. Bruce's expression didn't change.

Hudson kept going.

"We're building a power system. Real electricity. It's going to take time and it's going to take work and some of it is going to be unpleasant." He looked at each of them. "But when we're done you'll know how to do something most people on this planet don't know how to do anymore."

Theo nodded. "I'm good with my hands. Whatever you need."

Gideon said nothing. He was looking past Hudson toward the mansions, and his expression was the particular expression of a man thinking about someone who wasn't there.

Hudson looked at him.

"Gideon," Hudson said.

Gideon came back. Blinked.

"Sorry," Gideon said. "I'm here."

"Where'd you go?" Hudson asked. Not harsh. Just straight.

Gideon's jaw shifted. "I had a son," he said. "Five years old. Every time I see a house with a yard I think about whether he would have liked it."

Nobody said anything for a moment.

Gideon looked back at Hudson. "I'm here," he said again. "I just do that sometimes."

"That's fine," Hudson said. "Do it on your own time. When we're working I need you in the room."

"Understood," Gideon said.

Shaz spoke up from the end of the line.

"I have a question," she said.

Sloan glanced at her sharply, like questions weren't part of the expected behavior.

"Go ahead," Hudson said.

She looked at him directly. "The work we do here. Who does it belong to?"

The question landed in the middle of the group like something dropped from a height.

Misty shifted her weight. Theo looked at his boots.

Bruce was still standing nearby. He said nothing.

Hudson looked at Shaz for a moment.

"That's the right question," he said.

She waited.

"The knowledge belongs to whoever learns it," Hudson said. "Nobody can take that from you."

Shaz held his gaze for another second, reading him.

Then she nodded. One nod. Decisive. Like she'd made a decision about him and was done deliberating.

Bruce smiled beside them, satisfied, as if the exchange had gone exactly as he wanted.

Which was the thing that bothered Hudson most.

He hadn't expected Shaz's question to make Bruce happy.

He turned to the group.

"I'll come by in the morning, about an hour after sunrise. Be ready to get dirty."

Kmart

He walked back to his truck the same way he'd come, on foot, past Pickle, past the gate, back into the world that was broken and real rather than intact and wrong.

The group came together before he reached the fire.

Mae was first. She didn't ask how it went. She looked at his face and read it.

"He agreed," she said.

"Everything," Hudson said. "Faster than he should have."

Dwight's eyes narrowed. "What does that mean."

"It means he already has something planned," Hudson said. "I don't know what yet. But he was waiting for this conversation. He knew it was coming before I walked onto that green."

The circle was quiet.

"Then why go through with it," Moses asked.

"Because Ester is in that house," Hudson said. "And Mae gets access starting tomorrow. And the camp stays untouched." He paused. "Those things are real even if the rest of it isn't."

Mae nodded, jaw tight, already thinking about what she'd need.

"He's giving me workers," Hudson said. "Four of them."

Dwight made a sound.

"They'll report back to Bruce," Dwight said.

"Yes," Hudson said. "And I'll use that."

Dwight stared at him.

"Information runs both ways," Hudson said. "I need eyes inside Bruce's operation. Those four people are going to be in rooms I can't get into. If I earn their trust, they'll tell me things."

Tony leaned forward. "And if Bruce has already told them what to do."

"Then I figure that out too," Hudson said. "One of them asked the right question today."

Stephanie looked at him. "What question."

"She wanted to know who the work belongs to," Hudson said. "Bruce seemed pleased by it. That's interesting."

"Interesting how," Stephanie asked.

Hudson shook his head. "I don't know yet. But she's either very good at reading a room or she's been put there to do something specific."

"Or both," Stephanie said.

"Or both," Hudson agreed.

Jerry raised his hand.

"Mae goes to see Ester tomorrow?" he asked.

"First thing," Hudson said.

Jerry looked at Mae. "Is Ester going to be okay?"

Mae looked at Jerry for a moment, the nurse in her and the person in her both trying to answer at the same time.

"That's what I'm going to find out," she said.

Jerry nodded. He put his hand on Shadoe's back. Shadoe stayed still, ears slightly forward, reading the air the way he always did when the humans around him were worried.

Hudson looked at the group one more time.

"We got what we needed," he said. "Be careful about thinking that means we're safe."

Moses almost smiled. "Nobody ever thought that."

Hudson nodded.

"Good," he said. "Keep thinking that way."

Twenty-Two

Lynn

Chicago, Illinois. 1952

Lynn was seven years old the first time he stole something.

It was not hunger. Not desperation. Not a kid trying to survive.

It was curiosity.

His mother had brought him to the neighborhood grocery store on a gray Saturday morning, the kind of small place with narrow aisles and buzzing fluorescent lights. Everything smelled like floor cleaner, onions, and the faint stale bite of cigarette smoke that clung to the cashier's sweater.

His mother pushed the cart slow, studying price tags like they were insults. Lynn walked beside her with his hands in his jacket pockets, eyes roaming over shelves that looked like a museum of things his family never had money for.

Near the register there was a rack of small toys. Cheap plastic things on pegs, bright colors and smiling cartoon faces, placed right where a child could reach them.

Lynn stopped.

He picked up a small toy car still sealed in plastic. It wasn't big. It wasn't expensive. But to a boy who had learned to want quietly, it felt like a treasure.

He looked back at his mother. She had her back turned, comparing two boxes of powdered milk. The cashier was talking to someone at the counter.

No one was looking at him.

Lynn stared at the toy. His heart thumped harder, not with fear, but with something sharper. A thrill he didn't have a name for yet.

He slid the toy into his pocket.

It went in smooth. No struggle. No sound.

Nothing happened.

That was the strangest part. He expected something. A shout. A hand on his shoulder. Something in the world to announce that he had crossed a line.

But the world stayed quiet.

They made it home. His mother unpacked groceries. Lynn slipped to his room and pulled the toy out. A plastic car. Nothing fancy. But in his hands it felt like a prize.

He rolled it along the carpet and smiled in a way he did not often smile.

That afternoon his father came home. Boots. Heavy jacket. The smell of sweat and oil. He spotted the car immediately.

"Where'd you get that," his father asked.

Lynn's mind moved fast. "Mom bought it."

His father turned toward the kitchen. "Hey. You buy him that toy?"

His mother appeared in the doorway. "What toy?"

The room went still.

His father's eyes came back to him, sharper now. "Lynn. Did you steal it?"

"Yes sir," he whispered.

His father didn't snatch the toy away. He made Lynn carry it.

That was part of the lesson.

They drove back to the grocery store in silence. His father walked Lynn inside with a hand on his shoulder, steered him to the counter, and spoke to the cashier in a steady voice.

"My son took something from your store. He's here to return it."

Lynn held the toy out with both hands. "I'm sorry."

The cashier took it and nodded once, expression tired more than angry.

Outside, his father looked down at him.

"You don't take what isn't yours," he said. "You understand me?"

Lynn nodded. "Yes sir."

But even as he said it, another thought was forming behind his eyes.

He had done it. He had taken something and made it all the way home.

The only reason he got caught was because he showed it off.

And that was a different lesson entirely.

Stealing wasn't impossible.

It was simple.

All you had to do was be smart enough not to get caught.

Chicago, Illinois. 1959

By fourteen, that lesson was no longer a warning.

It was a system.

Lynn didn't think about stealing the way other boys did. To him, it wasn't reckless. It was efficient. He watched the city closely and saw two kinds of men: the ones who worked hard and still looked beaten down, and the ones who always seemed to have money, nice cars, and people around them. Lynn knew which kind he wanted to be.

Outside school one afternoon, he recruited a restless boy named Marco and brought him to a convenience store. Lynn explained it simply. Don't act fast. Act normal. Don't look guilty. Distract the cashier. Take what you need. Walk out like you belong there.

They did it.

Marco was thrilled. Lynn wasn't. He was satisfied.

That mattered more.

The thrill wasn't in the items. It was in the control. The planning. The fact that someone else followed his lead and it worked.

That was how it started. One store became several. Small thefts became things they could sell. By sixteen, Lynn had a small crew around him. He never called it a gang. He called it a team.

But the way they looked at him told the truth.

He liked being the one they waited on.

He liked it too much.

Chicago, Illinois. 1963 – 1974

His father tried for years to pull him back, not with tenderness, but with rules, warnings, and long talks after hard days at work. Lynn never respected any of it. All he saw was a man who had worn himself down for a world that gave him almost nothing back.

One night, Lynn came home after midnight and found his father waiting in the dark with a stolen wallet on the table.

This time, Lynn didn't bother denying much. His father pressed him, and Lynn finally admitted it. Not with shame. With attitude.

That was the end of it.

His father told him to get out.

Lynn waited for the softening, for the compromise, but it never came. So he packed a bag, took his cash, and walked out. His mother cried. His father didn't stop him.

As the apartment door closed behind him, Lynn didn't feel abandoned.

He felt free.

Once he was out, his life sped up.

He moved in with men who weren't friends so much as hungry opportunists. They stole, fenced goods, and built routines around other people's property. Lynn learned quickly. He studied neighborhoods, businesses, schedules, locks, patrol patterns, and people. He dressed better. He learned how clothes changed the way the world treated you.

By his early twenties, he wasn't stealing for fun anymore. He was organizing crews, picking targets, moving larger goods, and staying just far enough from the actual risk to keep his own hands clean.

That became his real talent.

He didn't just like money. He liked control. He liked telling other men what to do and watching them do it. He liked seeing fear in someone else's eyes and knowing he was the calm one in the room.

His arrests piled up in the background, but nothing held him long. He always had a lie ready, always had someone else closer to the crime than he was.

For a while, it worked.

Too well.

He reached the point where he felt untouchable.

Then the city finally caught up.

A police unit had been building a case quietly for months, watching shipments, routes, buyers, and patterns. Lynn didn't see it coming until the trap was already closed. A staged trailer full of high-value goods drew his crew in, and the moment they started unloading, the lights hit.

The trial came quickly. His lawyer argued. The prosecutor laid out his record like a biography. The judge gave him thirty years.

Lynn didn't beg.

As they led him away in chains, he made one quiet decision.

This wasn't the end.

Galesburg, Illinois. 1975 – 1987

Prison taught Lynn that rules were real.

Not the rules written in law books. The rules carved into men.

He arrived at the medium to max security prison in Galesburg and spent the first week being tested. Not always with fists. Men bumped his shoulder in the chow line to see if he'd flinch. Men stared too long, waiting for him to look down first. Lynn answered carefully. Didn't talk too much. Didn't act scared.

He found the men who mattered and made himself useful.

Not weak. Useful.

He brokered favors. Quiet trades. Cigarettes for phone calls. Information for influence. Men started coming to him with problems, not because he was kind, but because he was efficient. He learned the difference between being feared and being respected. Feared men died quicker. Respected men lasted.

Men called him Boss before he ever asked.

He collected a circle around him and trained them the same way he always had.

Do what I say and you'll eat. That's how this works.

He told himself every day it was making him better. Other inmates talked about getting out and living quiet, finding work, starting over. Lynn thought about power. About what kind of man he would be when he walked out those gates.

He was still thinking about it when the Liberty Flu appeared on the television in the common area.

At first it was just something on the news.

A tight-faced anchor talking too fast. A map with red dots spreading like a rash. Words like *outbreak* and *quarantine* and *mutation*.

Some inmates laughed. Some said the government was lying again.

Lynn stood near the back, arms folded, watching men react.

He didn't laugh.

He watched the anchor wipe sweat from his forehead on live television, and Lynn understood something the others didn't.

This wasn't politics.

This was real.

A week later the coughing started. A sharp hack in the night that echoed off the walls. Most men didn't look up. Coughing was normal in prison, from cigarettes, from mold, from the constant stale air.

But this cough had a different sound.

Wet. Deep. Like it came from the bottom of the body.

Then another man started coughing. Then another.

Within days it moved like fire through dry grass. Men stumbled down the tier holding their stomachs. Men collapsed in showers. And then the first one died, a man who had been complaining at the chow line the day before, suddenly on the floor, eyes open, mouth slack, skin gray.

The guards started coughing too.

They tried to hide it at first. Kept working. But fear spreads faster than any virus. One guard didn't show for shift. Then two. Then ten. The ones who remained wore bandanas over their mouths and scanned inmates like every one of them carried death in their lungs.

Food service slowed because kitchen staff were dead or too sick to work. Chow lines turned into fights. Men fought over bread. Men fought over water. Men fought over nothing, just to feel alive.

Lynn told his circle to stay close. Don't drink after nobody. Don't touch nobody. Keep your space.

They listened. Because even in chaos, men needed somebody to listen to.

Then one morning the prison went quiet.

Not peaceful quiet. Dead quiet. The kind that meant something had broken.

Lynn walked out onto the tier and saw guards standing in clusters, some crying, some shouting, none of them looking like officers anymore. They looked like trapped animals.

Then he saw it. A door that wasn't normally open. A gate unlocked. A guard walking fast, not stopping to correct anyone, just moving like he wanted to get away from the building.

A guard came to the cell block doors with a ring of keys in shaking hands.

"Get out," he yelled, voice cracking. "If you're gonna die, die out there. Don't die locked in these damn cells."

The keys hit metal. Locks snapped open. Doors swung wide.

For a few seconds nobody moved, because the idea was too big to trust.

Then the unit erupted.

Men poured out like water released from a dam. Some ran. Some fell to their knees crying. Some screamed in victory. Some started fighting immediately because they couldn't imagine freedom without violence.

Lynn walked to the yard with his head up, moving through chaos like he owned the path beneath his feet.

The yard was full of noise at first. Then it started thinning. Not because people left. Because people were dropping.

Men fell face-first into dirt. Men sat against the fence and slid down slowly. The virus moved through them like smoke.

Hours passed. Then a day. Then another.

The yard became a field of bodies.

Lynn stood among them like a shadow that refused to lie down. He coughed once, only once, and his own fear tried to rise in his throat.

But the cough passed. His lungs held. His body stayed strong.

When the sun dipped low and the yard had gone silent, Lynn understood the truth.

He was alive. He was the only one alive.

He walked across the yard slowly, stepping around the dead, the smell thick around him. He reached the fence. Razor wire shining faintly in the evening light.

He looked around at the bodies scattered in the dirt and found what he needed. A piece of plywood from a broken bench. A torn blanket. A jacket.

He threw them over the wire and climbed.

His boots slipped once. The wire bit into his palms anyway, sharp and hungry. Blood ran down his fingers. He hissed through his teeth.

But he kept climbing.

Because Lynn didn't quit. Not ever.

He dropped down the other side and stumbled to his knees in the dirt outside the fences.

Free.

The world had ended.

And it had ended in the perfect way for a man like Lynn. Because when society collapsed, the law died with it.

He started walking toward Galesburg, blood drying on his hands, a strange calm in his chest. Not afraid. Not grieving.

He felt something he hadn't felt since he was a boy sliding a toy into his pocket.

A thrill.

Galesburg, Illinois. 1987

Lynn moved through the empty town like a man inheriting an estate.

Food first. He found a bakery, tore into stale bread with both hands, ate until his stomach ached and kept going. Then clothes. He stripped off the prison uniform in a department store and dressed himself in a black coat, fresh shirt, pants that didn't smell like bleach and sweat. He stood in front of a mirror and looked at the man staring back.

Not an inmate. Not a thief running from police.

He looked like somebody important.

He liked that.

By afternoon he had found the mansion neighborhood. Wide lawns. Stone walls. The kind of streets that had always felt like a different planet. He heard the low hum before he saw the lights.

Power.

Whole house generators. The rich had planned for emergencies the poor weren't allowed to survive.

Lynn found the largest home on the street, broke a small window to reach the lock, and stepped inside. Warmth. Clean air. Carpet. Furniture too expensive to imagine. He stood in the kitchen and laughed out loud, the sound echoing off high ceilings.

That night he cooked steak on a stove that still worked and drank whiskey from a crystal glass, slowly, not to get drunk but to taste luxury. He slept in a bed so soft it made him angry.

Angry because it had always existed.

Angry because men like him were never meant to touch it.

But now he could. Now he owned it.

A week later he went to Kmart for supplies.

He was filling a cart when he heard it. An engine. A vehicle rolling into the lot.

Lynn froze.

A man stepped out of the car and looked around the way people did now, like death might jump from behind anything. Then he spotted Lynn and raised a hand.

"Hey. Don't shoot. I'm not looking for trouble."

He walked closer, hands visible, trying to appear harmless. "My name's Pickle. I know it sounds stupid. It's just what people called me growing up."

Lynn stared at him and made a decision so fast it barely counted as thought.

He lifted his chin slightly. "What did you say your name was?"

"Pickle," the man repeated.

Lynn nodded once. "It fits you."

Pickle laughed nervously, not sure if that was an insult or acceptance.

Lynn stepped closer, just close enough for the man to feel his presence.

"My name is Bruce," he said.

The name came out smooth. Powerful. Simple.

"Bruce," Pickle repeated. "Nice to meet you."

Lynn held his gaze. "You want to live through this?"

Pickle nodded fast. "Yes. I do."

Lynn nodded toward the cart of supplies. "Then you do what I say."

Pickle hesitated only a second. "Alright. Tell me what to do."

Lynn smiled, slow and satisfied.

That was the moment Bruceville began. Not with a committee. Not with a plan built by good people. It began with one predator realizing the world was empty enough to shape.

Bruce walked Pickle out of the store and pointed toward the mansion neighborhood.

"That's where we live," he said.

Pickle stared. "Those houses. Wow."

"Power still runs over there," Bruce said. "Generators."

Pickle's face lit up. "That's incredible."

Bruce looked at him. "You're going to help me build something. A community. Tomorrow you start painting signs. Directions. Anything that tells survivors to come here."

Pickle swallowed. "Why?"

Bruce smiled like a preacher. "Because people need hope. They need structure. They need leadership."

Pickle nodded like that made sense.

Bruce's eyes narrowed just a fraction. "And because when they come, they bring things I can use."

Pickle didn't quite hear that last part. He only heard the tone. Confidence. Safety. Purpose.

He wanted it badly enough to follow a man who didn't deserve it.

That night Bruce stood on the back deck with a cigar burning between his fingers. The golf course stretched below him like a kingdom made of quiet green. He exhaled smoke and watched the empty road in the distance, imagining headlights coming.

Survivors arriving.

Men and women desperate for safety.

The old world had laws. The new world had nothing. Nothing except people who were scared. And scared people always looked for someone to follow.

Bruce had been training for this his whole life.

The world was finally ready for him.

Twenty-Three

Airport Blood

Bruceville 1987

Pickle sits inside the security booth, boots up on the desk, chewing something steadily. A rifle leans within reach against the wall. He squints as Hudson's truck rolls forward.

"Well I'll be," Pickle says, pushing the door open. "The power man."

Hudson eases the truck to a stop.

Pickle circles once, looking into the bed, then at Mae in the passenger seat. "Bruce said you might come."

"He here?" Hudson asks.

"Always is."

Hudson nods. He kills the engine.

He and Mae step out. The truck stays at the booth. No one drives through Bruceville without permission.

Pickle jerks his thumb down the road. "Clubhouse end. Big house with the stone lions. That's where he's holding court today."

Hudson and Mae walk side by side down the paved drive. The homes rise around them, oversized and proud. Expensive brick. Massive garages. Wide windows looking out over the course.

The backyards open onto rolling green space that once held tee boxes and sand traps. Now deer tracks cut through tall grass.

Mae glances toward one of the houses. Curtains shift slightly.

"They watch everything," she says quietly.

"They have something to lose," Hudson replies.

They reach the largest house near the clubhouse. Two stone lions guard the front steps.

Bruce stands near the driveway, arms folded. A few of his men linger nearby, casual but observant.

Hudson steps forward.

"Bruce."

Bruce nods once. "You said you had a solution."

"I do."

Bruce gestures toward the edge of the drive where they can see the backs of the mansions sloping toward the old fairway. "Talk."

Hudson speaks carefully.

"There are three wind turbines standing east of Galesburg. Jacobs machines. Thirty kilowatt class, based on tower height and rotor diameter."

Bruce narrows his eyes slightly. "You've seen them."

"I've inspected them from the ground. The towers are intact. The nacelles are sealed. No visible blade damage. The foundations are commercial grade, not farm homemade. The underground conduit is already run. Whoever put them up meant for them to operate as a group."

Bruce listens.

"They were shut down clean. Brakes engaged. No sign of catastrophic failure. That tells me they were operational when things stopped. Equipment that new doesn't get abandoned mid failure without visible damage."

Bruce studies him. "And they'll power this."

"Three units that size will comfortably handle every home here if loads are managed properly. Lighting, refrigeration, tools. More than enough margin for growth."

Bruce glances toward the homes behind him.

"You're certain."

"I'm certain of what I observed. Steel doesn't lie. Neither does wiring."

Bruce nods slowly.

"Get me power," he says. "Real power."

Bruceville

Mae steps inside as Paula opens the door.

The interior of the mansion still smells faintly of polish and old money. Hardwood floors shine. A chandelier hangs overhead, dusted recently. Someone has been trying to keep the old world alive inside these walls.

"Hello, Ms. Mae," Paula says softly. "Ester has been waiting since she heard you were coming."

Mae gives her a gentle smile. "Then let's not keep her waiting."

Paula hesitates. "Before we go up, would you like some breakfast? I can make something quick. Eggs maybe."

"I ate with the group before we left," Mae says. "Thank you."

Paula nods and leads her toward the staircase.

They climb slowly.

At the top of the stairs, Paula stops in front of a closed door. A heavy key hangs from a hook on the wall beside it.

Mae notices.

"Is the door kept locked?"

Paula's fingers linger on the key. "Yes. Bruce thinks it's better like that. Ester is more important than she can understand."

Mae studies her face. "Still, people should make their own decisions, don't you think."

Paula exhales slowly. "I do believe so. But this is Bruceville. Bruce makes the decisions here."

She unlocks the door and steps aside.

The room is large and bright. Curtains are drawn back so sunlight spills across a neatly made bed. Fresh water sits on a side table. Folded blankets are stacked nearby. Ester sits upright against pillows, hands resting on the curve of her stomach.

She looks stronger than Mae expected. Tired, but healthy.

"Hello, Ester," Mae says gently. "You're looking well."

Ester's smile flickers, then fades. "I should have listened to all of you."

Mae moves closer. "Tell me what's happening."

"He says I have to stay in this room until I give birth. Then I can leave."

"Leave where."

"Anywhere. Just not here. Alone." Her eyes well slightly. "I can't have a child and leave. You know that, right."

Mae pulls a chair beside the bed and sits. "Don't you worry, honey. We'll walk through this together. You and your baby. But you have to trust me."

Ester nods.

"I've had pregnancies before," Ester continues quietly. "Never any problems starting out. I just never made it to term."

Mae takes her wrist gently, feeling her pulse. Steady. She places a hand against Ester's abdomen, listening, watching her breathing.

"Do you know how much longer?" Mae asks.

"I'd say about eight weeks."

Mae nods slowly. "Eight weeks is something we can work with."

Paula shifts near the window. "You've done this before? Delivered babies, I mean."

"I've helped," Mae says calmly. "More than once."

Paula swallows. "You can handle it by yourself, right? I'm not good with things like childbirth. I can boil water. Get blankets."

Ester looks at Paula. "If Bruce expects me to leave after the baby is born, who do you think he'll expect to take care of it."

Paula stiffens. "I don't know anything about babies. If I wanted one, I would have had one."

Mae's eyes move between them.

"I suppose that's something worth thinking about," Mae says quietly. "Sometimes the choice is not whether you want to be a mother. Sometimes it's whether someone else decides you are."

Bruceville

Hudson stands near the edge of the old cart path where the fairway begins to slope away from the houses. Bruce's men linger at a distance, listening without appearing to.

Gideon, Shaz, Theo, and Misty gather around him.

"The turbines are east of town," Hudson begins. "Three Jacobs units. Thirty kilowatt class based on rotor diameter and tower height. Commercial foundations. Not backyard builds."

Theo nods. "You think they were part of something organized."

"They were," Hudson replies. "Underground conduit is already run between towers. Whoever set them up intended them to operate together."

Shaz crosses her arms. "And you're sure they'll still run."

"They were shut down properly. Machines that size don't just fail quietly. You see the evidence when they do."

Gideon glances toward the horizon. "What do we need."

"Capacitor banks most likely," Hudson says. "Possibly replacement contactors. Bearings and lubrication. We will not know until we open the nacelles. But the heavy work is done."

Misty kicks at the gravel. "So we just flip a switch."

Hudson gives her a look. "We don't flip anything. We inspect. We test. We isolate the load. Then we bring them online carefully."

Bruce steps closer. "How long."

"If the parts are where I think they are, we could have one unit turning within weeks. All three within a month or so."

Bruce nods once. "You have access. Take what you need. But I want progress."

"You will have it."

Hudson turns back to his crew.

"We split up. Meet back up at the Kmart parking lot in two hours."

Theo and Misty, you head west. There was a secondary storage building near the maintenance yard when I drove past. Look for electrical cabinets, spare breakers, heavy gauge cable."

Theo grins. "Finally something simple."

"Do not assume simple," Hudson says evenly. "Assume careful."

Theo nods and heads for the truck.

Hudson looks at Gideon and Shaz. "The airport."

Shaz raises an eyebrow. "Airport."

"Small rural field," Hudson explains. "Backup generator systems. Possibly battery racks. Utility testing equipment sometimes ends up stored in places no one thinks to check."

Gideon glances at Shaz. "And nobody would think anything useful is there."

"Exactly."

Hudson hands Gideon a folded sheet of paper with a rough sketch of what to look for. "Large metal cabinets. Industrial battery racks. Capacitor assemblies. Do not dismantle anything you do not understand. If unsure, leave it."

Shaz smirks slightly. "You worry too much."

"I calculate," Hudson replies.

The teams move toward their vehicles.

Theo and Misty pull away first in one truck.

Gideon and Shaz follow in the second.

Airport

The road to the Galesburg airport is narrow and cracked, weeds pushing through the asphalt. Gideon drives with one hand on the wheel, the other resting loosely near the gear shift. Shaz watches the tree line as they approach.

"This place ever busy?" she asks.

"Before," Gideon says. "Crop dusters. Small private planes. Nothing fancy for these small town airports."

They roll through the open gate. No chain. No sign of disturbance.

The runway stretches ahead, long and empty. Hangars sit in a row to the left. A smaller utility building stands near a fenced equipment yard.

"That has to be it," Shaz says, pointing toward the squat brick structure.

Gideon parks close to the door. The air feels still, heavy.

They step out, laughing lightly, talking about how Theo will probably grab the wrong part and bring back something useless.

Shaz nudges him. "First time I've ever been to an airport."

"Awesome," Gideon says. "You probably thought there'd be more to it."

He glances toward the large hangar at the far end of the row. Its wide metal doors are closed, but a small side window catches sunlight.

Something flashes.

He frowns.

Pop.

The sound cracks the air.

Shaz jerks backward and falls hard to the pavement.

For half a second Gideon does not understand what happened.

Then he sees blood spreading across her thigh.

"Shaz."

Another shot strikes the concrete near her shoulder.

He runs for the small power building, throwing the door open and diving inside.

"Get up," he shouts from the doorway. "Crawl. Crawl."

Shaz grits her teeth and begins dragging herself forward. Her hands leave streaks of red behind her.

Pop.

Concrete chips scatter inches from her head.

"Come on," Gideon yells. "You can make it."

She pulls herself another foot. Then another.

Pop.

She jerks again, this time clutching her arm. Blood spills through her fingers.

"I'm hit," she gasps.

"I know. Just keep moving."

Her strength is fading. Her leg barely responds. Her arm trembles uselessly.

She looks up at him, fear breaking through the toughness.

"I can't," she says. "I can't make it."

Gideon stands frozen in the doorway. If he steps out, he is exposed. The shooter has a clear line from the hangar window.

"I'll be killed," he says, voice shaking. "Then we're both dead. Just crawl."

Pop.

Another round strikes nearby.

Shaz tries again. Moves inches.

Her head lowers to the pavement. Blood pools beneath her thigh and arm.

"I'm done," she whispers. "Please."

Gideon feels his chest tighten. His breath comes fast.

He counts in his head without meaning to. One. Two. Three.

Then he runs.

He sprints into the open, grabs her under the arms, and drags her across the remaining distance.

Another shot cracks past.

He pulls her inside and slams the door shut.

For a moment they both lie there on the concrete floor, breathing hard.

Shaz's eyes flutter.

"Stay with me," Gideon says.

He yanks off his belt and wraps it high around her thigh, pulling until his hands shake. He twists it tighter. Blood slows.

He strips off his shirt and wraps her upper arm, tying it down as firmly as he can.

"Stay awake," he says. "You hear me."

Her breathing is shallow now. Her eyes close.

He presses two fingers to her neck.

Pulse.

Still there.

He leans against the wall, staring at the doorway, listening for another shot.

Outside, the airport sits silent again, as if nothing happened.

Kmart

Back at the RV camp, Theo and Misty return in a cloud of dust.

"Found your prize," Theo says, wiping sweat from his forehead. "Capacitor housing. Looks intact."

Hudson looks toward the truck bed, and scans the components with a practiced eye. "Good," he says. "Very good."

Misty looks down the road. "Where are Gideon and Shaz? Airport is closer than where we went."

Hudson checks his watch out of habit, though time has lost much of its old meaning. “They should have returned by now.”

Theo shrugs. “Maybe they found more than you expected.”

“Or misunderstood what I asked for,” Hudson replies calmly.

Misty stretches. “Well they better hurry. It’s past lunch and I need something decent to eat.”

Hudson stands slowly. He studies the road a moment longer.

“Go enjoy your lunch,” he says. I’ll drive over to the airport and see what’s holding them up.”

Theo looks at the sun overhead. “How long do we get for lunch?”

“An hour,” Hudson says. “If they are just delayed, we will all be back here within that.”

Theo nods. “Works for me.”

Misty gives a small wave. “Don’t bring back extra work.”

Hudson allows the faintest smile. “No promises.”

He climbs into his truck and starts the engine.

The road toward the airport stretches quiet and empty.

He drives at a steady pace, not rushing. Delay does not automatically mean danger.

But something in his chest feels unsettled.

He presses the accelerator slightly harder.

Airport

Hudson turns onto the airport drive and immediately spots Gideon’s vehicle parked near the small power building.

That alone is not alarming.

The open door is.

He slows the truck.

Gideon stands in the doorway, waving. Not a normal wave. Sharp. Urgent.

Hudson eases forward.

Then he sees it.

Dark red across the pavement.

At first his mind registers hydraulic fluid. Equipment leak. Broken line.

Then the shape resolves.

Too wide. Too thick.

Blood.

Pop.

Glass explodes inward from the passenger side window.

Hudson does not duck blindly. He accelerates.

He drives past the small building, makes a tight circle on the gravel, and repositions the truck so the structure shields the cab from the hangar.

He stops with the nose angled close to the building wall.

Another shot cracks. Metal rings from the truck bed.

Hudson keeps his breathing steady.

He opens the driver door slowly and stays tight against the building's edge.

"You two okay in there?" he calls.

Gideon's voice comes back strained. "Shaz is shot. Twice. She's got a pulse but she's out."

"Where's the shooter."

"Hangar window. Left side."

Hudson peeks carefully around the building corner. The hangar stands a hundred yards away. Small rectangular window. Dark interior.

He cannot see movement.

"I'm going to reposition the truck," Hudson says. "The bed will give us cover. I'll crawl under and reach you."

"I don't like this," Gideon says. "He keeps firing."

"Angle of fire matters," Hudson replies evenly. "He can't hit beneath the truck without changing position. That exposes him. Physics favors us."

Another shot slams into the tailgate as Hudson backs the truck slightly to adjust alignment.

He shuts the engine off.

Then he drops flat and slides beneath the frame.

Concrete scrapes his elbows. He moves methodically, not rushing.

A round strikes metal above him. The truck absorbs it.

He reaches the doorway.

"I'm here," he says quietly.

Gideon's face is pale. Shaz lies motionless, blood soaked into the fabric around her thigh and arm.

Hudson grips her wrists. "On three. You move her legs."

"One," Gideon says.

"Two."

They drag her forward, inch by inch.

Another shot rings out, striking somewhere behind them.

Hudson does not look back.

They clear the open doorway and slide her beneath the truck.

From there, they move together toward the protected side of the building.

Once fully shielded, Hudson stands and moves quickly to reposition the truck again, angling it tight against the wall.

Another shot cracks as he shuts the door.

He returns to Gideon.

"Load her," he says.

They lift her carefully into the bed, keeping the tourniquet tight.

Hudson checks her pulse himself.

Still there.

Gideon's hands shake. "I froze. I just stood there. I thought if I stepped out I'd die."

Hudson meets his eyes. "You got the tourniquet on. That's what matters. You did not abandon her."

Gideon swallows hard.

A distant shot echoes again but misses entirely.

Hudson climbs into the driver seat.

The truck pulls away from the building and accelerates down the runway drive.

Another round cracks behind them.

It does not hit.

The airport falls away in the rearview mirror.

The shooter remains unseen.

The truck bounces hard as Hudson clears the edge of the runway and hits the broken access road. Gravel spits behind them.

Gideon kneels in the truck bed beside Shaz, one hand braced against the side panel, the other pressing fabric tight against her upper arm. Blood has slowed from the thigh wound but still seeps around the makeshift tourniquet.

"She's breathing," Gideon calls over the engine. "Shallow. But steady."

Hudson nods once, though Gideon cannot see him.

He checks the mirrors briefly. No vehicle follows. No figure appears from the hangar.

The road curves away from the airport fence line.

Gideon's voice drops. "I should have run sooner. I just stood there. I watched her crawl."

"You did what you could," Hudson says through the back window.

"I panicked."

"You moved when it mattered."

Silence fills the cab except for the hum of the engine and the rattle of loose tools in the back.

Gideon looks down at Shaz's pale face. "If she dies, it's on me."

Hudson's jaw tightens slightly. "If she survives, it is because you tied that belt."

Gideon does not answer.

The truck gains speed on the open stretch of road.

Hudson's mind runs ahead. Blood loss. Time. Infection risk. They will need water, clean cloth, someone steady with hands.

Bruceville lies several miles ahead.

Behind them, the airport shrinks into a thin line against the trees.

Power projects can wait.

Right now, survival outranks everything.

Twenty-Four

Hacksaw

Bruceville 1987

Hudson pushes the truck harder than he should on the broken road. Gravel snaps against the undercarriage. In the bed behind him, Gideon braces himself with one hand and presses down hard on Shaz's arm with the other.

"Stay with me," Gideon says, his voice cracking. "You hear me. Stay with me."

Shaz does not answer.

Bruceville comes into view.

The brick columns. The chained gate. The small security booth just inside.

Pickle sits inside with his boots on the desk, hat tilted back, rifle leaning in the corner.

Hudson leans out the window as he approaches.

"Pickle. Gate. Now."

Pickle squints, annoyed at first. Then he sees Gideon's shirt front covered in blood.

"What in the world—"

"Gate," Hudson shouts.

Pickle jumps up and yanks the lever. The gate arm lifts halfway before Hudson drives through under it.

The truck roars into the subdivision.

People look up from porches. Curtains shift in tall windows. A dog starts barking somewhere.

In the back, Gideon presses harder on the wound.

"She's cold," he calls toward the cab. "Hudson, she's getting cold."

"Keep pressure on it," Hudson answers. "Do not loosen that belt."

"She's barely breathing."

They pass the manicured driveways and stone facades. The golf course rolls wide and empty behind the houses.

"There," Gideon says. "The lions."

The mansion rises ahead, stone lions flanking the front steps like sentries.

Hudson lays on the horn.

The sound echoes across the fairway.

The truck slides into the circular drive and stops hard.

Jordy steps out onto the porch first. Sloan follows behind him.

"What's going on," Jordy calls.

Hudson is already out of the cab.

"Help me."

Sloan looks into the bed and freezes.

"Oh no."

Jordy climbs up without another word.

"Easy," Hudson says. "Keep her level."

Gideon's hands are red to the wrists.

"She was shot," he says, voice shaking. "Airport."

Jordy looks at the blood soaking through cloth. "Who did this."

"Later," Hudson says. "Right now we move."

Bruce steps out of the front door, drawn by the horn.

"What's this."

Hudson does not look at him.

"Get Mae."

Bruce hesitates for a fraction of a second, then turns and runs back inside.

Gideon climbs down from the truck bed.

"She was crawling," he says to no one in particular. "I told her to crawl."

Hudson grips his shoulder once.

"Carry her," he says. "Back deck."

The men lift Shaz and move quickly around the house toward the open space overlooking the golf course.

Behind them, neighbors stand silent, watching the blood drip across expensive stone.

The world in Bruceville has just shifted.

They carry Shaz up the back stairs onto the back deck that overlooks the wide, uncut fairway. The wind moves softly through tall grass below, almost peaceful.

It does not match the blood soaking into the wooden planks.

"Here," Jordy says, clearing the large outdoor table. "Lay her flat."

They ease her down.

Gideon keeps pressure on the arm. His hands shake.

"She was shot from the hangar," he says. "Window on the left side."

Hudson kneels briefly and checks her neck.

"Pulse is weak," he says. "But it's there."

The back door opens.

Bruce steps out first.

Behind him, Mae moves quickly but without panic.

"Oh my goodness," Mae says when she sees Shaz. "What happened."

"Airport," Gideon answers. "Arm and leg."

Bruce's jaw tightens. "Who would shoot someone living under me. We will find him and—"

"It doesn't matter who," Hudson says sharply. "Not right now."

Bruce looks at him.

"It matters what we can do to save her."

Mae is already assessing.

"Move your hand slowly," she tells Gideon. "Let me see the arm."

He does.

The cloth falls away.

Mae inhales once, controlled.

"Do you have any medical supplies here," she asks without looking up. "I need basics at the least."

Sloan speaks quickly. "We have a medical bag. Took it off an ambulance."

"Go get it," Mae says. "Now."

Sloan runs.

Mae moves to the leg wound next. She cuts away fabric with trauma shears pulled from her own small pouch.

The thigh wound is messy but clean through.

"She will survive this," Mae says quietly.

Bruce looks at the arm again. "And that."

Mae's hands pause.

"That's the problem."

Hudson watches her face carefully.

"What do you need," he asks.

"Light," she says. "As much as you can give me. And room."

Jordy drags lanterns closer.

Bruce stands at the edge of the deck, looking from the blood to the golf course beyond.

Sloan returns with the large red duffel bag and drops it beside Mae.

She opens it.

Inside, neatly packed supplies from another world.

She begins pulling items out with practiced hands.

"Morphine," she says. "Good."

She looks up at Hudson.

"Hold her steady."

He moves to Shaz's shoulders.

Mae works quickly.

"She is going into shock," she says. "We have to move fast."

Gideon steps back, staring at the ruined arm.

"Is she going to make it," he asks.

Mae does not answer immediately.

She looks at the shattered bone, the torn muscle.

Then she meets Hudson's eyes.

"The arm will be fatal if we don't take it off."

Silence falls across the deck.

Bruce speaks first.

"Take it off."

Mae nods once.

"Then we don't waste time."

Mae works quickly through the duffel, laying items out in careful rows on a clean section of the table.

"IV kit," she says.

Hudson finds it and hands it to her.

She inserts the line with steady hands. Clear fluid begins to drip.

"Keep that bag elevated," she tells Jordy. "Higher than her heart."

He nods and holds it up.

She draws morphine into a syringe.

"Shaz," she says softly. "If you can hear me, I'm giving you something for pain."

There is no response, but her breathing shifts slightly as the medication enters her system.

Bruce watches, silent now.

Mae cuts away the rest of the sleeve. The damage is undeniable. Bone fragmented. Tissue crushed.

"There is no way to repair this here," she says. "Even in a hospital this would be difficult."

Gideon swallows hard. "You can't fix it."

"No."

She looks at Hudson.

"If we leave it, she bleeds out or infection takes her within days."

Hudson nods once. "Then we do what keeps her alive."

Bruce steps closer. "What do you need."

Mae speaks clearly, like she is back in a clinical room decades ago.

"We need a saw. Something strong enough to cut through bone. Clean sheets. Boiled water. Every towel you can find. Alcohol or iodine. And more light."

Theo appears from the side yard. "We have a hacksaw. It will cut metal."

"It will cut bone," Mae says. "Bring it."

He runs.

Mae tightens the tourniquet high on the upper arm.

"We can't rush this," she says quietly. "But we can't hesitate either."

Gideon steps forward. "I can hold her."

"You will," Mae says. "All of you will help. No one faints. No one looks away when I need them."

Bruce turns toward the house.

"Get what she asked for," he calls inside. "Everything."

Footsteps scatter.

The wind brushes across the deck again, lifting the edge of a blood-soaked towel.

Hudson stands beside Mae.

"You sure you can do this," he asks quietly.

She does not look at him.

"I have done worse with less."

Then she lifts her eyes.

"And she is not dying on my table."

The hacksaw arrives.

Mae takes it, studies the blade, then nods once.

"All right," she says. "We begin."

Theo hands Mae the hacksaw. He has wiped it down with alcohol.

"It's clean as we can get it," he says.

"It will do," Mae replies.

Jordy returns with an armful of sheets.

"Boiled water coming," Sloan calls from inside.

Bruce steps back toward the railing, jaw tight, hands clasped behind him.

Mae turns to the men around her.

"I need space. Only those helping stay close."

Hudson remains at her side.

Gideon moves to Shaz's legs.

"You hold her steady," Mae tells him. "No matter what."

He nods, though his face is pale.

She checks the tourniquet again, pulling it tighter.

"Higher," she mutters to herself. "Above the destruction."

She looks at Hudson.

"When I say, you brace her shoulders."

"I will."

She draws another measured dose of morphine.

"Shaz," she says softly. "I'm giving you more. Stay with us."

The IV fluid continues to drip.

Sloan returns with steaming pots and sets them on a side table.

"More towels," Mae says.

They appear.

She pours alcohol over her hands and pulls on fresh gloves from the duffel.

Bruce watches the men move at her command. No argument. No delay.

"Is she going to live," he asks quietly.

"If her heart keeps beating and infection stays away," Mae answers without looking up, "she has a chance."

Theo stands near the door, unable to look directly but unable to leave.

"Tell me what to do," he says.

"Keep the flies off her," Mae replies. "And keep the light steady."

He nods and positions himself near the lantern.

Hudson looks around once.

"All right," he says quietly to the group. "Listen to her."

Mae takes a steady breath.

"We begin now."

On the table, Shaz's chest rises and falls.

Mae speaks before she moves.

"No one rushes me. No one pulls away unless I say so."

Hudson braces Shaz's shoulders, leaning his weight gently but firmly.

"I've got her," he says.

Gideon grips her legs at the knees.

"I'm here," he whispers to Shaz, though she cannot answer.

Mae checks the tourniquet one last time.

"Pressure is high enough," she says quietly. "That will slow the bleeding."

She makes her incision above the destroyed tissue. Her movements are steady, deliberate. No wasted motion.

Bruce turns slightly, unable to look directly but unwilling to leave.

Sloan hands her what she asks for without question.

"Clamp," she says.

A hemostat is placed in her hand.

"Gauze."

It appears instantly.

She works through the layers carefully.

Theo keeps the lantern steady despite his shaking arm.

Hudson does not speak.

When the time comes for the bone, Mae pauses only long enough to position the hacksaw.

"Hold her firm," she says.

Gideon tightens his grip.

The sound of metal teeth against bone fills the deck. It is not loud, but it is unmistakable.

Bruce closes his eyes briefly.

No one moves.

Mae works steadily until the bone separates above the fracture site. She sets the saw aside and immediately returns to the tissue.

"More suture," she says.

Sloan hands it to her.

She folds muscle carefully over the cut bone and begins stitching. The closure is firm but not tight, leaving room for drainage.

She finishes by wrapping the stump with clean gauze and binding it securely.

The entire deck is silent except for Shaz's shallow breathing and the faint wind across the fairway.

Mae removes her gloves slowly.

"It's done," she says.

Hudson releases Shaz's shoulders carefully.

Gideon steps back, staring at the empty space where her arm had been.

Bruce exhales, long and controlled.

Mae checks the IV and then Shaz's pulse.

"Still there," she says quietly.

For now, she is alive.

Bruceville

Mae keeps her fingers at Shaz's neck for a long moment.

"Pulse is weak but holding," she says. "Keep that fluid flowing."

Jordy adjusts the IV bag higher.

Hudson studies Shaz's face. "She's still with us."

"For now," Mae answers. "The bleeding is controlled. The real danger begins now."

Gideon looks at the wrapped stump and then away again.

"I should have gone sooner," he says quietly. "I stood there and watched her crawl."

Mae looks up at him. "You tied the tourniquet. Without that, she would have bled out before we ever saw her."

Hudson nods. "You bought her time."

Gideon swallows hard but says nothing.

Bruce steps closer, careful not to touch anything.

"What happens next," he asks.

Mae wipes her hands and looks directly at him.

"Shock is the first enemy. If her blood pressure drops too far, her body shuts down. We keep fluids going. We keep her warm."

"And after that."

"Infection," Mae says. "If bacteria takes hold, we may lose her anyway."

Bruce glances at the medical bag. "There are antibiotics in there."

Mae opens the duffel again and checks. "Some. Not many. We will use them carefully."

She turns back to the group.

"I need clean dressings twice a day. Boiled saline for cleaning. No one touches the stump unless they have washed and disinfected their hands."

Jordy nods. "We can set up a rotation."

"Good," Mae says. "Keep her elevated. If she wakes, she may thrash. You must hold her steady."

Theo finally speaks. "Will she wake."

"She might," Mae says. "Or she might sleep for many hours. That depends on how much blood she lost."

Hudson looks out across the golf course.

"She is strong," he says quietly.

Mae meets his eyes. "Strength will help. But discipline will save her."

Bruce studies the deck. The towels soaked red. The hacksaw lying silent on the side table.

"You saved her," he says to Mae.

"I gave her a chance," she replies. "Saving her happens over the next few days."

A breeze moves across the deck, lifting the edge of a sheet.

Inside the house, faint footsteps echo upstairs.

Life and death now sit side by side in Bruceville.

No one feels secure anymore.

“She will never be the same,” Bruce says.

“No,” Mae answers from the table. “But she will be alive.”

Bruce studies her.

“You cut it off without hesitation.”

“I hesitated,” Mae says calmly. “I just did not let it stop me.”

Bruce looks sharply at Hudson.

“You still intend to bring those turbines online.”

“Yes.”

“After this.”

“Especially after this.”

Bruce folds his arms.

“Someone shot at my people,” he says. “That changes things.”

Bruce exhales slowly.

“Keep her here,” he says. “This deck. My house.”

Mae nods. “She isn't moving.”

Bruce looks at Hudson once more.

“You bring electricity,” he says. “She brings life back from the edge.”

Hudson answers, "It's a crazy new world."

Twenty-Five

Battle of the Airport

Bruceville 1987

Morning light spills across the abandoned fairway and climbs slowly onto the back deck of Bruce's mansion. The air is cool. Quiet. Too quiet after the night before.

Shaz lies on the large deck table, bandaged, pale, unmoving. The IV still drips steadily. The wrapped stump rests elevated on folded blankets.

Mae sits beside her, hands folded loosely in her lap. She has not slept.

Hudson stands near the railing, watching the tree line beyond the golf course.

The back door opens.

Bruce steps out in boots and a dark shirt, hair still damp from washing his face. He stops when he sees them both there.

"You stayed," he says.

Mae looks up. "She needed watching."

Bruce glances at the IV bag. "All night."

Hudson turns toward him. "Yes."

Bruce studies them a moment.

"Your people will worry," he says. "Probably think I kidnapped you both."

Hudson shakes his head slightly. "I drove back after midnight. Explained what happened."

Bruce lifts an eyebrow. "You left."

"For twenty minutes," Hudson replies. "They were relieved."

Bruce walks closer to the table and looks down at Shaz.

"She still breathing."

"Yes," Mae says. "Stronger than last night. But she is not safe yet."

Bruce nods slowly.

Hudson adds, "Stephanie is coming this morning. She agreed to give Mae a break."

Bruce looks at him sharply. "Stephanie."

"Yes."

"I'm surprised. She is not overly fond of me. Or this place."

Hudson gives a faint, controlled smile. "She does not trust you. Or a few of your men. But she is fine with most of the people here."

Bruce lets that sit.

"And she is willing to walk into my house."

"She is willing to help," Hudson says. "That's the difference."

Bruce folds his arms and looks out over the fairway.

"We talked during the night," he says. "The guys and I."

Hudson waits.

"We are driving to the airport."

Mae's eyes lift briefly but she does not interrupt.

Bruce continues. "We don't believe in allowing an injustice to go unanswered if we can help it."

Hudson studies him carefully.

"I understand," he says. "The world is different now. But sticking your arm into a hornet's nest is still a bad idea today just like it was yesterday."

Bruce turns toward him, a faint edge in his voice.

"Not when you're the hornets."

Hudson holds his gaze for a long moment.

"Just make sure you know what you're swarming."

Bruce gives a short nod.

"We will."

Behind them, Shaz exhales softly. The IV drips again.

One drop at a time.

Bruce steps away from the deck and into the side yard where Mitchell, Jordy, and Sloan are already waiting. A fifth man stands slightly apart, broad shouldered, calm, observant.

Bruce gestures Hudson to follow.

"This is Omar," Bruce says. "He came in from the south. A couple years removed from active duty, Army."

Omar gives Hudson a short nod. "Sir."

Hudson studies him briefly. "You know how to move quiet."

"Yes."

Bruce folds his arms. "We're not rushing in blind."

Mitchell speaks up. "Two vehicles. Park well off the access road."

Jordy adds, "Approach on foot. Stay out of the line of sight from the hangar windows."

Sloan adjusts the vest he is wearing. "We have the equipment. Sheriff department locker room was a gold mine."

They are dressed differently this morning. Dark green clothing. Bullet resistant vests. Tactical helmets. Gloves. Rifles slung properly.

Hudson notices the detail. They are not pretending. They prepared.

Bruce looks at him. "You think this is unnecessary."

"I think anger moves faster than reason," Hudson replies. "And reason is what keeps people alive."

Mitchell shrugs. "He shot first."

"Yes," Hudson says. "And that tells you something."

Omar steps forward slightly. "Tells us he was afraid. Or territorial."

Bruce's jaw tightens. "He shot my people."

Hudson nods once. "Then bring him in. Don't create more dead."

Jordy checks his magazine. "We're not there to negotiate."

Bruce looks at each man in turn.

"We go in quiet," he says. "We see what we're dealing with. If he fights, we finish it."

Hudson meets Bruce's eyes.

"If he doesn't fight."

Bruce holds the look for a moment.

"Then we decide what to do."

Mitchell gestures toward the vehicles. "Time."

Bruce turns back toward the house briefly, glancing at the deck where Shaz lies.

"We end this," he says quietly.

Omar opens the passenger door of the first truck.

Two vehicles roll out of Bruceville ten minutes later, heavy tires humming low on the road.

On the deck, Mae adjusts Shaz's bandage.

Hudson watches the trucks disappear down the drive.

"Bring them back," he murmurs to himself.

The wind moves softly across the empty golf course.

Airport

The two vehicles stop nearly a quarter mile from the airport entrance. Bruce cuts his engine first. The second truck follows.

No one speaks for a moment.

Omar scans the tree line through binoculars.

"Clear from here," he says quietly. "No visible movement."

Mitchell adjusts the straps on his vest. "We go on foot."

Bruce nods. "Stay spread. No bunching."

They move through the tall grass along the edge of the access road, boots quiet against dirt and weeds. The airport buildings rise ahead in still silence.

The hangar sits long and gray against the sky.

Jordy keeps his rifle low but ready. Sloan checks the corners with each step.

Omar motions toward the opposite side of the hangar.

"Side door there," he whispers. "Opposite from the window line."

Bruce nods.

They circle wide, keeping the hangar between themselves and the window from which the shot had come.

The wind rattles a loose metal panel somewhere above.

Mitchell freezes.

"Just the wind," Omar murmurs.

They reach the side door.

Bruce places a hand on the handle and looks at the men.

"No firing unless necessary," he says quietly. "We bring him in if we can."

Jordy nods once.

Bruce eases the door open.

It swings inward without a sound.

The hangar interior stretches wide and cavernous. Planes sit like shadows in the dark.

In the far corner, a small orange glow flickers.

A fire.

The men slip inside, hugging the wall.

The door closes softly behind them.

They listen.

A voice carries across the empty space.

"We got them," the voice says. "Don't you worry."

The men exchange glances.

Jordy whispers, "He's not alone."

Mitchell tilts his head. "I only hear one."

Bruce raises his hand for silence.

They move slowly along the wall, staying in the shadow of an old crop duster wing.

The orange light flickers again.

The voice continues.

"Dying ain't what people want. Stay away, stay alive. That's what Otra always said."

The men pause.

Omar leans close to Bruce.

"He's talking to someone," he whispers.

Bruce studies the flickering corner.

"Let's find out who," he says quietly.

They advance, step by careful step, toward the fire.

The men move closer, staying behind the shadow of a small single-engine plane. The flicker of the fire throws long, uneven light across the concrete floor.

The voice continues, steady but strained.

"I know, I know. You don't have to keep saying it. I did what was needed."

Jordy leans toward Bruce. "He's arguing."

Mitchell whispers, "I still only hear one."

They advance another ten feet.

The stranger shifts in a folding chair near the fire. A lantern sits on a crate beside him. In his hand is a telephone handset. The coiled cord dangles freely, not connected to anything.

Omar narrows his eyes. "He's talking into a phone."

Bruce studies the scene.

Stranger continues, nodding as if listening.

"We got them. Nobody coming back here. They'll stay away now."

He pauses, tilting his head as though responding.

"Last dog's gone. Wasn't much meat. Traps'll catch something. Cats maybe. Possum. Protein's protein."

Sloan whispers, "He's alone."

Mitchell nods slowly. "Not quite right."

Omar keeps his rifle steady but low. "He hasn't looked up once. Firelight blinds him to the dark."

Bruce's voice is barely audible. "Solitude breaks some men."

The stranger speaks again, softer this time.

"Stop being mad. I kept us safe."

Bruce's jaw tightens.

"He shot ours."

Jordy shifts his weight. "We move."

Bruce watches the man a few seconds longer. The rifle that had fired at Shaz lies propped against a crate behind him. Too far for him to reach quickly.

Bruce whispers, "On my count."

Mitchell nods.

Omar adjusts his grip.

Bruce holds up three fingers. Two. One.

They step out of the shadows.

"Now."

The men surge forward all at once.

The stranger jerks up from his chair, the handset falling from his hand and swinging against the crate.

"What—"

Omar reaches him first, kicking the rifle away before the man can turn.

Mitchell grabs his shoulders and drives him forward. The chair crashes to the concrete.

Jordy forces his arms behind his back.

"Don't move," Sloan says sharply.

"I didn't mean nothing," the stranger blurts. "I was protecting."

Bruce steps in, calm but firm. "You shot my people."

"I thought they were robbers," the man says, eyes wide. "You don't know. You don't know."

Omar snaps cuffs around his wrists.

"He's secure."

The stranger looks around wildly. "I was just keeping us safe."

Bruce crouches in front of him.

"Who is us."

The man's eyes flick toward the fire, then back to Bruce.

"Me," he says after a moment.

Mitchell exhales slowly. "He's alone."

Bruce stands. "Bring him outside."

They lift him and guide him toward the open hangar door.

The sunlight outside is harsh after the darkness.

The man squints.

The fire crackles behind them, forgotten.

The rifle lies untouched where it fell.

Bruce pauses just beyond the doorway and studies the man more carefully.

"Name," he says.

The man swallows.

"Dougie," he answers. "That's what everybody called me."

Bruce nods once.

"Dougie," he says evenly. "You are coming with us."

Dougie's eyes widen. "You ain't going to hurt me, are you."

Bruce looks at his men, then back at Dougie.

"That depends," he says quietly.

Airport

They sit Dougie down on an overturned crate just outside the hangar. The morning sun hits his face. He squints, breathing fast, wrists cuffed behind his back.

Bruce stands in front of him.

"Dougie," he says evenly. "Explain why you shot my people."

Dougie swallows. His eyes dart from one armed man to another.

"I didn't know who they were," he says. "They came onto my place. I thought they was robbers."

Mitchell folds his arms. "They were looking for parts."

"How would I know that," Dougie shoots back, panic rising. "Otra always said folks take what ain't theirs if you let them."

Bruce studies him carefully. "No one was hurting you."

"They would have," Dougie insists. "You don't see it until it's too late. That's what Otra said."

"He," Bruce repeats.

Dougie nods toward the hangar. "Otra."

Jordy glances back at the empty building.

"He ain't there," he says quietly.

Dougie frowns. "He is. He don't talk much anymore. But he's there."

Omar keeps his voice calm. "How long you been alone out here, Dougie."

Dougie hesitates. "Since everything went bad."

"Before that," Bruce says. "What did you do."

Dougie looks at the ground. "Worked at the video store. Otra owned it. I rented out movies. I made recommendations."

Mitchell shifts slightly. "And after the flu."

Dougie shrugs. "People stopped coming. Otra got sick. I stayed. Kept the lights on till they went out."

Bruce looks at the hangar again. "And now you guard this place."

"It's ours," Dougie says quickly. "Food's here. Tools. Shelter. I kept it safe."

"You shot a woman," Bruce says.

Dougie's face tightens. "I didn't mean to hurt nobody. Just scare them. Make them leave."

Jordy steps closer. "She lost her arm."

Dougie blinks. "What."

Bruce does not soften.

"She may still die."

Dougie looks down at his cuffed hands. "It was misunderstanding."

Bruce straightens.

"You're coming with us."

Dougie's head jerks up. "Where."

"To face the people you harmed."

Dougie's voice trembles. "You ain't going to hurt me."

Bruce holds his gaze.

"You will speak," he says. "And they will decide."

Mitchell nods toward the vehicles. "Time to move."

They lift Dougie to his feet and guide him toward the trucks.

Behind them, the hangar sits open and empty, the small fire burning down to ash.

The airport is quiet again.

Bruceville

The two vehicles roll back toward Bruceville in tight formation.

Dougie sits in the back seat of the lead truck between Mitchell and Omar. His cuffed hands rest awkwardly in his lap.

He keeps glancing out the window.

"You ain't going to shoot me," he says quietly.

Mitchell does not look at him. "No one said that."

Dougie swallows. "I didn't mean to hurt nobody."

Omar speaks calmly. "Then you'll have a chance to say that."

In the second truck, Bruce stares ahead, jaw set.

Jordy finally breaks the silence. "You sure about this."

Bruce keeps his eyes on the road. "Yes."

"You could've handled it there."

"I could have," Bruce agrees. "But that makes it mine alone."

Sloan nods slowly. "You want the group to see."

"Yes," Bruce says. "They need to know the threat is over."

"And if they want blood."

Bruce exhales slowly. "Then we listen."

The vehicles reach the subdivision gate.

Pickle steps out of the booth, surprised to see the convoy returning so soon.

He spots Dougie in cuffs.

"Well I'll be," Pickle mutters.

Bruce rolls down his window. "Open it."

Pickle lifts the gate without question.

As the trucks move through, word begins to spread. People step out onto porches. Children who once played in the park area stand still now, watching.

Dougie shifts nervously.

"Why they all looking at me like that," he whispers.

Mitchell answers flatly. "Because you shot one of ours."

They pull into the community center area near the large burn pit. What once was a well kept park now serves as gathering ground for meals and meetings.

The trucks stop.

Bruce steps out first.

"Bring him," he says.

They guide Dougie from the vehicle.

His feet drag slightly.

"I said I didn't mean it," he repeats.

No one responds.

They walk him slowly through the open space toward the large oak tree near the burn pit.

Residents gather quietly, forming a circle at a distance.

Bruce turns to Jordy.

"Secure him."

Jordy nods.

Rope is wrapped around Dougie's torso and arms, binding him firmly to the trunk. Not cruelly. Not gently either.

Dougie looks around at the growing crowd.

"You ain't going to kill me," he says, voice thin.

Bruce stands before him.

"That will not be my decision alone."

The murmuring grows louder as more people arrive.

On the far side of Bruceville, lanterns remain lit on the back deck of the mansion.

Shaz is still alive.

Twenty-Six

Knuckles

Bruceville 1987

Morning light spreads slowly across the abandoned golf course, turning the tall grass gold. The air carries that early quiet that comes only after a long night.

On the back deck, Shaz lies on the table where she was operated on. Her face has more color now. The bandages are clean. Her chest rises in steady rhythm.

Stephanie finishes checking her pulse and nods.

"Strong," she says. "Much better than I expected."

Mae exhales for what feels like the first time in hours. "Her pressure held through the night. That was the biggest hurdle."

Hudson stands at the railing, arms folded loosely, watching the tree line.

Stephanie glances toward the house and then back to Hudson.

"How ironic," she says. "Bruce wanted the RV folks gone. Said you were useless."

Hudson gives a small smile. "Life works like that."

"One of those useless people saved his pregnant prize," Stephanie continues. "Another saved one of his people. Not exactly fitting his narrative."

Hudson nods. "You never know who matters most until you need them."

Stephanie lowers her voice. "I'm worried he's going to decide Mae needs to stay here."

Mae snorts softly. "He can decide all he wants."

Hudson shakes his head. "He would have better luck fighting a rabid mountain lion."

Stephanie smiles faintly at that.

Hudson nods toward the community park. "Sounds like they're back from the airport."

Mae looks at Shaz again. "Whatever they found, it will not be good."

"No," he says quietly. "It probably won't."

Bruceville

By noon the community center area begins to fill with people.

The burn pit sits cold in the center of the open space. Picnic tables have been dragged into loose rows. What used to be a park for families now feels like a gathering ground for something heavier.

Dougie is strapped to the large oak tree near the edge of the clearing.

His wrists are bound behind him. Rope wraps around his chest and waist. Another line secures his legs to the trunk so he cannot kick or run.

He shifts awkwardly, testing the restraints.

"I ain't going nowhere," he says nervously. "You don't gotta tie me so tight."

No one answers.

People walk up in small groups, looking at him, whispering.

Bruce stands nearby with Mitchell, Jordy, Sloan, and Omar. There is a quiet pride in the way they hold themselves.

They brought the shooter back.

Dougie's eyes move from face to face.

"I didn't mean to hurt nobody," he says. "It was a misunderstanding."

A small voice cuts through the murmurs.

"Dee, look at him."

Olivia stands beside Deanna, staring openly.

"He's short," Olivia continues, studying Dougie like he is something in a zoo. "But his belly is really big. He must eat lots."

Deanna gently touches her shoulder. "It's rude to talk about how people look, honey."

Olivia squints up at Dougie again. "But his head is shiny. He doesn't have any hair at all."

A few nearby adults shift uncomfortably.

Deanna pulls Olivia a little closer. "Come on. Let's go back to the house."

"But I want to stay," Olivia protests. "I want to talk to the new person."

"Not today," Deanna says firmly. "Let the adults handle this. We still have that puzzle to finish."

Olivia looks disappointed but allows herself to be led away. She glances back once more at Dougie before disappearing toward the houses.

Dougie watches her go.

"I like puzzles," he says softly to no one in particular.

Bruce ignores him, scanning the growing crowd.

Word has spread quickly.

The trial will not be small.

The sun climbs higher, warming the open space around the oak tree. People drift in and out, whispering, pointing, studying Dougie from a distance.

For a brief stretch, the area clears.

Hudson walks toward the tree alone.

Dougie watches him approach, eyes nervous but curious.

Hudson stops a few feet away.

"I'm Hudson," he says calmly. "I'm the one who drove the truck you were shooting at yesterday."

Dougie blinks. "You was the driver."

"Yes."

Dougie nods slowly. "I didn't want to hit nobody. I was just trying to scare you off. Make you leave."

Hudson studies him for a moment.

"You hit someone," Hudson says. "She lost her arm."

Dougie's face falls. "The other man said that too."

"It's bad," Hudson continues. "Real bad."

Dougie swallows hard. "I don't shoot good. My eyes ain't the best. I was aiming near you, not at you."

Hudson lets the silence sit for a moment.

"The man who runs this place is going to talk to you in front of everyone," he says. "You need to tell the truth. No matter how bad it sounds."

Dougie nods quickly. "Otra always said tell the truth. No matter what. Lying makes life harder."

Hudson gives a faint, almost sad smile.

"That's good advice," he says. "But I need you to understand something."

Dougie tilts his head.

"That is not how most people live," Hudson says quietly.

Dougie frowns. "Why wouldn't they."

Hudson does not answer immediately.

"Fear," he finally says. "Pride. Anger. Sometimes power."

Dougie shifts against the ropes. "I ain't got none of that."

Hudson studies him carefully.

"No," he says. "You probably don't."

Dougie looks relieved for a moment.

"I was just protecting my stuff," he says. "Otra said people would take it."

Hudson nods once. "I understand why you thought that."

He pauses.

"But people were hurt. That part is real."

Dougie lowers his head. "I know."

Hudson steps back slightly.

"When you talk to them," he says, "tell them who you are. What you did before the sickness. What you've been doing since. Let them see you."

Dougie looks up. "You think that helps."

"It's your best chance," Hudson replies.

Dougie nods slowly.

"I'll tell the truth," he says. "Just like I was told."

Hudson turns to leave, then stops.

"Dougie," he says without looking back. "Whatever happens next, stay calm."

Dougie swallows.

"I'll try."

Hudson walks away toward the tables being arranged for noon, the weight of what is coming settling heavily in the air.

Community Center

By afternoon the clearing is full.

Tables have been arranged in rows facing the oak tree. People sit shoulder to shoulder, murmuring quietly. Some stand along the edges, arms folded, waiting.

A murmur moves through the people.

Bruce is approaching.

He steps into the clearing dressed differently than anyone has ever seen him. A black suit. Crisp white shirt. Black tie. Shoes polished to a mirror shine.

He walks slowly, deliberately, letting the moment build.

Mitchell, Jordy, Sloan, and Omar spread out behind him like silent pillars.

Bruce stops in front of the crowd and turns to face them.

"Welcome," he says, voice steady and projecting. "People of Galesburg. And our streets of Bruceville."

The murmuring fades.

"I look forward to a day when thousands live here again," he continues. "But today we gather for something more immediate."

He gestures toward Dougie without turning fully.

"One of our own was gunned down yesterday while trying to secure parts that would bring dependable electricity to all of us."

He pauses.

"A woman who offers value. Skill. Contribution."

Then he turns fully toward Dougie.

"And this is the man responsible."

Dougie flinches slightly.

Bruce's tone hardens.

"Look at him. A manchild. Little to offer. Yet he tried to take someone who offers much."

A ripple moves through the crowd.

Bruce lets the silence stretch before speaking again.

"I believe in fairness," he says. "So I will allow this man to explain himself."

He turns his head toward Hudson.

"Hudson will serve as a neutral voice. He does not belong to our community. He was also placed in danger by this individual. That makes him the most fair representation we have."

All eyes shift toward Hudson.

Hudson steps forward calmly.

Bruce folds his hands behind his back and nods once.

"The floor is yours," he says.

The stage is set.

The trial of Bruceville versus Dougie has started.

Hudson steps forward into the open space between the tables and the tree. He turns so both Dougie and the crowd can see his face.

"This man's name is Dougie," Hudson says calmly. "Before everything fell apart, he worked at a video store."

A few people shift in their seats. The detail feels almost unreal in the new world.

"He lived a normal life. Was close friends with the store owner. Took care of him until he died. After the sickness came, he survived the only way he knew how."

Hudson turns slightly toward Dougie.

"Dougie," he says. "Tell them about yourself. Whatever you want them to know."

Dougie looks out at the crowd, overwhelmed. Dozens of faces stare back at him.

He swallows.

"I was born in nineteen sixty five," he begins slowly. "My daddy died in Vietnam. Fighting communists for America. Momma said he was a hero."

He nods once, as if confirming it to himself.

"She always said I was like him reincarnated. I think she meant I looked like him. I wasn't no fighter at anything."

"Momma died long before the sickness hit, Otra stepped in as my guardian."

A faint murmur passes through the audience.

"I worked at the video store," Dougie continues. "Rewound tapes. Rented movies. Made popcorn. Did what Otra said."

He pauses, thinking.

"I had a dog when I was seven. Black and white. Ran around my feet all the time. Came to the store with me every day. People liked him more than me."

A few soft chuckles break through the tension.

"He got hit by a car in the parking lot," Dougie says quietly. "That was the second worst day of my life."

He lowers his head.

"Otra dying was the worst. I was all alone."

The crowd grows still.

Hudson waits a moment, then speaks gently.

"Dougie," he says. "Can you explain why you shot at us yesterday. Were you angry. Were you trying to hurt someone."

Dougie shakes his head quickly.

"No. No sir. I never wanted to hurt nobody. I don't see good. I was aiming near you. Just to scare you off."

He looks out at the people.

"Otra always said robbers would come. Said people take your stuff and hurt you if you don't protect yourself. I was just doing what he told me."

The audience reactions split.

Some faces soften.

Others harden.

Hudson nods once, letting the words settle.

The man tied to the tree is no longer just a shooter.

He is something more complicated.

Bruce steps back and spreads his hands slightly.

"The floor is open," he says. "What should justice look like."

The crowd hesitates.

Then Gideon stands.

His face is tight, voice rough.

"I was there," he says. "I watched Shaz crawl while he was shooting at us. I could not help her. I say we shoot him. Same way he shot her."

A murmur moves through the crowd.

Bruce nods slowly. "I understand how you feel."

Deanna raises her hand.

"I think we need to be better than the world we came from," she says clearly. "We lock him up. We rehabilitate him. He has been alone. That does things to people."

Sloan leans forward.

"And how do you expect to lock him up," he asks. "Put him in the county jail and post guards twenty four hours a day. That is not realistic."

Misty speaks next.

"We don't need the county jail," she says. "We have capable people here. We can use a basement. Keep him secure. Feed him. Monitor him. It would not take much effort."

Deanna nods. "That's right. We set an example. Crime has consequences, but we still help people become better."

Hudson steps forward slightly.

"I don't live here," he says. "I'm neutral. But humanity being humane should be what we all aim for in this new world."

Bruce watches the faces in the crowd carefully.

"Let's be realistic," he says.

He steps closer to the tables.

"Everybody here who has spent time in a county jail, raise your hand."

Several hands rise. Some sheepish smiles.

"Simple things," Bruce continues. "Possession. DUI. Arguments that got out of hand. Bad days."

A few people nod.

"Now," Bruce says, voice sharpening, "raise your hand if you served time in a state or federal penitentiary."

No hands rise.

Not one.

Bruce spreads his arms.

"Thank you. That explains this idea of rehabilitation."

He turns toward Dougie.

"In the real world, prison did not reform monsters. It kept them behind bars. It kept evil contained until release. And what happened when they got out."

He answers his own question.

"They committed crimes again."

His voice hardens.

"It is in the DNA. It cannot be trained out."

Dougie shakes his head frantically. "I ain't no monster."

Bruce ignores him.

"I need to see the hands of those who want this monster locked up and fed daily. Raised like a pet in someone's basement."

There is hesitation.

Then hands begin to rise.

More.

More.

Most of the crowd raises their hands.

Only Bruce's core men remain still.

Bruce's jaw tightens slightly.

Paula speaks from near the back.

"Bruce," she says gently. "I think people want to try a peaceful way. We want to be something better than before the flu. We're not against you. We just don't want more violence."

The crowd murmurs agreement.

Bruce stands motionless.

His control is slipping.

The moment is turning against him.

Bruce stands very still.

For a moment, no one speaks.

The wind moves across the clearing, stirring dust around the burn pit.

Dougie shifts against the ropes, hopeful now.

"I can stay in a basement," he says quickly. "I'll be good. I promise. Just give me a phone so I can talk to Otra. I'll show you how nice I can be."

A few people glance at one another, uncertain but sympathetic.

Bruce slowly reaches into his jacket pocket.

At first, no one understands what he is doing.

Then he pulls out two sets of brass knuckles.

The metal flashes in the sunlight.

Before anyone can react, Bruce steps forward and drives his fist into Dougie's face.

The crack echoes across the clearing.

Gasps erupt from the crowd.

Bruce hits him again.

And again.

Dougie cries out, blood already running down his chin.

"Please," Dougie sobs. "I didn't mean it."

Bruce does not stop.

Each blow lands harder than the last. Rage that has been building all morning pours out of him.

People shout.

"Bruce stop."

"That's enough."

Children begin crying.

But Bruce keeps going until Dougie hangs limp against the ropes.

When Bruce finally steps back, his suit is splattered red. His face is streaked with blood.

He turns toward the crowd, chest rising and falling.

"You all listen to me," he says, voice shaking with fury.

"I try to be good to you. I give you food. Shelter. Protection. I am working to bring electricity. A future. A real community."

He points toward Dougie.

"And you return that with cowardice."

No one speaks.

"Our person was shot," Bruce continues. "And you want to pamper the shooter."

His voice drops lower, more dangerous.

"I am the leader. I decide punishment. I cannot trust any of you to make the right decision."

He sweeps his arm toward Dougie's broken body.

"Look at him. If any of you think you can replace me, remember this moment. Remember what happens when I'm finished."

Silence grips the clearing.

Bruce turns toward the houses.

"Go home," he orders. "All of you. Stay there until I say otherwise."

He looks at his men.

"Make sure they do."

Mitchell and the others nod, spreading out to enforce the command.

Hudson steps forward slowly.

"I think Mae, Stephanie and I should return to our group," he says calmly.

Bruce looks at him, breathing still heavy.

"Yeah," Bruce says. "You do that. Be back in the morning. Work moves on."

Hudson nods once.

Around them, people begin to disperse in stunned silence.

Dougie hangs against the tree, no longer breathing.

The community of Bruceville has just changed forever.

Twenty-Seven

A Jump Ahead

Kmart 1988

The morning air over the RV camp carries the smell of coffee and wood smoke. The sun is still low, casting long shadows across the gravel clearing between the trailers.

Ten weeks have passed since the day Shaz was shot.

Things feel different now. More organized. More purposeful.

Hudson stands near the folding table that serves as the camp's meeting spot. A handful of tools sit beside him along with a rolled set of wiring diagrams.

People gather slowly.

Tony brings a chair and sets it down with a scrape against the snow cleared gravel. Dwight walks over wiping his hands on a rag. Moses follows, coffee mug in hand. Mae steps out of her RV and joins them. Stephanie arrives with two mugs and hands one to Hudson.

Jerry stands close beside him, hands stuffed into his coat pockets, watching everyone with anticipation. Shadoe lies nearby, head resting on his paws, eyes alert.

Hudson clears his throat.

"I wanted to give everyone an update," he says. "We're almost there."

Tony straightens. "Almost there as in lights coming on soon."

Hudson nods. "Yes. The turbines checked out. We've been running tests for weeks now."

Mae folds her arms. "So what is left."

"Final connections," Hudson says. "And safety verification before activation. Once those are complete, we can bring the system online."

Stephanie studies his face. "You're being careful."

"I am," Hudson replies. "Once we start them, they need to run correctly. We can't afford a major failure."

Tony nods slowly. "That makes sense."

Jerry shifts beside Hudson, clearly wanting to speak.

Hudson glances at him. "Go ahead."

Jerry looks around at the group, nervous but excited.

"I helped," he says.

Mae smiles gently. "We know you did."

"No," Jerry says quickly. "I mean real helped. Hudson showed me how to carry the wires and hold the ladder and bring the right tools. I learned the names of stuff."

Hudson's expression softens.

"You did more than carry tools," he says. "You helped run conduit lines. You checked connections. You followed instructions exactly."

Jerry beams. "I did good."

"You did very good," Hudson replies.

Moses leans forward with a grin. "You mean he was actually useful on the job."

Hudson nods. "Very useful."

Jerry's chest lifts with pride.

Stephanie smiles warmly. "I'm proud of you."

Jerry glances down, smiling shyly. "I like helping."

Dwight chuckles. "Careful Hudson. You might have yourself a permanent assistant."

Hudson looks at Jerry. "I would be lucky to have that."

Jerry laughs softly.

Tony turns back to Hudson. "So when do you flip the switch."

Hudson pauses before answering.

"A few more days or weeks," he says. "There are details I want correct before we start anything."

Stephanie studies him carefully. "Details or timing."

Hudson meets her eyes briefly. "Both."

Tony catches the meaning immediately. "Bruce pushing."

"Yes," Hudson says. "He wants it on yesterday."

Mae rolls her eyes. "Of course he does."

Hudson continues calmly. "Power changes things. Once the lights come on, expectations change. Control shifts. I want everything stable before that moment happens."

Jerry looks confused. "Why would lights change people."

Hudson kneels slightly so he is eye level with him.

"Because electricity makes life easier," he says. "And when life gets easier, people start thinking about who made it happen."

Jerry nods slowly. "You made it happen."

Hudson shakes his head gently. "We made it happen."

Behind them Tony calls out, "Breakfast is ready if you two engineers are done saving the world."

Laughter ripples through the group.

Jerry laughs too, full and genuine.

Hudson watches him walk toward the others, shoulders a little straighter than before.

A month ago Jerry had simply followed along.

Now he is part of the work.

Bruceville

The walk up the stone path toward Bruce's mansion feels longer than it used to.

Mae notices things now that she did not notice a couple months ago.

Two men standing near the garage watching everything.

A rifle leaning against the wall beside the door.

People moving quieter. Speaking softer.

Fear has a sound.

It is the absence of normal noise.

Paula opens the front door before Mae even knocks.

"Mae," she says with relief. "I'm so glad you're here."

Mae smiles warmly. "How's our girl doing today."

Paula steps aside to let her in. "She's resting. It was a rough night. Her back is hurting more and she says the baby feels heavy."

Mae nods. "That is normal this close. Let me take a look at her."

They walk upstairs together.

Ester is lying on the bed, propped up on pillows. Her ankles are swollen and her face looks tired. She smiles when she sees Mae.

"You came," Ester says softly.

"I always come," Mae replies.

She sets her bag down and moves beside the bed, placing gentle fingers against Ester's wrist to check her pulse.

"How are you feeling," Mae asks.

"Tired," Ester says. "And hungry all the time. And sometimes I just want to cry for no reason."

Mae smiles gently. "All perfectly normal. Your body is working hard right now."

She presses lightly against Ester's abdomen, feeling the baby's position.

"The baby is sitting low," Mae says. "That tells me we are getting close."

Ester exhales slowly. "Good. I am ready."

Mae checks her ankles, nodding to herself.

"A little swelling," she says. "Nothing alarming. Are you drinking enough water."

Paula answers from the doorway. "I make sure she does."

Mae looks back at Ester. "Any headaches. Blurred vision. Dizziness."

"No," Ester says. "Just tired."

"That is good," Mae replies. "Very good."

She finishes her check and helps Ester shift into a more comfortable position with the pillows.

"You rest," Mae says softly. "Your job right now is growing that baby."

Ester smiles faintly and closes her eyes.

Mae and Paula step quietly out of the room and pull the door mostly closed behind them.

The hallway is dim, sunlight filtering through a window at the far end.

Paula exhales, tension leaving her shoulders.

"I worry about her," she says.

"She is doing fine," Mae reassures. "This is a healthy pregnancy. Her body just needs rest."

Paula nods, but her expression remains troubled.

After a moment she says quietly, "It is not just the baby."

Mae studies her face. "What is it then."

Paula hesitates before speaking.

"Bruce," she says.

Mae does not look surprised.

Paula lowers her voice even more.

"He has changed," she says. "Since that day with Dougie. Something is different. Dangerous tension."

Mae listens without interrupting.

"People are scared of him now," Paula continues. "They try not to show it, but I can see it. Nobody questions him anymore. Nobody disagrees with him out loud."

She swallows.

"He gets angry faster. Little things set him off. Yesterday he yelled at one of the guys for moving a chair without asking."

Mae nods slowly. "Fear makes people hold tighter to control."

Paula looks at her. "Do you think he is dangerous."

Mae considers her answer carefully.

"I think he believes he is protecting what he built," Mae says. "But when someone starts believing they are the only one who knows what is right, that can lead to dangerous choices."

Paula looks down at her hands.

"I did not like what happened to Dougie," she says quietly. "I know he hurt Shaz, but that man was not right in the head. He was like a child."

Mae places a gentle hand on her arm.

"You are not wrong," Mae says.

Paula's voice trembles slightly.

"I am afraid," she admits. "Not just for me. For everyone here. For the baby. What kind of place is this going to be."

Mae squeezes her arm gently.

"It is still becoming," she says. "Nothing is set in stone yet."

Paula looks at her with searching eyes. "You are not afraid."

Mae gives a small, honest smile.

"Oh honey," she says softly. "I have lived a long life. Fear does not scare me the way it used to."

Paula lets out a small laugh through her nerves.

Mae continues more seriously.

"But I do pay attention," she says. "And right now what matters most is keeping Ester calm and healthy. Stress affects the baby. We focus on what we can control."

Paula nods slowly.

"I'm glad you're here," she says. "I don't know what I would do without you."

Mae smiles warmly.

"You would do just fine," she says. "But I am glad I am here too."

From upstairs, a faint sound comes from Ester's room as she shifts in bed.

Mae turns her head slightly, listening with practiced awareness.

"She will not be pregnant much longer," Mae says quietly.

Paula's eyes widen slightly. "You think it will be soon."

Mae nods.

"Yes," she says. "Very soon."

The afternoon sun stretches across the lawns of Bruceville, reflecting off of the snow. The golf course behind the houses lies quiet, the fairways covered over.

Shaz walks carefully along the stone path behind the house where she has been staying.

Her steps are slow but steady.

Deanna walks beside her, close enough to catch her if she stumbles but careful not to hover too much. A few feet behind them, Olivia skips along, occasionally stopping to pick up rocks.

Shaz's left arm ends just below the shoulder in a neatly wrapped bandage. The swelling is gone. The wound is mostly healed over.

It still looks shocking.

But she no longer reacts to it.

She stops and takes a breath.

"That is enough," Deanna says gently.

Shaz shakes her head. "No. I want to make it to the bench."

"You don't have to push," Deanna says.

"I know," Shaz replies. "But I need to know I can do it."

They continue slowly.

Each step takes effort. Her leg still aches where the bullet passed through, muscles tight from weeks of limited movement. But she keeps going.

They reach the wooden bench near the edge of the yard. Shaz lowers herself carefully onto it, breathing heavier now.

Olivia runs up beside her.

"You walked farther today," the girl says proudly.

Shaz smiles. "I did."

"You are getting better," Olivia says with certainty.

"I am trying," Shaz replies.

Deanna hands her a water bottle. "Drink."

Shaz takes a sip and leans back slightly.

After a moment she looks at Deanna.

"I heard what happened," she says quietly.

Deanna knows immediately what she means.

"With Dougie," she says.

Shaz nods.

"He's dead," Deanna confirms softly.

Shaz looks out toward the empty golf course for a long time before speaking again.

"I don't like that," she says.

Olivia tilts her head. "Why. He was bad."

Shaz shakes her head gently. "No. He was scared."

Deanna watches her carefully.

"He shot you," Deanna says, not arguing but stating the fact.

"I know," Shaz replies. "And I'm not saying it was right. But he thought we were going to hurt him. He was alone for months. That does things to people."

She pauses, choosing her words.

"I would have preferred a peaceful resolution," she says. "Even if he had to leave. Killing him did not fix anything."

Deanna exhales slowly.

"Some people feel justice was done," she says.

"I understand that," Shaz replies. "Gideon probably does too."

Deanna nods. "He does."

Shaz looks down at her shoulder.

"But violence does not bring peace," she says quietly. "It just makes more violence."

Olivia sits down beside her, studying her face.

"Are you sad," the girl asks.

Shaz smiles faintly. "A little."

Olivia thinks for a moment, then leans her head gently against Shaz's arm.

"That's okay," she says.

Shaz's expression softens.

"Yes," she says. "It is."

Deanna watches the two of them, something protective settling inside her.

Shaz is healing.
The community is not.

Kmart

The evening settles over the RV camp in slow layers of orange light and cooling air. Tony is tending a pot over the fire while Dwight chops vegetables on a makeshift cutting board. Moses sits nearby with a cup of coffee, watching the flames and humming softly under his breath.

Hudson and Stephanie sit at the folding table reviewing notes from the turbine site. Jerry sits beside them, carefully cleaning dirt from a pair of pliers with a rag.

Footsteps approach from the tree line.

Theo and Misty emerge into the clearing.

One look at their faces tells Hudson something is wrong.

Tony notices too. "You two look like you walked through a funeral."

Theo exhales. "We need to talk. All of us."

That brings everyone closer.

Dwight wipes his hands and steps over. Moses sets his cup down. Jerry looks between the adults, sensing the shift in mood.

Hudson gestures to the chairs. "What happened."

Misty does not sit. She folds her arms tightly across her chest.

"Bruce tied a man to the torture tree today," she says.

The words land heavy.

Hudson's expression sharpens. "Who."

"Julian," Theo answers. "One of the guys from the second house near the clubhouse."

Tony frowns. "Why."

Theo pulls out a chair and drops into it.

"Lunch gathering," he says. "Bruce was talking about work assignments for next week. Julian spoke up. Said people should have a right to express opinions instead of everything being dictated."

Stephanie's eyes narrow slightly. "And Bruce reacted."

Misty nods. "Immediately. He had his guys grab Julian. They tied him to the same tree Dougie was tied to."

Jerry's head snaps up. "The tree."

"Yes," Misty says quietly.

Dwight shakes his head slowly. "That's not good."

Theo continues. "Bruce told everyone Julian would stay there until he came to his senses. Said he had to apologize for his wrong thinking."

Tony's jaw tightens. "Wrong thinking."

Misty adds, "Not just apologize privately. Bruce said Julian would make a formal announcement to the whole community. He has to say Bruce always does what is best for everyone."

Silence spreads across the group.

Moses speaks first, voice low. "That's not leadership. That's a scared man losing control."

Hudson leans back slightly, processing.

"How did people react," he asks.

Theo answers. "Nobody stepped in. Some people looked uncomfortable. Some agreed with Bruce. Most stayed quiet."

Stephanie looks at Hudson. "Fear again."

"Yes," Hudson says.

Jerry looks confused and upset. "But Julian just talked. He did not hurt anyone."

"That's correct," Moses says gently.

Dwight rubs his chin. "And Gideon."

Theo exhales. "Gideon stood with Bruce. Said discipline keeps order."

That confirms it.

The fracture line is clear now.

Tony looks around the group. "So we have two sides forming."

Hudson nods slowly. "Yes."

Misty glances at Jerry, then back to Hudson. "We didn't tell Gideon we were coming here tonight."

Jerry looks up. "Why."

Theo answers bluntly. "Because he would tell Bruce."

The reality settles heavily.

Hudson studies each face around him.

"We need to stay calm," he says. "Division inside a small population can destroy everyone."

Stephanie nods. "But ignoring this will not help either."

"No," Hudson agrees. "It will not."

Moses folds his hands together. "Power changes people. Always has."

Tony looks toward Hudson. "Once the turbines start running, Bruce is going to think he owns the world."

"That is why he keeps pushing me," Hudson says. "He wants the victory."

Dwight speaks quietly. "You holding back on turning them on."

Hudson meets his eyes. "Yes."

Jerry looks between them, worried. "Are we in danger."

Hudson answers honestly.

"Not yet," he says. "But the situation is moving in that direction."

Theo leans forward. "Bruce is not the same man that welcomed me."

Misty's voice is firm. "He showed us who he is."

East Galesburg, The Day After

The wind moved steadily across the field, pushing against the idle turbine blades. Hudson climbed down from the tower, wiping his hands on a rag as the sound of an approaching truck cut through the open space.

Bruce stepped out first.

Gideon followed.

That alone told Hudson everything he needed to know.

Gideon used to walk beside him out here, asking questions, learning the system piece by piece. Now he stood just behind Bruce's shoulder, quiet, watching, no longer part of Hudson's work.

Bruce didn't waste time. "You're still not done."

Hudson set the rag aside. "We're close."

Bruce looked past him at the turbines. "They look done."

"They're not operational," Hudson said. "Not safely."

Gideon stepped forward slightly. "We've been saying that for weeks," he said. His tone wasn't hostile, but it wasn't neutral either. "At some point, close has to mean something."

Hudson looked at him. "It does. It means we don't rush the part that matters."

Bruce folded his arms. "People are starting to talk."

"They can talk," Hudson said. "Or they can have power that actually works."

Gideon shook his head. "You're thinking like an engineer. He's thinking like a leader."

Hudson didn't respond right away. He studied Gideon for a moment, noticing the difference. The hesitation that used to be there was gone. The need to understand had been replaced with something else.

Certainty.

"Power isn't leadership," Hudson said finally. "It's responsibility."

Bruce took a step closer. "Power is control. And control is what keeps people alive."

Hudson met his eyes. "Until it doesn't."

The wind pushed through the towers again, a low mechanical groan echoing across the field.

Gideon spoke again, more firmly now. "People need to see something working. Right now all they see is delay. That makes them nervous."

Hudson nodded once. "They should be nervous if this goes wrong."

Bruce's voice lowered, steady and controlled. "Holding this back, makes me look weak."

"I'm finishing it correctly."

Bruce watched him, measuring the answer. "You built something valuable," he said. "Something people are going to depend on. That means it doesn't just belong to you anymore."

Hudson didn't look away. "It never did."

Gideon stepped in closer now. "Then act like it. Turn it on."

Hudson shook his head. "Not until it's ready."

Silence settled between them, heavier than before.

Bruce broke it. "You have your days," he said quietly. "Not many."

He turned and walked back toward the truck.

Gideon lingered for a moment.

Hudson expected something. A word. A look. Something from the man who had stood beside him through every step of this.

Gideon didn't give it.

He simply nodded once, short and distant, then turned and followed Bruce.

Hudson watched them leave, the truck disappearing down the dirt road.

Jerry stepped closer. "He's different now."

Hudson nodded. "Yeah."

Kmart

By the time Hudson made it back to camp, the fire was already going and the smell of food carried through the air. The sound of voices reached him before he even stepped into the clearing, familiar now in a way it hadn't been two months ago.

Stephanie looked up first.

She didn't say anything right away, just watched him walk in, reading his face the way she had learned to do. Then she stood and crossed the space between them without hesitation.

"You took longer than I expected," she said, her voice quiet but steady.

Hudson handed her the empty water bottle from his pack. "Ran into Bruce."

She nodded once. "Of course you did."

Her hand brushed his arm as she took the bottle, a small, natural contact that didn't go unnoticed by anyone around the fire. It wasn't new anymore. It was understood.

Tony glanced over with a half-smile. “You bring trouble back with you, or did you leave it out there.”

“Still out there,” Hudson said.

"Has Mae not made it back yet, It's not normal for here to be this late," Hudson asked.

"She sent a message earlier. Ester is close, she is going to stay until the birth." Stephanie replied.

"Does she have everything she needs in Bruceville?" Hudson asked.

“For now,” Stephanie added.

"Good."

Hudson looked at her, just for a second, and there was something shared in that look. Not spoken. Not explained. Just there.

They sat down side by side near the fire.

Not across from each other.

Not separate.

Together.

Jerry noticed it and smiled to himself before going back to cleaning the pliers.

Tony pointed toward them with his spoon. “I remember when you two didn’t sit that close.”

Stephanie didn’t look up. “You also remember when we didn’t have power or food figured out.”

“Fair point,” Tony said.

Hudson leaned back slightly, the tension from earlier still there but quieter now. Stephanie handed him a plate without asking what he wanted. He took it the same way.

Routine.

Familiar.

Earned.

For a little while, the camp felt steady again.

But out past the firelight, beyond the reach of voices and warmth, the turbines turned slowly in the dark.

And everything tied to them was still waiting.

Bruceville, After Midnight

Inside the house, Paula is sitting beside Ester's bed when Ester suddenly grips the sheets.

"Paula," she says sharply.

Paula leans forward. "What is it."

A wet warmth spreads across the mattress.

Ester's eyes widen. "Something happened."

Paula pulls the blanket back and freezes.

"Oh," she says. "Oh my."

Ester looks down. "Is that."

"Yes," Paula says quickly. "Your water broke."

Another contraction hits.

Ester gasps and grabs Paula's arm.

"It hurts," she says.

Paula stands abruptly. "I am getting Mae."

She rushes from the room and down the hallway, nearly slipping on the stairs as she hurries.

Mae is downstairs sorting supplies when Paula bursts in.

"It is time," Paula says breathlessly. "Her water broke."

Mae stands instantly, all calm focus now.

"Alright," she says. "We move quickly but we do not panic."

Bruce appears from another room. "What is happening."

Mae answers without slowing. "The baby is coming."

Bruce's eyes widen. "Now."

"Yes," Mae says. "Now."

Upstairs, Ester cries out again as another contraction grips her body.

Mae reaches her bedside and begins issuing instructions immediately.

"Paula, clean towels. Boiled water if you have it ready. Bring the bag."

Paula runs to comply.

Bruce stands in the doorway, stunned by the reality unfolding.

Mae turns to him briefly.

"Send someone for Hudson," she says. "And Stephanie. I may need extra hands."

Bruce nods and rushes away.

Outside, a runner is already heading toward the RV camp under the dark sky.

Back in the room, Mae places a steady hand on Ester's shoulder.

"You are alright," she says calmly. "Your body knows what to do."

Ester grips her hand tightly. "I'm scared."

Mae leans closer.

"I know," she says softly. "But you are not alone."

Twenty-Eight

Birth Day

Bruceville 1988

Theo passed the news along to Hudson and the others without delay. By the time they were on the road, the drive to Bruceville felt longer than usual, stretched by everything waiting for them there.

Hudson and Stephanie speak very little as they drive. The road runs through farmland that was once carefully kept, now left to fall into quiet neglect. Snow covers the fields, and the wind moves across it under a dark winter sky. It is just past midnight, and the only light comes from the truck.

Theo sits in the back seat, leaning forward slightly.

"She was hurting pretty bad when I left," he says. "Mae looked calm though. Real calm."

"That's good," Stephanie replies. "Mae being calm is exactly what you want."

Hudson keeps his eyes on the road.

"Did Bruce say anything," he asks.

Theo lets out a breath. "Mostly orders. He kept asking if the baby was coming yet. Like anyone could answer that."

Stephanie shakes her head. "He's scared."

"Yeah," Theo says. "But he doesn't show scared like normal people."

They reach the outer road leading into the subdivision.

The security booth comes into view.

Pickle is sitting inside, feet propped up on a chair, radio beside him. He straightens immediately when he recognizes the truck.

Hudson slows.

Pickle steps outside and lifts the gate arm without being asked.

"Mae has been working with her, and Bruce, one would think he was a caged animal."

Hudson nods. "Thank you."

Pickle leans closer slightly. "Hope it goes alright."

"So do we," Stephanie says.

They drive through and park near Bruce's house with the stone lions at the entrance.

The neighborhood feels quiet.

Too quiet.

As Hudson steps out of the truck, something catches his eye across the lawn.

The tree.

Julian is still tied to it.

His arms are pulled behind the trunk. His head hangs forward, chin resting against his chest. His legs look stiff from standing too long. Even from a distance Hudson can see the exhaustion in his posture.

For a moment Hudson just stands there.

Stephanie notices his focus and follows his gaze.

"Oh no," she says softly.

Theo mutters under his breath. "He's been there all day."

Hudson feels a tightening in his chest that has nothing to do with the coming birth.

This isn't discipline.

This is cruelty.

He forces himself to turn away.

Inside the house, voices echo faintly from upstairs. Ester cries out in pain, the sound sharp and real.

Stephanie moves quickly toward the door. "Come on."

Hudson follows.

The air inside the house feels warm and tight, filled with the faint smell of antiseptic and nervous energy.

Another cry echoes from upstairs.

Stephanie moves quickly, taking the steps two at a time. Hudson and Theo follow close behind.

At the bedroom door they find Paula standing just outside, wringing her hands together.

"She is hurting," Paula says. "Mae is inside. I'm getting things when she asks but I can't stay in there. The blood makes me dizzy."

"That's alright," Stephanie says gently. "You're helping."

Paula nods, relieved not to be judged.

Stephanie pushes the door open.

Inside, Mae is already working with quiet focus. Supplies are spread neatly across a table nearby. Clean towels. Medical tools. Bowls of water. Everything organized with practiced efficiency from years of nursing experience.

Ester lies on the bed, hair damp with sweat, gripping the sheets as another contraction builds.

Mae looks up briefly when Stephanie enters.

"Good," she says. "I could use another set of hands."

Stephanie moves beside her immediately. "Tell me what you need."

Hudson stays near the wall, out of the way but present.

Bruce stands at the foot of the bed.

Watching.

He looks tense, restless, hands opening and closing at his sides.

"What's taking so long," he demands. "Is the baby coming."

Mae does not even glance at him.

"It takes the time it takes," she says calmly. "Babies do not follow schedules."

Ester cries out again as pain grips her body.

Mae leans close. "Breathe. Slow breaths. You're doing fine."

Stephanie wipes Ester's forehead with a damp cloth.

"You're strong," Stephanie says softly. "Stay with us."

Ester nods weakly, tears in her eyes. "It hurts so much."

"I know," Mae says. "But this pain has a purpose. Each contraction brings the baby closer."

Bruce paces a few steps.

"Why is it not out yet," he says. "Something should be happening."

Mae checks Ester again, her expression tightening slightly.

The baby isn't descending as easily as she would like.

She keeps her voice steady.

"We're progressing," she says. "But slowly."

Bruce hears only the word slowly.

"That's not acceptable," he says. "We can't have complications."

Stephanie glances at him sharply but says nothing.

Mae continues working, her calm presence filling the room.

Outside the door Paula waits, ready to run for anything needed.

Inside the room tension builds with every passing minute.

This birth would be routine in the old world.

Here, it feels dangerous.

Delivery Room

Time begins to blur inside the room.

Contractions come closer together now. Ester's breathing grows heavier, more desperate between waves of pain. Sweat beads across her forehead and runs into her hairline. Her hands grip Stephanie's arm with surprising strength.

"I can't do this," Ester gasps. "I can't."

"Yes you can," Mae says firmly. "Your body was made for this. Stay with me. Push when I tell you."

Mae checks again.

Her calm expression does not change, but Stephanie sees the concern in her eyes.

The baby is not moving down properly.

Mae leans closer to Stephanie and speaks quietly so only she can hear.

"The head is not advancing enough," she says. "We may need assistance."

Stephanie nods. "Tell me what you need."

Bruce hears the word assistance.

"What does that mean," he demands. "Is something wrong."

Mae does not look up.

"It means I'm evaluating options," she says. "Please stay calm."

Bruce's voice rises. "Calm. How am I supposed to stay calm if something is wrong with my child."

Stephanie answers before Mae can.

"The best thing you can do right now is let Mae work," she says. "Stress helps no one."

Bruce glares at her but says nothing.

Another contraction hits.

Ester cries out loudly, body curling forward with the effort.

Mae guides her. "Push. Now. Good. Again."

Ester strains with everything she has, then collapses back against the pillows, exhausted.

Mae checks again.

Still not enough progress.

Bruce sees the pause.

His voice sharpens.

"If that baby is harmed," he says, pointing toward Mae, "you'll answer for it."

The room goes still for a moment.

Stephanie looks up slowly, anger flashing in her eyes.

Mae does not react at all.

She continues working as if he never spoke.

Hudson watches from the wall, tension building in his chest. He sees clearly what is happening. Fear is turning Bruce into something dangerous.

Mae speaks calmly to Ester again.

"We're going to help the baby a little," she says. "You keep pushing when I tell you."

Ester nods weakly. "Okay."

Stephanie moves to retrieve a device from the supply table.

Bruce watches every movement, breathing faster.

"You better know what you're doing," he says.

Mae finally glances at him.

"I do," she says simply.

Then she turns back to Ester.

Competence fills the room.

While panic waits just beneath the surface.

Mae positions herself with steady hands, her movements deliberate and practiced despite the circumstances. Stephanie hands her the vacuum extractor from the supply tray. The device looks strange and primitive compared to modern hospital equipment, but it is functional.

Mae speaks calmly to Ester.

"I am going to place a cup on the baby's head," she says. "It will help guide him out while you push. You focus on your breathing and do exactly what I say."

Ester nods weakly, tears sliding from the corners of her eyes.

"Okay," she whispers.

Stephanie squeezes her hand. "You're doing amazing."

Bruce stands rigid at the foot of the bed, eyes locked on every movement.

Mae positions the cup carefully.

"Next contraction," she says. "You push hard."

The contraction hits.

Ester cries out and pushes with everything she has left.

Mae pulls gently, controlled.

For a moment there is resistance.

Then suddenly the suction breaks.

The cup releases with a loud pop.

The sound echoes sharply in the room.

Bruce jumps back in shock.

His face twists instantly into rage.

"What did you do," he shouts. "What did you do to him."

He slams his fist into the wall hard enough to shake a picture frame.

"You killed him," Bruce screams. "You killed him."

Stephanie turns sharply. "Stop."

But Bruce is already spiraling.

"I will have you tortured," he shouts at Mae. "Slowly. You understand me. Slowly."

Mae does not even look at him.

Her focus remains on Ester.

"Push again," she says calmly.

Ester obeys through tears and exhaustion.

With the next effort, the baby's head emerges.

A second later the shoulders follow.

Mae lifts the infant free.

For a brief moment there is silence.

Then a cry fills the room.

Strong.

Sharp.

Alive.

Mae's expression softens.

"Healthy baby boy," she says.

Stephanie exhales in relief. "Thank God."

Bruce freezes.

The rage drains from his face as the sound registers.

The baby is alive.

His posture changes instantly.

Shock becomes wonder.

Wonder becomes pride.

"My son," he says softly.

Mae continues working, clearing the airway and checking the infant with efficient movements.

The crisis has passed.

But the emotional damage remains hanging in the air.

Mae wraps the baby in a clean towel, working quickly but gently. The infant's cries settle into small, rhythmic sounds as he adjusts to the world.

Ester lies back against the pillows, exhausted beyond words, tears streaming down her face.

"Is he okay," she whispers.

Mae smiles warmly. "He's more than okay. He's strong."

She places the baby carefully against Ester's chest.

The infant quiets almost immediately, instinct guiding him toward warmth and heartbeat.

Ester's face changes.

Fear disappears.

A deep, stunned joy takes its place.

"My baby," she whispers.

Bruce steps forward quickly.

"Let me see him," he says. "Clean him off so I can hold him."

Mae does not move.

"The mother holds him first," she says calmly. "They need to bond. That's important."

Bruce waves a hand dismissively. "I don't care about bonding. This child belongs to Bruceville. The community will raise him. One day he will be the heir of this kingdom."

Mae looks at him with mild amusement.

"Can you explain how you intend to breast feed this child," she asks.

Bruce blinks. "What."

Mae nods toward Ester. "He needs his mother. That is not optional."

Bruce shifts, regaining his composure. "Yes. Of course. She should breast feed. It will make him stronger."

Stephanie cannot resist.

"Great job in leadership," she says. "Making sure the people are fed."

Mae laughs softly under her breath.

Community Center

Hudson steps outside into the evening air, the coolness a sharp contrast to the heat of the bedroom.

Voices drift faintly from inside the house as Mae and Stephanie finish cleaning. Somewhere in the distance a door slams. The neighborhood feels quiet again.

His eyes move immediately toward the tree.

Julian is still there.

Hudson walks across the grass slowly, checking once over his shoulder to make sure no one is watching too closely. The shadows from the setting sun stretch long across the yard.

As he gets closer, he can see how bad Julian looks.

His arms are bound behind the trunk. His shoulders slump forward from exhaustion. His chin rests against his chest. His legs tremble slightly just from standing.

Hudson stops a few feet away.

"Julian," he says quietly. "It's me. Hudson."

Julian lifts his head with effort.

"Yeah," he says weakly. "I know your voice."

Hudson pulls a water bottle from his pocket and raises it.

"I brought you water," he says. "And some food."

Julian's eyes brighten slightly.

"That would be nice," he says.

Hudson helps him drink, holding the bottle carefully so he does not choke. Then he tears open a small package of jerky and feeds him a piece at a time.

Julian chews slowly.

"I'm tired," he says after swallowing. "Standing like this... no way to rest."

Hudson nods. "I can imagine."

Julian looks up at him.

"I agreed to do what he wanted," Julian says. "I told him I would apologize in front of everyone. Say he was right. Say I was wrong."

Hudson frowns slightly. "Then why are you still here."

Julian gives a tired laugh.

"He said I needed a few more days," he says. "So I never question him again."

Hudson feels anger rise in his chest.

"You should tell people that," he says. "Everyone thinks you are refusing."

Julian shrugs weakly. "What does it matter. Everybody is scared. Nobody will say anything."

Hudson leans closer, voice low.

"If people knew you agreed and he is still punishing you, they would see the truth. He's lying. He can't be trusted."

Julian shakes his head slowly.

"Man," he says, "I just want to be free. Then I want to leave this place as fast as I can. Being alone was better than this."

Hudson studies him for a moment.

"I could untie you," he says quietly.

Julian's eyes widen. "Absolutely not."

"Why," Hudson asks.

"I don't have the strength to run," Julian says. "Bruce would kill both of us. Right here."

Hudson nods slowly.

"Alright," he says. "Then listen to me. Do what he wants. Say the words. Survive."

Julian closes his eyes briefly. "That is the plan."

Hudson gives him one last sip of water.

"I need to go back before anyone notices," he says.

Julian nods faintly. "Thanks for the food."

Hudson turns and walks back toward the house.

Hudson reaches the porch just as Paula steps outside, closing the door quietly behind her. The faint sound of the newborn crying drifts through the house for a moment before the door settles shut.

Paula smiles nervously.

"It's a boy," she says. "Mae said he is healthy."

Hudson nods. "That is good news."

Paula glances back toward the hallway, lowering her voice.

"Bruce is in there watching like he is some kind of king," she says. "I don't even think he blinked."

Hudson studies her face for a moment.

"Paula," he says quietly, "would you leave this place if you had the chance."

She blinks in surprise, caught off guard by the question. For a moment she studies his face, as if trying to decide how honest she can be.

"Are you kidding," she says softly. "Almost everyone here would leave if they could. Except Bruce's cronies."

Hudson nods once, letting that settle between them. Then he glances toward the deck door to make sure they are still alone.

"You passed me a note once," he says.

Paula goes still.

"It just said one word," Hudson continues. "Help."

Her eyes widen slightly, and for a second she looks like she might deny it. Then her shoulders drop, the truth easier than pretending.

"I didn't think you even saw it," she says quietly.

"I saw it," Hudson replies.

She looks down at her hands, fingers tightening together. "Then why didn't you say anything."

Hudson takes a breath before answering. "Because of Ester. Because of the baby. If I moved too soon, if anything went wrong, it would have put all of you in a worse position than you already are."

Paula nods slowly, the logic landing even if it is not what she wanted to hear.

"I figured that might be it," she says. "Still felt like I was talking to a wall."

"You weren't," Hudson says. "I just couldn't answer you yet."

She looks back up at him, searching his face.

"And now," she asks.

Hudson holds her gaze. "Now I'm telling you I heard you."

"When the time is right," he says, keeping his voice low and steady, "I will help you."

Paula studies him for a long moment, measuring whether she believes it.

Then she nods.

"Thank you for being honest," Hudson says. "Let's keep this between us."

Paula nods quickly. "Of course."

Hudson steps back inside.

Upstairs the room is calmer now. Ester lies against the pillows with the baby resting on her chest. Mae and Stephanie finish gathering supplies. Bruce sits in a chair near the bed, staring at the infant with possessive intensity.

Hudson smiles gently.

"Congratulations," he says.

Ester smiles weakly. "He is a gift. I never thought I would live to see this day. Thank goodness for Mae. If I had been alone, I don't know what would've happened."

Bruce immediately inserts himself into the moment.

"You were blessed to live here," he says. "I made sure you had everything you needed. The community needed something great to happen. Now we have a new baby and electricity coming. No one can say I'm not a great leader."

Mae shakes her head slightly.

"You should stop before your head explodes," she says.

Bruce ignores the comment.

"I don't see where any of you are needed the rest of the day," he says. "Hudson and Mae can come back tomorrow to check on things. Hudson, I expect the power to be on within a few days."

Hudson answers evenly. "We're close. A few days more and it should be ready."

He pauses, then adds casually, "How about the man tied to the tree. That seems like severe punishment."

Bruce's expression hardens instantly.

"That is not your concern," he says. "Goodbye. That means return to your camp."

The dismissal is clear.

Bruceville

Hudson, Mae, and Stephanie leave shortly after.

Outside, the night air feels cooler. The walk back to the truck is quiet.

None of them notice the figure watching from a nearby house.

Sloan.

He has been standing in the shadows, eyes fixed on the tree and the conversation that happened there.

Once the truck disappears down the road, Sloan walks toward Bruce's house.

He finds Paula in the kitchen.

"Go tell Bruce I need to speak with him," Sloan says.

Paula hesitates. "He said not to disturb him. He's upstairs with the baby."

Sloan shakes his head. "He will want to hear this. If he's mad, I take responsibility."

Paula exhales. "Okay. It's on you."

She goes upstairs.

A moment later Bruce comes down, irritation on his face.

"These people think everything is an emergency," he mutters. "It's amazing they survived this long."

He steps outside.

"What is it," he asks Sloan.

Sloan points toward the yard.

"I was watching from my house while the birth was happening," he says. "I saw Hudson walk straight over to the tree."

Bruce's eyes narrow immediately.

"What did he do," Bruce asks. "Did he release Julian."

"No," Sloan says. "Julian is still tied up. But Hudson talked to him. Looked serious. I think he gave him water and something to eat."

Bruce's jaw tightens.

"Julian can't be trusted," he says. "What do you think Hudson asked."

"I couldn't hear," Sloan replies. "But it looked important."

Bruce nods slowly.

"Let's find out," he says.

They walk together toward the tree.

Julian's head hangs forward again, exhaustion pulling his body down.

Sloan kicks lightly at the ground near his feet.

"Wake up," Sloan says. "The boss wants to talk."

Julian lifts his head weakly.

"I'm awake," he says. "Can I be released. I'll say whatever you want. Just tell me."

Bruce steps closer, voice calm but cold.

"Just tell me what Hudson said to you," he said. "That man brings problems with him, and I'd rather get ahead of it. You help me out here, and you can go home. I'll make sure you're fed and comfortable."

Julian swallows.

Hope flickers across his face.

He nods slowly.

"This is what he said," Julian begins.

Twenty-Nine

Julian

Bruceville 1988

Morning arrived quietly over Bruceville.

The ground was hard with frost, the dead grass brittle beneath it as the early sun cast long, pale shadows across the open community area. Omar walked beside Deanna and Olivia, the three of them moving toward the tree without much conversation. The tree had become something no one could ignore anymore, even when they tried.

Olivia saw it first.

She stopped walking.

"Julian is gone."

Omar followed her gaze. The rope still hung from the branch, swaying slightly in the breeze, but the man who had been tied there for days was nowhere to be seen.

Deanna stepped closer, scanning the ground around the trunk.

"Maybe Bruce released him," she said, though her voice carried uncertainty.

She looked at Omar.

"Did you hear anything about that?"

Olivia's face brightened with relief.

"He must be back at his house. I was worried about him. I like Julian. He pushes me on the big swing."

Deanna smiled gently at her.

"I know, sweetie. He acts like a big kid most of the time."

Omar nodded slowly.

"We need that in this world," he said.

Movement caught his attention.

Jordy stepped out onto the back deck of Bruce's house, stretching as if he had just woken up. When he noticed Omar near the tree, he walked over casually.

Omar did not waste time.

"Jordy, you have any idea what happened to Julian?"

Jordy shrugged.

"Yeah, man. Bruce decided he had been strapped to the tree long enough. We untied him. He asked Bruce if he could leave the community. Said he did not want to be a distraction anymore. Bruce was more than happy to let him go."

Omar studied his face.

"You helped him get out of town?"

"Absolutely," Jordy said confidently. "I drove him to the Ford dealership. He picked a Lincoln Continental. I filled the tank and off he went. Looked like he headed toward Peoria. Some people do better alone."

Deanna nodded, satisfied enough for Olivia's sake.

"There you go. He decided to go it alone."

Olivia's shoulders dropped slightly.

"I'm going to miss him. He was really nice."

"I understand," Deanna said softly. "More people will arrive someday. Maybe someone your age."

Olivia's mood lifted again.

"That would be great."

As Deanna and Olivia walked away toward the houses, Omar lingered behind with Jordy.

He lowered his voice.

"Okay. Tell me the truth. Bruce would never just let Julian leave."

Jordy's expression hardened immediately.

"Julian drove away. That is all you need to know. Don't ask about it again."

Omar held his gaze for a moment, then nodded slowly.

"Alright. I understand."

Jordy leaned a little closer.

"Bruce is going to have a meeting later today. He will tell everyone Julian decided to move on. That's the story."

Omar gave a small nod.

"I got it. Julian is moving on. End of story."

But the words felt wrong even as he said them.

Kmart

Back at the RV camp, the morning carried the familiar sights and sounds of a new day.

Mae moved from trailer to trailer, knocking lightly on doors as she went.

"Morning. Time to wake up."

Inside one of the RVs, Jimmy groaned loudly.

"Too early."

The door swung open a moment later, and Shadoe shot past him like a black streak of energy. The German Shepherd ran straight into the open field, nose down, tail high, already searching for a place to relieve himself.

Jimmy laughed and stepped outside, stretching his arms over his head.

"He's ready for the day."

Hudson emerged a moment later. His hair was still slightly mussed from sleep, and he rubbed his face with both hands before looking around the clearing.

"I need strong coffee," he muttered. "Yesterday wore me out. I'm still tired. Stress is harder than working."

Jimmy shook his head.

"Working makes me tired too, but it's a good tired. Stress makes your brain tired."

Hudson nodded.

"That's exactly right."

Stephanie was already at the cooking area, crouched near the small propane grill. She turned the valve and struck the igniter until a blue flame appeared.

"There we go," she said. "Heat coming."

Moses approached carrying a bowl and a bag of flour like a chef entering a kitchen competition.

"Get that grill hot," he said with authority. "Pancakes are on the menu."

Dwight stepped out of his trailer and stretched his back.

"What's everyone doing today?"

Mae answered while tying her hair back into a loose knot.

"I'm heading to Bruceville to check on Ester and the baby. Make sure both are doing well after the birth."

Hudson nodded.

"That's a good idea."

Tony walked over carrying a folding chair and dropped into it with a satisfied sigh.

"Dwight and I are going to Rio," he said. "Small place but might still have supplies worth grabbing. Tools. Hardware. Anything useful."

Dwight gave a thumbs up.

"We might get lucky."

Moses pointed a spatula toward Hudson.

"And you?"

Hudson looked toward the distant horizon where the turbines stood beyond the trees.

"Jimmy and I are heading to the turbines. Theo and Misty will meet us. Final checks today."

Jimmy grinned.

"I'm going with Hudson and Shadoe. We're going to do hard work and then come back for good lunch."

Moses laughed loudly.

"Hard work and good lunch. That's the correct order of life."

Moses smiled as he poured batter onto the hot griddle.

Mae looked toward Hudson again.

"When I get to Bruceville, I'll also check on Julian. Make sure he's alright."

Hudson nodded but his expression turned slightly serious.

"Do that. But be careful. Don't do anything risky."

Stephanie stepped closer to Mae.

"I'm going with her. Two people are better than one."

Mae gave a small smile.

"I'll not say no to that."

Tony leaned forward in his chair.

"You still think Bruce is stable enough to deal with?"

Hudson hesitated before answering.

"I think Bruce is under pressure. Pressure changes people."

Dwight snorted.

"That man was strange before pressure."

Hudson did not disagree.

Jimmy returned from the field with Shadoe trotting beside him proudly.

"He chased something," Jimmy announced.

Hudson laughed softly.

"I'm sure he did."

Jimmy looked at Hudson with sudden seriousness.

"Shadoe needs a dog friend?"

Hudson nodded.

"He has you as a friend."

Jimmy's face lit up.

"He's my best friend, but he needs a dog friend. I'm human, silly."

"I agree, if we find a good fit for Shadoe, we will think about it," Hudson said

Jimmy looked around the camp, excitement building in his expression.

"That would be amazing."

Hudson studied him for a moment, then nodded.

"Yes," he said quietly. "Amazing."

For a few minutes the camp felt normal.

Almost like the old world had not ended.

But underneath the morning routine, unease still lingered.

None of them knew yet what had happened to Julian.

And none of them realized how close everything was to changing.

Bruceville

Inside Bruce's mansion, the air smelled faintly of clean linens and bleach from the night before.

Morning light filtered through the curtains, soft and warm, landing across the bed where Ester rested with the baby against her chest. The infant slept peacefully, tiny mouth moving occasionally as if still nursing in his dreams.

Paula sat nearby in a chair, watching with quiet fascination.

"I stayed up most of the night," she said gently. "Just in case you needed anything. He did really well. I even changed his diaper."

She made a face.

"It was awful."

Ester smiled faintly, her voice still tired but warm.

"The first one always is. He's strong. He's feeding well."

Bruce entered the room just then, already dressed and composed, his hair neatly combed. He moved closer to the bed, looking down at the baby with open satisfaction.

"How's my sweet baby boy this morning?"

Paula answered quickly.

"He's doing great. Strong lungs too. He cried a little during the night but it never lasted long."

Bruce nodded proudly.

"The community will be excited to meet him today."

Ester's smile faded.

"I don't think that's a good idea yet."

Bruce looked at her, surprised.

"Why not?"

"He's only a day old," she said softly. "He needs to stay here. Quiet. Safe."

Bruce waved a hand dismissively.

"I will be the only one holding him. Everyone else will be keep at a distance. This boy is a morale builder. People need something positive."

Paula hesitated, then spoke carefully.

"If people were happy, morale would not need building."

Bruce's eyes shifted toward her, his expression sharpening slightly.

"You need to be more respectful, Paula. We just survived a civilization killing virus. People lost families. Babies always help morale."

Ester shifted uncomfortably against the pillows.

"I'm still not comfortable with him leaving the room."

Bruce's smile tightened.

"The best part of being the leader is I do what I want."

A knock sounded at the door.

Mae stepped inside with Stephanie just behind her.

"Knock knock. Your friendly nurse is here."

Paula's face brightened with relief.

"I'm so glad you came. We were just talking about whether to bring the baby out to meet people today."

Mae did not hesitate.

"He stays in this room."

Bruce's jaw tightened.

"It was not a debate. He will meet the community."

Stephanie stepped forward calmly, her voice controlled but firm.

"The mother should decide. She carried him and delivered him. You just watched from the sideline."

Paula added quietly.

"Bruce, could you rethink this for me?"

Bruce turned toward Stephanie, irritation now fully visible.

"I might have reconsidered. But since Stephanie likes to act like she runs things, my decision stands."

Mae ignored the tension and moved to the bedside, gently checking Ester's pulse and examining the baby.

"He looks good," she said. "Strong color. Good breathing."

Stephanie smiled at Ester.

"You did amazing."

Ester's eyes softened with gratitude.

"I couldn't have done it alone."

Mae glanced toward the window that faced the community area. The empty tree stood clearly visible from the room.

"I noticed the man who was tied out there is gone. What happened?"

Bruce answered immediately, his tone smooth.

"He apologized last night. We both agreed it was best for him to move on. He packed his things and left."

Mae nodded slowly, though something about the explanation felt incomplete.

"I hope he finds a place that makes him happy."

Bruce smiled confidently.

"He's a happy sort. I'm sure he will be fine."

Stephanie exchanged a brief glance with Mae.

Neither of them fully believed it.

But neither said anything.

The baby stirred softly against Ester's chest, letting out a small sound before settling again.

East Galesburg

The turbine field stretched wide under the late morning sun, the tall steel towers rising against the blue sky like monuments from another world.

A steady breeze moved across the open ground, turning the blades slowly with a low rhythmic sound that felt almost alive.

Jimmy ran ahead through the field with Shadoe racing beside him, both of them laughing in their own ways. The dog leapt forward, nose low, chasing some invisible scent, while Jimmy tried to keep up.

"He smells something," Jimmy called back over his shoulder. "Probably a rabbit."

Hudson watched them for a moment, a faint smile breaking through the tension that had been building in his mind all morning.

"Dogs enjoy running," he said quietly. "That is reason enough."

Jimmy stopped and turned, breathing hard but still grinning.

"Can I just run with him for a while?"

Hudson nodded.

"Sure. I doubt you will stay with him long."

Jimmy laughed and took off again, Shadoe immediately accelerating ahead like a black arrow across the field.

Theo and Misty pulled up in the truck a few minutes later, dust trailing behind the tires as they parked near the base of the nearest tower.

Theo stepped out carrying a toolbox.

"You ready to finish this thing?"

Hudson nodded.

"Final checks today. If everything passes, we're done."

Misty leaned against the truck door, studying the turbines for a moment.

"It still amazes me," she said. "All this running again after the world ended."

Hudson followed her gaze upward.

"The equipment was built to last. We just had to wake it back up."

Theo hesitated before speaking again.

"As we were leaving Bruceville this morning, I noticed Julian was missing."

Hudson turned toward him.

"What do you think that means?"

Misty answered quietly.

"I don't think it means anything good."

Hudson's expression grew serious.

"Did anyone say where he went?"

"Pickle mentioned a community meeting planned for lunch," Theo said. "That's all."

Hudson looked toward the distant tree line in the direction of Bruceville.

"That doesn't sound positive for Julian."

Theo nodded.

"You're probably right."

For a few seconds none of them spoke. The slow turning of the turbine blades filled the silence.

Finally Hudson clapped his hands lightly.

"Let's finish the work. One problem at a time."

They moved toward the base of the tower, opening panels and checking connections with practiced motions.

Jimmy returned a few minutes later, flushed and breathing hard, Shadoe still bouncing with energy beside him.

"I almost caught him," Jimmy said proudly.

Hudson smiled.

"I believe you."

Jimmy watched Hudson work for a moment, then spoke more quietly.

"Boss man."

Hudson glanced over.

"Yes."

Jimmy hesitated.

"Are we really totally done with the windmills?"

Hudson nodded slowly.

"Yes. After today, we could turn it on."

Jimmy's eyes widened.

"Your saying, no more job."

"Don't worry about that, work will always be plentiful," Hudson replied.

Jimmy looked across the field toward the distant town.

"The lectricity is going to make people happy."

Hudson paused before answering.

"Yes," he said quietly. "It will."

But as he looked toward Bruceville, a heavy feeling settled in his chest.

Something had changed there.

And he was not sure Jerry's "lectricity" would fix it.

Thirty

Morale Meeting

Torture Tree 1988

By midday, the community of Bruceville had gathered near the large tree at the center of the open park. Long picnic tables were lined with food, and the smell of cooked meat and fresh bread drifted through the cool winter air. Children moved between the adults, laughing and chasing one another, while older residents stood in small groups, talking quietly and waiting for whatever Bruce had planned.

The tree stood behind the tables, still and silent.

No one mentioned Julian.

Bruce emerged from his house a few minutes later carrying the infant in his arms. Paula walked beside him, watching carefully in case the baby stirred. Conversations faded as people noticed them approaching.

Bruce climbed onto the small wooden platform that had once been used for community announcements before the world changed. He looked out over the crowd with a satisfied expression.

"Everyone," he called, his voice carrying easily. "Today is an important day for Bruceville."

He lifted the infant slightly so people could see.

"This child represents our future. Proof that humanity survives."

A murmur moved through the crowd. Some smiled. Others did not.

Bruce continued. "The mother has not yet chosen a name, but I believe we already know what he should be called."

He paused, letting the moment stretch.

"This is Junior. The future heir of our town."

Several people glanced at one another. Ester stood nearby, supported by Mae, her expression tired but protective. She did not correct him.

Bruce continued without noticing. "He is healthy. Strong. The Liberty Flu had no effect on him. That means we can rebuild. That means we must rebuild. Every one of you should start thinking about having children. That is how we save humanity."

Paula shifted beside him, uncomfortable, but Bruce kept moving.

He handed the baby back. "Take him to his mother."

Paula nodded and carried the infant to Ester, who pulled him close with quiet relief.

Bruce turned back to the crowd, his tone shifting slightly. "I also want to address something from yesterday. The situation with Julian."

The air tightened.

"During the night, Julian came to his senses," Bruce said smoothly. "He admitted I had been correct about everything. He apologized for the trouble he caused and said he understood now why discipline was necessary."

A few people exchanged looks.

"We both agreed it would be best for him to move on. He said he wanted to spend time alone. Reflect. Find his own path."

Jordy stepped forward. "I drove him to the old Ford dealership. Helped him gas up a Lincoln. He headed toward Peoria. Said he would be fine."

The explanation landed unevenly. Some nodded. Others said nothing.

Bruce clapped his hands once. "Now for the good news."

His voice rose again. "Power will be turned on before the day is over."

This time, the reaction came immediately, but it wasn't what Bruce expected. Conversations broke out across the crowd, not unified, not directed at him, but scattered.

"No more generators," Bruce said louder. "No more uncertainty. Stable electricity."

He spread his arms toward the homes behind him. "We will grow. Expand. Fill Galesburg again. We will become the largest and safest community in the Midwest."

He paused, smiling. "And don't think you need to thank me. This is simply what real leaders do."

No applause came.

The people shifted where they stood. Some sat. Others leaned toward each other, voices low, uncertain. The moment broke apart instead of building.

Bruce felt it immediately.

He kept his expression steady, but something tightened behind his eyes. They were not looking at him the way they had before. Not with the same confidence. Not with the same trust. Whatever he had built was slipping in ways that were harder to control than open defiance.

Julian was in the room, even without being named. In the glances. In the hesitation. In the quiet conversations.

The explanation should have been enough.

It wasn't.

Bruce drew a slow breath and held it. He reminded himself what he had done. Food. Shelter. Order. This place existed because of him.

That should have mattered more.

Instead, they were questioning it.

His jaw tightened slightly. They didn't understand what it took to hold something like this together. They wanted safety without accepting the cost.

And now even this, power, progress, something that should have united them, was being met with hesitation.

The shift inside him hardened.

If they would not give him the respect he had earned, then it would have to be reinforced another way.

He nodded once to himself.

They would understand.

"Return to your designated tasks," he said. "We will meet again for dinner."

The crowd began to disperse, but the conversations did not end. They changed shape. Smaller groups. Lower voices. Glances that lingered too long.

The celebration had not taken hold.

Something else had.

Paula stood near the edge of the park, watching Ester walk back toward the house with Stephanie and Mae. Relief settled in knowing they were not alone.

Deanna approached with Olivia. "That was something."

Paula nodded. "He should not have taken the baby out like that."

Olivia looked up. "Junior is a funny name."

Paula managed a small smile. "I think his mother will decide."

Deanna waited, then lowered her voice. "Does the Julian story make sense to you?"

Paula hesitated. "No. He could barely stand yesterday."

Deanna glanced toward the tree. "Exactly."

Omar joined them. "Everything alright?"

Paula studied him. "Do you believe what Bruce said?"

Omar hesitated. "I don't know what to believe."

He lowered his voice. "Jordy said he drove him out. But Bruce doesn't usually let people like Julian walk away."

They stood in silence.

Nearby, others whispered.

No accusations. No open resistance.

Just doubt.

Paula leaned closer to Deanna. "I'm scared."

"You're not the only one," Deanna said.

Across the park, Jordy and Sloan watched the crowd carefully.

People were beginning to choose sides.

East Galesburg

The turbines turned steadily in the afternoon wind, their long blades slicing the air with a low rhythmic sound that carried across the open field.

Hudson stood at the base of the control cabinet with Jimmy beside him, reviewing the last set of readings. Theo and Misty were working near the second tower, checking connections one more time before closing the panels.

Jimmy wiped sweat from his forehead with the back of his arm.

"It looks like it's already running," he said, looking up at the blades. "Why don't we just turn the power on?"

Hudson smiled slightly.

"Because spinning does not mean ready. There is a difference between movement and stability."

Jimmy nodded slowly, absorbing that.

A vehicle approached across the gravel access road, dust trailing behind it.

Hudson turned toward the sound.

Bruce's truck.

It pulled up hard and stopped near the work area. Jordy and Sloan stepped out first, both scanning the surroundings automatically. Bruce followed, already looking irritated.

He walked directly toward Hudson without greeting anyone.

"I just told the entire community the power would be on today," Bruce said.

Hudson remained calm.

"It's not ready yet."

Bruce stopped a few feet away.

"The turbines are spinning."

"They are in test mode," Hudson replied. "We still have final synchronization checks and load verification."

Bruce's jaw tightened.

"People need to see results."

"They will," Hudson said. "When it's safe."

Bruce stepped closer.

"I promised them today."

Hudson met his eyes.

"If I activate before everything is stable, we risk system failure. That could damage equipment permanently. Then nobody gets power."

Jordy shifted slightly behind Bruce, watching Hudson with narrowed eyes.

Bruce's voice dropped.

"Are you refusing me?"

Hudson answered evenly.

“I'm protecting the system. A few more days. That's all.”

"You said a few more days earlier in the week. The people need hope." Bruce said in an excited tone.

Bruce stared at him for several seconds. The wind moved between them, carrying the slow whoosh of the turning blades overhead.

Finally Bruce stepped back.

“You're playing a dangerous game with my leadership,” he said quietly.

Hudson did not respond.

Bruce turned sharply toward his truck.

“Come on,” he said to Jordy and Sloan.

The three men climbed back into the vehicle. The truck roared to life and pulled away, gravel spraying behind the tires.

Jimmy watched them leave.

“He looked mad.”

Hudson exhaled slowly.

“Yes,” he said. “He did.”

Bruceville

The afternoon sun sat high over Bruceville as Shaz walked slowly up the path toward Gideon’s house. Her gait was steady now, though still careful, her balance slightly different without her left arm. The empty sleeve of her shirt was pinned neatly, and the bandage beneath had begun to shrink as healing progressed.

She paused at the door for a moment before knocking.

Inside, she heard movement. A chair scraping. Something being moved quickly.

The door opened.

Gideon stood there, looking surprised.

"Shaz."

"Hey," she said simply.

He stepped back immediately.

"Come in."

She walked inside and stopped.

The house was a mess.

Clothes on the floor. Dishes stacked on a table. Trash gathered in corners. The air smelled stale, like someone who had not cared enough to clean in a long time.

Shaz turned slowly, taking it all in.

"I have noticed you have been avoiding me," she said.

Gideon looked down.

"I'm sorry."

She met his eyes.

"I lost my arm. Not my head."

He swallowed hard.

"I know. Things have just been... depressing."

Shaz stepped closer.

"I'm alive. I'm healing. Other than missing an arm, I'm still the same person."

Gideon nodded but did not look convinced.

"I still feel guilty," he said quietly. "I froze. I didn't know what to do. And I never want to be in that position again."

Shaz studied him.

"So your plan is to hide in your house until what. You do something stupid."

Gideon shook his head quickly.

"I don't hide all the time. I spend time with Bruce every day. He tells me what he plans on doing. He asks what I think."

Shaz blinked in surprise.

"You are Bruce's guy now?"

"It's not like that," Gideon said defensively. "We're all under Bruce. He's the leader. He takes care of us."

He paused, emotion rising.

"The man who almost killed you. Bruce handled him. Everyone else wanted to treat him like a guest. Feed him. Protect him. Only Bruce stood up and punished the criminal."

Shaz's expression softened but remained firm.

"The group voted to lock him up," she said. "After time, maybe help him become part of the community. He was protecting himself. Just like anyone would."

Gideon shook his head.

"No. He was trying to kill people. He didn't care about anything. He just wanted the experience of killing and we were there."

Shaz sighed quietly.

"I'm sorry you feel that way. But I see it differently."

Gideon looked at her with conviction.

"Bruce understands it the way I do. That's why we get along. He is the best person to lead."

Shaz held his gaze for a moment.

Then she nodded slowly.

"Okay," she said. "Okay."

She stepped toward the door.

"I'll be leaving then. Don't be a stranger. If you see me out, say hi."

Gideon nodded.

"Yeah. I will."

She walked outside into the sunlight, closing the door behind her.

As she moved back toward the street, her face showed something deeper than sadness.

It was the realization that the community was no longer whole.

People were dividing.

And Gideon, she worried about him.

Kmart

Night settled slowly over the RV camp, bringing with it the faint rustling of wind through the trees. A small fire burned in the pit near the center of the clearing, its glow lighting the faces gathered around it.

Hudson sat beside Stephanie on one of the folding chairs, a mug of hot tea cooling in his hands. Tony, Moses, Dwight, Mae, and Jerry formed a loose circle nearby. Shadoe lay on the ground at Jimmy's feet, though the dog's ears twitched constantly, picking up sounds no one else noticed.

The mood felt different tonight.

Heavier.

Tony leaned forward, resting his elbows on his knees.

"I don't like this," he said.

Moses nodded slowly.

"Me neither."

Hudson looked up.

"What part."

Tony answered without hesitation.

"Bruce."

The fire popped softly as a log shifted.

Moses spoke next.

"I've seen men like him before. Not the exact same situation, but the personality. Power gets in their blood. Once it's there, they do not give it up."

Dwight added quietly, "They start thinking they are the only reason everyone survives."

Stephanie glanced toward Hudson.

"If turning the power on would calm things down, maybe we should do it."

Hudson shook his head.

"It might calm things for a few days. But it will also solidify him as leader. Permanently."

Tony nodded.

"That's what I am worried about."

Jerry shifted uneasily in his chair.

"That Bruce is bad, he shouldn't be the leader of nothing, not even a town with no people in it."

Moses pointed at the fire with a stick.

"Bad men with power are dangerous," he said. "Especially when they view themselves as the hero."

Shadoe suddenly lifted his head, ears forward, low growl rumbling deep in his throat.

Jimmy looked down at him.

"What is it, boy?"

The dog stood slowly, scanning the darkness beyond the firelight.

Jerry shifted nervously.

"He feels something."

Stephanie reached over and touched Hudson's arm.

"You don't think Bruce would do anything tonight."

Hudson hesitated.

"No," he said finally. "I don't think so."

But even as he spoke, unease settled deeper in his chest.

The fire crackled.

The trees moved in the wind.

And somewhere beyond the edge of the clearing, shadows shifted.

It happened fast.

One moment the camp was quiet, the next the darkness exploded with movement.

Figures stepped out from between the trees, weapons already raised.

"Do not move," a voice shouted.

Stephanie jerked upright, instinctively grabbing Hudson's arm.

Jordy, Mitchell, and Sloan stepped into the firelight, rifles pointed directly at Hudson. Behind them were two more armed men Hudson recognized from Bruceville.

Tony stood halfway from his chair.

"What the hell is this."

"Sit down," Jordy snapped. "Nobody gets hurt if you cooperate."

Hudson rose slowly.

"What do you want."

Mitchell answered coldly.

"You."

Two men moved forward immediately, grabbing Hudson's arms before anyone could react.

Stephanie lunged toward them.

"Stop."

A rifle swung toward her chest.

"Back up," Jordy warned.

She froze, breathing hard, eyes wide with fear.

Jerry stood beside the fire trembling, confusion and panic flooding his face.

"Leave him alone," he said weakly.

Shadoe growling at the men caught their attention, quickly.

"Retarded boy, better grab that dog before he gets a bullet," Mitchell said.

Jerry quickly put his arms around Shadoe's neck, "I'm not retarded, I just have an extra special chromosome."

One of the armed men shoved Hudson forward toward a waiting truck at the edge of the clearing.

Tony took a step forward but Moses grabbed his arm.

"They are armed," Moses whispered urgently. "We can't win this right now."

Hudson looked back once toward Stephanie.

"It's alright," he said calmly. "Don't fight them."

Stephanie's voice broke.

"Hudson..."

They forced him into the truck bed.

The engine roared to life.

Gravel sprayed as the vehicle turned and accelerated into the darkness.

Within seconds the headlights disappeared beyond the trees.

Silence fell over the camp.

Stephanie stood frozen near the fire, shock written across her face.

Jerry began to cry quietly.

Tony stared into the darkness with fury building in his eyes.

"They just made a very big mistake," he said.

The night closed in around them.

And Hudson was gone.

Thirty-One

Interrogation

Community Center, Morning, 1988

Pain arrived before awareness.

Hudson felt it first in his shoulders, then his ribs, then the dull pounding at the back of his head. His wrists burned where the rope pulled tight above him. For a few seconds, his mind drifted between sleep and consciousness, trying to make sense of the sensation before anything else came into focus.

Then he heard voices.

And he remembered.

His eyes opened slowly, the light hitting him harder than expected. Sunlight forced him to squint as the world swam and then began to settle into something recognizable. Melting snow. Dirt. The open park. The houses of Bruceville beyond.

And the tree.

He was tied to it.

His arms were pulled back around the trunk, rope wrapped tight across his chest and wrists, holding him upright. His legs were secured near the base, forcing him to carry his own weight instead of resting against it. He inhaled carefully, testing his ribs. Bruised, but not broken. His lip tasted like dried blood.

A shadow moved in front of him.

Bruce stepped into view.

"Well," Bruce said calmly. "You're awake."

Hudson met his eyes but didn't answer.

Bruce studied him for a moment, as if assessing something mechanical rather than human. "You know why you're here."

Hudson's voice came out rough. "No."

Bruce gave a faint smile. "Sabotage."

Hudson blinked slowly, letting that sit without reacting.

"You're delaying the power," Bruce continued. "Undermining leadership. Creating doubt in the community. Conspiring against me."

Hudson let out a slow breath. "I'm making sure the system works."

Bruce's smile faded. "You're making sure you stay important."

Hudson shook his head slightly. "That's not how I think."

Bruce stepped closer. "You underestimate people. They follow results. If you control the power, you control loyalty."

Hudson held his gaze. "I'm trying to keep everyone safe."

Bruce's voice hardened. "You're trying to control what belongs to me."

By now, movement had started around them. Doors opened. People stepped outside. The sight of Hudson tied to the tree pulled attention immediately, drawing them in whether they wanted to look or not.

Bruce raised his voice. "Everyone come here."

Residents began to gather, confusion spreading as they realized what they were seeing. Hudson stood against the tree, bruised and bound, but still steady. Still present.

Bruce turned toward the crowd, his expression shifting into something more formal, more controlled. "This man has been sabotaging our progress."

Murmurs spread outward.

"He has delayed activation of the power grid," Bruce continued. "He has undermined leadership. He has conspired to weaken this community."

Hudson watched the faces in front of him as they processed it. Shock. Fear. Disbelief. None of it settled cleanly.

Bruce stepped close again, lowering his voice so only Hudson could hear. "You should have turned it on when I told you."

Hudson didn't look away. "No."

Bruce straightened and addressed the crowd again. "He will remain here until he decides to cooperate. My men will stand guard over him in case someone makes a poor decision."

People moved closer now, stepping off porches and into the open space, drawn by something they didn't fully understand yet. The closer they got, the harder it became to ignore what they were seeing.

Paula was among the first to arrive.

She stopped when she saw him. "Oh my God."

Her hand went to her mouth as she took in the bruises, the rope, the way he was being held upright by force instead of choice. Hudson looked exhausted, but conscious, his breathing steady despite everything.

She turned toward Bruce immediately. "What are you doing."

Bruce didn't look at her. "He's being disciplined."

"For what," she demanded.

Bruce answered without emotion. "For delaying the power. For undermining leadership. For conspiracy."

Paula stared at him. "That's insane."

Bruce turned his head toward her, his eyes cold. "Be careful."

She stepped back slightly, but she didn't apologize.

Behind her, Deanna arrived with Olivia holding her hand. Olivia stopped when she saw Hudson. "Why is he tied to the tree," she asked quietly.

Deanna didn't answer. She was looking at Bruce.

Across the open space, Ester stood near the edge of the gathering with the baby held tightly against her chest. Shaz stood beside her, one arm steadying her.

Ester's voice was barely above a whisper. "He helped me."

Shaz nodded slowly. "Yes. He did."

The baby stirred, unaware of anything around him.

Omar approached from the opposite side, his steps slowing as the scene came into full view. His eyes moved from Hudson to Bruce, then to Jordy and Sloan standing nearby, watching everything.

The murmuring began to change.

"This is wrong."

"What happened."

"He was fixing the power."

"Why is he tied up."

Fear settled over the group, not loud, but heavy. No one stepped forward. No one openly challenged Bruce. But something underneath it all had shifted.

Bruce noticed.

He raised his voice again. "This man refuses to cooperate with the activation of our electrical system. Until he decides to help this community, he will remain here."

Hudson said nothing.

He stood there, breathing slowly, his eyes moving across the people he recognized.

Some looked ashamed.

Some looked frightened.

Some looked angry.

Paula stepped forward again despite herself. "You can't do this."

Bruce leaned slightly toward her. "I do as I want, you should already be aware of that."

She looked at the ground.

Around them, the community stood in silence.

And more than one person realized something they had been trying not to admit.

Bruce was dangerous.

Community Center, Morning

Omar stood near the back of the crowd with his arms folded across his chest, his eyes fixed on Hudson.

The scene in front of him didn't make sense.

Or maybe it made too much sense.

Hudson tied to the tree. Julian gone. Bruce standing there as if he had the right to decide what happened next. The pieces began to fall into place whether Omar wanted them to or not, each one settling in a way that left less room for doubt.

He shifted slightly, stepping to the side where Jordy stood watching the crowd with that same guarded expression Omar had noticed before.

"You really drove Julian out of town," Omar said quietly.

Jordy didn't look at him. "I told you what happened."

Omar studied him for a moment. "He could barely stand the day before."

Jordy's jaw tightened. "Drop it."

Omar let it go.

He didn't need to push any further. The answer was already there, just not spoken out loud.

He stepped back and looked at Hudson again.

Hudson had come here to help. He had fixed the turbines, repaired the power system, and done what no one else could. He had saved Shaz when things went bad. He had brought something close to order into a place that had been barely holding together.

And now he was tied to a tree.

Because he refused to obey Bruce.

Omar felt something shift inside him, not sudden, but steady and undeniable.

This wasn't discipline.

This was control.

Bruce's voice cut through his thoughts. "He will remain there until he decides to cooperate."

Omar looked back at Hudson.

For a brief moment, Hudson met his eyes.

There was no anger there.

No panic.

Only calm.

That unsettled Omar more than anything else.

Because it meant Hudson wasn't afraid.

And if Hudson wasn't afraid, then maybe Bruce wasn't as powerful as he wanted everyone to believe.

The realization settled in, clear and unavoidable.

Julian had not left on his own.

Bruce had lied.

And now Hudson was next.

Kmart, Sunrise

Morning light spread across the Kmart parking lot, reflecting off broken glass and faded painted lines. The RVs sat in their usual arrangement near the garden center entrance, but without Hudson moving between them, the place felt still in a way it hadn't before.

Tony stood near the edge of the lot with his arms crossed, staring toward the road where the vehicles had disappeared earlier. Dwight stood beside him, his jaw tight, scanning the distance as if Hudson might somehow walk back into view.

Stephanie remained in the same folding chair she had been in when Hudson was taken. Her posture was upright, almost rigid, her hands clasped tightly together. She had not cried. Not yet.

Jerry stood close beside her, shifting nervously, his face pale. "They had guns," he said again, his voice low. "Big guns."

No one corrected him.

The sound of an engine broke through the quiet as Theo's truck rolled into the lot. It slowed as he took in the group, the silence, the way no one moved toward him. Misty saw it at the same time he did.

Something was wrong.

Theo stepped out of the truck. "What happened."

Tony didn't soften it. "Bruce's men came last night. They took Hudson."

Theo stopped where he stood. "What."

Stephanie nodded, her voice controlled. "They surrounded us. Five of them. Rifles. Tactical gear. Jordy. Sloan. Two others. Pickle was with them."

Misty's expression shifted. "Pickle."

Dwight nodded grimly. "He'll do anything for Bruce. Always has."

Theo ran a hand across his face, trying to put it together. "We left early. Still dark. Everything looked normal on the road. But Pickle wasn't at his shack."

Misty nodded slowly. "That stood out. He's always there."

Tony glanced toward the road. "He wasn't there because he was helping with the abduction."

Stephanie's voice stayed steady. "They moved fast. Hudson didn't fight. He knew someone would get shot if he did."

Jerry nodded quickly, the memory still fresh. "They grabbed him and pushed him into the truck. Just like that."

Dwight added, "They had angles on all of us. One wrong move and we would have lost people."

Theo looked toward the empty road leading back to Bruceville, his focus sharpening. "That's where they took him."

Tony gave a single nod. "That's where he is."

Silence followed.

It settled heavier this time, not shock anymore, but something else beginning to take shape.

Moses spoke into it. "That man just crossed a line."

Dwight didn't hesitate. "He sure did."

Stephanie lifted her head, her voice calm but unshakable. "We're getting him back."

Kmart Loading Dock, Three Hours Later

The group gathered near the loading dock entrance of the Kmart, using the concrete overhang for shade and a sense of cover. The open parking lot stretched out around them, empty except for their vehicles and scattered debris left behind by a world that no longer existed.

Tony leaned against one of the pillars with his arms folded, his eyes fixed somewhere beyond the lot as he worked through the problem. Moses sat on an overturned crate with his elbows on his knees, staring at the ground in quiet concentration. Dwight paced slowly, stopping now and then to glance toward the road that led back to Bruceville, as if expecting something to come from it.

Stephanie stood nearby with Jerry beside her, one hand resting lightly on his shoulder. Shadoe sat at her feet, ears up, reading the tension in the air better than any of them.

Theo and Misty joined the group, both carrying the weight of what they had been told.

Tony spoke first. "We are going to have to fight."

No one argued.

Dwight nodded once. "That's where I landed."

Moses lifted his head. "We can't rush in blind. Bruce has numbers, weapons, and position. If we go in without a plan, we lose before we start."

Stephanie's voice cut through the air, steady but tight. "Hudson is probably tied to that tree."

The words settled heavily over the group.

Tony met her eyes. "Yeah. I'm thinking that."

Jerry swallowed hard. "They're hurting him."

Stephanie tightened her hand gently on his shoulder. "We're going to fix it."

Theo stepped forward slightly. "Then we do it right. We need information. How many men he has, where they're placed, and who is actually loyal to him."

Misty nodded. "And who isn't."

A voice came from the edge of the loading dock.

"I can help with that."

Every head turned at once.

Omar stepped out from behind one of the concrete pillars, his hands raised slightly, not in surrender but enough to show he wasn't reaching for anything.

Theo's eyes narrowed immediately. "You followed us."

Omar shook his head. "No. I came here on my own. I didn't know you two were here."

Dwight stopped pacing and faced him fully. "Then explain why you're here. And be real clear about it."

Omar looked at each of them before answering. "Because Bruce is dangerous. And what he's doing to Hudson isn't right."

Tony didn't move from where he stood. "That's not enough of a reason to trust you."

"I'm not asking you to trust me," Omar said. "I'm telling you what I know."

Stephanie stepped forward slightly. "Then start talking."

Omar nodded once. "Bruce has six men that are fully with him. Jordy, Sloan, Mitchell, and Pickle. The other two were deputies before everything fell apart. They know how to handle weapons and they follow orders."

Moses leaned forward slightly. "And Gideon."

Omar hesitated just long enough to matter. "Gideon is close to Bruce now. He listens to him. But he's not like the others. He's not violent unless he feels like he has to be."

Dwight absorbed that. "Weapons."

"Mostly rifles," Omar said. "Some body armor from the sheriff's department. Helmets. They keep most of it in Bruce's garage."

Tony's focus sharpened. "And Hudson."

"They'll keep him at the tree," Omar said. "At least for now. Bruce wants people to see it. He thinks it keeps control."

Stephanie's jaw tightened, "I knew that sick monster would tie him to that damn tree."

Tony studied Omar carefully. "And why are you helping us."

Omar didn't look away this time. "Because Julian didn't leave."

The group went still.

Omar lowered his voice. "I know it. I didn't see him leave. No one did. And Bruce doesn't let people walk away from him."

That was enough.

Moses nodded once. "Alright."

Tony pushed off the pillar and stepped forward. "Then you're in this with us."

Omar gave a small nod. "I am."

Dwight moved closer, the pacing gone now, replaced with focus. Theo and Misty stepped in as well. The circle tightened.

Stephanie stayed beside Jerry, but her attention locked in.

Tony spoke, his voice calm and direct. "We move tonight. Fast and quiet. Surprise is the only advantage we've got. We hit hard, pull Hudson out, and take control of the situation before Bruce can react."

Moses nodded. "We need to split assignments. Entry, extraction, and containment."

Dwight added, "And we need to know who we don't shoot. Not everyone up there is the enemy."

Theo looked at Omar. "You'll guide us in."

"I will," Omar said.

Tony glanced around the group, making sure everyone understood what this meant.

"This doesn't go halfway," he said. "Once we start, we finish it."

Moses gave a small smile. "Times like this, I remember you were a Marine."

Tony shrugged slightly. "Once a Marine, always a Marine. We don't retire. We just get older."

That drew a few small smiles, but they didn't last long.

Shadoe stood suddenly, tail stiff, his attention fixed on the dark edge of the lot. The shift in the group had changed something.

They all felt it.

The line had been crossed.

And now they were moving toward it together.

Bruceville, Afternoon

The mansion was quiet in the afternoon light, the kind of quiet that came from people staying where they were told to stay.

Bruce stood near the window in the main room, looking out over the community. From here, he could see the open park, the tree at its center, and the slow movement of people trying to go about their day while pretending nothing had changed.

Behind him, Sloan stepped into the room and closed the door.

For a moment, neither of them spoke.

Bruce didn't turn around. "He's still refusing."

Sloan nodded once. "Didn't expect anything different."

Bruce shifted slightly, his hands resting behind his back. "The goal is simple. We get him to turn the power on. However that happens, it happens."

Sloan leaned against the wall, arms relaxed but his attention sharp. "And if he doesn't."

Bruce finally turned. "Then we do it ourselves."

He let that settle before continuing.

"Either way, by tomorrow, this community has power."

Sloan gave a faint nod. "And Hudson."

Bruce's expression didn't change. "He's already made his decision."

Sloan understood immediately. There was no hesitation in him when he answered. "Then I don't have a problem finishing it."

Bruce studied him for a moment, as if confirming something he already believed. "Good."

Sloan pushed off the wall and stepped closer. "He's too full of himself anyway. Walks around like he's the only one who knows anything. Like everything depends on him."

Bruce gave a small, controlled smile. "That's the problem. He thinks he's important."

Sloan nodded. "He carries it. You can see it in how he talks. How he looks at people. Like he's above it."

Bruce turned slightly, looking back toward the window. "People like that forget something important."

"What's that," Sloan asked.

"They only matter as long as they're useful."

The room went quiet again for a moment.

Then Bruce spoke, his tone shifting, more measured now. "We're not like that."

Sloan shook his head. "No."

"We serve the community," Bruce continued. "Everything we do is for them."

Sloan nodded in agreement. "Always."

Bruce glanced back at him. "That's why this works. People trust leadership when leadership puts them first."

Sloan gave a faint smile. "And when leadership is willing to do what needs to be done."

Bruce didn't respond to that directly, but he didn't disagree.

His attention shifted again, this time more focused.

"There's something else."

Sloan's posture changed slightly. "The RV group."

Bruce nodded. "They're a problem."

"They'll come for him," Sloan said.

"Yes," Bruce replied. "And we don't let that happen."

Sloan waited.

Bruce continued, calm and deliberate. "In the morning, after we deal with Hudson, you, Jordy, and Mitchell go down there."

Sloan understood exactly what that meant. "You want it clean."

"I prefer it quiet," Bruce said. "But I'm not concerned with how it gets done. Just that it gets done."

Sloan gave a single nod. "It will."

Bruce stepped closer, lowering his voice slightly. "If the community asks questions, we give them an answer they can accept."

Sloan's expression didn't change. "They attacked first."

Bruce nodded. "They were informed Hudson was executed for betrayal. They reacted. We defended ourselves."

Sloan almost smiled. "The sheep will accept it, even if they question it."

"It doesn't have to be perfect," Bruce said. "It just has to be enough."

Sloan turned slightly, already thinking ahead. "Timing."

"Morning," Bruce said. "After Hudson."

Sloan nodded again. "I'll get Jordy and Mitchell ready."

Bruce looked past him toward the door, then back to the window.

"By this time tomorrow," he said, almost to himself, "this place is stable again."

Sloan didn't question it.

He opened the door and stepped out, leaving Bruce alone in the quiet room.

Bruce stood there a moment longer, looking out over the community he believed he controlled.

In his mind, everything was already decided.

Community Center, Evening

The community gathered near the tree, no one lingered near the front. People stood back, forming a loose circle with space between them and the platform. Conversations were low and brief.

Hudson stood at the base of the tree, his hands bound behind him. His shoulders were squared, but the strain showed in the way he held his breath a second too long and the tension that stayed locked in his jaw. Blood had dried along his lip, and the cut on his cheek had darkened as the air cooled.

Bruce stepped forward slowly, taking his time, making sure every eye followed him.

But before he addressed the crowd, he stopped in front of Hudson.

Close enough that no one else could hear.

For a moment, he just looked at him.

"I didn't trust you the moment I met you," Bruce said quietly. "Not at that dinner. Not for a second."

Hudson met his eyes, saying nothing.

Bruce continued, his tone calm and controlled. "You walked in like you already knew how things should work. Like you were evaluating everything. People like that are a problem."

Hudson let a breath out slowly. "First thing I thought when I met you at that dinner," he said, just as quietly, "was that you were either in prison when the flu hit, or you had just gotten out."

Bruce's expression didn't change right away.

But something behind his eyes shifted.

Hudson kept going. "The skin tone gave it away first. You've got that look. Not enough sun. Not enough time outside. But it wasn't just that."

Bruce didn't interrupt.

"It was how you carry yourself," Hudson said. "The way you talk. The way you watch people. I've been around enough of it to recognize it. Long-term incarceration leaves a mark. You don't lose it."

Bruce's jaw tightened slightly.

"You don't know anything about me," he said.

Hudson gave the smallest shake of his head. "I know enough."

A brief silence passed between them.

Then Hudson added, almost evenly, "Looks like I hit a nerve."

Bruce leaned in just slightly, his voice dropping lower.

"Be quiet," he said. "If you know what's best for you, you stop talking right now."

Hudson held his gaze.

But he didn't say anything else.

Bruce straightened, the moment closing as quickly as it had opened. Whatever had passed between them stayed there, unseen by the crowd but felt in the shift of tension.

Then Bruce turned away from Hudson and faced the community.

His voice rose, controlled and clear.

"Let's try this again," he said calmly. "Will you turn the power on."

Hudson met his eyes. "No."

Bruce didn't react immediately. He gave a small nod, as if acknowledging the answer rather than resisting it.

Then he stepped slightly to the side.

"Sloan."

Sloan moved without hesitation. His fist drove hard into Hudson's midsection, the impact sharp and controlled. Hudson folded forward, the air leaving him in a sudden rush as his body tried to recover.

The crowd shifted.

No one stepped forward.

Hudson stayed bent for a moment, pulling air back into his lungs, forcing himself upright again. His breathing was uneven, but his eyes lifted back to Bruce.

Bruce waited until Hudson was steady.

"Will you turn the power on," he asked again, his tone unchanged.

Hudson shook his head once. "No."

Bruce gave another small nod.

"Jordy."

Jordy stepped in and struck Hudson across the mouth. The sound carried. Hudson's head snapped slightly to the side, and a thin line of blood appeared along his lip before running down his chin.

A few people in the crowd looked away.

Hudson swallowed, straightened again, and faced Bruce.

Bruce studied him for a moment, then stepped closer.

"One more time," he said quietly. "Will you turn the power on."

Hudson didn't hesitate. "No."

Bruce reached into his coat slowly, deliberately, and pulled out a knife.

The movement drew the crowd's full attention.

He stepped close enough that Hudson could feel the presence of him without touching. The blade came up slowly, stopping just in front of Hudson's eye. Bruce moved it slightly, not enough to cut, but enough to make the point clear.

Hudson didn't flinch.

The knife hovered there for a moment, the silence stretching across the entire space.

Then Bruce lowered it.

In one quick motion, he dragged the blade across Hudson's cheek, opening a shallow cut. Blood surfaced immediately, running down along the side of his face.

Bruce stepped back.

"Will you turn my power on," he said, louder now.

Hudson's voice was steady despite the blood and the pain. "No."

The answer landed harder than anything else.

Bruce turned away from him then, shifting his focus to the crowd. His voice rose, not shouting, but carrying clearly.

"You all heard him," he said. "Hudson has made his decision."

No one spoke.

No one moved.

Bruce let the silence sit, then continued.

"In the morning, I will ask him one more time. One last opportunity to do what is right for this community."

He paused, letting his eyes move across the faces in front of him.

"If his answer is still no, he will be executed."

The words settled heavily over the group.

"And I will turn the power on myself."

Bruce's gaze hardened slightly as he looked over them.

"This community will move forward. With or without him."

He stepped back toward the platform.

"Return to your homes," he said. "All of you. Stay there until morning."

This time, people moved.

Slowly at first, then more steadily. No one argued. No one questioned it. They turned and walked away in small groups, voices quiet, heads lowered.

Hudson remained at the tree.

Bruce watched them go, his expression calm again, as if everything had returned to order.

But the silence that followed was different now.

It wasn't obedience.

It was something else.

Kmart, Night

Night settled heavy over the Kmart parking lot, the wide stretch of asphalt reflecting faint starlight. The RVs sat quiet in their usual positions, but nothing about the camp felt normal anymore.

Hudson was gone.

The absence felt physical, something that could be felt in the air between them.

Tony stood near the folding table with a hunting rifle leaning against his leg. Dwight checked shells beside him, working methodically and without wasted motion. Moses sorted gear with practiced efficiency, laying out flashlights, extra ammunition, and knives wrapped in cloth to keep them quiet.

Stephanie stood near the fire pit with her arms folded tightly across her chest, her eyes fixed somewhere beyond the camp. Theo and Misty moved between the vehicles, gathering supplies and checking equipment one last time.

Mae stepped out of one of the RVs, concern written plainly across her face. "Tell me what the plan is," she said.

Tony looked at her. "You are staying here."

Mae opened her mouth to argue, but Dwight spoke first. "We need someone here. If Hudson comes back injured, or if anything goes wrong, we need medical help ready. That is you."

She hesitated, weighing it.

Moses added gently, "You are just as important here as we are there."

Mae let out a slow breath and nodded. "Alright. But you bring him back."

"We will," Tony said.

Jerry stood nearby with Shadoe, watching the preparations with wide, anxious eyes. "I'm going too. He's my friend," he said suddenly.

Tony stepped over and knelt in front of him. "No," he said calmly. "You have a very important job here."

Jerry frowned. "What job."

"You protect Mae," Tony said. "And you protect Shadoe. If something happens here, you are the one in charge."

Jerry straightened slightly, the weight of it settling on him. "I protect them," he repeated.

Dwight nodded firmly. "That's right."

Jerry looked down at Shadoe, then back up. "I can do that."

"We know you can," Tony said.

A few moments later, Omar emerged from the darkness, moving quickly but carefully between the vehicles. Theo met him first.

"You made it."

Omar nodded. "Barely. Bruce ordered everyone to stay inside their homes until morning."

"Tell us everything."

Omar leaned over the table and traced the layout with his hand as he spoke. "Sloan and Jordy were near the community center when I left, both armed with rifles and sidearms. Mitchell was moving between the houses and the tree with a shotgun. Pickle was at the guard shack earlier, but after Hudson was tied up, he started rotating watch."

He paused briefly before continuing. "There are two former police officers with Bruce, Chris and Jason. Both carrying handguns and rifles. They know tactics. They are the most dangerous."

Dwight nodded slowly. "Good to know."

Theo looked at him. "Did you see Gideon."

Omar shook his head. "No. I assume he is at his house."

Tony crossed his arms, thinking it through. "When is the best time."

Omar answered without hesitation. "Before dawn. Around four in the morning."

"Why then," Moses asked.

"Because exhaustion hits hardest right before sunrise," Omar said. "They will have been awake most of the night. Early on, they are alert. Later, they get tired. That is when mistakes happen."

Dwight nodded. "He's right."

Tony looked around the group, making sure everyone was with him. "We go in at four."

Stephanie stepped forward. "I'm coming."

Tony started to object, but Theo spoke first. "She needs to. Hudson will respond when he hears her voice."

Tony exhaled slowly, then nodded. "Alright. But you stay behind us unless we say otherwise."

She nodded without hesitation.

Weapons were distributed quietly. Hunting rifles. Shotguns. Handguns checked and loaded. Flashlights wrapped to dull the beams. Every movement was controlled, deliberate.

Dwight slung his rifle over his shoulder. "I never thought I would be doing this again at my age," he muttered.

Moses gave a faint smile. "Life has a way of bringing things back around."

Tony looked at Omar. "Once this starts, there is no going back."

Omar nodded. "I know."

Tony turned to Mae and Jerry. "Lock the RV doors after we leave. No lights. No noise. If we are not back by sunrise, you stay put until we return."

Mae stepped forward and gripped Tony's arm. "Bring him home," she said quietly.

Tony nodded. "We will."

Jerry knelt beside Shadoe and wrapped his arms around the dog's neck. "Stay with me," he whispered.

The German shepherd pressed against him, sensing the shift in the air.

Tony looked around one last time, taking in each face.

The weight of what was coming settled over them all.

They understood the truth.

By morning, some of them would not be coming back.

Thirty-Two

War!

Kmart, Before Sunrise, 1988

The sky over the Kmart parking lot was still dark, a deep blue that had not yet surrendered to morning. A thin line of pale gray rested low on the horizon, promising sunrise but not delivering it yet. The air felt cool and heavy, carrying the quiet that comes before something important happens.

Two trucks idled near the edge of the lot with their headlights off.

Near the RVs, Mae stood beside Jerry and Shadoe. The German Shepherd paced in a slow circle, sensing tension that the humans were trying to hide. His ears stayed upright, alert to every sound.

Jerry shifted his weight nervously but forced his shoulders back.

"Don't worry, Mae," he said. "I will protect you and Shadoe if anyone comes."

His voice trembled just slightly, but his eyes were serious.

Mae saw both the fear and the courage. She placed a gentle hand on his arm.

"You are doing exactly what we need," she said. "Guard duty is serious work. You stay alert, keep Shadoe close, and you keep this place safe."

Jerry nodded quickly.

"I can do that," he said. "I will not let anything happen."

Shadoe pressed lightly against Jerry's leg as if agreeing with the responsibility.

Across the lot, Theo finished loading gear into the back of his truck. Misty stood beside him checking a shotgun. Dwight and Moses spoke quietly near the tailgate, their voices low and focused.

In the second truck, Omar slid behind the wheel while Tony climbed into the passenger seat. Stephanie moved toward the rear door but paused for a moment, looking back toward Mae and Jerry.

Mae walked over to her.

"You stay close to the others," Mae said softly. "And you bring him home."

Stephanie nodded, emotion tightening her throat.

"I will," she said.

Tony leaned out of the truck window. "We approach from the far side of the golf course," he said quietly to the group. "No headlights once we leave the road. We park out of sight and move on foot."

Theo nodded from his truck. "We get eyes on them before anything else."

"Exactly," Tony replied. "No rushing. We identify positions first."

Stephanie climbed into the truck, gripping her weapon tighter than usual.

This was not just a rescue mission for her.

This was Hudson.

Theo started his engine first. The low rumble sounded loud in the quiet morning air. Omar followed a second later.

Mae stepped back beside Jerry as the trucks began to roll.

"Eyes open," she reminded him.

Jerry nodded firmly. "Yes ma'am."

Golf Course, Before Sunrise

The trucks rolled to a slow stop along the far edge of the golf course where the terrain dipped slightly and a line of trees provided cover. Engines shut down almost at the same moment. The sudden silence felt heavy after the low rumble of travel.

Doors opened carefully.

No one spoke above a whisper.

Theo motioned with two fingers, and the group moved out across the grass. The ground was damp with morning dew, soaking the cuffs of their pants as they walked. Ahead, the large homes of Bruceville rose against the faint glow of early dawn, their outlines dark and still.

Stephanie stayed close to Tony as they approached the first row of houses. Dwight moved slightly to their left while Moses and Omar angled toward a position that would give them a view of the mansion. Theo and Misty remained farther out in the open field, watching the spaces between homes where anyone might appear unexpectedly.

They reached the shadows behind a hedge line and dropped low.

Tony raised binoculars slowly and looked toward the center of the community.

The torch illuminated torture tree.

Hudson.

Even from this distance they could see his shape tied upright against the trunk.

Tony lowered the glasses and passed them to Stephanie. Her hands trembled slightly as she lifted them.

"He's still alive," she whispered.

Tony nodded.

Dwight studied the area carefully. "Mitchell is at the table."

Sure enough, Mitchell sat slouched in a chair facing the tree. His rifle rested across his lap. His head dipped forward once, then jerked back up.

Sleepy.

Not alert.

Moses shifted his attention toward the mansion.

"Back doors," he murmured.

Chris stood near one entrance, Jason near the other. Both armed. Both awake. Their posture showed discipline compared to Mitchell's fatigue.

Omar pointed quietly toward the guard booth.

Pickle was pacing a slow line between the booth and the tree. Every few minutes he stopped, rubbed his face, then continued walking. When he reached the booth he opened the door, stepped inside, and sat down for a moment before rising again.

"He's tired," Omar whispered. "Not paying attention."

Tony nodded slightly.

"Jordy or Sloan?" Dwight asked.

Theo scanned the homes again. "Not visible. Could be anywhere."

That uncertainty hung over the group.

Tony studied Pickle's pattern another moment.

"When he sits," Tony said quietly, "that's the window."

Omar understood immediately.

"I can reach him without being seen," Omar said. "From the back side of the booth."

Tony met his eyes. "Quiet."

Omar nodded once.

"Quiet."

Positions formed quickly after that.

Tony and Dwight set up with a clear line toward the tree where Hudson was tied. Stephanie stayed near Tony, ready to move the moment an opening appeared. Moses positioned himself with Omar's original angle toward the mansion so they could watch Chris and Jason.

Out in the field, Theo and Misty took positions where they could see movement from any of the surrounding homes. If Jordy or Sloan appeared, they would be the first to know.

Everyone settled into place.

No one spoke.

The faint light of dawn crept slowly across the rooftops as they waited.

Pickle reached the booth again.

Opened the door.

Stepped inside.

And sat down.

Tony glanced at Omar.

Omar moved.

Omar moved low along the back side of the homes, keeping close to fences and landscaping that broke up his outline. Every step was slow and deliberate. The faint light of dawn helped him just enough to see without needing artificial light, but the shadows still worked in his favor.

Ahead, the guard booth came into view.

Pickle sat inside with his head tipped back against the wall, rifle resting loosely across his knees. His eyes were closed. Exhaustion had finally caught up with him.

Omar slipped behind the booth where the thin siding blocked the view from the tree and the mansion. He paused, listening.

No voices.

No movement.

He reached the door handle and pulled it open just enough to slide inside.

Pickle's eyes opened halfway.

Recognition flashed.

"Omar?"

That was all he managed to say.

Omar moved fast and silent.

Seconds later, Pickle slumped forward, motionless.

Omar eased him down carefully so nothing would fall or make noise. He stepped back out of the booth, closed the door, and disappeared into the shadows the same way he had come.

Within moments he was back beside Moses.

"Done," he whispered.

Tony did not look at him. His attention remained locked on Mitchell.

The moment had arrived.

Tony exhaled slowly and squeezed the trigger.

The rifle cracked across the quiet community.

Mitchell jerked violently in his chair and fell backward onto the pavement, the chair tipping with him. His rifle clattered beside him.

For a split second, everything froze.

Then chaos erupted.

Chris and Jason reacted instantly.

Both men moved toward each other on the back deck near the mansion doors, shouting quick words Tony could not hear from the distance.

Jason moved into the shadows, heading toward the tree.

Chris stayed near the back entrance.

From the left side of the neighborhood, a door burst open.

Jordy.

He stepped out with a rifle already in his hands, scanning the area wildly.

“Sloan,” Jordy shouted. “We got movement.”

But Sloan did not appear.

The mansion door opened again.

Bruce stepped onto the deck beside Chris, confusion and anger on his face.

“What's happening,” Bruce demanded.

At that exact moment Omar fired.

The shot cracked past Bruce’s shoulder and struck the siding behind him.

Bruce froze for half a heartbeat.

Then instinct took over.

He dove back inside the house.

The door slammed.

From inside they heard his voice, loud and furious.

“Find them,” Bruce shouted. “Kill them all.”

"Sloane, protect the front of the house, people are trying to assassinate me. Do your job."

The stillness of stealth was gone.

War had begun.

Torture Tree, Before Sunrise

The moment Mitchell hit the ground, Stephanie moved.

Tony saw her break from cover and sprint toward the tree before he could say a word. Dwight swore under his breath and shifted his aim to cover her path.

Hudson lifted his head as she reached him.

His eyes widened.

"What are you doing," he said hoarsely. "You're going to get yourself killed."

Stephanie dropped to her knees beside him, already pulling a knife from her belt.

"I'm getting you out of here," she said.

The rope around his wrists was thick and pulled tight. She pressed the blade against it and began sawing.

It barely made progress.

"Hurry," Hudson said quietly. "They are going to see you."

Tony fired a controlled shot toward the mansion deck to keep Chris pinned down. Dwight shifted his aim toward the left side of the houses where Jordy had appeared.

Movement.

Theo saw it first from his position in the field.

Jordy advancing.

Theo fired.

The muzzle flash gave away his location instantly. Jordy dropped behind the edge of a house wall, then leaned out and returned fire.

The shot cracked across the open space.

Theo jerked backward and fell onto the grass, severely wounded.

Misty screamed his name.

She raised her rifle and fired toward Jordy's position, but her shot went wide, striking siding several feet from him.

Jordy moved fast.

He disappeared around the side of the house, using the structure to break line of sight. Misty tried to reposition, but she was too exposed.

Jordy came around behind her.

Two shots.

Misty dropped where she stood.

Back at the tree, Stephanie was still cutting.

The rope fibers were fraying slowly, but not fast enough.

Hudson's voice grew more urgent. "Stephanie, you have to move."

Footsteps approached.

Stephanie turned her head just in time to see Deanna running toward them.

In her hands was a machete.

"This will work better," Deanna said breathlessly. "Move your hands."

Stephanie shifted aside while Deanna swung.

The blade struck the rope hard.

Once.

Twice.

Fibers snapped.

Nearby, Jordy after circling back, fired a finishing shot into Theo, then began moving back toward the tree.

Tony shouted. "Move. Move now."

Deanna swung again.

The rope gave way.

Hudson sagged forward as his arms came free. He nearly collapsed, but Stephanie caught him under one shoulder.

"I can't feel my hands," he muttered.

"You're alive," Stephanie said. "That's enough."

Deanna grabbed his other side.

"Come," she said. "My house."

They moved as quickly as Hudson's weakened legs allowed, half dragging, half carrying him across the yard and toward Deanna's front door.

Behind them, gunfire continued to crack through the neighborhood.

Inside the house, Olivia crouched behind a couch, eyes wide with fear.

Deanna shoved the door closed and locked it.

"You are safe," she told Hudson.

For the moment, it was true.

Outside, the war continued.

Bruceville, Before Sunrise

Jason had been moving toward the tree when the shot near the mansion changed everything.

He pivoted instantly.

If attackers were near the house, that was the real threat.

He slipped into the shadows along the side of a hedge line, circling wide, trying to come up behind Omar's position. His steps were quiet, controlled. He almost made it.

Almost.

Moses saw him first.

A flicker of movement that did not belong.

"Jason," Moses muttered under his breath.

Jason raised his weapon at nearly the same moment.

Moses fired first.

The blast caught Jason square in the chest. Jason staggered backward and collapsed onto the grass, rifle falling from his hands.

Omar exhaled sharply.

"Thank you," he said.

But the shot had given away their position.

From the mansion deck, Chris leaned out just enough to fire.

The round struck Moses before anyone could react.

Moses dropped instantly.

Omar shouted his name, but there was no response.

Chris shifted again to fire a second shot.

That movement exposed him.

Omar fired.

Chris jerked backward and crumpled onto the deck beside the doorway, motionless.

For a brief moment, silence settled over that part of the battlefield.

Then Tony and Dwight reached Omar's position.

Tony looked down at Moses.

His jaw tightened.

"Bastards," Tony said quietly. "We finish this."

Behind them, the cost of the conflict was becoming clear.

Pickle dead.

Mitchell dead.

Jason dead.

Chris dead.

Misty dead.

Moses dead.

Theo dead.

Inside the mansion, events unfolded very differently.

The moment the first gunshot cracked through the morning air, Paula ran to Ester's room.

"You have to come with me," Paula said urgently. "Now."

Ester clutched the baby against her chest. "What's happening."

"Hudson's people," Paula said. "They're here."

She pulled open the closet door in the master bedroom and revealed the hidden safe room behind it.

"There," Paula said. "Inside."

They stepped into the reinforced space, and Paula locked the door from the inside.

"This lock only works from in here," Paula said quickly. "No one can open it from outside."

Ester nodded, holding the baby tightly.

"It will keep us safe," Ester whispered.

Outside the room, Bruce moved very differently.

He had rushed to the back door when the shooting began, shouting toward Chris.

"Chris," Bruce called. "Did you get any of them."

A voice answered faintly.

"Yeah, I got..."

Bruce frowned.

"What did you say," he called.

He cracked the door open just enough to see the deck.

Chris lay on his back, staring into the sky. Blood was pooling quickly.

Bruce slammed the door shut.

"Incompetence surrounds me," he muttered.

Instead of going outside, he turned and hurried toward the front of the house.

At the front window, Sloan stood watching through a narrow gap in the curtain.

"Chris is down," Bruce said. "What do we do."

Sloan kept his rifle ready.

"We stay inside," Sloan said calmly. "The guys will handle it. If not, I will make sure no one gets in."

Bruce nodded quickly.

"Yes," he said. "Yes. That's right."

Outside, Tony and Dwight joined Omar near Moses's body.

They had seen Stephanie and Hudson reach Deanna's house.

For now, Hudson was safe.

Tony looked toward the mansion.

"Time to end this," he said.

Across the neighborhood, Jordy had also seen Hudson enter Deanna's home.

His face twisted with anger.

"I knew she was a traitor," he muttered. "Should have removed her before she became dangerous. Her and that sniveling kid."

He turned and ran toward his own house.

Bruceville, Sunrise

Back inside the safe room, Paula and Ester sat in the dim quiet with the baby.

Paula gave a small nervous laugh.

"Bruce never told me about this place," she said. "I found it exploring. When you live in a big house with nothing to do, you learn every corner."

She tapped the lock lightly.

"It's all locked up," she said. "Bruce will be in for a surprise."

Ester nodded.

"Thank goodness," she said.

Paula listened to the distant gunfire echoing through the neighborhood.

"I think Hudson's friends are taking exception to Bruce kidnapping him," Paula said.

Ester looked down at her child.

"I hope so," she whispered.

Paula nodded slowly.

"It's time somebody stopped Bruce," she said.

Jordy moved quickly through his own home, grabbing the large keyring from the table where Bruce had insisted it always remain. Every house in Bruceville. Every door. Control over everyone.

He stepped outside and crossed the yard toward Deanna's home.

The fighting sounds echoed faintly across the neighborhood, but this part of the street felt strangely still. Jordy reached the back door, slid the correct key into the lock, and turned it slowly.

The door opened without a sound.

Inside, he paused, listening.

Voices.

Hudson and Deanna.

Jordy's jaw tightened when he heard Hudson speaking.

"Bruce has to be dealt with tonight," Hudson said. "He already decided to execute me. That's not something you come back from."

Jordy felt anger rise in his chest.

Bruce had given him purpose.

Bruce had protected him.

Bruce had made him important.

He moved deeper into the house, rifle ready.

Stephanie had just come down from checking on Olivia when she heard the faint movement near the hallway. She froze and leaned slightly around the corner.

Jordy stood there, focused toward the voices ahead.

He had not seen her.

Stephanie raised her handgun.

"Jordy," she said firmly. "I have you in my sight. Drop it now. Don't do anything stupid."

Jordy turned slowly, surprise flickering across his face.

"Come on, Stephanie," he said. "You try to pretend you are a tough cookie, but I don't believe you're a killer. It takes a lot to actually pull that trigger and take a life."

Stephanie did not lower the weapon.

"Are you saying you have killed before," she asked. "Maybe Julian."

Jordy shook his head quickly.

"Oh no," he said. "Do not pin that on me. Sloan killed him. Only after Bruce told him to. I had nothing to do with that. I wanted him released. I thought that other guy should have been released too, but you know how Bruce is."

Stephanie's voice hardened.

"That other guy had a name. Dougie. He deserved to live."

By then Hudson and Deanna had stepped into the hallway behind Stephanie.

Jordy glanced between them.

"I'm going to put this down," he said. "Just don't shoot me."

He bent slightly, lowering his rifle toward the floor.

Quickly, he reached inside his boot, pulling out a small .38 snubnose.

He moved fast.

The silver revolver started to rise.

Stephanie fired first.

The shot echoed through the house.

Jordy staggered backward and collapsed onto the floor, the revolver falling from his hands. He gasped.

"You didn't have to shoot me, we could have been friends before."

He coughed up blood, inhaled a shallow breath, then expired.

Upstairs, Olivia screamed.

Deanna rushed past Hudson toward the staircase.

"It's okay," she called upward. "It's okay, honey."

Stephanie stood frozen, her hands trembling violently, the gun still pointed toward where Jordy had fallen.

Hudson stepped forward slowly and placed his hand on her shoulder.

"You had to do it," he said quietly. "Do not beat yourself up. He would have killed all of us."

Stephanie shook her head, tears forming.

"I've never done anything like that," she said. "It's not right to be in this position. I blame Bruce."

Hudson nodded once.

"So do I," he said.

Footsteps approached outside.

Tony entered the house moments later, breathing hard but controlled.

"The sun is coming up," he said. "We have Bruce in his house. Sloan is believed to be inside with him. No one else outside."

Hudson looked toward the door.

Then back at Stephanie.

"It's almost over," he said.

But everyone in the room knew the hardest part was still ahead.

The Mansion, Sunrise

Tony crouched near the corner of the mansion, breathing steady, watching the windows for movement. Hudson stood beside him, still weak but upright, his face tight with focus. Stephanie and Omar positioned themselves where they could see both the front entrance and the side of the house.

Tony spoke quietly.

"Bruce and Sloan are still inside," he said. "No movement out here. That means this ends here."

Hudson nodded once.

"We try talking first," he said. "There are innocent people in that house."

Stephanie glanced toward the upstairs windows.

"Paula and Ester," she said. "And the baby."

Hudson looked at Omar.

"You're the one Sloan might listen to," Hudson said. "Try."

Omar moved forward into the yard, stopping behind a low stone planter that gave him partial cover.

"Sloan," he called out. "I know you're inside. I'm guessing you are near the front door. Bruce is not worth dying over."

Inside the mansion, Sloan stood near the front window with his rifle ready. Bruce paced behind him.

"Sloan, it's your job to keep me safe," Bruce said. "These people want to destroy what we built."

Sloan kept his eyes on the curtains.

"We're not in great shape," Sloan said calmly. "This house has windows everywhere. Back doors. Too many angles. I'm one man."

Bruce shook his head.

"We have Ester and the infant," he said. "They will not risk hurting them."

Sloan gave a small sigh.

"Sometimes you realize when it's time to negotiate," Sloan said.

Bruce snapped.

"It's not your job to negotiate," he said. "It's your job to protect me and dispose of anyone who comes after me. Remember that."

Outside, Omar continued.

"You have a choice," Omar called. "Drop your weapons, open the door, and walk out. I promise we will let you leave this area and start over. That is more than you gave Julian."

Sloan hesitated.

"You forget," Sloan called back. "We have three hostages that guarantee Bruce and I leave safely."

Omar shook his head.

"No," he said. "Bruce will not be leaving. Only you get that option."

Bruce leaned toward Sloan and spoke quickly.

"Tell them no deal," Bruce said. "Tell them I will allow Hudson and his friends to live here. I will make this place a democracy. People will vote and I will respect it. I made mistakes but I'm still a good leader."

Sloan began repeating the offer through the door while Bruce quietly slipped away toward the stairs.

Upstairs, Bruce hurried into his bedroom and opened the closet that hid the safe room.

He tried the handle.

Locked.

His face twisted.

He rushed to Ester's room.

Empty.

"Paula," he called toward his bedroom door. "I know you're in there. Unlock it. Let me in, I'm the only one that can protect you."

From inside the safe room, Paula's voice came back calm and steady.

"We hear you, Bruce," she said. "But Ester and I are safe. You might think about negotiating."

Bruce's anger flared.

"Those crazed people will kill all of us including you," he said.

Ester answered softly.

"We will take our chances," she said.

Back outside, Tony and Dwight moved toward the rear deck while Omar continued keeping Sloan focused at the front.

Dwight smashed a window near the back door with the butt of his rifle.

Glass shattered loudly.

Inside, Sloan turned his head toward the noise.

"I heard the window break," Sloan called. "You come in and I start shooting."

Sloan moved upstairs, where he had heard the deck doors window broken.

Omar answered calmly.

"Too many people are coming inside," he said. "You might hit someone, and if that happens, we'll have no choice but to take you out."

The broken window had been a diversion.

While Sloan had retreated, Omar smashed the front window and slipped inside, unlocking the door for Hudson.

Stephanie broke a side window and stayed outside watching for movement.

Hudson entered cautiously with his handgun raised.

The downstairs was empty.

"Omar," Hudson whispered. "Where."

"Upstairs," Omar said quietly.

They paused near the base of the staircase.

Hudson spoke low. "We can't rush that. He will have the angle."

Omar nodded.

"I make noise here," Omar said. "You get Dwight and be ready at the back. We hit him from two directions."

Hudson slipped outside to relay the plan.

Moments later, Omar slammed a chair against the wall at the bottom of the stairs.

The crash echoed through the house.

Sloan moved instantly.

But he had anticipated the back entry.

When Dwight came through the rear opening, Sloan fired first. The shot hit clean, and Dwight dropped hard to the floor. Hudson reacted without hesitation, bringing his weapon up as Sloan fired again. This time the shot went wide, grazing Hudson's ear, while Hudson's return shot found its mark.

Sloan jerked backward, his rifle slipping from his hands as he fell against the stair railing and slid to the floor.

Silence filled the house except for heavy breathing.

Hudson approached slowly.

"We didn't want to have to do that," Hudson said quietly. "All you had to do was surrender."

He glanced at Dwight's body.

"Dwight is dead," Hudson said. "And you're about to be. Why?"

Sloan's eyes struggled to focus.

"Bruce gave me purpose," Sloan whispered. "And power."

His gaze went empty.

Upstairs, the final defender of Bruce was gone.

The house was no longer a fortress.

Only Bruce remained.

The Mansion, Sunrise

Hudson called down the staircase.

"Omar," he said. "Come up. Bruce isn't here."

Omar appeared moments later, breathing hard from the fight.

"Bruce is hiding," Omar said. "That guy is a rat. He isn't coming out unless we drag him."

Stephanie moved down the hallway toward the master bedroom. The room looked disturbed, drawers partially open, furniture shifted. Her eyes moved across the space until they landed on the large silver metal door set inside the closet wall.

She stepped closer and tried the handle.

Locked.

She knocked lightly.

"Bruce," she said. "If you are hiding in there, it's time to come out. All of your guys are gone."

A pause.

Then she spoke again.

"It's not Bruce," she added gently. "It's us. I have Ester and the baby with me."

The lock clicked.

The door opened slowly.

Paula stood there with Ester behind her holding the infant.

Relief washed over Stephanie's face.

"You are okay," she said.

Paula nodded. "We're fine."

Ester looked past her. "Is it over."

"Almost," Stephanie said. "Have you seen Bruce."

Paula shook her head. "No idea. He was trying to get into this room earlier."

Tony and Omar entered the hallway behind Hudson.

"Ester," Hudson said softly. "Take the baby to Deanna's house. Stay there until we come get you."

Ester nodded and moved quickly down the stairs with Paula guiding her.

Once they were gone, Hudson turned back toward the rooms.

"He will hide somewhere he feels powerful," Hudson said quietly.

Omar understood immediately.

"The office," Omar said.

They moved downstairs together.

The office door stood closed.

Hudson opened it slowly.

The room looked untouched. The large desk sat centered on the rug, antique furniture arranged with the same show of authority Bruce had always preferred.

Hudson stepped inside, scanning.

"Looks empty," Tony said.

Hudson crouched and checked behind the desk.

Nothing.

Then he noticed the large wooden cabinet against the wall.

Two heavy doors.

Tony stepped to one side.

Hudson took the other.

They opened the doors at the same time.

Bruce sat crammed inside, sweating, eyes wide with fear.

For a moment, no one spoke.

Tony stepped back slightly.

Omar entered behind them, followed by Stephanie.

Bruce slowly climbed out and sat in the desk chair, trying to regain composure.

Paula appeared in the doorway, watching silently.

Hudson looked at Bruce for a long moment.

"What should we do with you," Hudson said. "Tie you to the tree and let everyone take a turn with your brass knuckles."

Bruce swallowed.

"I suppose it would be best for everyone if I moved on," he said quickly. "I can go to another part of the country. Out west. Far away. You will never hear from me again."

Omar shook his head.

"I don't see that happening," he said.

Hudson nodded slowly.

"We're going to gather everyone," Hudson said. "We will have a vote. What happens to you will be decided by the community."

Bruce opened his mouth to protest, but Hudson continued.

"Unlike you," Hudson said, "the vote will be honored."

Hudson's voice hardened.

"We will also collect the dead," he said. "The people need to see exactly what you caused. No one had to die. Everyone could have lived peacefully if you had not been power hungry."

Bruce looked down, saying nothing.

Outside, the first full sunlight of morning spread across Bruceville.

Doors began opening cautiously.

People stepped onto porches.

Neighbors looked toward the mansion, toward the tree, toward the bodies lying in the streets.

Whispers spread quickly.

Bruce's men were gone.

The fighting had stopped.

The reign of fear was over.

At Deanna's house, Ester held her baby close while Olivia watched from the window.

In the mansion doorway, Paula stood with her arms folded, staring at Bruce without fear for the first time.

Hudson stepped outside onto the front steps and looked across the community.

The sun had risen.

The war was over.

Thirty-Three

Community Justice

New Galesburg 1988

The morning came slowly over New Galesburg.

The first light of dawn spread across the quiet streets, touching rooftops, trees, and the large open community area near the tree where Hudson had been tied only hours earlier. Smoke from spent gunfire still lingered faintly in the air, mixing with the cool dampness of early morning. For a few long moments, the town felt frozen between two worlds, the violence that had just happened and whatever came next.

No one spoke as the group began their work.

Hudson, Tony, Omar, and Stephanie moved methodically from place to place, collecting the bodies. There was no triumph in their movements. No sense of victory. Only exhaustion and sorrow.

Theo was found first.

He had fallen near the edge of the field where he had tried to cover Stephanie. His rifle still lay nearby in the grass. Misty was not far from him. The two had died within minutes of each other.

Stephanie stopped when she saw them.

Her breath caught in her chest, and for a moment she could not move forward.

Tony stepped beside her quietly.

"We will carry them," he said gently.

Stephanie nodded, though tears were already forming in her eyes.

They lifted Theo carefully onto a blanket, then Misty. The motions were slow, deliberate, respectful. No one rushed.

Next came Moses and Dwight.

Moses had fallen near the mansion, still positioned where he had tried to protect Omar. Dwight lay inside the back entrance, where he had attempted to breach the house. Both men had died fighting to save someone else.

Mae had not arrived yet, but Hudson already felt the weight of what she would face when she saw them.

"They were good men," Hudson said quietly.

Tony nodded.

"The best."

The group then moved to the others, the men who had followed Bruce.

Mitchell still sat slumped near the table where he had been shot. Chris lay near the back deck. Jason was found not far from the rear of Bruce's home. Sloan remained upstairs inside the mansion. Jordy had died in Deanna's home. Pickle's body lay inside the guard booth.

They were placed on blankets too.

No one separated them.

Death had erased the lines Bruce had drawn between people.

As they worked, the sun continued rising, casting long shadows across the community area. One by one, the bodies were laid out in rows beneath the tree, the same tree that had been used for punishment, humiliation, and control.

Now it became something different.

A place of truth.

When the last body was carried into position, Hudson stepped back and looked at them all.

Ten lives gone in one morning.

Friends. Enemies. Neighbors. Survivors of the same broken world.

All equal now.

Behind him, Bruce sat handcuffed to a wooden chair placed directly in front of the tree.

Tony had secured the cuffs tightly. Bruce's wrists rested in his lap, his shoulders slumped forward. His head hung low, avoiding eye contact with anyone around him. For the first time since Hudson had met him, Bruce looked small.

Not powerful.

Not commanding.

Just a man who had run out of control.

Tony stood a few feet behind him, shotgun held across his chest, eyes never leaving Bruce for more than a second.

Bruce shifted slightly in the chair but said nothing.

No one spoke to him.

Hudson exhaled slowly and looked toward the streets of New Galesburg.

"It's time," he said.

Omar nodded.

"I will get everyone."

Omar turned and began walking toward the houses, his voice soon echoing down the quiet roads.

"Everyone come to the community center! Important meeting! Now!"

As his voice carried through the community, doors began to open.

People stepped outside cautiously, unsure of what they were about to see.

The reckoning had begun.

By the time Omar finished calling people from their homes, more movement was beginning across New Galesburg.

Residents stepped outside slowly, many wrapped in blankets or still wearing what they had on when the gunfire started. At first, their faces showed confusion. Then they saw the bodies beneath the tree. The confusion gave way to alarm. Quiet conversations began, then faded just as quickly as people started to understand what had happened.

Stephanie's vehicle returned just as the first small groups gathered.

Mae climbed out quickly, followed by Jerry. Shadoe jumped down beside them, immediately alert, ears up, sensing the tension in the air. Jerry had tried to be brave during the drive, but the moment he saw the blankets on the ground, he stopped walking.

Mae saw them too.

Her steps slowed, then stopped completely.

"Oh no," she whispered.

She already knew.

Hudson moved toward her, his face heavy with sorrow. He did not need to say anything. Mae's eyes searched the blankets until she recognized Moses' boots sticking out from beneath one corner.

Her hand went to her mouth.

"No... no..."

Stephanie reached her first, wrapping her arms around her shoulders. Mae leaned into her, trembling.

Jerry stood frozen.

His eyes moved from one body to another until he recognized Dwight's hat resting beside a blanket. Dwight had joked with him just the day before. Dwight had promised to teach him how to clean a rifle properly.

Jerry's face crumpled.

Hudson stepped forward and pulled Jerry into a tight embrace.

"It's okay," Hudson said softly. "It's okay to be sad."

Jerry buried his face against Hudson's chest.

"They were my friends," Jerry said, his voice shaking. "They helped me... they were nice to me."

Hudson held him tighter.

"They were proud of you," Hudson said. "All of them were."

Mae finally gathered enough strength to walk forward.

Tony moved aside quietly so she could approach Moses. She knelt beside the blanket and pulled it back just enough to see his face. Tears fell freely down her cheeks, but she did not cry out. Her grief came in silence, the kind that carried deeper weight than any scream.

"He was always smiling," she said softly. "Even when things were bad."

Stephanie knelt beside her and placed a hand on her back.

Around them, the rest of the community continued arriving.

Deanna came with Olivia, keeping a protective arm around the girl's shoulders. Olivia looked frightened by the number of people gathered but more confused by the stillness of the bodies.

"Are they sleeping?" Olivia asked quietly.

Deanna knelt down beside her.

"No, sweetheart," she said gently. "They died."

Olivia's eyes filled with tears.

"Like my parents?"

Deanna swallowed.

"Yes. Like your family."

Paula arrived next, walking slowly from the mansion area. Her eyes moved from Bruce to the bodies and back again. Shock washed over her face as she began to understand how many people had died because of the conflict.

Ester did not come.

She remained inside Deanna's house with the baby, still recovering, fully aware of the violence that had unfolded overnight.

More residents gathered until nearly the entire community stood in the open area beneath the tree.

The air felt heavy.

No one spoke loudly.

The presence of death had silenced everything.

Bruce remained seated in front of them all, head lowered, hands cuffed. For the first time, people looked at him not as a leader but as the source of what had happened.

Fear was still there.

But something else had begun to replace it.

Doubt.

And anger.

Hudson stepped forward slowly, looking across the faces gathered before him.

"We are going to talk," he said. "All of us."

The moment of decision was coming.

When the last of the community had gathered, a heavy silence settled over the clearing.

The bodies lay in a row beneath the tree. Blankets covered them, but everyone knew who was there. Friends. Neighbors. People who had shared meals together only days before.

Omar stepped forward first.

"Everyone is here," he said, turning slowly so his voice carried to the entire group. "We need to decide what happens next."

He paused, then looked directly at Bruce.

"You will be given a chance to speak," Omar said. "After that, the community will decide."

Community Center

Bruce lifted his head slowly.

For a moment he looked smaller than anyone had ever seen him. The confidence, the swagger, the certainty that had defined him for weeks seemed gone. His hair was disheveled, his face pale, his eyes tired.

When he spoke, his voice was softer than expected.

"I know you are all angry," he said. "I understand that."

He swallowed.

"I was in prison before all this happened," he continued. "For a long time. Years. And prison is not what people think it is. You live every day knowing someone stronger might hurt you. Guards treat you like you are nothing. Other inmates test you constantly. You survive by becoming hard."

Some people shifted uncomfortably.

Bruce continued.

"I suffered in there. More than any of you know. I am pretty sure I have PTSD from it. When the world collapsed and I got out, all I could think about was never being controlled again. Never being powerless again."

He looked down briefly.

"So yes. I made decisions based on fear. Fear that everything would fall apart. Fear that someone else would take control and I would end up back under someone's authority."

He lifted his eyes again.

"But I was not alone in this," he said quickly. "Sloan was a big part of what happened. He was bigger than me, more aggressive. I leaned on him. He pushed things further than I wanted. The kidnapping of Hudson was not even my idea. I knew the power would come on eventually. Sloan was the one angry about delays. He was the one pushing for force."

A murmur moved through the crowd.

Bruce pressed on.

"I'm not a monster," he said. "I was scared, same as all of you. I was put in a situation I couldn't control. Sloan was the one pushing the violence. I was trying to hold things together."

He leaned forward slightly in the chair.

"I'm not proud of what happened," he said. "But I'm not the villain you think I am. I was trying to protect this community. I was trying to keep some kind of order in a broken world."

He paused, then added quietly,

"I'm actually a coward who got put in a bad position."

No one spoke.

The silence that followed felt heavier than before.

Tony did not move his eyes from Bruce.

Omar stepped forward again.

"That's enough," he said calmly. "You'll be quiet now."

Bruce started to respond, but Omar raised a hand.

"I said enough."

Bruce closed his mouth.

The moment for others to speak had arrived.

For a moment no one moved.

Then Paula stepped forward from the edge of the crowd.

She looked smaller than usual, but there was a steadiness in her face that had not been there before. Weeks of quiet fear had been replaced by something stronger. Something resolved.

Omar nodded to her.

"You can speak," he said.

Paula took a slow breath and looked directly at Bruce before turning to the community.

"When I first came here," she began, "I thought I had finally found somewhere safe."

Her voice trembled slightly, but she continued.

"Bruce told me I was welcome. That everyone looked out for each other. That this was a place where people mattered."

She swallowed.

"But very quickly, things changed."

She glanced briefly toward Bruce, then back to the group.

"He told me I needed to live in his house. Said it would be easier that way. Safer. I did not think much about it at first. I was just grateful to have a roof over my head."

Her hands folded together in front of her.

"But then it became clear I was not free to leave," she said quietly. "He made me do things, repulsive things, I did not want to do. It was everyday sometimes twice a day. If I said something, he promised me that I would be given to his group of men, as a toy. He made it clear that I belonged to him."

A ripple of discomfort moved through the listeners.

"I lived every day knowing I could not make my own choices," Paula continued. "I smiled when he was around. I agreed with him. I did what he wanted. Because I was afraid."

She turned and pointed toward Bruce.

"Sloan was not the leader," she said firmly. "He was just another follower. Bruce made the decisions. Bruce told people what to do. Sloan did what Bruce wanted."

Bruce shifted in his chair, but Tony's presence kept him silent.

Paula's voice grew stronger.

"He controlled everything. Where people lived. What they did. Who they talked to. And everyone was scared to question him because they saw what happened when someone did."

Her eyes filled with tears.

"I am standing here today because other people were brave enough to stop him," she said. "Not because he protected me. Not because he cared about anyone."

She wiped her cheek.

"He wanted power. That is all."

The clearing remained silent.

Omar stepped forward again.

"Thank you, Paula," he said gently.

Paula nodded once and stepped back beside Mae, who reached out and squeezed her hand.

The truth had been spoken aloud.

And everyone had heard it.

Omar stepped forward slowly, his eyes moving across the faces of the community.

He looked tired. Older than he had just days before. The weight of what had happened rested heavily on him, but there was also clarity in his expression.

"I need to say something," he said.

The murmurs faded.

Many people knew Omar had worked closely with Bruce. He had been one of the men people assumed supported him. That made his words carry weight now.

"I did things for Bruce," Omar continued. "Jobs he asked me to do. Protection. Running errands. Keeping order when he wanted something handled."

He paused, then shook his head slightly.

"But I always felt something was off," he said. "I could not explain it at first. Just a feeling that things were not right."

He glanced toward the empty space near the tree where Julian had once stood tied.

"After Julian disappeared, that feeling became certainty."

Several people shifted uneasily.

"I knew Bruce would never just let someone leave," Omar said. "Not after being challenged publicly. Not after being embarrassed."

Bruce lifted his head slightly, but Tony's presence kept him quiet.

Omar continued.

"While we were negotiating this morning, I learned the truth from Sloan," he said. "He told me exactly what happened."

The air seemed to tighten around the group.

"Bruce ordered Julian to be cut down from the tree," Omar said. "Not because he was forgiven. Not because he was free. Because Bruce had already decided what would happen next."

A few gasps escaped the crowd.

"They drove Julian out to an old cornfield," Omar said quietly. "Sloan shot him in the back of the head. Execution style. Just like Bruce ordered."

A shocked silence fell over everyone.

"They left his body there," Omar added. "For animals. Like he was nothing."

Several people covered their mouths. Others stared at Bruce in disbelief.

Omar's voice hardened.

"I hate that so many people died today," he said. "I hate that it came to violence. But at the end of the day, all of this rests on Bruce's shoulders."

He pointed toward the chair.

"Dougie. Julian. Hudson nearly killed. The men who followed him. Our friends who died stopping him."

His voice lowered.

"He is too dangerous to ever be free again."

Omar stepped back.

The truth about Julian hung in the air like smoke.

And there was no taking it back.

Hudson stepped forward slowly, his body still stiff from the rope and the beating he had taken, but his voice steady.

He looked down the line of blankets first.

Theo.

Misty.

Dwight.

Moses.

His throat tightened.

"All of them were my friends," he said quietly.

The words carried across the crowd.

"They did not have to come," Hudson continued. "They did not have to risk their lives for me. But they did anyway."

He paused, swallowing hard.

"If they had not come... I would be dead right now."

Stephanie lowered her head. Jerry stood beside her, holding her hand tightly.

Hudson turned his gaze toward Bruce.

"And Bruce would still be ruling this place with fear," he said.

He looked back to the community.

"How many more people would have died if nothing changed," he asked. "We will never know. Because these men and women stopped it today."

His eyes moved down the second row of bodies.

Mitchell.

Jordy.

Sloan.

Pickle.

Jason.

Chris.

"I did not know these men," Hudson said. "Not really. To me they were Bruce's enforcers. The ones who stood between people and freedom."

He paused again.

"But before the world ended... they were probably just normal people. Neighbors. Fathers. Brothers. Coworkers. People with families who cared about them."

A few people nodded slowly.

"They got pulled into Bruce's orbit," Hudson said. "Into his fear. Into his anger. Into his need for control."

He looked back at Bruce.

"I blame him for their deaths too."

The statement landed heavily.

Hudson took a breath.

"Dougie. Julian. The people we lost today. Maybe others we do not even know about."

His voice grew firmer.

"This man cannot ever be free again."

He turned toward the community.

"You have to decide what happens next," he said. "Not me. Not any one person. All of you."

He gestured around the gathering.

"This is your community."

He nodded once.

"And whatever you decide… will be honored."

He stepped back.

The responsibility now rested fully with the people.

For a long moment, no one spoke.

The wind moved lightly through the trees. The blankets on the ground shifted slightly with the breeze.

Bruce slowly lifted his head.

His face looked different now. The confidence was gone. The authority gone. What remained was fear.

"I understand that you are all upset," he began. "Emotional. Angry. I get that."

He looked around at the crowd.

"But you all believed in compassion before," he continued. "You believed in second chances. In rehabilitation instead of death."

His voice softened.

"I would prefer to live," he said. "I made mistakes. But I still choose life."

No one responded.

The silence stretched.

Then movement came from the back of the crowd.

Gideon stepped forward.

Shaz walked beside him.

People turned to look.

Gideon's eyes were tired, his posture heavy, like he had been carrying something for a long time.

"I need to say something," he said.

Hudson nodded once.

"Go ahead."

Gideon took a breath.

"When Shaz got shot," he said, "I was full of anger. All I wanted was revenge. That was it. Nothing else mattered."

He looked toward Bruce briefly.

"I believed Dougie deserved to die. That is what I thought. That is what Bruce believed. And that is what happened."

His voice dropped.

"I was wrong."

Shaz reached over and took his hand.

"Revenge did not help me feel better," Gideon continued. "It made everything worse. I shut myself inside my house. I stopped talking to people. I only talked to Bruce because I thought he was the only one who understood."

He shook his head slightly.

"I was dealing with depression. Anxiety. Panic attacks. Still am."

The honesty surprised people.

"But after talking with my friend," he said, nodding toward Shaz, "the person who actually got hurt... I realized something."

He swallowed.

"Violence doesn't fix pain. It spreads it."

Shaz squeezed his hand.

"We're going to get through it," she said softly. "Together. No more hiding."

Gideon nodded.

"Yeah," he said quietly. "Together."

The moment shifted something in the crowd.

Fear gave way to reflection.

Reflection gave way to resolve.

A path forward was forming.

Deanna stepped forward slowly.

She looked around at the people gathered in front of the tree. At the blankets. At the bodies. At Bruce sitting in the chair with his wrists bound.

Her voice was calm, but firm.

"We should be better than what the world was before," she said. "We should not answer violence with more violence."

She paused, letting the words settle.

"I would like to see the hands of everyone who believes Bruce should be kept alive, but imprisoned here so he can never hurt anyone again."

For a moment, no one moved.

Then a hand rose.

Then another.

Then another.

Within seconds, every hand in the crowd was raised.

Hudson looked across the group, emotion visible in his face.

"I believe you have all made the right decision," he said. "Let us hope this ends the violence from this day forward."

He took a breath.

"There is something else I need to tell you," he continued. "The power system is ready. It has actually been ready for a couple of weeks. I held off because I would not help strengthen a dangerous leader."

Murmurs moved through the crowd.

"I can have electricity running this afternoon," Hudson said. "It will take about thirty minutes to bring everything online."

Bruce lifted his head sharply.

"I knew you were lying," he snapped. "All of this could have been avoided if you had just done the right thing."

Hudson met his eyes without anger.

"I was never going to help you control people," he said calmly. "I'm confident in that decision."

Mae stepped forward next.

"I would like to ask something of everyone," she said. "All of these people who died today deserve proper burials. If we work together as a community, we can give them the respect they deserve."

Heads nodded across the crowd.

Tony and Omar moved behind Bruce and lifted him to his feet.

He didn't resist.

They walked him toward the mansion.

The bedroom that had once been used to confine Ester had already been cleared. The door was solid. The windows secured.

It would serve as a temporary cell.

As Bruce disappeared inside, the weight of his rule seemed to lift from the entire neighborhood.

Outside, sunlight spread fully across New Galesburg.

People began moving again.

Talking.

Planning.

Helping.

Hudson stood near Jerry, pulling him into a hug.

"Don't be ashamed to cry," he said quietly."

Jerry nodded against his shoulder.

"I'm going to cry, not because I'm a baby, okay. It's because I will miss Dwight and Moses, the most.

"Later, when it's quiet and I finally let myself think about everything that's happened, I know I'll cry too," Hudson said.

THIRTY-FOUR

Time Moves On

NEW GALESBURG 1988

Two months had changed everything.

The community gathered beneath a simple wooden arch near the old tree, the same place that had once held fear now filled with something entirely different. The structure had been built by Kimberly using salvaged lumber, its rough edges smoothed just enough to feel intentional. It wasn't elaborate, but it didn't need to be.

People stood close together, not out of caution, but because they wanted to be there.

Hudson stood beneath the arch, steady and composed, dressed in clean work clothes that passed for something formal in this new world. Beside him stood Jerry, shoulders straight, doing everything he could to take the role seriously.

Shadoe sat at his side, calm and alert, as if he understood the importance of the moment.

Across from them, Stephanie stepped forward, Paula at her side.

Paula looked different now. Lighter. At ease in a way she had never been before. She stood beside Stephanie not as someone surviving, but as someone living.

Mae stepped forward to begin, her voice calm and clear as she spoke the words they had agreed on. There was nothing complicated about it. No long speeches. Just promises, spoken simply and meant completely.

Hudson took Stephanie's hand. "I choose you," he said. "No matter what comes next."

Stephanie smiled, her eyes steady. "And I choose you. Every day from here on."

That was enough.

Mae nodded once. "Then you are married."

The reaction came immediately. Applause. Laughter. Relief. Something that had been building for weeks finally finding its release.

Jerry turned to Hudson, unable to hold it in. "I did it," he said. "I was the best man."

Hudson smiled and rested a hand on his shoulder. "You were perfect."

Shadoe gave a single bark, drawing laughter from the group.

The celebration moved naturally from there.

Tables were set up. Food was brought out. People gathered in small groups, talking, laughing, reconnecting in ways that hadn't been possible before.

Hudson found Gideon and Shaz sitting together near the edge of the lawn.

"You two look settled," Hudson said.

Gideon glanced at Shaz, then back at Hudson. "We are."

Shaz smiled. "We made it official."

Hudson nodded. "Congratulations. You'll be the next wedding."

Gideon laughed. "One step at a time."

Nearby, Mae and Tony stood with Paula near the porch of her small home at the edge of the community.

"How's it feel out here," Tony asked.

Paula looked out toward her garden, rows already beginning to take shape despite the season. "Quiet," she said. "In a good way. No one watching me. No one telling me what to do."

Mae nodded. "That takes getting used to."

Paula smiled faintly. "I wake up sometimes expecting someone to be standing over me giving orders. Then I remember it's just me."

Tony leaned against the railing. "You earned that."

"I've been thinking about getting some goats," Paula added. "Something to take care of. Something that's mine."

Mae laughed softly. "That sounds wonderful for you."

Across the yard, Deanna stood watching a group of children run through the grass. Olivia led the way, two younger kids close behind her. Not far off, the teenage boy who had arrived weeks earlier stood nearby, still adjusting to what it meant to be part of something stable.

He had found them by accident.

He stayed because he finally felt safe.

The Jail

Omar stood near the garage with Kimberly, looking over the reinforced structure she had built.

"You never told Bruce you could do this," he said.

Kimberly shook her head. "I wasn't about to make myself useful to him."

She gestured toward the cell. "I built places like this before everything fell apart. Funny how that came back around."

Inside, Bruce sat on a narrow bed with a small television glowing in front of him, an old VCR tape flickering across the screen. He spoke now and then, mostly to himself, repeating the same story to anyone willing to stand there long enough to hear it. He had been a great leader. He had been misunderstood. He had only done what was necessary.

Outside the cell, no one stopped for long anymore.

Topher was standing nearby with a clipboard in his hand, not because anyone needed one now, but because old habits had a way of surviving. Before Bruce fell, Topher had been the man asked to interview new arrivals and score them for usefulness. Bruce had loved that system. He loved reducing a person to a number, loved the way it made judgment sound official.

Bruce looked up when he saw them. "Well," he said, trying to sound casual, "what's mine."

Topher did not answer right away. He looked through the bars at the man who had once controlled the whole neighborhood, then down at the paper in his hand.

"You really want to know?"

Bruce gave a thin smile. "Course I do."

Topher nodded once. "Eleven point two one."

The smile faded.

Bruce stared at him. "That's wrong."

Topher shook his head. "No, it isn't."

He said it plainly, without cruelty. "Hudson scored a ninety-five when you had me rate him. You remember that. You liked the number because it proved how valuable he was to the community. You liked having a man that useful under your thumb."

Bruce's face hardened, but he said nothing.

Topher went on. "Your number is low because you don't actually bring anything. No trade. No skill set that keeps people warm, fed, or alive. You can't build. You can't fix. You can't heal. You can't teach much beyond fear." He glanced down at the page again. "If you were released someday and judged by the same standard you made me use on everyone else, you wouldn't be accepted here. At best, you'd qualify for the most basic labor."

Bruce looked away then, his jaw tight.

The little television kept playing, voices from another time filling the silence for him.

Topher stood there a moment longer, taking in the cell, the screen, the man on the bed. Then he turned and walked away.

Illinois & Tennessee

The decision to leave had not come suddenly.

It had been building quietly inside Hudson for weeks, a pressure behind the sternum that he had learned to recognize. Not panic. Not urgency. Something older and more patient than either of those things.

Greeneville.

Carla.

Harry.

He had accepted the probability long ago. The Liberty Flu had been too devastating. Entire cities wiped out in weeks. Families gone overnight. He had told himself the story of acceptance so many times that he had almost started to believe it.

But probability was not certainty. And as long as uncertainty existed, the question would keep finding him in quiet moments. Standing at a window. Lying awake before dawn.

Watching Jerry laugh at something across the room. *What if.*

One morning, Hudson stood near the vehicles. Stephanie, Jerry, and Shadoe waited beside him without being asked. That was the thing about the people he had found. They understood before he spoke.

Stephanie studied his face. "You're thinking about it again."

"I need to see it," Hudson said. "Even if there's nothing left. I need to put my own eyes on it."

Jerry shifted his weight. "We're going with you. Right?"

Hudson looked at him, this young man who had become something he didn't have a word for anymore. Not a son. Not quite. Something the old world hadn't needed a name for because it hadn't required surviving the end of the world to exist.

"Of course," Hudson said. "You're part of this."

Jerry's shoulders dropped with relief, and he looked away quickly, the way he always did when something hit him too squarely.

Mae found Hudson by the vehicles the morning they departed.

She didn't say much. She put her hand on his arm and held it there for a moment, the way a person does when words would only get in the way.

"If you find something," she said finally. "Or someone. You come back here."

"I know."

"This is home, Hudson."

He looked at her. "I know that too."

Tony gave him a long handshake and didn't let go immediately. Then they climbed in. Stephanie in the passenger seat. Jerry in the back with Shadoe draped sideways across his lap like he had no bones.

As they pulled away, Jerry watched the people waving from the road until they disappeared behind the tree line.

"I like New Galesburg," he said quietly.

Hudson looked at him in the rearview mirror. "So do I."

The drive south was almost peaceful.

Roads cracked and buckled in places, but passable. Abandoned cars sat rusting on shoulders, grass pushing up through the asphalt around them in patient green lines. The world was not dead. It was just becoming something else, slowly, without asking permission.

They stopped to clear debris, siphon fuel, let Shadoe run in open fields that had once been rest stops. No danger. No other people. Just the three of them and the dog and the long quiet of a country that had mostly emptied out.

Stephanie watched the hills roll past. "It feels like we're the only ones left sometimes."

"Not the only ones," Hudson said. "Just far from the others."

Jerry leaned forward between the seats. "Do you think there are more communities like ours? Somewhere?"

"Yes," Hudson said. He believed it. He had to.

He recognized Greeneville before the signs confirmed it.

The hills came first, the particular shape of them against the sky, a silhouette he hadn't realized was still stored somewhere in his body. Then the roads. The intersections. A gas station he'd stopped at a hundred times, its canopy collapsed now on one side, weeds splitting the concrete around the pumps.

His hands tightened on the wheel without him deciding to.

They reached Carla's neighborhood in the late afternoon, the low sun cutting long shadows across the overgrown lawns. The house was still standing. Of course it was. Houses didn't need people to keep standing.

Hudson sat in the driver's seat and didn't move.

The engine ticked as it cooled.

"Take all the time you need," Stephanie said.

He nodded. But he knew that time wasn't the thing he needed. He just needed to make his legs work.

The front door was unlocked.

Inside, the dust had settled over everything in a thin gray film. The counters, the furniture, the framed photos on the side table. But the shape of the life that had been here was intact. Shoes by the door. A coffee mug on the counter, long dry. A book left open on the couch, spine cracked to hold the page.

She had been reading something. She had meant to come back to it.

Hudson stood in the living room for a long time. Then he turned to the wall.

The photos were still there. All of them.

Carla at the beach, laughing at something off-camera, squinting in the sun. Harry at maybe six years old, holding up a fish he'd caught with both hands like it was the greatest thing that had ever happened. Harry in the backyard on a Thursday afternoon, it had seemed ordinary at the time and now felt almost sacred in its smallness.

I miss you, he thought. Not said. Thought, in that deeper register where grief actually lives.

He stayed with the photos until the light in the room changed. Stephanie and Jerry didn't hurry him. They sat on the porch steps outside with Shadoe between them and waited the way people wait when they love someone, without watching the clock.

They stayed in Greeneville for several weeks.

They searched the neighborhoods in widening circles. Checked the nearby towns. Looked for any sign that someone had been here recently. A fire pit. A disturbed door. Tire tracks in the mud. They found nothing. Not tragedy, exactly. Just absence. The particular quiet of a place that had been emptied out and left to its own slow rhythms.

On the last night, Hudson sat outside watching the sun go down behind the mountains he had grown up seeing from a distance. The light turned the ridgeline orange and then purple and then dark.

Stephanie sat beside him, close enough that their shoulders touched.

For a while neither of them spoke.

"I got my answer," Hudson said.

"Yeah."

"It's not the one I wanted."

"No."

He was quiet again. The mountains went black against the last of the light. Somewhere in the grass, something small moved through the dark.

"I'm glad I came," he said. And he meant it, not in spite of the grief, but because of it. Because he had stood in that house and looked at those pictures and let the loss be real instead of probable. That was something. That was actually something.

Stephanie didn't say anything. She leaned her head lightly against his shoulder for a moment, then lifted it again.

"So," she said. "What now?"

Hudson thought about it. He thought about Mae saying *this is home.* He thought about the road back north, and the people waiting there, and the particular pleasure of a life that was still being built.

He smiled, and it was a real smile, the kind that lives just underneath something heavier and earns its place by being there anyway.

"Florida," he said.

Stephanie turned to look at him.

"Beach time," he said.

From somewhere behind them, Jerry's voice came out of the dark: "Did you just say *beach?*"

Hudson laughed. Genuinely laughed, the kind that starts in your chest and doesn't apologize for itself.

"Water and sand," he confirmed.

There was a brief pause. Then the sound of Jerry telling Shadoe they were going to the beach, as if the dog needed advance notice, as if this was very important information that could not wait.

Hudson stood up. Stephanie stood beside him. The mountains were dark now and the stars were coming out and somewhere down the road, others were doing the same. Humanity would live on.

Epilogue
Florida

Destin, Florida. 1988

By the time they reached Destin, the air itself felt different.

Salt. Warmth. Relaxation.

The roads into town were quiet like everywhere else, but the Gulf didn't know anything had happened. The water rolled in its steady rhythm. The tide had not heard of the Liberty Flu. The horizon stretched unbroken and wide and completely indifferent to everything that had come before.

They parked near the shoreline and pulled two old beach chairs and an umbrella from the back of the vehicle.

Jerry looked at the sand and then looked at Hudson.

"Can I go?"

"Go ahead."

He was gone before Hudson finished the sentence.

His shoes came off somewhere between the parking area and the waterline, left behind without ceremony, and then he was sprinting, arms out a little for balance, laughing before he even hit the water. Shadoe blew past him and got there first, barking once at the foam rushing over his paws, then dancing backward as the wave pulled out.

"It's cold!" Jerry shouted. "Hudson, it's cold!"

"That's how it works!"

"I know that!" He ran deeper anyway, turning sideways as the next wave hit him at the hip. "It's really cold!"

Shadoe snapped at the foam like it had personally offended him, retreated, then charged the next swell with the same misplaced confidence.

Hudson and Stephanie set up the chairs beneath the umbrella. The sun came down warm and unhurried. Stephanie leaned back and closed her eyes and didn't say anything for a little while, which was its own kind of statement.

"You didn't tell me it would be this beautiful," she said finally.

Hudson watched Jerry stumble in the shallows, catch himself, laugh at himself. "I forgot," he said. "I forgot what it felt like to just sit somewhere."

Then Shadoe stopped.

His whole body went still. Head up. Ears forward. Gaze fixed on something down the beach.

A German Shepherd was picking her way along the edge of the surf. Moving carefully, ribs faintly visible, fur gold and black in the sun. Alone.

Jerry waded out of the shallows and stood watching her with his hands clasped in front of him, very still, the way he got when something mattered.

Shadoe moved toward her slowly. She didn't run. They circled, nosed at each other, worked it out the way dogs do. Then the tension was just gone, and they were moving together along the waterline like the matter had been settled.

Jerry cupped his hands around his mouth. "Sandy!" he called.

The female's ears turned toward him.

He looked back at Hudson, satisfied. "Her name's Sandy."

Within a minute they were all three running the surf together, Jerry soaked to the chest, both dogs chasing the same waves, nobody keeping score.

Stephanie reached over and found Hudson's hand.

"He deserves this," she said.

Hudson nodded. He didn't trust himself to say much more than that.

Hudson stood and pulled his shirt off.

"Going in?" Stephanie asked.

"Yeah," he said. "I think so."

He walked down to the water where Jerry and both dogs were waiting, none of them standing still. The sand was warm under his feet. The tide came in cool and steady around his ankles.

Jerry was grinning, soaked, completely at home in a way that some people never managed even before the world came apart.

"Hudson," he said.

"Yeah."

"This is the best day."

Hudson looked at him. Then out at the water, wide and still going.

"Yeah," he said. "It really is."

Also by Todd Thorne

Released:

The Skinner
New Cardano: Origin of the End
Forgiveness Road: A Family's Reckoning
A Banana, Blue Jeans and Bubba: A Southern Memoir About Earning Your Place

Coming Soon:

The Skinner 1978
The Contest: Only One Survives

About the author

Todd Thorne is a storyteller drawn to the edges of human experience, where ordinary people are forced into extraordinary circumstances. His work explores survival, morality, and the choices people make when the structures of society fall away.

Born in Louisiana and shaped by years living in the South, rural Montana and the Midwest, his writing reflects a strong sense of place, from small towns to wide open landscapes where isolation and resilience go hand in hand. His stories are grounded in realism, with characters who feel authentic and situations that push them to their limits.

He is the author of *The Skinner, Forgiveness Road,* and the *New Cardano* series, with each project exploring different aspects of human nature under pressure.

Todd is the husband of Candida and the father of four daughters and two sons. He currently lives in the Midwest, where he writes full time and continues to build immersive worlds that challenge, entertain, and stay with readers long after the final page.

www.ingramcontent.com/pod-product-compliance
Lightning Source LLC
LaVergne TN
LVHW050918080826
845145LV00001B/123

* 9 7 8 1 9 6 8 3 8 1 1 2 7 *